La Contessa

S. Nano

La Contessa
Published in 2024 by
House of Erotica
houseoferotica.uk

an imprint of
Andrews UK Limited
West Wing Studios
Unit 166, The Mall
Luton, LU1 2TL
andrewsuk.com

La Contessa

S. Nano

HOUSE OF EROTICA

Contents

HOUSE OF EROTICA

1: Roberto

This is a favourite place to ply my trade. Leaning against the flaking stucco of this dilapidated warehouse, the flickering wall lamps transform me into a shadowy figure of mystery as my alluring silhouette entices clientele into the dark passages of Venice.

From this spot I can see down the alleyway to a landing stage where gondolas are moored. If I glance to the left, I have a view of Campo di San Canciano with its numerous taverns and brothels, and the customers of Il Toro Nero as they stumble drunk into the night air. There can be no doubt in anybody's mind what I'm offering when they see my slender, well-toned frame leaning against the wall, and the seductive glint in my eye. Oh yes, the Cannaregio is notorious. No-one scouring the alleyways in this district is ignorant of the erotic delights on offer here.

Tonight is unusually quiet. From this location there are many places I can take my clients depending on what perverse desires they have. There are the hidden, arched entrances of the disused warehouses and dilapidated merchant houses, once thriving and bustling, but long empty since the decline of trade through Venice. Occasionally it's possible to sneak down to the gondolas bobbing restlessly on the canal for an encounter requiring more comfort. Often I've been chased off by an irate gondolier. Others know me well and, when it's quiet, will let me use their gondola in exchange for a few *soldi*.

I could choose to work in the comfort of a brothel or a tavern like Il Toro, but why should I have my hard earned money creamed off by the madam of a bawdy house? No, I can make a fair charge for my special kind of service and keep the proceeds. And business is good.

You'd think anybody looking for a sexual liaison would yearn for a soft feather bed and a warm fire but no, often that's not the case. Many of my clients prefer the debauched excitement of being fucked against the wall in an alleyway or having their cock sucked in the gloomy light. The frisson of being discovered is part of the allure. I know I'm good at what I do. I'm young, fit and in good shape. I know my boyish good looks appeal not only to the women seeking sexual excitement, but also to those men whose sexual preferences are for other men. I cater for them all.

My clientele is more varied than you might imagine. You'd think offering myself on the alleyways of Venice would only attract the lowest classes, but that's not so. Eighteenth century Venice is an open minded, many would say decadent, city. You find all classes here, from nobility, who fancy a dalliance with the perverse, to working men, who will blow their wage on an encounter with a prostitute. They'll all happily wander the lanes of the Cannaregio to satiate their sexual needs. Yes, I know; I've fucked duchesses and countesses, sucked the cocks of dukes and counts.

And then Venice has many foreign visitors on the Grand Tour. They may profess their motive for visiting the city is the magnificent architecture and brilliant art, but the underlying reason is far more risqué. It's surprising how these aristocrats open up to a street-boy offering sexual services. It's as if they have a perverse excitement in doing so. I can smell their anticipation as they scour the streets choosing the right woman or man, depending on their preference.

Don't make the mistake of thinking it's only men. Oh no, I've had countless young aristocrats, married off to an ageing heir by their families, who come to the streets of Venice solely to get fucked. You can hear the sly arguments they put forward, "Oh but Lord Chichester, we simply must go to Venice. It's the most fashionable place to be seen and the buildings and art are a marvel to behold. Why I was only speaking to Lady Sykes the other day. She has recently returned from a tour of the Alps and Northern Italy, and Venice was the indubitable highlight of her trip." Yes, I've heard the stories. "I'm going to midnight mass in Santa Croce, my love," she will say, and a compliant servant will chaperone her whilst my cock thrusts into her willing cunt. No other city offers the same range of erotic delights as *La Serenissima*, the serene Republic.

Mind you, I *can't* do this for the rest of my life. There's only so long you can be on the streets at night in all weathers and it not take its toll. The prostitutes in the Cannaregio have a longer working life; they can use layers of make-up to disguise their age, but in my game youth is everything. I care for my body and groom myself well as it's essential for the success of my trade but I know I can only do this for so long. I'm careful with what I earn and keep it stashed away in my lodgings, hoping one day I'll earn enough to buy myself into an apprenticeship, perhaps in the glass blowing works in Murano, since I'm especially good at blowing. In the meantime, I enjoy my work. I revel in the thrill of the unexpected and get a buzz out of the dark and dangerous side of my occupation.

The sound of two revellers turning out of the square and into the back-lane in my direction disturbs my reverie. Their bulky frames are silhouetted in the gloomy lamp light of the alley, a twin vision of bustles, busts, and

2

curly wigs teetering on Italian leather shoes, waddling purposefully down the alleyway. A less expert eye might be fooled by them. Being familiar with the clientele who frequent these alleys, there's no disguising what these two figures are. Something in their demeanour betrays them, as if they are trying too hard to walk with effortless, feminine grace without quite succeeding. It's a familiar sight in the Cannaregio. After all, this is Venice; the dark underbelly of its decadence is never far beneath the surface. However much they try to hide their maleness, it's obvious they are transvestites.

As they approach I play along with their game.

"Greetings ladies," I take my hat off and bow extravagantly, "and what service can I give you tonight?"

I can't fault their make-up, it's flawless, but the lie of their Adam's apple betrays their true gender. The night air becomes infused with powder and sweet perfume as their magnificently coiffured wigs bob to and fro before me.

"What a sweet boy, isn't he Lucretia?" he says, admiring my good looks and sleek black hair tied into a queue which hangs on my neck.

"Yes, but is he old enough to be on the streets of these parts of Venice? Does your mother know you're here?"

I smile benignly and play along with their joke, "I promise you ladies, I appear younger than I am. I assure you I'm old enough not to need my mother's permission to service any needs you ladies might have... for a price."

"Oh, he's a cheeky one, isn't he Viola?" giggles Lucretia.

"And you'll do anything we ask of you?"

"Oh, yes my lady, I'm willing and very... adaptable, as I say, for a fair price."

After a brief exchange we agree upon a price and a silver *ducat* is passed into my palm. The charade of seduction begins.

Lucretia, the taller of the two transvestites in a blonde wig, runs a fingernail along my cheek. The fingers are expertly painted but there's no hiding the roughness of his skin. Venice is a tolerant city, but even here there are risks for homosexuals and transsexuals. Sodomy is illegal in Venice, frowned upon by the ruling Council of Ten and the church, though it's hard to believe, given how prevalent it is. But they must still be careful, hence the extravagant disguise, and why they come to this place to satisfy their sexual urges. Viola, the second transvestite who is thicker set and has a black wig, reaches his hand down to my breeches and runs his fingers along them, feeling the line of my hardening cock. I have no problems responding. Male or female client, my member is always ready and willing and my powers of recovery are renowned, which is necessary in my trade.

"Come, let's retire to a more secluded place," I urge. "If we go into the alley, there's a porch where we're less likely to be disturbed."

The two transvestites readily comply with my suggestion. I link my arms with theirs, one on either side of me, and lead them towards a hidden alleyway. I flatter their beauty extravagantly whilst we walk and they respond with delighted amusement, revelling in the belief their secret has not been discovered.

But as I glance around to check everything is clear in the entrance to the alley, I detect a shadow in the dark. A wide-rimmed hat and a slim, female figure darts behind a Doric pillar, the entrance to a deserted merchant's residence. It registers with me for a fleeting moment, and my curiosity is aroused. Who could be watching me? It's not the typical behaviour of the prostitutes working these alleyways, but I push it to the back of my mind; after all, I have my clients to think about.

I hustle the two transvestites under the portico of a once grand house whose façade is now crumbling like many buildings behind the Grand Canal. The dark haired transvestite wastes no time in forcing me into the corner, pressing me against the stone work with the billowing spread of his gown and the thrust of his false bosom. He takes my face between his hands and pushes his lips eagerly onto mine, his tongue exploring my mouth. He pins me against the wall. The overwhelming aroma of sickly perfume and powdered wig invades my senses.

Meanwhile, Lucretia is on his knees pulling at my breeches to release my, now, fully erect cock. I have no problem with this. I know what I'm paid for; to provide a service to my clients. I can't even claim there isn't some perverse way I enjoy it. I warm to the touch of sticky saliva around my cock as Lucretia takes the full length of my member into his mouth and sucks on me. I groan in exaggerated pleasure.

"Oh yes, suck me lady, suck me!"

I'd be lying if I say I don't get sexual gratification from this. Besides, the transvestite is a skilled practitioner in the art of oral sex and it does no harm to enter into the role. My clients expect a performance. I don't have to pretend too much in this case as the expert tongue wraps itself around the tip of my cock, licking its glans. He'll bring me to a climax soon unless I can control myself. He pulls his lips away from my member leaving me teetering on the edge of release.

"He's an eager one, isn't he my dear?" says Lucretia.

"Oh, yes, he's enthusiastic. Shall we see how far he'll go?"

"He promised to service us in any way we pleased."

"Yes, he did, didn't he? We must take you at your word, boy."

"Yes, get down on your knees."

4

I anticipate what will come next. I obediently kneel in front of Viola. He pulls up rolls of silk material from his dress and layers of petticoats and lowers his silk knickerbockers to allow a blue-veined penis to spring free.

I feign shock to play along with their game. I'd done nothing to betray that I'd seen behind their disguise, and I don't want to spoil their pleasure in revealing the surprise beneath the layers of material. The pair of them giggle in delight as they reveal their secret.

"You said you'd service us. All the sucking's made me horny. Are you ready for this boy?"

"And there's another hard cock needs satisfying when you've finished there."

I take Viola's cock into my mouth, drawing the unyielding flesh deep until it gags at the back of my throat. I suck on it vigorously, pulling my lips over its taut hardness, revelling in the pleasure I'm giving my client. I know I'm good; I can tell the transvestite is surprised at how good. He groans in ecstasy.

"Ah, yes," he gasps. "You've done this before, boy. You dirty little slut. Oh that's good boy, come on, suck me."

I slow my pace as I sense his excitement, and the tension building up in his cock. I don't want him to come too quickly. I like to give my money's worth, then clients will come back. So I suck him with long, slow strokes, occasionally rolling my tongue over the tip of his cock to his moans of delight.

Whilst I'm pleasuring him, Viola reaches out to take hold of my cock, still slimy with a mixture of saliva and pre-cum. He closes his fist around it and pulls on my hardness, rubbing in synch with my sucking motions. This only serves to excite me and increase the pace of my lips sliding along Viola's cock.

Lucretia teases me, "I can tell what a naughty boy you are. Oh, I'm going to enjoy taking you! Get on your hands and knees boy."

I momentarily release the cock from my lips. It's red raw now and screaming out for release. I grasp Viola's balls into my hands and kneed them as I run the tip of my tongue along his throbbing cock to the sound of his euphoric groans. By now my breeches are around my ankles, and I get down as I've been ordered. The granite of the porch is hard and cold but I barely notice. I imagine the scene, me on my hands and knees like a bitch in heat, sandwiched between these two extravagantly dressed transvestites with their vast wigs and layers of make-up. I know what Lucretia wants. I know he wants his cock up my arse.

Viola drops onto her knees so I can continue sucking his cock. I open my mouth wide for him so he can thread his member into my mouth again. The debauched scene is set for its frantic climax, the two transvestites aroused and eager for release. As for me, yes, you might think my behaviour disgusting, but in a perverse way I'm enjoying myself with these two men, helping them act out their sexual fantasies. There's something gloriously decadent about offering myself up in such a wanton way. It's strangely liberating.

I continue sucking on Viola's cock as I sense Lucretia searching for the little hole of pleasure in my backside with his finger. I gasp through a mouthful of hard penis as he pushes a finger inside me, rotating it roughly around my arse to prepare me. He extracts his finger. I raise my arse into the air and wiggle it invitingly. Lucretia runs his hand over my backside and gives me one hard slap with his palm. I let out a muffled grunt which amuses both of them.

Lucretia moves his hands over my groin and grasps my hips firmly to steady himself, ready to penetrate me. The hardness of his erection presses against my flesh as it seeks out the hole. He soon finds it and eases his penis into me. I endure its girth stretching me, and his urgent nudges as he pushes deeper. I offer no resistance. I'm experienced enough to know the best thing to do is relax my anal muscles and let the hard flesh push past the tight ring of my arse-hole. With one more thrust the whole length of Lucretia's cock is inside me. I groan with pleasure. I don't need to pretend or exaggerate. It's a muffled moan, the kind you can only make when you've a mouthful of hard cock. It's strange and bizarrely fulfilling to have a penis deep inside you, pressing against the sensitive nerves deep in your anus.

Lucretia warms to his task. His cock nestled inside my arse, he sets about the task of fucking me, repeatedly withdrawing and pumping inside me. His strokes get deeper, and his grunts of exertion and pleasure louder. As he thrusts harder, my sucking on Viola's cock gets firmer. I'm oblivious to anything now, except the debauched physicality of what the two transvestites are doing.

I sense Viola's orgasm building up first. His groans increase in intensity as he builds up to his climax. Before he comes, he pulls his cock out of my mouth and masturbates. He wants to watch as he comes in my mouth. He expels a loud groan as he reaches his climax and his cum spurts into my waiting mouth whilst other globs of his spunk splatter onto my face. How deliciously depraved! I taste the saltiness and roll the disgustingly thick substance around my mouth before swallowing it. All the time Lucretia pumps his cock into my backside. Seeing the show his companion has put on tips him over the edge, grunting in ecstasy as he releases himself into my back passage. The three of us collapse onto the floor of the porch in exhaustion and fits of laughter.

You don't judge people in my game; you accept them and their desires for what they are. I'd never mock them for how they choose to dress or for trying to satisfy their sexual desires, however strange they appear. On the contrary, over the course of my brief encounter, I've acquired respect for them.

"You're good boy," gasps Viola, "we'll look out for you when we're next in the Cannaregio.

"He's bloody good," echoes Lucretia, still panting with the exertion.

They both show their appreciation for my service by giving me a kiss and a hug. Then my two transvestites adjust their dresses and walk away, two more satisfied customers, and me a silver *ducat* and a generous tip better off for my troubles.

I turn back to the lane… to see the broad-rimmed hat disappear behind the corner. Now my curiosity is piqued. I have to investigate this mysterious figure who's been spying on me.

2: Julia

I dash in pursuit of my mysterious, cloaked and hatted follower before she disappears into the shadows of the Calle Miracoli. Turning the corner, I catch her up and grab her arm. She makes no attempt to escape my clutch or run off, so I loosen my grip. She turns towards me and two luminous, brown eyes and attractive face looks up at me. I'm taken aback. This girl is certainly a beauty, there's no mistaking. And she's no working girl. Her cloak is made of thick velvet and finely cut, and her face is naturally pretty with no need for the layers of rouge the prostitutes around here use. My initial anger melts away when I see the girl who's been pursuing me.

"Why are you spying on me?" I ask gently, "do you want servicing? I can do that for you."

"No, no, you misconstrue my intentions sir, I am here on an errand for my mistress," she replies with more than a hint of indignation.

"Oh yes, and who is your mistress and what is your errand?"

"Have you heard of La Contessa? La Contessa di Nemesia. My name is Julia and I serve in her household as her personal maid. Her reputation is well known in Venice I believe."

"La Contessa, yes her name is notorious," I reply.

Indeed, her name is renowned in Venice. In a city which takes a certain pride in its decadence, La Contessa's name is the epitome of all that's sexually debauched. The reputation of her balls and parties is high amongst those with an interest in the sexual or bizarre. I've never met her. Our social circles are poles apart, but her antics are the talk of the taverns and brothels of the Cannaregio. It's even said she enters the district masked or in disguise. So, the girl's story possesses some credibility. But what interest could she have in a male street walker like me, who prostitutes himself to all and sundry?

"But what does she want with me?" I ask.

"Ah, you see, this is my errand. She asked me to scour the alleyways of Venice for a new slave to serve in her household."

"And you think she'd be interested in me?" I ask, my curiosity aroused by the possibility.

"She's most particular. She wants slaves who can commit completely to her service. She's after fresh blood and is looking for a young and willing male slave. You have the physical attributes," she teases, "good looking... well-endowed."

Her eyes flash with appreciation as, seeing me close up, she casts an appraising glance over me.

"And your enthusiastic performance with the two transvestites would intrigue her. Her interests are, how can I say, extremely perverse, and servants who can offer a range of different services interest her."

"So, is she looking for a stud to service her?" I enquire, flattered at the compliments.

Julia bellows with laughter, and I'm not a little deflated at her reaction. Surely that's what her mistress wants?

"No, you misunderstand. Don't flatter yourself with such vanity, those are not her inclinations. She'll manipulate and control. She'll use your body how *she* desires, not to satisfy your sexual needs, great though I'm sure they are," she adds with a sly smile.

"But, I don't get it, what's in it for me? Why should I give this up for her?"

"The pay is good, if you are prepared to accept her rules and serve her obediently and diligently. You will have a patroness who, in her own way, will support you if you are loyal. And give all what up? Standing on street corners in all weathers until your youthful good looks fade, is that where you want to be in five years-time?"

I look hurt, but she's right, as I understand only too well. I can't do this for the rest of my life. The shelf life of a street worker is short. If the life-style doesn't wear you down, then there's the risk of syphilis and other diseases. Despite the offence I've taken, her point is well made.

"I have other plans," I mutter defensively.

"I don't mean to cause offence sir, but you must see the weight of my argument. I won't deny life serving my mistress is not without its challenges. She's an exacting mistress and I've seen how she uses her sexual slaves and servants, but the rewards are considerable. She's also generous and, as I've said, the pay is good."

The offer is an intriguing one. The arguments advanced by La Contessa's maid are powerful ones. How much more sense it makes to do what I do now but receive a regular income and live in the opulence of La Contessa's palace. I'm aware of her reputation as a strict madam and organiser of sexual games. It's known she's a wealthy, powerful and formidable lady with connections amongst the aristocracy and ruling elite in Venice. There must surely be opportunities for advancement in such a household.

Then my attention is drawn back to the delectable Julia, exotic and sensuous in her rich cape and wide brimmed hat. Perhaps La Contessa's household will hold opportunities of another kind.

"Are all the servants in La Contessa's service as pretty as you? Because, if so, I reckon I'd enjoy working in her household."

It's corny I know, but I can't resist making passing the comment. It invariably works; few girls can resist a compliment. Julia smiles knowingly, and blushes.

"You flatter me, sir. Beware if you think working for La Contessa will offer an outlet for your own flirtation or you will get a rude awakening. Remember you would be there only to serve La Contessa. So, tell me, are you interested in entering her employment?"

It's decision time. I can't help but be intrigued by such a curious offer. To be plucked from the back-alleys of the least salubrious district of Venice and transported into one of the grand palaces on the Grand Canal to serve a wealthy lady, albeit one known to have extreme and bizarre tastes. I know in my heart Julia's right when she says my life on the streets is a short one. And then what? I might earn enough for an apprenticeship to a trade. Is this what I want to do with my life? No, the proposal put before me now is far more enticing.

"Yes, I'm interested in your offer."

"Excellent," exclaims Julia, "but remember La Contessa won't accept you into her household until she has assessed you, and put you through an initiation. She's trusted to my judgement and I'm sure you won't disappoint, will you?" she adds slyly.

"So, what happens? Do I come back with you straight away?"

"Yes, but there's one other little test you must face. La Contessa's instructions were clear. She said, "you must be sure to find a young male who can submit to me completely. Make sure he can accept punishment from you as a trial so he understands the nature of the duties I will expect him to perform.""

Julia looks at me with a wicked smile.

"So, you're saying you have to punish me before I can come back with you?"

I'm shocked but excited at the prospect of receiving punishment from the lovely Julia.

"Yes, if you can't pass this test, then you'll be no use to La Contessa. Come sir, I'll make it as fun for you as I can. Tell me, what's your name?"

"Roberto, my name is Roberto. Follow me. If I have to submit to punishment, let's find a place we can play out your game in a modicum of comfort."

I take Julia by the hand, encased as it is in the softest kid-leather gloves. If this young lady is her mistress's maid, then she must be well looked after to afford such luxurious accessories.

As we stumble along the poorly lit alley heading for a spot of light at the end of a dark tunnel, I take the opportunity to wrap my arm around her waist. She shoots a quick glance at me but does nothing to resist, pulling herself into the warmth of my body.

We reach the canal side. The water laps against the crumbling steps leading towards the canal-basin where a handful of gondolas are moored. The moon casts a baleful glow off the surface of the canal-waters. If you were an artist, you might see a romantic scene. The black-lacquered gondolas rocking gently on the water bathed in moonlight, and a young and attractive couple, cloaked and mysterious. But this is Venice, decadent and full of surprises, where nothing is quite what it seems.

"Is this OK? Will we be disturbed here?" enquires Julia.

"Not at this time. Most of the gondoliers will be working off Ponte San Leonardo where they can pick up trade from the taverns around the square. This place is only for mooring. I know many of the gondoliers; a few will offer me use of their gondolas for a *soldi*."

"Here, take care," I say whilst taking her hand to guide her into a gondola.

I've chosen one with a canopy to afford greater privacy, designed for erotic liaisons. The sights and sounds these gondoliers must witness as masked strangers seduce and copulate under their noses!

"We'll have a little privacy in here," I explain, as I part the drapes and invite her into the gondola.

The weight of our bodies and the nervous carelessness of our steps cause the gondola to rock, and Julia to lose her balance. As she stumbles and falls onto the cushions scattered on the floor of the gondola, I collapse on top of her. It's an opportune piece of timing. We both fall in a heap of excited giggles. We know where this is heading, have both been anticipating this from the moment our eyes met minutes ago.

The weight of my body presses on her and I feel the excited heaving of her breasts against my chest. My face is over hers and I admire her pert little nose and sensuous ruby lips curled into a knowing smile. Her bright hazel eyes invite me to kiss her. She's lovely, there's no doubt about it. It's been a long time since I've desired a woman for *my* pleasure, and not merely to satisfy a client. I lower my lips onto hers and they are met with an aroused passion matching my own. She puts her arms around me and squeezes me tighter, dislodging her hat in the process. A swathe of chestnut hair tumbles onto the shoulders of her burgundy cloak. We kiss and cling to one another using the heat of our bodies to ward off the midnight chill.

As our mouths part for a moment she puts a finger on my lips and whispers, "Wait Roberto. Stop for a moment. I must carry out the trial La Contessa has set for me. I must do this. She will question me and she sees all, she'll suspect if I've not carried out her instructions. I've never done this before. She enjoys playing with people. I think she wants to see if I'll go through with it."

My curiosity is aroused. "Go through with it? What do you mean?"

"She told me, "I have a special task for you, girl. I want to find a new slave. Go into the lanes of the Sestiere di Cannaregio. I hope you have the stomach for this Julia, for the alleys around the Campo di San Canciano are renowned for their decadent goings-on. I'm looking for a young man who'll perform for me, who'll do anything I desire. He must be able to take punishment, and you must test him for me because he's no use if he's not willing to suffer for his new mistress. You can choose any implement you like." At first I protested, but believe me Roberto, as you will soon find out, you do not resist a command from my mistress. Besides, I'm devoted to her, I'd do whatever she asks of me. I think she set the task as a test for me too."

I can't deny I find the thought of the delectable Julia inflicting corporal punishment on me intensely arousing.

"She means for you to spank or whip me?" I ask.

"Yes, that's her intent. I won't deny I'm passionate and hot-blooded, but it's not my natural inclination. I'd rather have a man's cock inside me than have him tied up. But, I think my mistress has asked me to carry out this task deliberately. I've no experience of domination but I've to go through with it. La Contessa will interrogate me in detail about what I've done and how you responded to it."

Julia's tale has made me even more intrigued about the mysterious La Contessa and convinced me entering into her employment could prove to be a lot of fun.

I spread my arms in an inviting pose, "Well go on then Julia, I'm all yours... dominate me, punish me!"

Julia looks apprehensive and apologetic, "Honestly, I've never done anything like this, but my mistress did give me one or two tips."

She inhales a deep breath to prepare herself and get into the right frame of mind.

"Ok, for the next few minutes you will be my slave and do as I say..." she announces trying to be serious, "... and then, if you please me, you can fuck me!"

"Oh, I'll look forward to that bit," I smile.

"Stop Roberto, this is serious. If I fail in my task, I'll get punished... I know I will. You must help me by entering into this."

I put on a deliberately serious face, "Mistress, your wish is my command."

She stretches her hand out towards me, her gloved fingers held out tantalisingly before me.

"Kiss my hand," she commands.

I glance up into her eyes. The hints of playfulness have deserted her. She has a doggedly determined stare as she takes on the role of mistress.

"Yes, madam," I reply.

I take the kid gloves into my hand and draw in the intoxicating aroma of leather. I put the hand to my lips and kiss the glove. The leather is soft and pliable against them. I've kissed a woman's hands on many occasions but it has been done mechanically, as a greeting, and never in such a sexually charged atmosphere. Julia holds out her hand like a Duchess.

"Now," she mutters breathlessly, affected by the sexual tension between us, "remove the glove with your teeth."

I find this a delectable and sensuous little twist. I take the leather at the tip of the middle finger between my teeth and tug gently. I'm expecting this might be a tricky task but such is the luxurious smoothness of the leather, the glove slides easily forward. After a few gentle pulls with my teeth the glove drops silently onto the cushions. Her immaculately manicured hand is offered and I press my lips against it, no command needed for me to understand the unspoken instruction. My heart beats fast, and I sense Julia, having entered fully into the role, is aroused by what she's made me do.

"You understand my instruction is to inflict punishment on you, don't you?"

"Yes, madam."

"Undo your breeches and pull them down."

I obediently comply with the request.

"Now, your knickerbockers... "

I accede to the command until both breeches and knickerbockers are hanging around my ankles. I surprise myself at how easily I give in to the whispered orders. It's like I'm in a dream. I'm beginning to think Julia is rather good at this, or perhaps she's touched a submissive side of me?

"Now, get down on all fours."

By now, as I get into position, my heart is racing and my cock is definitely aroused. There I am; my leggings around my ankles and my arse exposed, in full view of the beautiful Julia, in anticipation at the erotic delights she'll inflict on me.

Her hand runs over the fleshy mound of my arse. I have to confess, the delicious touch of Julia's soft fingers is extremely arousing. Then I hear the slap of flesh upon flesh as she spanks my bare backside. I know I'm expecting this, know Julia has explained the need to punish me but, nonetheless, I'm still surprised. Maybe I expected a gentle half-hearted slap, thinking the girl who, on her own admission, is doing this for the first time, would only deliver a few gentle slaps. She spanks me several times more with her bare hand and I expel a gasp as the stinging spreads over me. It's not intensely painful, but it's still a hard stroke. Julia delivers another four or five slaps. I hear her breathing, heavy with the physical exertion of the strokes and, dare I say it, the feeling of arousal they trigger in her. After another few strokes, and with my arse stinging in a sensuously erotic way, Julia finishes by running her hand gently across my glowing backside.

When she moves her hand away I get up from my crouching position, but Julia grasps my ponytail of black hair in her hand and pushes me onto the silk cushions again.

"No, I haven't finished yet. I'm sorry," she whispers apologetically, "but I must leave my mark on you. My mistress will inspect your backside tomorrow and will seek for evidence I've carried out her instructions to the letter. She'll look to see I've put my mark on you. I must go further. The redness will fade by tomorrow morning and she won't believe I punished you severely enough to truly test you."

On hearing this my emotions are mixed. My cock is hard and I yearn to turn Julia onto her back and take her, yet I'm both fearful and excited at the prospect of further punishment.

"You must do whatever your mistress instructs," I reply, my bottom still hanging invitingly in the air.

"She must be convinced you can receive punishment or she won't take you into her employment."

The more I hear, the more excited I am of the opportunity to spend more time with Julia, and of meeting her mysterious and sadistic employer. I've not great experience of submission in my work, but the touch of Julia's palm on my arse is convincing me it's something I could warm to.

Julia bends over me, the velvet of her cloak rubbing against the bare skin of my backside. She presses her body against mine so closely I feel the excited rising of her breasts against my back.

"Before I departed, she told me, "Leave a token on him so I can see what punishment he is prepared to take. Only then can I be assured he might be fit to join my household." She invited me to choose an implement from her collection of whips, paddles, and tawses, and described the marks they leave. I selected her leather flogger. She said, if I hit you hard enough with it, it would leave a nice scarlet glow across your arse."

What a night it's turning out to be, offering more intriguing possibilities than any other I've experienced whilst scouring the alleys of the Cannaregio.

I repeat, "Then you must do what your mistress asks of you."

Julia pulls the flogger out from under her cloak. She touches my cheek with it tantalisingly. On its end is a black piece of leather in the shape of an ace of spades. She offers it to me, and I kiss its surface in the knowledge it will soon be striking the peachy flesh of my backside.

Julia rises and stands over me, my face and body still buried in the cushions but my backside still exposed like a sacrifice. Julia sets her legs apart to steady herself and assumes a standing position to afford greater purchase for a swing.

The first stroke comes cracking down on my arse, and I hear the slap of the rounded piece of leather on my skin. If the touch of Julia's bare hand delivered a delicious sting, the flogger is seriously painful. She delivers another few strokes and then runs the leather against my glowing flesh. She definitely knows how to do this. Making me wait and anticipate the next round of strokes, offering me a hint of sensuality before the pain. If it's her first time, then she's a quick learner, or maybe her mistress has provided her with tips before she set her off on this bizarre errand.

The flogger comes down hard on me again. Julia raises it high above her head and brings it down with all the force she can muster. Who'd have thought her delicate frame could deliver such a powerful stroke, yet it did. The pain is excruciating, but deliciously so. It does nothing to subdue my ardour. My cock is still erect. Indeed, with every stroke it gets harder, and my desire to lie with my tormentor ever greater.

Julia gives me a real beating by the end. My arse stings like nothing I've experienced before. I've no doubt Julia has left her mark on me.

"There, I'm sorry. It's not my natural inclination, but it had to be done."

I roll round onto my back so I can face Julia for the first time since she began my punishment. Her face is flushed, her hair dishevelled, and she's panting. She looks ravishing, and I want to take her now. My punishment at her hands has only made me want her more.

"And what is your natural inclination, if it's not to be dominant?" I probe suggestively.

"I want a man to take me. I want a man who'll ravish me and fuck me," she laughs wickedly.

Within a fleeting moment I flip her onto the cushions and throw the weight of my body onto her.

"That's an invitation I can't refuse," I say.

15

I press my face against hers and our lips meet in a passionate kiss, our tongues exploring each other's. How nice it would be to part the heavy velvet and seductively unlace her bodice to expose the lovely flesh of her breasts, but our need is too urgent. I'll save that sensual pleasure for another occasion.

"Are you ready? Do you want me to take precautions? There are certain things I use in my work…"

"No, I know the time of my month and it's safe… that's probably why I'm so randy," she giggles. "Just do it. Enter me!"

I pull her cloak aside, lift up her skirt, pull down her satin drawers to her knees and thrust myself into her. She's ready for me. Her cunt is sopping. The game at playing dominant has aroused her. She's as desperate for me as I am for her. I pump my cock into her. The moment is right for a quick fuck. There are occasions when you take time to seduce, but this isn't one. My cock has been hard for ages and is ready to burst, which it does as I pommel her with a succession of hard thrusts. It's exquisite to empty my spunk into Julia's expectant pussy. I carry on pumping inside her, grinding against her sex to bring her to ecstasy.

We both collapse onto the cushions laughing. The gondola is still rocking to and fro in the water at the exuberance of our short, but glorious, fuck.

"Mother of Mary, I needed that," she gasps, her breaths still heavy from the exertion of her climax.

"You needed it!" I exclaimed. "I was desperate for it. Desperate to have you from the moment you lifted your head and showed your face from under your hat!"

After a few minutes Julia sits up and adjusts her clothes.

"I should be returning. Are you coming with me? Will you join my mistress's household."

There's no question in my mind, "If it means being in the same household as you, then yes, it's a resounding yes."

A look of concern flashes across Julia's eyes.

"You must always remember you will be there to serve La Contessa. There may be opportunities. God, I hope so, and I'll do what I can to create them. But we have to be careful. If La Contessa finds out we are having sexual relations in her household behind her back, then she'll be angry. I warn you… she can be quick tempered, capricious and sadistic. She'll have you performing all kinds of depraved acts. I've seen and heard. What I've done tonight is nothing… believe me, it's a trifle to what *she's* capable of. And never forget your first loyalty must always be to her. Are you still willing to come?"

My mind is made up. Despite the hints and warnings Julia gives me, I'm curious to find out more about La Contessa and intrigued to discover what it will be like to serve her. Then there are the enticing possibilities offered up by the proximity of the lovely Julia. The prospect of sampling more sexual delights with her, however furtive and secretive, cannot be overlooked.

3: La Contessa

It's the early hours of the morning by the time Julia and I reach the Palazzo Cavalli, the residence of her mistress, La Contessa di Nemesia. The Grand Canal is well-lit even in the pitch black of night and in the dim glow I cannot fail to be impressed. It's an imposing four story palazzo occupying a prominent position right on the edge of the canal. Its vast and elegant portico is approached from a grand sweep of stone stairs leading from its own landing stage on the canal where La Contessa's private gondolas are moored. Given her reputation as one of the wealthiest and most powerful women in Venice I expect her residence will be grand, and I'm not disappointed. We enter by the servants' entrance at the rear of the palace.

The palazzo follows a typical design. The tradesmen's entrance is at ground floor level. There will be state rooms and, no doubt, knowing her reputation, a grand ballroom on the first floor, La Contessa's private quarters and guest bedrooms will be on the second and third floors with the servants' quarters on the fourth. It's to these Julia directs me, following the servants' staircase at the back of the palazzo. My appetite is whetted. Though I recall visiting several grand merchant's houses in my childhood, I've never crossed the threshold of such a magnificent palazzo.

Julia tends to my needs and gets bread, cheese, and wine for supper.

"You'll wait here. I'll come and fetch you in the morning as soon as I've helped La Contessa dress and given a report back to her on my search."

I try to steal a goodnight kiss by pinning Julia against the wall but, to my surprise, she brushes me to one side. I can't help but betray my disappointment at being so brusquely dismissed after our moments of passion on the gondola.

Her eyes flash at me, "We must be careful," she urges, "the walls of the palazzo have ears and her servants are everywhere. It's dangerous; trust me, we must do nothing to provoke my mistress's wrath."

Reluctantly I back away and release Julia from my grip.

True to her word, Julia comes to fetch me the next morning after I've bathed and put on the clean tunic she laid out for me. Her manner is still distracted as it was when we parted last night. She appraises me carefully, brushing fluff off my jacket, smoothing my black hair and straightening my queue. I notice how tense she is about my introduction to her mistress.

"I've given my account of last night. La Contessa seems satisfied," she adds nervously, "but she wants to see you now."

I follow her down the servants' stairs. Emerging onto the floor below, we enter a wide corridor sumptuously decorated in baroque style. Most strikingly, the whole corridor is lined with a series of marble sculptures of naked girls in provocative and erotic poses.

Julia breaks into a smile when she sees my reaction, "The Nereides, sea nymphs from Greek myth," she explains. "They were a commission from Giuseppe Torretti. You'll get used to it. La Contessa collects... interesting works of art."

"Torretti, I'm impressed, your mistress has excellent taste. I've seen his work in the Basilica di Santa Giovanni but I've never seen anything like this before."

"You've heard of him?" Julia sounds surprised.

"Why yes, I received a good education. I haven't been a street bum all my life you know. My father was a wealthy merchant until trade declined and his debts mounted and... well, then he took his own life, and I was left orphaned and on the street. But, contrary to what you might think from the circumstances you found me in, I'm well educated."

Julia's eyes glow with interest and a new respect, "Not just a pretty face and a hard cock then," she laughs. "Good, La Contessa will like that."

Julia stops me half-way along the corridor. We stand directly in front of a marble statue of a naked girl holding a conch shell, nipples thrust out like a challenge, seducing me into the depths of the sea, and the untold erotic pleasures awaiting me there.

She shifts nervously from one foot to the other gesturing with her hands.

"Listen, this is important," she implores. "There are a few things you need to know. La Contessa is a strict mistress. You must do everything she says. And don't act cocky or answer back,"

"Cocky, me?" I say.

"No, I'm serious. If you want to please her do as she orders... and she is exacting and very particular. If you don't do what she says... then she will make you do it, believe me, until, well you want to do it. If you understand what I mean."

"Don't worry, I've got it. Don't offend her. I'll be on my best behaviour."

"No, there's more. Oh, never mind. You'll either get it or not. If she's not satisfied with you, she'll soon sling you out, which would be a shame really..."

I catch her sly, meaningful glance... "Because you want me to fuck you again?"

"Shut up, Roberto... and don't ever let La Contessa hear you flirting with me!"

As we approach the end of the corridor Julia taps gently on a door decorated with gilded ivy leaves. I hear a muffled voice from the other side. I'm nervous now. The hints from Julia about what to expect have made me wary about this meeting with my new mistress.

The door swings open and we enter La Contessa's boudoir. I soak in the air of opulence. My eyes are immediately drawn to the figure sat in a sumptuous, gilt chair lined with rich, scarlet velvet. I'm stunned at the figure sitting imperiously on the chair casting a detached, almost disdainful, glance across my body. Her unsmiling face stares at me like an accusation of weakness and frailty. At the corner of her red lips is a fake mole. Its position, pointedly to anybody familiar with Venetian fashion of the day, is the *assassina*, the murderess. The haunting, yet deadly, beauty of the face wearing it makes it apparent the positioning of the mole is no mere affectation.

She wears a *moretta* mask in black across her eyes, which only serves to accentuate her piercing green eyes bearing down on me like a lion stalking its prey.

Her dress, or perhaps I should more accurately say, lack of it, is designed to provoke and seduce. She wears nothing more than a basque, its whale bone stays and black and scarlet satin panels press her stomach in but thrust her naked breasts upwards. And what magnificent breasts she possesses, perfect mounds of alabaster flesh.

Her hair, contrary to the fashion of the day, tumbles seductively over her breasts in rich auburn waves. Around her elegant neck is a necklace of delicate and exquisite pearls. I've seen many beautiful women... and many painted hags in my time amongst the prostitutes and courtesans who ply their trade in the Cannaregio, but never has a woman made such a deep and immediate impact on me. On a person less controlled and elegant it might appear wanton but on this impressive figure it's provocatively seductive.

"Come here, boy," she commands.

I shuffle forward nervously, my heart thumping with a mixture of excitement and anticipation. As I approach I'm overwhelmed by the intense and sensuous scent of her perfume, which surrounds her body in a haze.

"Take your clothes off for me, boy."

I shuffle and hesitate slightly, which is all La Contessa needs to repeat the command.

"Now!"

I start to loosen my jerkin.

"And what do you say?"

I stop, initially wondering what she means, and then stumble to find the right words,

"Yes… madam."

"Yes, mistress," she corrects. "My maids are permitted to call me madam, but my male servants must call me mistress. Do you comprehend?"

"Yes, mistress."

"Then go ahead."

She watches every movement intently as I discard my clothes in a dishevelled heap until I'm down to my long-johns.

"Come boy, there's no place for modesty here. If you want to enter my household then you must expose yourself… completely."

I'm still nervous but, exposed to the withering gaze of La Contessa, I shuffle out of my knickerbockers. How many times have I stripped naked in front of clients without hesitation? Yet, this is different; like I'm offering myself up.

When I'm finally naked, she gets up from her chair and takes a few steps forward, casting her eyes over me. She circles me a few times inspecting me. I'm conscious of the curves of milky flesh close to my body. The feeling is disconcerting but also highly charged and erotic. I feel a surge of arousal through my cock under the concentrated inspection of my new mistress.

She turns to Julia, "You've chosen well. He's an excellent specimen. He has the physique and physical attributes I need. I can see why you were drawn to him. You've done well to find such a young man in the alleyways of the Cannaregio. The question is… does he possess the right mental qualities to serve me?"

She walks another circuit as I stand pensively, small and insignificant. A painted fingernail drags down my back causing a tingle of arousal as it runs along the curves of my muscular backside. She comes back to face me, the flesh of her breasts, thrust up by the tight corsetry, heaves under my nose. Her hands explore my torso, brush underneath the sac of my balls and come to rest on the tip of my erect cock. She's teasing me, testing me. I know it, but there's nothing I can do to stop the blood surging through my cock.

"Ah, Julia, I see he has rather a beautiful cock. Did you inspect it for me before you chose to bring him back?"

"Yes, madam."

She runs her finger along its length and my cock twitches and throbs in response. I say nothing.

"Look at it Julia. It's splendid. I bet you'd like it inside you. I think you'd love to have it in your cunt, moving inside you, filling you, satisfying you, wouldn't you?"

"I hadn't really thought about it, madam."

Julia's face reddens.

"Oh no, really, it never crossed your mind when you were inspecting him for me... a hot-blooded girl like yourself," she teases. "I bet he could give you a good fucking. Did you try him Julia? Did you have him inside you?"

"No madam!" is the indignant reply.

We exchange a furtive glance which I swear La Contessa notices. Julia is sweating and shifting uncomfortably from one foot to the other. She looks guilty. I can't help but think La Contessa knows she's lying and is toying with her.

"I don't blame you, girl. I bet he could make you come. I think he could make you squeal in ecstasy when he thrusts inside you. But you know my rules don't you? You know I don't permit sex between my servants. You have to save yourself up for me and my perversions, don't you?"

By now La Contessa's hand has strayed under Julia's skirt, seeking out her cunt. Julia lets out a small whimper and groan as La Contessa's fingers find the spot. She smiles.

"It's a shame isn't it? The discipline I impose on those who serve me."

She removes her fingers from Julia's cunt and turns her attention to me. She holds them up to my nose.

"Can you smell her cunt juices? I bet you'd love to gorge on them wouldn't you?"

I squirm in silence.

"Well?"

My discomfort is intense. What do I say? Yes I would of course, but surely that's not the answer to give.

"No, mistress."

"Liar!" she accuses, her voice sharp with reprimand. "Yet your cock tells a different story, doesn't it? Look at it. Well it's no matter. You will taste them for me."

She puts her fingers to my mouth and gently, enticingly, runs them along my lips, forcing them to part so she can ease them into my mouth. I suck on her fingers and drink in the salty juices from Julia's cunt. My cock is throbbing with need, and I swear I could come any second.

She takes the fingers, wet with my saliva and Julia's juices, out of my mouth and wraps them around my penis. She squeezes my cock tight.

"It's still hard. So, what is turning you on? Is it my tits, slave?"

I'm in turmoil. I don't know what to answer. If I say no, is it an insult? If I say yes?

"They're beautiful mistress. I'd love to touch them, if I'm permitted."

Out of the corner of my eye I catch Julia roll her eyes and shake her head. Wrong answer, I suspect.

"For such an impertinence on my personal honour, you must be punished. You see this object; it is an offence to me. It must be aroused only when I need it for my own amusement."

La Contessa steps back to her chair. With her back towards me I can admire her shapely figure. The whale bone stays of her corset pulling in her mid-riff tight and accentuating her curves erotically. Her legs, long and slender, emerge from the fringe of her silk corset.

She returns with a riding crop. At one end is a shovel of brown leather whilst at the other, a handle wrapped in cords. She turns to face me, her green eyes peering from behind the mask. She grips the cord handle tight in her long fingers and taps it gently against her hand. My stomach twists in fear and anticipation. I've no doubt of her ability to wield this instrument with dramatic effect, and I have a suspicion of where the strike will fall.

What have I let myself in for? Perhaps for the first time I have doubts about the decision. La Contessa´s reputation is well known, and to knowingly offer myself into her employment, aware this is only an appetiser for what other plans she might have for me. But the fear passes as I steel myself for the first hit, realising I need this. I want the strike of the leather but, above all, I want to create a good impression on my new mistress.

Her proximity is overwhelming. The feathers on her mask brush against my chest as she leans forward. The purse of soft leather at the end of the crop is run tantalisingly along the taut skin of my cock.

I know she's playing with me, teasing me with an aperitif before the main course.

"Such a lovely cock," she whispers in my ear almost regretfully, "but from now on it must learn to come out only for my pleasure."

She raises the crop high above her shoulder and brings it crashing down, the leather slapping against the hard flesh of my member. I flinch with the pain but still meet the hard stare of my mistress from behind the mask. The second stroke is as harsh, more so, but this time I'm prepared and hold my ground not yielding to the pain throbbing through my cock. It's still erect though, and now La Contessa pays attention to its tip, glistening with pre-cum. She plays with me again, rolling the soft leather around my glans before striking it ferociously with a series of staccato strokes. The pain is excruciating but I know I must not flinch. I sense La Contessa is testing me and does not want a slave who squeals or succumbs to the slightest

23

pain. She lifts her arm again, this time high above her shoulders. I visualise the muscles of her wrists tightening around the corded handle before it's brought crashing down on my cock, not once, but five times. I stand firm, but see Julia in the background flinch for me at the severity of the strokes. By now my cock has lost its potency. She lifts it up with the tip of the riding crop in triumph, soft and forlorn, and lets it flop.

"That's better, you see. This is how I want to see you until I'm ready to play with you… or offer you up to my guests."

"And did you test him as required?" La Contessa asks Julia

"Yes madam."

"And how did he respond to it?"

"Very well, madam, he showed himself willing to take his punishment and submit to me."

"Did you get sexual pleasure from it?" she asks me, "from having your arse flogged by such a pretty girl."

I hesitate, "Yes, I would be lying if I said it didn't arouse me mistress."

"You will need to learn that your first duty is to your mistress's desires, not your own sexual needs. Still, I would not expect anything less. The first time your arse is spanked and whipped arouses complex emotions, does it not? Submission, humiliation… wonderfully exotic feelings when you embrace them. Are you capable of doing this for me?"

"Yes, mistress," I reply, "I'm ready to try so I can serve in your household."

"And Julia, did it excite you?"

Julia flushes, "Well, yes, a little madam."

"A little," she exclaims. "Come now my maid, you can't hide anything from me. I bet your cunt was sopping, wasn't it? The feeling of domination, of having a hot young male submit to you is a delicious one, I find."

"Well, yes madam, I suppose it did." Julia squirms with embarrassment.

"And did you strike him hard? Did you leave your mark on him?"

"Yes, madam. I did exactly as you asked. You can see the marks for yourself," she replies, inviting La Contessa to inspect my backside.

She steps around me to inspect Julia's handiwork with the flogger. She runs her sharp painted fingernail across each deep red welt mark. I flinch slightly as my arse is still sore, and the marks left by the whip still inflamed.

"Keep still boy," La Contessa hisses as she digs her fingernails into the red marks.

I tighten my buttocks and try my utmost to remain still during La Contessa's examination.

"Excellent. Good work, Julia. I love how you've created a criss-cross pattern of stripes. You know I appreciate a bit of artistic flair. Red and raw without breaking the skin or causing bleeding, that's precise work, my maid. Perhaps I will make a dominatrix out of you yet," she smiles.

"I don't know, madam, though I must confess, I did rather enjoy it."

"Naturally you did! What hot-blooded female would not enjoy having a firm muscular arse offered up for her pleasure! You have done well Julia. I think this young man has potential."

"Thank you madam," Julia sighs in relief.

"As for you boy, this has only been a taster. I understand Julia has warned you of what will be expected of you, has she not?"

"Yes, mistress."

"I guarantee it will be extreme and exotic. Julia's trial and my little test today are mere trifles compared to the punishment and humiliation I'm capable of inflicting. I expect my specially chosen male slave to be open and willing to submit to anything for me, and to show discipline in his own sexual appetites. Are you capable of that I wonder? The trials you will face will be extreme but I expect complete obedience. You will be served up for all manner of sexual perversions to my friends and guests, and expected to carry out whatever I desire, however perverted. Are you prepared for that?"

I tremble in fear. But what have I got to lose. Surely whatever La Contessa throws at me can't be any more debauched than what I'm already used to? And then there's the domineering presence of La Contessa herself. It would be cowardly to turn away now. Finally, there's Julia. I've heard La Contessa's undisguised warnings, but do I dare to balance service to this mistress whilst still pursuing Julia? As she's warned, it's fraught with risk. La Contessa lays down strict rules for her household staff, yet I'm already committed to taking the risk. I know Julia is attracted to me, and she's a prize which, unlike the unattainable Contessa, can be won. These thoughts flash through my head before I answer.

"Yes, mistress, I'm ready and willing to serve in your household, whatever that may entail."

"Excellent. I hope you live up to your promise. I have in mind a special test for you, a challenge in which you can show me how suited you are to serve me. If I am satisfied then you can be accepted as a permanent member of my household. Very good, you may take leave of me now. I have to catch up on my correspondence." Turning to her maid, she continues, "Julia I won't need you now until I get dressed for dinner. I'm dining out this evening at Florian's. In the meantime," she adds with a knowing glint in her eyes, "I will leave my new charge in your capable hands."

4: The Palazzo

"How do you think it went?" I ask Julia, as we trace our steps back along the passage past the thrusting marble breasts of the Nereides, their faces appearing to smile with satisfaction that I'm prey, lured and captured by their subtle wiles.

"Ok, I think. There were a couple of moments where I thought she might turn against you, but she didn't. And she's offered you a further test of servitude, which will be challenging for you. But, if you pass, I believe she'll welcome you in her household as her slave. So, yes, it was encouraging."

"Have you any idea what she has in mind?" I ask.

"No, I don't, but be warned her desires are decadent and perverse, so prepare yourself. What did you make of La Contessa?" Julia enquires.

"Mesmerising," I laugh, and Julia laughs with me, understanding precisely what I mean. "That presence. I've known plenty of beautiful women in my time but she has something special. Her gaze can turn you into clay, moulding you to her needs, and there's nothing you can do to resist. It's both disconcerting but fascinating; you don't want to be drawn in but you can't help yourself."

Julia stops and shoots a glance at me, "Very perceptive Roberto, that's exactly how it is. She's a remarkable woman. I feel the same, even though I'm her maid and don't play an active part in her games. Yet, I'm still drawn to her."

"And what about us?" I ask.

"Do you think she knows? It was unsettling how she questioned you about our meeting and the way she teased me as if she knew what we did in the gondola."

"I don't see how," I reply, "she's guessing. I mean... her sexy maid and a horny young man... it doesn't take much to work out what might happen."

"Maybe, but there's more. It's scary, she understands things instinctively. She definitely suspects something."

"You worry too much," I say pinning her up against the corner of the passage. I run my hand under her skirt and up her leg whilst planting a kiss on her lips. At first her lips are soft and yielding as if she wants to give in to the kiss, but then she breaks suddenly from my clasp.

"Not here, Roberto. You've got to learn. What if a servant sees us and reports back to La Contessa? It's too risky."

"When, then? You've got the rest of the day to show me around, she said so herself."

"Later maybe, but for now, I've got to give you a tour of the palazzo."

I get over the disappointment, and am encouraged by her hint of the possibility of finding some place to make love later in the day. I concentrate on what she has to say. Julia proceeds to describe the rooms of the palazzo and introduce me to its staff.

The opulence of the palazzo, which was obvious last night, is confirmed by the tour Julia gives me. The palace, built entirely from the best Italian marble, is symmetrical, divided into two halves by a splendid marble staircase and a sweeping set of stairs leading to the reception rooms on the first floor. Julia explains that we are on the second floor, the rooms to the left of the central staircase being La Contessa's private chambers: her boudoir, dressing room, office, private sitting room and bedrooms. Julia tells me it's the part of the palace she's most familiar with as La Contessa's personal maid.

The grand staircase is only used for special occasions and is normally out of bounds, but we are able to use the back staircase. The state rooms are on the first floor; the doors to these rooms stay locked but Julia describes them and their uses. One side of the main staircase is taken up entirely by the grand ballroom, used only for balls and concerts when La Contessa wants to impress the rich and powerful.

"Oh," Julia gasps, "you must see it Roberto. I'm sure you will one day if La Contessa accepts you into her employment. It's so magnificent, it really is. You'll never have seen anything so splendid."

On the other side of the staircase there's another set of public rooms: a salon used for more intimate functions, a games room with card tables and a billiard table, a private reception room and even a little theatre. All I get to see is the massive entrance hall, its roof reaching up two floors to the roof of the palace. The doors leading from it are embellished with gold leaf, and the cupola set up high in the domed roof. I strain my neck. The symbols painted as frescoes on the ceiling are clear, the twelve signs of the Zodiac.

I raise a quizzical eyebrow. I'm intrigued. I'd expect a religious theme or classical allegory, "I can't see that going down too well with the Archbishop or the Council of Ten. They are renowned for their conservatism."

"La Contessa is a law unto herself," Julia explains. "She's extremely powerful. She only accepts the outward forms of the Catholic Church when it suits her, which is infrequently. As to the Doge and the Council of Ten, well," she whispers secretively, "to tell you the truth she has a hold over them. I don't know how, though they attend her parties and indulge themselves in whatever La Contessa has to offer."

I'm intrigued. The politics of Venice are complex. You have *La Serenissima,* the serene republic, this city of indulgence and sexual promiscuity, the Doge and the ruling Council of Ten at its head. Nominally conservative, but having lost control of what goes on in the city decades ago, they allow the decadence to flourish. Perhaps the proclivities of the political elite are closer to its people and its visitors than might be expected or, maybe, as Julia hints, La Contessa has a hold over them.

At the rear of the palace is a patio and private garden screened from the prying eyes of the overlooking palaces by a line of palm trees, with a cool fountain in the middle.

I cannot help but comment on another aspect of the palazzo and its decoration, the art work. As I've already seen from the marble statues of the Nereides it's openly libidinous, if not entirely debauched. In the guest quarters and public galleries it's more aligned with the tastes of the day. I know a lot about art from my adolescence when my father, a minor collector himself in more prosperous times, passed on all he knew. This awareness convinces me La Contessa has a large and magnificent collection.

There are frescoes by Tiepolo, canal scenes by Francesco Guardi and Canaletto, portraits by Rosalba Carriera and paintings by Sebastian Ricci, Pietro Longhi and other prominent artists of the age, all seemingly private commissions. This is an unrivalled art collection of great taste and magnificence. The pride of place in the entrance hall is a huge canvas by Canaletto occupying the whole back wall of the landing between the staterooms and the private apartments. It's obviously a private commission. It depicts the Grand Canal during the *Carnevale* in exquisite detail, the throngs of revellers in different masks painted with exacting accuracy and vibrant colours. At the centre of the painting is the palazzo taking pride of place with La Contessa on its balcony overlooking proceedings in an elaborate mask decorated with ostrich feathers.

After exploring the state rooms we descend into the bowels of the palace. Julia introduces me to the other members of the household. It's hard to remember all the names of the staff I meet. We sit around a huge table in the kitchen surrounded by brass pans and jelly moulds hanging from the ceiling sharing pots of strong black coffee and cakes. Julia chats amiably with the other kitchen and domestic staff and appears to have a rapport with them. I get the impression that, though La Contessa is a firm mistress who requires everything to be done to the exacting standards she demands, she's also a fair employer, and looks after her staff well. The household appear to accept the bizarre nature of her behaviour.

I comment on this to Julia and she agrees with my assessment. She does give me a word of warning and advice though.

"Yes, I've a good relationship with the other staff but then, you have to remember, I'm La Contessa's personal maid. I don't do any management of the household but passing on her personal wishes is mostly down to me. I have a powerful position, and to cross me would be a slight to La Contessa. I should warn you there can be tension between the household staff and those chosen as her play-things as they're called. It's as well to be aware. Everybody's familiar with her predilections and, whether they approve or not is irrelevant, they'll never comment. Lucio is La Contessa's household manager. You must look out for him. He's La Contessa's eyes and ears in the palazzo. His influence is equal to mine but in a different way. He manages the household; I manage La Contessa's wishes. But he has spies everywhere. This is why we must be so careful if..."

"If what...?" I interject with a smile.

"If we are to continue, with our... dalliance."

"Ah, then it's possible," I add triumphantly.

"Only if we are careful and keep it secret. I'm not sure if you realise the dangers. La Contessa runs a strict house. She'll be furious if she finds out."

"So, do you know how much La Contessa is worth? This palace, the works of art alone, must be worth a fortune."

"No," Julia laughs, "I'm her maid not her accountant! Really, I couldn't say. There's all this you can see, there's her hunting lodge and country estate in Piedmont and other properties and business interests. I've heard the figure of 20,000 ducats a year mentioned, and that's only her personal income without the value of the properties or estates."

"Whew," I gasp, "that's a fortune."

"And she uses it to express her innermost desires."

After completing the tour, Julia takes me up to the fourth storey of the palazzo and the servants' quarters.

"These are the rooms for La Contessa's permanent staff. Many of the kitchen staff and domestics come in from other parts of the city. You'll be a member of her private retinue and live in the palazzo. Your role will be to serve La Contessa in her perverted sexual games but not all the time. In between times you will be given other household tasks to do."

Julia provides me with a uniform in La Contessa's livery, including a white tunic with a black swan on it, a symbol I've already seen around the palazzo.

Understandably, the decor in the servants' quarters is much plainer, but it's still comfortable. My own room is a reasonable size and perfectly adequate. I must remember to get permission to return to my lodgings to collect such belongings as I have. Julia explains that Lucio will arrange the terms of my contract with La Contessa, and payment.

The long corridor echoes to the sound of our feet. Julia casts an anxious eye up and down the passage.

"Quickly," she says ushering me through a door into her room.

It smells of her, of perfumed soap and her scent. Julia's quarters are not merely functional, they are positively commodious. She has her own sitting room with a writing desk, because she acts as La Contessa's personal secretary, a dressing room, and a bedroom with, I note with a smile of anticipation, a rather grand bed. I jump onto it and bounce up and down.

"Well this looks comfy Julia. You're well looked after. Here, come and join me," I say, patting the cover and inviting her to sit beside me.

"Yes, I know," she replies, "I consider myself lucky. After my parents died I was raised in an orphanage. La Contessa came there to choose children for her staff. I must have been about 11 or 12 at the time. I remember it vividly; this grand lady being paraded in front of the orphans in their tatters. Anyway, for whatever reason, she chose me, and I've never looked back. She seemed to take a liking to me. She had other staff teach me to read and write and I got ever more responsible jobs until she made me her personal maid. I was thrilled when she summoned me to tell me about my appointment. It was the best day of my life. She says she likes my sunny disposition... it's a balance to her darkness, at least that's what she says.

"I love my job, Roberto. I love serving her. I know she can be demanding and harsh but I don't care, and it's her right to make those demands. Everything has to be perfect for her and, when I see the results, it makes me feel good. For instance, I get to help her to dress. I handle her beautiful clothes and get to touch the gorgeous materials. And when I see how fabulous she looks and, believe me, she always looks amazing; to think I've had a part in creating that is satisfying."

I sit quietly, fascinated by Julia's speech and her openness. I put my arm around her and give her a hug and she nestles her head against my shoulder.

"We have one thing in common, Julia, and that's losing parents at a young age. I was too young to remember my mother when she died, but I still miss my father lots. He took me everywhere with him, even to his business meetings. What little sense I have, I got from him. As I've said, he taught me an appreciation of art and architecture, pretty valuable if you live in a city such as Venice."

"I remember nothing about my parents. To be honest, it's La Contessa who's rescued me from what would have been a miserable life."

"So, is she a bit of a mother-figure to you?" I prompt, aware La Contessa is a mature woman and could well be old enough to be Julia's mother.

She laughs hysterically at the suggestion, "No Roberto, really, no! She's not a mother figure. She's... oh, never mind, you ought to shut up now and kiss me!"

I would have been intrigued to hear how Julia did see La Contessa but I was not going to turn down the invitation to kiss her. I push her onto the bed and roll onto her, planting my lips onto hers. We lay there kissing passionately. This is what I've been anticipating all day; to have Julia to myself. I loosen the cords on Julia's bodice, remove it and pull her cotton chemise over her head. Her skin is golden brown.

I've been yearning to see her tits bared for the first time. I've seen breasts of all shapes and sizes and, I can't help it, I love them. Love the varying angles of their curves, how they hang, how the soft flesh feels in my hands. And Julia's are indeed lovely, up there with the best! They are beautifully rounded but not too large. They are pert but deliciously soft and pliable. I can't resist leaning over and smothering them with kisses, to Julia's delight.

"You're lovely, Julia," I murmur before rolling my tongue around the bud of her nipple.

"Mm, flattery will get you... well, quite a long way actually!"

I break off to remove my own jerkin and shirt to reveal my smooth olive skin, exactly the same tone as Julia's. I want her body pressing against my bare flesh. Now, it's Julia's turn to admire my body as she runs her hand across my cheek and then across my hairless chest.

"Yes, tasty," she's says in appreciation.

We lie next to each other touching. I wrap my arms and squeeze her against me, her breasts pressing against my flesh. I feel the swelling of them against my chest. And then we kiss passionately. Our ardour is definitely aroused now. She helps me by lifting her hips, inviting me to pull skirt, petticoat, and knickerbockers down to her ankles where she shakes them off onto the floor in one movement. There she is in all her naked glory. I lean over, burying my mouth into the bush of hair above her sex and smothering her in kisses as she gasps with anticipation.

In my excitement I frantically unbutton my breeches and pull them off, flinging them onto the floor. My cock is hard. It's been hard from the moment I was invited into Julia's bedchamber. Julia wastes no time in taking it in her hand and running her fingers along the hard flesh and rubbing its tip. She's handles it with desire and confidence, it's obvious this is not the first time.

"It's so nice to touch. I want it, Roberto. I want it inside me."

"And you shall have it, my love."

I gently manoeuvre Julia onto her front. I admire every delicious curve of her lovely body. I lie by her side and run my fingers from her shoulders over her back until they come to rest on the little hollow above her arse. I gently brush the delicate hairs with the tip of my finger.

She sighs contentedly, "Mm, lovely. Don't stop."

I let my fingers explore the secret corner of her body, allowing them to drift downwards along the curve of her backside to excited gasps of arousal. I kneel over her and lean down to kiss her shoulders then, planting kisses along her back until I come to the spot above her backside, which obviously arouses her. This is lovely. I've fucked countless women, often in back-alleys on stone floors or impaling them against the flaking, plaster walls. So it's wonderful to have the time to explore the body of a beautiful woman with touch and kiss. In the short time we've spent time together I feel drawn to Julia; I like her and respect her. The tenderness I show her isn't feigned. I kiss the hollow in the small of her back.

"Ooh, yes, that's good. Kiss me on the arse, please," she pleads

"With pleasure," I reply.

I press my lips against the soft flesh of her backside. Whilst doing this I let my hand drift towards her sex and allow my fingers to brush her bush of soft brown hair.

"Oh god, Roberto, that's *so* nice. Touch me there. Put your fingers inside me."

I will do, but I prefer to keep her waiting and play with her a little longer. I run my fingers through the hairs, getting tantalisingly closer to the folds of her sex. She moans in appreciation of every touch. I run my finger along the lips of her cunt and feel the juices from her sex on my fingers. Then I insert a finger into her and she gasps. I gather the moistness and seek out the bud of her sex rolling my finger over it and pressing against the bone beneath it.

"Oh, that's good," she groans.

"Do you want it inside you?"

"Yes, now. Take me from behind."

She crouches, burying her head into the pillow and gripping onto the bed with her hands. Then she raises her backside into the air, inviting me to penetrate her. I kneel up behind her and grip her hips in my hands. She is sopping and my cock slides into her. I move gently inside her and take her 'doggy style'. From this position I can put my hands underneath her and rub her clit whilst still pumping into her.

"I want you Julia,"

"Give it to me. Touch me! Fuck me!"

I slide my cock into her faster and harder whilst still tugging at the hard nub of her sex. I feel ripples of pleasure rolling down her back. Her breaths get heavier and her groans more intense. I know she's about to climax. I go for one final push and thrust my cock inside her more deeply. She lets out a guttural scream as the waves of orgasm pump through her. It doesn't take long for me to follow as I groan and come into her. We both collapse onto the bed, exhausted and exhilarated. We lie silently for a few minutes holding each other. Finally, Julia breaks the silence.

"That was brilliant. It's been such a long time, I needed it so much."

"It was special for me Julia. I do this so often I've almost forgotten what it's like to be with a woman I desire, not just to make a living."

"But you know we can't carry on having sex Roberto."

"Why, because of your mistress?" I ask.

"No, or at least not only that. I can't get pregnant. It would give away what we've been up to and, besides, I don't want to lose my position here. We'll have to be careful and restrain ourselves."

"Not necessarily. There are ways around it."

"What do you mean?"

"Well, you can do things to stop yourself getting pregnant. You can use half a lemon as a cap. The lemon juice kills the sperm. Or you can create a pessary using a sponge mixed with acacia tree bark and honey to bind it together."

"Ugh. I don't fancy that!"

"A lot of my clients say that. If you don't want to stick anything inside you, there's wild carrot or you might know it as bishop's lace. If you take its seeds after sex it stops you getting pregnant. The Ancient Greeks and Romans used it, so... if it's good enough for them. I always carry some with me. I offer it to all the women I fuck."

"How do you know this stuff?"

"Tricks of the trade, Julia! Everyone on the streets knows this stuff but the church won't tell you because they believe any contraception is a sin."

"Does it work?"

"Yes. How do you think courtesans maintain a career without having scores of babies? Bishop's lace has been around for centuries; it's effective, and it doesn't have any side effects."

Julia looks surprised. She has no idea such methods are available.

She looks thoughtful for a few moments before saying gleefully, "Well that opens up a lot of possibilities."

We continue laying there for a while, touching and muttering endearments. We both jump in shock when there's a knock on the door. It's Lucio's voice.

"Miss Julia, are you there? The mistress has been asking for you."

"Oh, it's ok. I'm on my way. I must have dozed off. I had a late night last night."

"Ok, Miss Julia, I'll tell her you'll be with her straight away."

We hear footsteps walking away from the door.

"Shit," mutters Julia, "I'll have to go. I daren't keep La Contessa waiting. I might get away with it. I don't think she gave me a specific time to attend to her. You don't think Lucio heard us do you?"

"Probably, I expect the scream of pleasure was heard through the whole palazzo. What if he did? You worry too much."

"We need to be careful, Roberto. It's all very well for you, you haven't as much to lose if we get caught. You'd better get yourself dressed," she says as she picks her velvet skirt up from where it had been tossed aimlessly onto the floor, and shuffles back into it. "And when you go, make sure nobody sees you leaving my room."

Now fully dressed, she gives me a final kiss and then scuttles out of the door to serve her mistress. I luxuriate in the warmth and aroma of sex in Julia's bed before eventually and reluctantly, I get myself dressed. What a first day at work!

5: The Party

The next day the palazzo is propelled into a hive of activity. Harassed servants are rushing around in a frenzy whilst the kitchen staff are busy preparing dishes for dinner. Julia, stressed with issuing mistress's commands to the rest of the staff, visits me to explain what's going on. I have to say Julia looks sexy when she's in a fluster; her hair dishevelled and her cheeks flushed red. How I'd love to fling her on the bed and take her there and then, but I know I won't be popular if I try, so I restrain my desires.

She explains in a breathless voice, "La Contessa has announced that she's holding a party. She can be capricious, just suddenly decide to do something. It's not a large one, like her famous masquerade balls in the grand ballroom, but an intimate party for a select group of her confidantes. La Contessa will want everything to be perfect. She's very particular, and it's important her parties have the right ambience; everything, the decoration of the salon, lighting, food, music, and her dress must be exactly as she desires. The success of her parties is founded on this attention to detail."

I know from her reputation that La Contessa di Nemesia's parties are renowned throughout Venice as being amongst the most risqué and erotic events in the city. For those in the social circle who favour the sexual and bizarre, it's a great privilege to be invited. I mention that I'm rather looking forward to seeing what goes on at them.

"Be careful what you wish for," laughs Julia, "I think you'll get a closer look than you might like. She wants you to be part of the entertainment for her guests!"

"Me. Have you any idea what she plans?" I ask.

"None at all, but she did warn about setting you a test. This will be it. She'll want to see how you perform for her guests, I expect. I have to go, I'm meeting with the florists to arrange the bouquets of roses to decorate her salon. Oh, I've an important message as well. You are to attend her private boudoir at six. I expect I'll see you there as I shall be helping her get dressed."

Julia leaves in a hurry, no doubt having a long list of tasks to do for her mistress in preparation for the party. That leaves me the rest of the day to complete the menial tasks I've been given and ponder what La Contessa might have in store for me.

The time for the arrival of her guests is fast approaching. In accordance with my instructions I go to La Contessa's boudoir and knock tentatively on the door. I hear Julia's voice ordering me to enter and wait until her mistress is ready for me. Julia is helping with her toilette and dressing in preparation for the party. I stand silently and patiently. La Contessa sits at her dressing table with her back to me as Julia brushes her hair. The table is scattered with ivory combs and brushes inlaid with mother-of-pearl. Julia is absorbed in her task but finds a moment to flash me a welcoming smile.

I watch intrigued at the interaction between the two women, especially Julia. She's brushing La Contessa's hair in long deliberate strokes with a care and tenderness bordering on intimacy. She stops every so often to gently stroke and re-arrange the striking auburn locks.

"Oh, you have such lovely hair, madam," whispers Julia.

"Thank you."

And it's true, La Contessa's hair is striking. It's thick and lush, and glows with a reddish hue in the candlelight.

"I could spend the whole evening brushing your hair. It smells delicious madam. I do love it when you let it cascade over your shoulders like this. It's such a shame to cover such lovely hair up in a wig, even though I know it's the fashion these days."

"Yes, Julia, I prefer to wear it this way, but regretfully the formality of certain occasions demand I wear a wig."

The dialogue is an insight into the relationship between Julia and her mistress. On my introduction she appeared tense, presumably anxious for her mistress's approval of her choice, but watching them now, there is an ease to their exchange. It's noticeable that Julia takes great pleasure in the intimate act of brushing her mistress's hair.

I'm jolted out of my observations by La Contessa's voice, now cold and hard, "Come over here, slave. Let me take a closer look at you."

I move forward and she appraises me quickly with a contemptuous glance.

"So you are my new slave, aren't you? Are you innocent of what goes on at my parties?"

"Mistress, your reputation proceeds you, I only know the rumours which spread throughout the city."

"I have chosen you to be the entertainment for my party. Go away and take a bath so you are clean and fresh for my guests, then return in another hour. After you enter my boudoir you will remove your bath robe and kneel before, naked. Do you understand slave?"

"Yes, mistress," I reply.

"Good, you are dismissed now," she says with a nonchalant wave of her hand.

Returning to the servant's quarters to bathe, I'm nervous about what La Contessa plans for me. I expect complete loyalty to her will be required. I don't have long to dwell on these thoughts. The hour passes, and it's not long before I'm tentatively knocking on La Contessa's boudoir door again.

"Enter slave," she commands.

I enter her room. Julia has gone and La Contessa is alone, still sat at her dressing table, but with her chair turned to face me. I drop my bath robe onto the floor so I'm naked, and drop to my knees.

Her voice is severe. "You will be the entertainment for my guests tonight. This is a great privilege for you. I expect complete obedience from you. You will follow my instructions precisely. You will not address me or any of my guests unless you are spoken to. To do otherwise will be considered the height of rudeness and will be punished accordingly. You will assume the role of slave and submit to whatever pleases myself or my guests. I trust this is clear?"

"Yes, mistress," I reply.

"First, I will collar you; to show that in my presence you are no more than a pet. Indeed, I treat my dogs with more attention than I do one of my slaves."

She takes a leather collar from her dressing table, puts it around my neck and buckles the collar tightly. Then she takes a lead and attaches it to the collar.

"First, you must be humiliated in front of the other household staff, so you know your place. You will walk to heel and follow behind me on all fours."

La Contessa stands up and walks towards the door, giving the lead a sharp jerk to make sure I follow. I get on my hands and knees and crawl behind her. We go along the corridor to the main staircase of the palazzo. At the bottom of the stairs the household staff is lined up, ready to serve at the party. I'm made to descend the stairs on all fours past the silent stares of La Contessa's staff, who stand on either side forming a corridor of humiliation. La Contessa leads me into her salon.

It's a large room, though presumably not on the scale of the palazzo's grand ballroom, and decorated sumptuously in a baroque style with rich colours and gold leaf. Most striking though is La Contessa's collection of erotic art adorning the walls. There are tapestries depicting naked Greek gods and goddesses in scenes of sexual debauchery. On another wall are sketches from India showing acts of sodomy and fellatio. In alcoves there are sculptures of naked men and women, their sexual organs shamelessly exposed or entwined in sexual acts. The whole salon exudes an air of richness and decadence. In the centre of the room is a dais, and by its side a large wooden chest with sliver clasps. In front of La Contessa's throne is a bench covered in red leather and suspended from the ceiling by chains. A chamber orchestra sits in a bay window patiently waiting for La Contessa's orders to play.

She mounts the dais and sits imperiously on her throne. La Contessa wears a stunning gown cut to enhance her ample decolletage, with her auburn hair swept back and decorated with pearls. A golden mask, adorned with emerald and ruby feathers, covers her eyes. With a single gesture of her hand I'm ordered to crouch at the foot of the dais, my mistress still holding the lead.

She issues a command to one of her servants by the door, "My guests may enter now and pay homage to me."

La Contessa's guests enter the salon. It's a select party with only eight guests. They are a stunning sight. They are dressed in cloaks and hoods of crushed velvet in rich, dark hues; deep blues, rich reds, purples, indigos, and maroons. They wear silk gloves in colours matching their cloaks. The guests are masked in white *morettas* with a variety of expressions.

La Contessa must have given precise instructions as to the dress code, and the impact is stunning. Dressed, as they are, in similar loose fitting cloaks and masks, it's impossible to tell which guests are male and which female. One by one each guest comes forward to La Contessa on her dais. She holds her hand out, and the guest is permitted to touch her hand gently with their masked lips.

"Thank you for coming," she announces. "I hope you will enjoy the entertainment and pleasures I have laid on for you. Join together in pairs and dance. Let the party begin!"

On her prompt the string quartet and harpsichord start to play. The guests form couples and dance a stately minuet around the dais where La Contessa sits, and also around me, still crouched obediently at her feet. It's a magical and intoxicating sight as the cloaked figures glide elegantly around me.

La Contessa claps her hands. The orchestra stops playing, the couples halt their dancing and the pair immediately in front of La Contessa advance towards her.

"This servant has recently entered my employment as my new slave and needs to learn the arts of subservience. For this evening he is our entertainment, a toy you can play with for your own amusement and pleasure. Slave, this guest needs some boots cleaning," La Contessa says, gesturing to one of the figures before her. "Make yourself useful and use your tongue to lick them clean."

I crawl nervously forward. The guest hitches up a cloak to reveal a pair of brown ankle boots of soft Italian leather. I stroke my tongue gently up to the top of the boot then back down again. Meanwhile, the other guests have gathered round to watch me undertake this demeaning task. The masked guest turns to La Contessa, and an indignant female voice rings out.

"Contessa, this is hopeless. If you wish to keep the hard earned reputation of your parties, you must find slaves who carry out their tasks more thoroughly. I expect my boots to be licked clean with more enthusiasm than this."

La Contessa replies. "You are right. I cannot have my guests offended by such dilatory service. Slave, get on all fours and spread your legs whilst you perform this task." She turns to her other guests, "he needs punishment to encourage him. Kick him in the balls whilst he performs this task."

I suffer a crushing blow of leather boot on my balls and gasp in pain.

"Slave, did anyone tell you to stop your task while you were being punished? No, they didn't, did they? Keep licking my guest's boots and don't stop until I order you."

This time I work my tongue up the leather more vigorously. I receive another kick in the balls from the other guest. Even though the pain is excruciating, I try not to let it distract me from the task at hand. I keep working my tongue across the leather boots, every so often receiving another kick. Eventually, La Contessa orders me to stop. She turns to her guest.

"Are you satisfied with this service yet?" she asks.

The guest answers, "Yes, this will do. After a poor start your servant has cleaned my boots thoroughly."

Leaning down from her dais, La Contessa examines the boots, "You are being generous. I still think he needs to be punished more, so he realises he must carry out his tasks with more enthusiasm from the start. Kick him in the balls again to teach him a lesson."

At first I experience several gentle blows to my balls from the other guest's boot. The intensity builds up as the blows get faster and harder until I'm in agony, and my balls throb with every kick.

"That will be enough for now," pronounces La Contessa, "change partners and let us have more dancing."

On her command the music starts up again, and the robed and masked figures start their parade around La Contessa and myself again. The dance is a *furlana,* currently popular in the ballrooms of Venice. It's a fast and furious dance as the guests fly around the salon their velvet cloaks a blur of vibrant colour. The dance mimics the behaviour of courtship and this version emphasises its flirtatious and erotic elements. La Contessa claps her hand and the dancers drop onto one knee with an extravagant wave of their hands.

"I think to get our enjoyment from this servant he should be put into bondage so he is completely at our mercy."

A man's voice replies from behind a mask, "Yes, Contessa, I agree. We like to see slaves tied up and defenceless so we can do whatever we like with them. We'll perform this task for you so your servant is prepared for our pleasure for the rest of the evening."

The two guests hold out a hand each and pull me up from my crouching position at La Contessa's feet. They lead me over to the red, upholstered bench suspended by chains from the ceiling, and place me on it, their masked faces leaning over me. Together they secure my ankles and wrists to the dangling chains and pull ropes through hooks in the side of the bench to secure me. I'm now at the mercy of La Contessa and her guests.

"Excellent. Now my servant is prepared, change partners, and let us have another dance."

The sound of the violins and cellos swell up around me. Once again the velvet-cloaked bodies swirl around the room, so close that I feel the lightest brush of the soft material against me. The same ritual is repeated with La Contessa clapping her hands and two guests coming forward, whilst the others gather around the bench to watch proceedings.

La Contessa announces, "Now my servant must pass through a trial of fire and ice."

A female voice calls out, "I'll apply the ice Contessa," and then a male voice, "And I'll apply the fire."

One of the guests moves forward. She carries a small pouch out of which she takes a handful of crushed ice into her silk-gloved hands. She holds the handful of ice against my cock. At first I'm startled as I react to the intense cold against such a sensitive part of my body. But she continues to press the pack of ice hard against my cock and the feeling increasingly becomes one of burning. I squirm and moan as the intensity of the pain builds up. I hear La Contessa and her guests, who are watching my humiliation intently, laugh at me. As the guest with the female voice withdraws, the guest with the male voice approaches carrying an ornate, brass candlestick.

"This should be amusing," he says, "let's see how he squirms when the hot wax touches his ice-cold prick."

La Contessa leans forward, "Don't hold back, hold the candle close to his cock so the heat of the wax is intense."

He holds the candle over me. The flame dances near my flesh, and then the hot molten liquid is poured onto the tip of my cock. I let out a squeal of surprise and pain at the shock of the heat on my cold penis. The warmth of the molten wax penetrates me in waves, a sensation both painful and deliciously exhilarating. Then I get another shock. As I'm concentrating on the attention given to my cock, I suddenly feel the silken hand of the female guest press ice against my nipples. The two guests work together alternating the ice and hot wax on these most sensitive parts of my anatomy.

"There's nothing like seeing a slave squirm with pain and discomfort inflicted by his mistress," one female guest laughs.

A male voice replies, "He almost looks as those he's enjoying it now he's got used to the sensations."

La Contessa intervenes, "I can't have that. He is not here to receive pleasure, he is here to entertain me and my party guests. Anyway, we must get the wax off now."

She reaches into her box and pulls out two whips passing them to two of her guests, "Hit him hard until all the hardened wax has been whipped off."

The two guests set about me, one whipping me on the cock and balls, the other on my already sensitive nipples. I shout out in pain.

"We can't have his noise disturbing our fun, you ought to shut him up Contessa," suggests one of her guests.

"Yes," she replies, "servants must suffer their punishments in quiet dignity not draw attention to themselves and disturb our peace."

La Contessa pulls another object out of her box and steps from her dais. She dangles it in front of my eyes and smiles cruelly. It's a gag, a ball wrapped in leather. She lifts my head, tells me to open wide and thrusts the ball into my mouth, fastening the strap behind my head. The ball fills my mouth and the only sound I can summon is a muffled grunt.

"That's better, now you can carrying on whipping him without any disturbance."

The two guests continue their whipping, the strokes getting harder and more frequent. There's no protest I can make. I'm completely under La Contessa's, control, and have to accept the punishment given me. Eventually, the wax is whipped off and my nipples, cock, and balls are left red and throbbing.

"Stop now, choose another partner, and we will do more dancing," La Contessa proclaims.

The guests pair up again and dance around the salon in time to the music. My head is throbbing with the intensity of the experience as the cloaked and masked bodies spin around me. La Contessa claps her hands again and another two of her guests step forward.

"Now, let us prepare this slave for a test of his endurance before we head off for the feast I have prepared for you," says La Contessa, handing out more objects to her guests.

"I am sure you know what to do with these."

"Yes, Contessa," says a female voice.

"Yes, Contessa," echoes a male voice, "we will make him suffer with these for your amusement."

The male guest ties my cock and balls up tightly whilst the female guest puts clamps on my nipples, sore from ice, hot wax, and whip. The pain is intense, but I can make no response. I'm completely at her mercy. With the clamps secure, she squeezes them tightly between her fingers. My body jerks. The pain is excruciating.

"I think that hurt," the guest laughs, and laughter echoes around the salon.

The male guest has the thin rope strapped tightly around my balls and cock and threads it through a pulley above the bench. He pulls the ropes hard and ties a lead weight onto the end of them stretching my cock and balls. The female guest does the same at the other end of my body, so the nipple clamps are pulled by another lead weight. To finish off, another guest applies pegs onto my stretched genitals. The pain is intense. Yet, because I know there is no way out of my predicament, I try to endure the punishment and humiliation.

La Contessa stands up and descends from her dais. She announces to her guests, "Now is time for feasting. Whilst this slave is left to suffer, we will retire to my dining room. Whilst we are drinking fine wine and feasting on a splendid banquet, this worthless slave will be left in isolation until we return, fed and refreshed, to take him to new levels of pain and humiliation."

At this La Contessa strides towards the door of the salon with her guests following in procession.

6: Humiliation

I'm left alone to suffer and contemplate what fate awaits me when La Contessa and her guests have finished their feasting. The pain from the weights on my cock, balls, and nipples lures me into a hypnotic daze, until eventually I hear animated talking and laughter from outside the salon door. Is my humiliation about to begin again?

The door opens, and I sense there's a different mood to La Contessa's party. Gone is the controlled dignity of the cloaked and masked figures from earlier in the evening. The wine and food has generated a more raucous atmosphere, and guests who are ready for more amusement. As the group enters the door of the salon La Contessa is still wearing the same gown and mask as before, but her guests have changed. They have disrobed and removed their masks. They are not entirely naked, as they wear some adornment: leather gloves, boots, belts, or straps. The men have beautifully proportioned bodies... and are well hung. La Contessa must have chosen them herself. The women are stunning, amply breasted, with long hair down to their waists. As the guests enter, other servants carry in large couches for the guests to lounge on and tables with crystal goblets and wine.

The guests start to pair up. There are no rules to this party. I notice various couplings; men with other men, women with other women, embracing and kissing with wild abandon. La Contessa watches proceedings with an engaged and satisfied expression, showing obvious delight in the world she's created for her guests' enjoyment.

La Contessa calls to one, "Mariana, release the slave from his clamps and weights so we can use him for our pleasure."

One of the female guests steps away from the mass of writhing bodies and stands over me. She removes the ball gag from my mouth. She squeezes the nipple clamps tight causing an adrenaline rush of pain, and tugs them off. I gasp in agony as the blood returns to the tips of my nipples causing a further wave of pain. She moves to my cock and balls, sharply removing the clamps and lead weights. Another female guest stands opposite her, leaning over me to give her a passionate kiss until their lips part and they break into light-headed laughter.

"I wonder if your servant is hungry, Contessa. He's been trussed up whilst we enjoy a marvelous banquet. I bet you'd like some desert, wouldn't you?"

"Yes, madam," I reply, wondering what to expect.

Mariana collects a crystal glass dish filled with a rich chocolate mousse. She leans over me, her long dark hair brushing against my body. She dips her finger into the bowl and runs it along my lips. I savour the bittersweet, dark chocolate. She slips her finger into my mouth so I can lick the chocolate from it. The taste is sensational. By now my cock has hardened; the eroticism of the guest's actions too sensuous to resist. She dips her hand into the glass dish again and removes it to smother my erect cock with chocolate dessert, running the creamy mousse along the shaft.

"Claudio," she calls, "you wanted seconds of Contessa's delicious dessert, didn't you? Well, I've got it here for you, but you'll have to lick it off this servant's cock if you want it."

"Mmm, yes, I'll suck this slave's cock for more of Contessa's chocolate mousse," he responds.

My heart's beating fast; never before have I been subjected to such humiliating treatment. Claudio leans over me and runs his tongue up the shaft of my cock, licking greedily until the chocolate has disappeared. Mariana smothers more of the chocolate mousse onto my cock. This time, Claudio takes the whole head of my cock into his mouth and slides his mouth up and down my shaft, sucking hard. The movements get faster and more intense. My balls are fit to burst as I sense my orgasm building up.

La Contessa intervenes, "Yes, Claudio, excite him and frustrate him. But remember, nothing we do here is for a servant's pleasure, only ours; use him how you wish, but deny him the satisfaction of his release."

At this, the strokes of the guest's mouth along my cock become slower until Claudio pulls his mouth away, having sucked every piece of the chocolate mousse off my cock. I'm left denied and frustrated.

La Contessa beckons two of her female guests, "Portia, Francesca, come here. I think I'm ready to have more fun with this slave. She reaches into the box by her dais and pulls out two strap-on dildos. My eyes water at what punishment I might have to face next. Portia and Francisca help one another on with the strap-on cocks, tightening the belts around their supple waists to hold them in place. To my eyes, never having faced such objects before, they appear fearsome. The strap-ons are long and thick. The two women stand over me, taunting me, the two false cocks bobbing above my face as they smile at me.

One of them gently strokes my hair and face with an expression combining amusement and pity.

44

"I think this slave is ready to receive us Contessa. To take these long, hard objects into his body so we can explore his orifices for our pleasure."

"Yes Portia," agrees La Contessa, "you know what you must do, penetrate this slave whilst I watch."

Portia moves into position by my head, pulls my face to one side and slips the strap-on into my mouth.

"Suck on it slave," she whispers in my ear, "suck on it nice and slowly, until we're both ready to work out on you."

The head of the strap-on is already in my mouth and I suck on it as I've been commanded. The act is humiliating, but it's also strangely comforting to suck on the hard object controlled by this ravishing, dominant woman.

I'm aware of Francesca at the other end of the bench where my legs are suspended in the air and strapped to chains. I feel something slimy being spread over my anus and a finger being inserted. I know what's coming next, but at least I know lubricant has been applied before I'm penetrated. My head is still to one side with the strap-on in my mouth, so I'm unable to see the moment of insertion when it finally comes. I endure the probing against my back passage until the strap-on pushes deep inside me. Now, I'm filled at both ends.

The two women work in tandem to penetrate me, with slow strokes at first, then more vigorously, so the two strap-ons thrust deep into me. By now, I've lost control over the momentum of the movement. I can only lie back, an object, abused and penetrated. One strap-on deep inside my anus, the other filling my mouth, making me gag and gasp for breath. Portia and Francesca continue to get pleasure from me until, my head swirling and my body exhausted, they simultaneously withdraw the strap-ons. My heart throbs, the blood pounding through my body; humiliated but strangely and exotically exhilarated.

La Contessa laughs, "Splendid. Thank you Portia, thank you Francesca. It is amusing to watch my slave being abused. Don't think your ordeal is over yet. Stephano, Lorenzo, come over here and join us."

Two young men rise from a couch where they have been kissing and fondling one another. They're already aroused with angry cocks. They come forward. I anticipate what will happen next. Far from any respite, I fear the performance I've endured will be repeated with two real cocks.

"Portia and Francesca have warmed him up for you. Now do what you want with him. Fuck his mouth and arse with flesh and blood cocks so my new servant understands what it means to be my slave."

Stephano's voice replies, "Yes, Contessa, whatever you wish. We'll fuck him as hard as we can, until he can take no more."

One hard cock is fed into my mouth, the other pushed into my stretched and sore arse. Then the movement begins. Thrusts, forceful and hard, the full weight of the two guests' powerful thigh muscles behind them. I don't know how much longer I can hold. Stephano and Lorenzo grunt and groan with exertion as they approach their climaxes. My mouth full of cock, I can do nothing to resist.

All of a sudden the thrusts stops and the two cocks withdraw from my orifices. Portia and Francesca move forward. Portia grasps Stephano's cock, whilst Francesca takes Lorenzo's. They hold the two cocks over me, one above my mouth, the other over my abdomen. The two men are at the peak of their excitement. They want release, and fast. They don't care where their cum goes as long as they reach their climax. Portia and Francesca rub the two cocks hard. The air in the room is expectant. La Contessa leans forward eagerly anticipating the humiliation being inflicted on me.

"Take it, slave. Receive the cum of my guests into your mouth and over your body."

I sense the two men have reached the point of no return. Simultaneously, there are two groans and hot, white spunk spurts into my mouth, and over my abdomen. I swallow the seed, and feel the thick, sticky substance oozing over my body.

The tension in the room is broken when La Contessa laughs at my predicament with her guests' cum all over me.

"Delightful, there is nothing more pleasing than to see a slave submit to such a decadent act. But I have not finished with him yet."

She pulls out another object form the wooden box by her side, "Bianca, take this and have your pleasure with my slave."

Bianca comes forward with what looks like another strap-on cock, but the design is slightly different. I realise it's a gag with a large cock protruding from one side and a smaller one on the other. Julia straps the object round my head. The smaller cock fills my mouth and I clasp onto it with my teeth as Bianca tightens the straps to secure the gag. She lifts herself up and straddles me. I watch as she lowers herself onto the cock and allows it to penetrate her. She lets out a gasp of pleasure as the object fills her to its full depth.

Two more male guests come forward; they gently touch and kiss her body and breasts as she works herself up and down on me. They kiss her and squeeze her nipples as she fucks herself on the gag. I'm helpless as she pushes her weight onto me, moaning loudly with pleasure until finally she lets out a scream, her body shuddering as she reaches her climax. She lifts herself off the cock gag, helped by the two men. Another guest releases me from the gag and unties the chains still holding me onto the bench.

La Contessa leans forward in her throne, "This is what my servants are for. To be used by me and my guests for our pleasure," she announces to the assembled guests.

She turns her gaze towards me. From behind the mask her eyes fix on me, "Now, slave, do you understand what it means to serve me. You must submit your whole body for *my* pleasure and amusement without complaint or objection. This is your role in life now. Do you understand, slave?"

"Yes, mistress," I reply.

"You have served us well, and I am pleased with you. But, be warned, whilst in my service you can be subject to punishment, humiliation, and abuse at any time. It gives me pleasure to see how pathetic slaves can be controlled and made subject to my will."

She claps her hand. The doors of the salon open and two of her servants come to lift me off the bench. I've been chained up for so long, exhausted from the ordeal and unsteady on my legs. Then there's a mental exhaustion. I'm in a daze, my head spinning with feelings of submission and devotion for my mistress. I collapse onto my knees.

"Thank you, mistress," I gasp.

"Your devotion is welcome, servant. You may be chosen to serve me again. Now, take him away from my presence."

The two servants carry me from the salon back to my room. I have tasted servitude to La Contessa and, whatever trials and humiliation I must suffer, I know my deepest need is to be summoned into her presence again to serve. I curl up on my bed, my head a whirl of emotions.

There's a gentle knock on the door. It's Julia with bread, a plate of cured meats and a tankard of beer.

"You look knackered," she observes. "How do you feel?"

Julia's concern is touching. Though I'd probably appreciate a quiet time with my thoughts, I don't want to offend her, especially as she's taken the trouble to bring food for me. I try to summon a reply from my frazzled brain.

"Oh, I don't know what to make of it Julia. It's too much to take in. My head's spinning and my whole body's throbbing. It was painful and humiliating but exhilerating and thrilling at the same time. Every part of me feels alive if you know what I mean."

"She's pleased with you, in her own way. I can tell," Julia reassures me. "She told me you performed well and said she'd be happy to have you in the palazzo as her slave."

"That's wonderful. I want that... I really do."

Julia is sensitive to my reflective mood and refrains from bombarding me with questions. When I've finished eating, she curls up alongside me on the bed where we cling on to one another in an affectionate hug.

I'm left with my own reflections on the events of the evening. I'm delighted to hear La Contessa will accept me as her slave. I've tasted servitude to her and, whatever trials and humiliations I must suffer, I know my deepest desire is to be summoned into her presence to serve her again.

7: Transformation

It's only a few days before I'm summoned to attend La Contessa again. As I stand in her boudoir waiting to hear what service she requires from me today, my gaze is drawn to the stunning gown draped across the back of a chair. A dress fashioned in glimmering emerald silk with a mantle in rich cream and embroidered with a design of orange flowers. The sleeves and hem are trimmed with the most delicate Belgian lace. It's decorated with golden brocade and *passementerie* embedded with Venetian pearls. It's as magnificent a gown as I've ever seen, hardly surprising knowing how La Contessa is admired for the style and opulence of her dress.

La Contessa turns away from her bureau where she's writing a letter. I can't resist the temptation to remark on the gown.

"If I may be so bold, mistress, I have been admiring your dress. I believe you'll be the toast of Venice in this gown."

She fixes her steely gaze onto me as I instantly realise how inappropriate my comment is. I prepare myself for the inevitable reprimand. Her voice is a torrent of enraged disdain.

"How dare you offer your opinion without being asked? I don't expect to receive compliments from mere servants. What place do you think you hold in this household? You are a slave. Your thoughts and feelings mean nothing. What are you?"

"Your slave, mistress."

"And what are you to me?"

"Worthless, mistress. My place is only to serve you," I reply.

"That's better. Don't ever forget your place."

Then the tone of her voice changes. An enigmatic glint appears in her eyes and the hint of a smile on her lips.

"Besides, who says the dress is for me?"

Now she turns around in her chair and faces me with an appraising glare.

"Today, my servant, you are to serve me in a different way. You will entertain me. I am going to take you on a little expedition."

She leans forward, her pearl white teeth breaking into a mischievous smile which is more disconcerting than being rebuked. I'm left wondering what wicked plans her fertile imagination has conjured up.

"I'm glad you appreciate this gown slave, because today it will amuse me to see you dressed in it as a high class noble woman. Then, we will go out together for a little promenade so the good residents of Venice can admire us."

So this is the game La Contessa desires to play today. It's an unusual request, but I know well enough by now the bizarre sexual demands for which she's renowned. My first reaction is one of unease. I've never held any wish to dress in a woman's clothes before and the idea is challenging. Maybe I should be thankful my task is only to dress up for La Contessa and not be subjected to a more severe punishment.

"I will offer Julia to assist you whilst I retire to my dressing room to get ready. When I return, I expect to find you transformed into a Venetian noblewoman. I suspect my maid will rather enjoy the task, won't you Julia?"

"Oh yes, definitely, madam," she replies, an amused sparkle in her eyes.

As La Contessa withdraws into the private dressing room adjoining her boudoir, Julia approaches. She casts a glance over her shoulder to make sure her mistress is out of sight then runs her fingers along the inside of my breeches. My cock twitches with the first yearnings of arousal.

"Mm, I'm going to enjoy this," she says cupping my balls in her hand and squeezing them. "I think madam's set you an interesting challenge. I think you'll look sexy in women's undergarments!"

Personally, I'm not so convinced.

She unties the cord around my breeches and gently lowers them to my ankles. She runs her hands back up my thigh and brushes her fingers against my cock, now fully erect. She puts one finger against my lips gesturing me to keep silent whilst a hand wraps around my cock and pulls at it. Her touch is exquisite. How I'd love her to carry on and masturbate me, so I come over the floor of La Contessa's boudoir. But Julia has a task to perform. She releases my cock and goes to fetch an item of clothing from a pile laid out on an occasional table. She tells me to take the rest of my clothes off, which I do hurriedly, so by the time she returns I'm naked. Smiling playfully at me, Julia dangles a pair of silk cami-knickers in the air.

"You must put these on," she teases, "La Contessa wants every piece of your dress to be perfect."

I pull them gently up, the satin texture of the silk rubbing against my leg, thigh and finally, my genitals. It's hard to describe the sensation. On the one hand I feel humiliated, standing in front of Julia, my manhood enveloped in silk. The pull of my hard cock straining against the smooth material is deliciously sensuous. I sense myself succumbing to a feminine side I didn't realise I possessed. The sight excites Julia. She seeks out the hardness underneath the silk with an arousing touch.

"The corset is next, I'm afraid," she says.

Julia's trying hard to suppress a laugh. Her blue eyes sparkle with amusement at my predicament. She's taking pleasure in my embarrassment and revelling in the sexual tension of this strange situation.

"The cut of the dress will give the appearance of hips," she explains, "and I'll find stuffing to create your breasts. But you must put the corset on to pull in your waist. La Contessa needs you to pass as a perfect lady."

I take offence at this. I'm young and lithe and have no spare flesh. Julia's hair brushes against my skin whilst she stands behind me to fit the stiff whale bone corset around my midriff. She tugs at the cords, pulling the corset tightly around me. When she finishes my waist feels pencil thin. How can women wear such things? Yet I know there's no point complaining, I must tolerate the discomfort to serve as La Contessa wishes.

Julia helps me on with the padded bra to help create the illusion of an amply breasted lady. Then she helps me into the magnificent dress. The weight of the layers of rich material lays heavy on me. I have to adjust my stance to stop myself from falling over. Again, I'm astonished by the encumbrances women have to endure. How can they move freely and go about their daily business in such dress?

"Oh, you look fabulous, my dear," Julia giggles.

"It feels weird. I don't know how you ladies manage."

"Believe me, it's nothing, court dress is even worse. You should try wearing *pannier* hoops. You end up out here," she explains holding her arms out, "and have to walk through doors sideways. La Contessa hates them though I've known her wear them for grand occasions when it's expected. And when you've a body as shapely as hers, why would you hide it beneath such a ridiculous thing?"

"Yes," I reply, "I couldn't agree more."

"We'd better get a move on as we're nowhere near finished."

Julia's face is a picture of concentration as she does my make-up. I've seen her do her mistress's, and the care and attention to detail she uses is remarkable. She applies white powder to my face, as is the fashion of the day, and uses her finger to smear rouge onto my cheeks before sensuously running her finger across my lips. Occasionally she permits herself a subtle glance and smile. She puts on long false-eyelashes and eye shadow and then applies a small patch of black taffeta in the shape of a half-moon to the top of my check bone.

"Do you know what this false mole means? It says come and fuck me! I'd love to, but madam will be furious if you're not ready in time."

Finally, she ties my ponytail up into a bun and perches a wig on top of my head. It's a full head of blond curls, built up high above my head in an elaborate hair piece. The whole experience has been made me vulnerable but also, I have to confess, aroused.

Julia stands back to admire her creation and smiles approvingly at me.

"There, we're finished now. Let's both hope La Contessa is pleased with how you look."

We don't have long to wait before she calls a command from her dressing room.

"Servant, I want you to stand in front of the mirror, close your eyes and wait for me."

I do as I'm told and wait expectantly for La Contessa's entrance. If the dress she's offered her servant is this luxurious, I try to imagine how stunning she will look. I sense movement behind me, then an arm pass under my elbow to take hold of my hand.

"Servants you have done a good job for me. I see my slave is transformed into the perfect image of a Venetian lady. What does it feel like to be turned into a woman?" she asks.

"Humiliated and emasculated, mistress, but it's also strangely sensuous," I reply.

"It is good you feel humiliated. You must surrender something for your mistress. You should realise your sexuality means nothing, and your mistress can change your gender at her whim. This is the start of a journey for you, slave. You must learn that slaves in my household must be prepared to give everything up for me, even their very manhood. And did he get aroused Julia?"

"Yes, madam. I'm afraid he did," she admits.

La Contessa raises a quizzical eyebrow, "And did you get aroused Julia? I could hear your merriment. I take it you were entertained by the task."

"Yes, indeed I was madam."

Turning to me she says, "You will be paraded and shown off. You will be taken through the canal sides and alleyways of Venice in full view of the public. They will stare at you. Will you pass as a finely dressed Venetian noblewoman or will they suspect the hidden secret under your magnificent dress? The time has come for me to reveal myself. Open your eyes and look into the mirror."

I open my eyes and, before me, reflected in La Contessa's ornate mirror are two figures standing arm in arm. La Contessa, transformed into an elegant Venetian patrician and, me, into a Venetian noblewoman.

She's wearing an azure and gold damask jacket trimmed with jewelled buttons, grey silk trousers, white breeches, and black leather, buckled shoes. Her auburn hair is straightened and swept back in a fashionable queue underneath a black silk, tri-cornered hat decorated with gold brocade.

Above her lips is a false black moustache. In her other hand she holds a sword stick.

Our respective transformations are indeed stunning, but will we pass as the perfect noble couple? La Contessa appears to be delighted.

"Come, the canals and lanes of Venice await us."

8: Deception

From the palazzo we set out on foot at a leisurely pace towards Ponte Rialto. La Contessa is in her element, nodding her head in greeting to every passing stranger as we stroll along the canal side paths and elegant squares of the city. It's as if she's inviting everybody to take notice of us, teasing them to guess if this perfect noble couple are not what they seem.

I can't help thinking everybody is looking at us, suspicious there's something not right about how we appear or carry ourselves. I feel uncomfortable dressed as a woman. Although our respective transformations are remarkable, I'm self-conscious of the flaws betraying the dark secret underneath the elegant clothes. I suffer the humiliation of being exposed to public view dressed in feminine clothing. I'm reminded of my encounter with the two transvestites on the night Julia found me. How many people can guess there is a hardening cock under my gown, rubbing against the silky smoothness of my cami-knickers?

La Contessa leads me along the Merceria and then into Campo di San Canciano. I recognise these alleyways from my youth. She's taking us into the Cannaregio district, the working class area of Venice where Julia found me. As we stroll deeper into this district, the lanes become narrower and the buildings shabbier. The flaking stucco betrays the fact that this part of the city has seen more prosperous times.

The people in the streets are dressed in their working clothes. The grand palaces of the Grand Canal, and the elegantly apparelled clientele on the Rialto, have been left far behind. I'm even more self-conscious now. Dressed like this we stand out, attracting curious stares from the local people going about their daily business.

I realise what La Contessa is doing. I know this area well and there's only one reason a nobleman would enter this district of Venice... to find a brothel. She strolls on purposefully.

La Contessa turns to me and says, "I see you recognise the alleyways of the Sestiere di Cannaregio. I told you we were going on a little expedition," she laughs, mocking my naivety. "You believed that after taking so much trouble to transform you I was merely going to take you on promenade, did you slave? Oh no, I have far more interesting things planned for you!"

I'm anxious at what further service La Contessa requires from me.

She turns into a narrow alleyway and then into a secluded square. Facing us is a tavern I'm familiar with, known by the name Il Toro Nero. It's one of my old haunts, and I can only hope nobody recognises me, though it's unlikely given my disguise.

"Now, my slave, I will see how well you can serve me."

When we enter the tavern, the buzz of drunken conversation dies down as curious eyes turn towards us. The air is heavy with the odour of beer, cheap wine, and tobacco. The tavern is populated by the strange mix of familiar characters; working class Venetians, the odd dandy, and a scattering of ample breasted courtesans flirting with the customers.

La Contessa steps forward to speak with the madam and proprietor of the establishment. I'm left by the door to face the leering stares of the clientele of Il Toro Nero.

This is the most humiliating experience for me to date. Is my transformation so convincing this tavern full of hot-blooded men, here to spend an hour with a whore, are mentally stripping me with their gaze? Are they really imagining me as a naked woman of noble birth, here to service their lusts?

Whilst I'm reflecting on my predicament, La Contessa is deep in negotiation with the madam of the house. I watch her empty a pile of *soldi* into her hands. She gestures for me to come forward. I walk with as much feminine grace as I can muster in the tight corset and heavy material. It's a curious sensation. It's as though I'm flirting with the drunken customers of the tavern, flaunting my femininity. Is part of me actually enjoying this? Am I getting a perverse pleasure from the attention being given me, and the deception perpetrated on this unwitting audience?

The madam leads the way, and La Contessa and I ascend the stairs to the gallery.

She turns and whispers, "Servant, remember you must act the role I have chosen for you convincingly and obey my instructions."

I nod my acknowledgement of La Contessa's wishes

"Francesco," the madam's voice calls along the upstairs gallery, "your clients are here." She turns to La Contessa, "I've personally chosen this one for your game, milady. I believe he has the sadistic streak you're looking for."

La Contessa weighs up the man. He's a few years older than me, perhaps in his thirties, and is thick set and muscular. There's a malicious glint his eyes as if he is looking forward to his meeting with La Contessa.

"Yes, most satisfactory. I am happy to trust to your judgement," she says.

"If that'll be all, sire, I'll take you to your room."

The madam leads the three of us into one of the upstairs boudoir rooms and withdraws. The room is surprisingly clean and pleasant. It's sparsely furnished and dominated by a large four poster bed.

La Contessa turns to the man, Francesco, and speaks to him in a deepened, husky voice.

"I need to teach my young wife the ways of the world. She is young and innocent and she must learn the true meaning of obedience. As part of her training, I want her to be punished. I will watch as you follow my directions and abuse her."

"She's a beauty, sir, there's no doubt about it. I'll give her a good fucking for you if you want."

My eyes widen in shock. My disguise is so skilfully executed that even at such close quarters this man believes I really am a nobleman's young wife. He lustily runs his hand up my body and gropes my false breasts. Surely the deception will be found out and I will be undone, but no, the layers of thick material are enough to hide the true nature of my false breasts. He puts his hand to my cheek and pulls my face towards his. Our lips meet and he thrusts his tongue deep into my mouth, eager with lust for me. I'm shocked but dare not pull away and risk angering La Contessa.

"I had a more perverse activity in mind than a good fucking. I have paid you well for my entertainment and I am particular as to my needs. You will follow my directions precisely," La Contessa pronounces.

"I'm yours to command, sir," he replies.

"I need her punished. She must learn obedience and trust. Tie her to the bed. You may be as rough with her as you need."

"Get onto the bed, you slut," he orders, "you've heard what your husband and master wants."

He pushes me face down onto the bed. I don't need to feign fear; it's real enough for me. He kneels over me and puts the full weight of his body over me.

"There's no point resisting my beauty. Your master wants you abused for his pleasure, and I'll enjoy doing it."

I lie down on the bed gasping for breath, my face buried into the pillow. He ties rope onto one my wrists, the knot secured so tightly I can feel the rough fibres of the rope digging into my wrists. My arm is stretched and the other end of the rope tied firmly onto one of the posts of the bed. I catch a glimpse of La Contessa. She sits in a chair and leans forward, watching proceedings intently. Her green eyes gleam with a mixture of malice and amusement.

"Make sure you tie her tight. She mustn't wriggle free. And gag her; I don't want to be disturbed by any of her screams."

Francesco soon has me spread-eagled, the ropes secured to a post at each corner of the bed. The ropes are drawn tight. There's nothing I can do but surrender to the fate La Contessa has conjured for me.

The weight of Francesco's sweaty body is heavy on me as he splutters in my ear, "You're going nowhere until your master and I have used you, my dear."

"Take this. I know I do not need to tell you how to use it. Beat her, pay no heed to her squeals of pain," La Contessa orders.

Francesco kneels over me. I feel the touch of soft leather as the end of a riding crop is run tantalisingly across my powdered cheek and across my neck. He lifts it and cracks it down hard-on the bed head, letting out a malicious laugh.

"You've heard what your master wants. I'll give you such a fucking whipping. I'll make you hurt, you slut."

My heart races and beads of sweat trickle down my forehead. Is La Contessa going to leave me in the hands of this sadist?

La Contessa orchestrates proceedings with firm instructions.

"Lift up her dress and pull her knickers down. Don't take them off. I want you to expose her pert arse. Don't uncover her cunt. I will save that hidden delight for later."

I'm party to her trick and hear the mocking tone in La Contessa's voice. She's delighting in the game. I've gained an insight into her perverse mind. I know she'll not reveal the dark secret underneath my silk knickers until she has acted out this little performance for her own amusement.

The weight of the man's body is off me. I feel the lick of a riding crop on my backside; a dozen gentle taps with the soft loop of leather at the end of the crop to warm me up and build up the tension. I know there's more to come. Sure enough the riding crop comes cracking down on my arse. I count six powerful strokes with the hard length of the crop. My backside stings like nothing I've felt before, and I fight back the tears welling up in my eyes.

"What does it feel like to be punished? Perhaps now you'll learn to obey your husband and master."

"I am not satisfied with your punishment," says La Contessa. "I thought madam called you a sadist. I believe you are holding back. I am sure you can strike her harder. How many more strokes do you think she should take?"

"Another six?" Francesco hesitates as he senses La Contessa is not satisfied with his reply, "perhaps ten, sire?"

"I want you to give her another twenty strokes, building up in intensity. I want the last five to be relentless with no break. Do you understand me?"

"Yes sire, I'll enjoy dishing out such punishment."

I overhear every nuance of the conservation. Six strokes were hard enough. Will I be able to endure another twenty? My body tenses in anticipation of the savage beating La Contessa has ordered.

I count the strokes in my head. The first few are excruciatingly painful, but by about the eighth I reach a plateau where each new stroke does not add greatly to my suffering. Finally, the last five rain down on me with a speed and ferocity that takes my breath away. By the end the stinging pain in my backside is being absorbed by my whole body. My head is spinning as my mind and body adjust to the beating I've taken.

"How's that, you bitch. That'll teach you," he barks in my ear. Then he turns to La Contessa, "Is sire satisfied with the beating?"

"Yes, I am pleased my wife has learnt a lesson about the meaning of true subservience. But, I have not finished yet. There is another act of pain and humiliation I want to observe."

I can guess what act La Contessa intends, and my suspicions are soon confirmed.

"I want to watch you take her up the arse. I need to see your hard cock inside her; fucking her back passage until I am satisfied her humiliation is complete. Fuck her as hard as you wish. Give her no mercy. If she squeals or begs for mercy, fuck her harder until you empty your load inside her."

"Yes, sire, it'll give me great pleasure to do that for you. My cock is getting hard just hearing you talk of it. You truly are a cruel master."

I sense him kneeling behind me. I'm tied down, unable to move, my legs spread wide and my arse exposed. There's no escape from this act of humiliation. His fingers enter me, playing with me, preparing me for penetration. His hard cock presses against me before forcing itself into my back passage.

He puts the weight of his body on me. I smell his hot breath against my face, reeking of beer and stale tobacco. I hear the grunts of exertion as he moves energetically inside me. It's a strange mix of pain and pleasure, humiliation, and satisfaction. Then I hear La Contessa's voice, cruel and playful.

"Fuck her harder. Thrust your cock into her. Show her the meaning of true obedience. Show her that unless she obeys me, she must suffer pain and humiliation."

There's no point resisting. I welcome the long thrust of his hard cock into my arse and resolve to embrace my punishment. Francesco's breathing gets heavier, his grunting more intense, and then I feel the spurt of hot spunk inside my arse as he comes inside me.

La Contessa encourages him, "That's it, come inside her, empty yourself into her arse for me."

Finally, Francesco is spent and silent as he lies on top of me his wilting cock still inside me.

I'm suddenly aware of movement. La Contessa has leapt up from her seat and is starting to untie me. She's already released my ankles and is now undoing the knots securing my wrists. She works quickly and urgently. Her game is not finished yet and I've learnt enough of her perverted imagination to know the poor unsuspecting Francesco will be her next victim.

Swiftly, silently, before he can even begin to suspect what's about to happen, his ankles are tied together with rope and his breeches lowered. La Contessa drags him off the bed onto the floor. I jump off the bed straight away to help her.

"What the fuck are you doing?" Francesco calls out.

I help La Contessa turn him around so he's sat on the floor against the end of the bed. Before he can offer any serious resistance, his wrists are tied to the bed posts.

He thinks La Contessa is merely a perverted husband who delights in seeing his wife punished. He's no awareness of how wickedly ingenious she can be.

"Let me go. I never agreed to this."

"You didn't think my entertainment was over, did you?" La Contessa says, standing over him with me by her side. "I have paid you well for your services, and I intend for you to do what I demand."

Now the tables have turned, I see the fear in his eyes.

La Contessa removes her blue silk jacket, and she pulls off the white linen shirt, tossing it onto the floor. Her chest is strapped in wide bands of cloth, which she now unwraps to uncover her breasts. She leans over him, her ample breasts hanging in front of his face tantalisingly out of reach.

La Contessa taunts him, "Would you like these? Do you want to touch my beautiful tits? How much do you desire them? How much would you like to plant kisses on my lovely white flesh? Oh dear, it seems you are a bit tied up at the moment. You will never sample the delights of my flesh."

Francesco is livid with rage, "You bitch! You bastard! You dirty lesbian sluts!"

La Contessa turns to face me, and laughs.

"Dirty lesbians are we? He's got an interesting lesson to learn hasn't he slave?"

I reply, entering into the spirit of La Contessa's teasing, "Oh dear, mistress, he thinks we're lesbians. I believe you still have another little surprise in store for him?"

I see the look of horror on his face as he realises how far he's been deceived.

"Lift your dress up and pull your knickers down, slave."

I raise the rolls of heavy material and slip the silk knickers down to show my hardening cock.

"You fucking perverts," shouts Francesco.

La Contessa strikes him hard across the cheek with her hand. He goes silent, fear taking over from anger.

"Listen to me. I'll take no more insults from you. You have gambled on a little sex game and now you will pay the consequences. I have paid handsomely for my entertainment. and I will get satisfaction. None of this performance is for your pleasure, only mine. Now, I expect you to perform for me. I want you to take my servant's cock in your mouth and suck it until he comes."

"No, that's sick, I'm not doing it," replies Francesco offering one last piece of resistance.

La Contessa takes hold of his hair and pulls it sharply, forcing his head back.

"You will do as I command." She gestures to me, "Enter him."

My cock is now hard and I force it into his mouth. I feel the wetness of his saliva round my cock, but also his reluctance to carry out La Contessa's order fully.

"Is he sucking on it?" she asks.

"No, mistress, he has it in his mouth, but he's not sucking."

"Then ram it into his throat till he gags. I'll teach you a lesson. When I say I want you to suck on cock, I expect you to do it."

I force my cock further in until Francesco's body starts to jerk with a gagging motion. I withdraw to give him a chance to recover his breath. La Contessa is still pulling his head back by his hair.

"Suck on cock or choke on it, which will it be?"

Francesco realises there's nothing he can do but give in to La Contessa's demands. Finally, I feel the bobbing movement of his head as, reluctantly, he starts to move his mouth along the shaft of my cock.

"Now, that's better. Don't even think you can cross me." Turning to me, she enquires, "Is he making you come yet, slave?"

"No, mistress, I'm not ready to come yet."

"I don't have the patience to wait for this. Give me your cock."

She grasps my cock, now wet with saliva, firmly in her hand, and starts to masturbate me. La Contessa is still bare breasted, and her tits jiggle rhythmically in time with the rapid movements of her hand. Now, I feel the inevitable climax build up.

"That's it slave, come for me, spunk over him."

"Oh mistress, yes, that's it. Oh yes."

My cock releases its load of hot sticky spunk over Francesco's face.

He looks crushed and bedraggled. His head droops onto his chest, my cum dripping from his face.

"Madam, you are twisted and sick," he finally gasps.

La Contessa looks at him with a malicious smile and then spits in his face. She laughs, mocking his plight.

"Yes, I know. I am La Contessa di Nemesia. I always get my way. I command men to do my bidding. I humiliate them, and they still end up worshipping me. Look at this miserable servant here. He's been abused by me, but still he stays in my household for more. Why? Because he would rather be in my presence and submit to my punishments than leave."

La Contessa is right. I can't deny what she's saying. After each perverse and servile task I complete for her, I go away yearning for more.

La Contessa dresses again as the perfect Venetian gentleman. I pull up my silk knickers, arrange the magnificent ballgown and adjust my dishevelled wig. Then I follow La Contessa as her servile noble wife.

We leave the unfortunate Francesco, his face covered in my cum and La Contessa's spittle, a victim of her perverted cruelty.

9: The Kitchen

After working in La Contessa's service for several months I've become accepted as part of her household. My days are a mixture of serving my mistress in whatever sex games she decides to use me for and a variety of domestic tasks.

Whenever the mood takes her, she will summon me to her boudoir to serve her. She enjoys administering corporal punishment and possesses a massive chest covered in erotic carvings, full of whips, paddles, floggers, tawses, and canes which she uses to deliver severe punishments. She has a choice of clamps and pegs for applying to nipples and genitals, which she takes delight in squeezing to make me twist and squirm.

She has ropes and cords to bind me and her skill at rope bondage is extraordinary. She will tie my balls up and put me in bondage so tight the knots leave marks where they've pressed into my flesh. She likes the pattern of white ropes against my olive skin. She puts me into a hog-tie position and all manner of predicament bondage.

She has a huge collection of dildos and strap-on cocks of varying lengths and girths to create different sensations, some in polished wood, others covered in kid skin leather. Her favourite, which she used once on me, is a dildo of solid Murano crystal. She keeps a selection of candles and one of her past-times is to watch me squirm as she drizzles hot wax over my bound-up cock and balls.

It comes as no surprise she takes pleasure in offering me up to her friends given how she involved her guests in my torment at her party. Often I'm blindfolded and have no idea whether it's a man or woman, a real cock, or other object being thrust into my orifices. I'm made to suck cock, and to lick cunt. Her visitors are often masked and dressed in costumes, so there's always a sense of theatre in her play. As for La Contessa, she always looks magnificent. She has a vast wardrobe but whether she wears corsetry or a gown, she always looks stunning.

I've come to relish serving her. I submit to her freely and offer myself for whatever she desires, and to whomsoever she invites to the palazzo.

In between those times when she seeks to use me for her pleasure, I'm given domestic chores to run for her. Typically, these involve things like cleaning the marble statues in the palazzo, polishing the silverware, or dusting the frames of her art collection. I enjoy these tasks, the last one in particular, as you can imagine. They give me a chance to scrutinise La Contessa's magnificent collection of erotica. I swear there's not an item in the palazzo that isn't suggestive if you look close enough. For example, her dinner service has images of seduction and fornication disguised within it.

I'm not confined to the palazzo though, and am often given errands to run, which take me into the vibrant and debauched streets of my beloved Venice. I collect dresses from her couturier, hats from her milliner, wigs from her wigmaker, fine wines, and champagne from her vintner, the best French perfume from her perfumer, cakes and sugared biscuits from the patisserie and even offal from the butchers to feed her dogs.

I'm even accepted by the rest of the household staff now and have established a good working relationship with them. I make an effort to be helpful. I'm mindful of Julia's advice on my first day concerning the tensions between La Contessa's household staff and slaves, but can't say I've experienced any hostility towards me. My easy going manner means I get on with most of them, the female staff appear to have taken a special shine to me!

The only exception is old Lucio, who's always watching me. I don't report to him for any of the tasks I undertake, only to Julia who conveys La Contessa's orders to me. I believe this is a source of resentment for him, even though I'm careful to do nothing to antagonise him. Julia is aware of it and, though agreeing I've done nothing to upset him, she warns me to be wary as she says Lucio is La Contessa's eyes and ears in the palazzo.

In between participating in La Contessa's sexual games, the various errands I'm given and Julia's service to her mistress, we steal as many opportunities to make love as we can, though not nearly enough for my liking!

Julia has no set work pattern as she is more or less permanently on call to serve La Contessa. She can be summoned at any time of the day or night, and is often called to her boudoir in the early hours of the morning after La Contessa has returned from a supper, ball, or visit to the theatre to assist with her undressing.

Julia doesn't mind in the slightest. Quite the contrary; she says she enjoys serving her at these times as La Contessa is often relaxed and chatty. She gossips to Julia about where she's been, the aristocratic Venice elite she mixes with and titbits about who's fucking who, often in a highly amusing way. Julia laughs, saying she often returns tipsy, having quaffed many glasses of champagne or *malvasia,* a delicate white wine popular in Venice these days. She says La Contessa is even more beautiful than ever when she's had a drink as she looks flushed. I comment, as a joke, that it sounds like Julia wants to go to bed with her, but Julia turns defensive, embarrassed by the suggestion.

Although a firm mistress who expects high standards of servitude, La Contessa is a fair employer and gives her staff days off. On the occasions when Julia and I have the same leave we will go into the city for a stroll or share a rich hot chocolate and pastries at Café Quadrie, one of Venice's supreme indulgences. La Contessa pays her slaves generously for the unique services she requires from them, so we can dress up in respectable clothes and frequent the cafes around Campo San Marco. Julia believes La Contessa indulges such behaviour by her special household staff because she's making a statement. She's so rich and powerful even her servants can be seen in fashionable places.

We often end up in one of the secret courtyard gardens I know of, and where I used to take clients when I was walking the streets. There we take the opportunity to indulge in *al fresco* sex if it's quiet enough. Julia will go out with no undergarments to make things easier, and we'll find a hidden corner of a garden where we can make love. Sometimes we get a chance to meet up in Julia's room either during the day when it's quiet or when Julia has finished work. I'm more than content with my life at the palazzo, and my decision to serve La Contessa.

I treat La Contessa with the submissive respect she's due and is expected from me, but this still allows for a modicum of social contact beyond serving as her sex toy. She is a cultured and engaging woman as well as an awesomely strict dominatrix. Although rare, these moments give me a great deal of pleasure and afford me an insight into La Contessa's mind beyond her sadistic cruelty. Having gained this, I can well imagine why Julia gets such satisfaction from serving her. I've seen them together and they have an easy rapport. I think Julia is the only person I've not heard La Contessa speak harshly to, though I'm assured by her it's happened on many occasions.

On discovering my interest in art, La Contessa is happy to discuss the subject with me. On one occasion she was thrilled when I told her about the secret frescoes of the Last Judgement hidden in a locked baptistry in the church of San Giovanni my father took me to see. As a youth I remember being shocked by their content but they left a lasting impression on me, and I guessed they would appeal to La Contessa's taste.

The frescoes depict the seven deadly sins and the punishments in hell meted out to the fallen who have succumbed to them. The scene portraying lust is particularly graphic and, when I describe the pictures of naked bodies on racks being punished by black devils with pitch forks, she insists on me taking her to the church there and then. The priest was reluctant to open up the baptistery at first, but nobody denies La Contessa! Through a mixture of cajoling, seduction and threat she soon has the priest eating out of her hand and only too eager to show the frescoes to her. She insisted it was for reassurance of how the sinful would be punished in hell, but I saw how her eyes lit up when she saw the scenes of debauchery before her.

"I'm most grateful to you. How satisfying to see how the sinful will be punished in hell. It is a lesson for all of us to heed," she commented to the priest, but she did so with a mischievous glint in her eye. And when we emerged from the church, she was thrilled.

"What a shame the artist died centuries ago. I would have him fill one end of my ballroom with a fresco so perverted it would shock everyone! My slave, I must act out these scenes with you! You saw how one was wrapped in chains and suspended from the ceiling and whipped with a flail, poked with knives and prodded with forks. How I should love to do that to you, my slave."

"Whatever you wish, mistress," I reply submissively, but secretly wishing she would!

"I'm sure you have many sins to atone for my slave. And not only those committed before entering my service," she added suggestively.

The visit to the church has been one of the highlights of my service to La Contessa. It gives me great satisfaction to have introduced those frescoes to her and brought her such pleasure.

The opportunities to share such intimacies with La Contessa are rare and most of my tasks are more mundane. Typical of such errands is one Julia announces one day. I'm to sit in the scullery in the basement of the palazzo adjoining the kitchens and polish La Contessa's shoes and boots. Now, at first I mistakenly think this should not be too onerous a task but I have grossly underestimated the sheer quantity of footwear in her wardrobe. So, when the maids appear with several barrow loads of shoes, I know this task will set me up for the day. The job comes with dire warnings from Julia.

"You must make sure every shoe is clean and polished. She will inspect them, and if any aren't shiny then you'll be punished for sure. She'll expect to see her face reflected in them."

"This sounds like one of those thankless tasks in which I'm set up to fail," I laugh, aware that I'm unlikely to polish every piece of footwear to La Contessa's impossibly exacting standard.

"That may be Roberto," Julia replies, "but it's as well to remember the scale of any discipline will be in proportion to how you've completed the task. So, I suggest you make a serious effort."

"Oh yes, I understand. Don't worry; I'll devote myself to doing a good job."

Julia leaves me with a mountain of shoes and boots, tubs with a greasy substance made from beeswax, lanolin and oils coloured with dyes, a bundle of rags and several soft, pig-hair brushes to aid me in the task before leaving.

I sigh deeply. I don't mind in the least. I'm happy to carry out these domestic errands for my mistress. I just think it'll be a bit of a chore. But that's before I pick up the first pair of boots. Before the smell of leather, mixed with the odour of the sweat of La Contessa's feet, hits my nostrils. Before that heady mixture combines with the aroma of the beeswax as I scoop a blob up onto a rag. And before I start handling the boots.

I caress the smooth leather and run my fingers along it feeling the creases left by the wearer. I get a hard-on. I have an iron hard stiffy within minutes of caressing La Contessa's beautiful boot with its pointed toe, and elegant shape. I finger the long heel with its shiny metal tip and visualise La Contessa's shapely calves inside the boot and the heel pressing on my balls and imagine the exquisite pain as the sharp metal digs in. I realise that, far from being an onerous task, I can turn it into an afternoon of sensuous fun.

As I work my way through the pile, I realise there are shoes and boots of every description. There are kid-skin slippers, ankle length boots made of red morocco leather, and riding boots with sharp spurs. There are all manner of buckles and eyelets in silver or brass to polish. Other shoes are made of material such as gold brocade or are embroidered in silk and need a gentle wash with soapy water.

I set about my task enthusiastically, taking time to polish, and buff every inch of leather and material methodically. I take time and care over each item of footwear, handling it lovingly and ensuring I do a thorough job. Around me the kitchen is a hub of activity as they serve tea and then evening meal. I break to take bread, cheese, and wine with the kitchen staff before resuming my labour of love long into the evening. Eventually, when there's only one pair left from the massive pile, Julia arrives to see how I'm getting on. "Are you still polishing shoes!" she exclaims.

"Yes, I've only one pair to go now."

"But it's 11 o'clock. You've been cleaning shoes for hours."

"Well, I wanted to do a thorough job. Anyway, you know La Contessa will punish me if her boots aren't polished properly. Besides, I'm enjoying it."

"Is this turning you on?" she asks with a mischievous grin.

"Well, a bit... maybe," I laugh. "I've saved my favourite pair for last."

It's a pair of boots. Their leather is as soft as kid gloves and they are so perfectly cut. They are knee length and obviously made to measure by

La Contessa's own shoemaker as you can see how the elegant curve of her calves would fit snugly in the boot. Both their pointed tips and long heels are tipped with silver. They are secured onto the leg with a series of eyelets and laces which run up the front of the boot.

"Can I help you?" asks Julia.

"Yes," I reply passing over one of the boots and then tossing her a rag.

"Oh, I remember her wearing those boots. I'm sure it was when one of the Council of Ten came to visit. I don't know why... I helped Madam get dressed. She looked magnificent though. I had to tighten up the laces whilst La Contessa sat back in her chair. I loved it!"

"They're an awesome pair of boots," I concur.

Julia is running her hands along the soft leather wistfully. She places her nose over the boot and breathes in deeply.

"Mm, the smell of leather mingled with La Contessa's perfume. How glorious!"

I'm a little shocked Julia would be so perversely risqué as to sniff her mistress's boots. But I should not be so surprised, after all, haven't I spent the best part of the day wallowing in the sensations of handling La Contessa's footwear.

"Yes, it's quite a turn on. At first I thought it would be a chore, but I've had an erection all day. I had to hide it from the other kitchen staff when I stopped to eat!"

By now we've both dipped the rags in the beeswax and are coating the leather in it.

She cast a sly glance across at me, "Well, maybe we ought to do something about your hard-on."

We both feverously rub the leather to bring out the shine, anxious to finish the job. We glance across at each other, satisfied we've completed the task to La Contessa's satisfaction. The silver glints in the candlelight and we can see our reflections in the shiny leather. The boots are carefully placed in the cart of now sparkling, and polished footwear. Whilst we are both still knelt on the stone slabs, I lean over and take Julia's face in my hands. I thrust my tongue into her mouth and we kiss passionately. I've been in a state of arousal for the best part of a day and I want her. I want her now. And I can't be bothered to climb four floors of steps to take her!

I take her in my arms, lift her up, and throw her on the huge oak table stretching the length of the kitchen. Luckily the kitchen staff have retired to the servants' quarters and cleared everything away. I climb onto the table on top of Julia. I pull down the layers of her petticoats and knickerbockers to reveal her delicious cunt.

She gasps, "Roberto… not here… not in the kitchen. What if somebody comes in?"

"I don't care. I want you now."

Julia succumbs, her own desires overcoming her caution.

"Go on then, Roberto. Fuck me now. Fuck me quick and hard."

She reaches her arms out gripping the iron frame set over the table from which sets of copper pots and pans dangle. I lower my breeches. My cock is hard, eager to penetrate Julia and get release. She arches her hips to receive me, and I thrust myself into her cunt. She moans in pleasure.

"Give it to me Roberto. Fuck me."

I push inside her cunt and fuck her on the kitchen table. She moves her hips in time with mine, inviting me to go deeper into her. I crouch over her, pinning her arms to the table with my hands, and crouch over her as I pump my cock into her. Her look is wild and abandoned as she grips the iron. I swear the heavy table shakes in time to our movements. Julia's knuckles are white with gripping the metal frame causing the copper pots and pans hanging above us to shake. Julia thrashes her head to and fro, moaning with pleasure.

She's close to coming, so I thrust myself into her even harder, grinding my hips against the sweet spot to tip her over the brink. She grunts, and her body bucks and twists. The vibrations of her climax ripple through her body until her hands shake the metal frame. A brass saucepan clatters onto the table with a thud narrowly missing my arse, which is still pumping into Julia's cunt. As I reach my climax, a couple of jelly moulds clunk onto the table falling with a loud clutter onto the stone floor.

"Oh god, yeah. I needed that," gasps Julia.

"Shit. Me too. That's been building up all day. God it was good."

"Shit, we've made a racket. I hope nobody heard."

"Don't worry, Julia. The kitchen staff left ages ago."

"Fuck, they prepare the food on this table," she laughs.

I put my finger in a damp pool of my cum and Julia's cunt juices.

"Well, the meat will have a nice tang to it tomorrow. I'm up for eating my share of it!"

Julia, now sat up on the kitchen table, took my fingers in her hand and licked them clean.

"Mm, tasty. Cook will wonder what the special ingredient in her stew is."

Our lusts satiated, we both climb off the table and pick up the copper kitchen equipment which has fallen onto the floor. As we do so, the kitchen door swings open. My heart jumps for fear it's La Contessa, though it's rare for her to be seen in the kitchens. It's old Lucio. I expel a relieved sigh though Julia looks distinctly uneasy. Luckily, she's adjusted her underwear. Lucio eyes us both suspiciously.

"Roberto has been cleaning madam's shoes. I came to give him a hand. I accidentally knocked the frame holding the pans, and a couple fell off," she explains nervously.

Lucio picks up the heavy copper pan, "You must have given it quite a shake to knock it off."

"Oh, it didn't take much," said Julia, more composed now. "You ought to get cook to find something better to secure them."

I admire what Julia did there, trying to twist the blame onto a member of staff under Lucio's authority.

"There's nothing wrong with how they're hung, Miss Julia. It'd take a lot to make them come off," was Lucio's acerbic reply, with the emphasis on the word *come*.

Once Lucio had gone, Julia started to panic.

"Do you think he heard us fucking? Even if he didn't, I'm sure he suspected."

"He wasn't very observant," I reply. "If he'd seen the glob of spunk on the table, we'd be done for!"

"It's not funny," says Julia. But the glint in her eye shows she sees the humorous side of the incident.

10: The Bath

Julia sends a message to let me know La Contessa wishes to see me. Apparently she has invited special guests today and wants to arrange an entertainment for them during the afternoon. I'm told by Julia to arrive naked and stand at the door until La Contessa is ready for me. I knock on the door, and Julia's voice confirms I can enter.

I'm taken aback when I enter the boudoir as La Contessa is still in her bath. There's a massive brass tub in the centre of the room and she's still wallowing deep in the steaming water. I see nothing indiscreet because she's covered in the foaming and perfume infused waters. Nonetheless, I'm surprised I should be invited into her chamber whilst she's in this state of undress. Julia tells me to wait whilst La Contessa finishes her bath.

I'm drawn into this little vignette, which reveals a lot about the relationship between Julia and her mistress. La Contessa is luxuriating in the hot water, her eyes closed, her head resting against the high back of the bath, her arms draped over the side as Julia bathes her. She has a sponge and perfumed lozenge of soap in her hand and is washing La Contessa. What strikes me is the tenderness and attention Julia gives her mistress. She's revelling in every touch as she runs the sponge over La Contessa's shoulders and breasts, her cleavage visible above the water.

"Mm, that feels delightful, Julia. It's so lovely to wallow in a hot bath."

Julia dips her hand further into the tub. I imagine her running the sponge across her mistress's crotch underneath the water, an image I can't get out of my head. It's hard to accept the little moans of pleasure coming from La Contessa's lips are solely from the luxuriant hot water. And Julia has a dreamy expression on her face suggesting she's getting sensual pleasure from the act of bathing her mistress.

"Your skin is so soft, madam."

"Thank you, Julia. The oils you got from the Chinese merchant at the Rialto Market have helped, and they smell gorgeous."

"I believe it's jasmine oil, madam."

"Yes, I recognise the aroma," replies La Contessa.

Once again I'm fascinated by this relationship between Julia and her mistress. I've heard her speak of the pleasure she gets from being La Contessa's personal maid. Seeing the way she touches her, and the mien of her face as she ministers to her mistress suggests more than mere job satisfaction. My suspicions are only added to by what happens next.

Julia finishes bathing her mistress, and La Contessa stands up in the bath. I get to see her naked body from behind for a fleeting moment before Julia wraps a white towel around her. For a second I get to admire the statuesque figure and the voluptuous curve of her hips and backside. Mistress and maid are both beautiful, but in different ways. Julia is shorter than her mistress and rounder and cuddlier whereas La Contessa is tall and imperious. Hers is a commanding presence, her maid is comelier.

Julia wraps the fluffy white sheet around her mistress enveloping her in an embrace. She pulls La Contessa's body close to hers and rubs her mistress attentively whilst drawing in the aroma of her freshly soaped and oiled skin. Again I'm struck by the sensuality of Julia's touch. I doubt such intimacy between a lady and her maid is normal nor would it be permitted in most aristocratic households. I'm drawn away from my musings by La Contessa's sharp words.

"Avert your eyes, slave."

Obviously I say nothing of my glance at her naked back. I turn away and hear Julia collect something from the dressing room. When I'm told I can look up, Julia has slipped a dressing gown onto La Contessa. It's Chinese silk and decorated with two dragons. Her breasts swell underneath the material where it's been pulled tight across her chest, offering a glimpse of her cleavage. I make an effort to restrain my natural urges and resist the erection building up in response to the sensual delights before me, or I'll get into trouble. With considerable willpower I manage to do so.

"So, my slave, now to the task I set you of cleaning my shoes."

I'm anticipating a severe reprimand and punishment for a failure in detail or minor blemish left on one shoe.

"Yes, mistress," I reply.

"I must say, slave, I have inspected a sample of my footwear and I'm extremely impressed. I could find no fault in the work you carried out for me. I have heard glowing reports from my household staff of the dedication to which you applied yourself to the task. I must say I'm delighted, as my shoes have never looked so shiny. You must have worked hard to achieve such outstanding results."

"Thank you, mistress."

"You worked so hard I suspect you must have enjoyed the task, my slave. Is this the case?"

I try to choose my words carefully, as I suspect a trap is being laid for me, "Yes, mistress, it's always a pleasure to do a service for you, mistress."

"So, my slave, did you get pleasure from handling my boots?"

"The pleasure is in serving you, mistress," I persist.

"No, slave, I believe you are wilfully misunderstanding me. Did you get sexually aroused? Did touching the soft kid skin leather turn you on? Did you get a hard-on dreaming of your mistress in her exotic footwear?"

Ah, I've been found out, and there's no point trying to hide it from her. I confess, "Yes, mistress, I did get an erection from handling your shoes."

"Yes, I thought so. So, there you are hidden in the scullery with a barrow load of shoes with a stiff cock as you imagine your mistress doing unspeakable things to you whilst wearing said footwear. And did you wank, slave?"

"No, mistress, I promise I did not," I say honestly, but hiding the fact of how I did get my relief.

"It's irrelevant; the mere thought of treating your mistress like a sex object or getting sexual pleasure out of visualising her, is enough. Do you understand this, slave? Having those thoughts alone is enough to anger your mistress."

"I'm sorry, mistress. I promise, I do understand."

"I'm not so sure you do. I think there has to be a punishment for having these filthy thoughts about your mistress. Fetch my slave a pair of boots, Julia; the knee length black ones with the row of silver buckles and laces, which I understand were my slave's favourites."

La Contessa sits on a chair as Julia hands me the boots.

"Now put them on me, slave,"

As I kneel before her, La Contessa's dressing gown parts slightly, enough for me to appreciate the elegant curve of her ankle and to get a peek up at her shapely legs. I loosen the cords and ease La Contessa's delicate foot inside, pulling it gently until it's nestled comfortably in the boot. I wind the laces around the silver hooks and tighten them. I repeat the same exercise for the other boot.

Once the boots are on, La Contessa stands up whilst I'm still left kneeling on the floor. She lets the silk dressing gown slide off her back until she stands naked, save for the leather boots. I take a peek and gasp. It's an awesome sight, and one I was not expecting to experience. She's an imperious and voluptuous figure, and acutely aware of it. And she uses it to full effect, teasing me with her untouchable sensuality. La Contessa sits down again.

"Yes, you did a good job of polishing these boots for me slave, but not good enough. I don't think the bees wax is adequate. These boots need special treatment. These boots need licking clean."

The handling of La Contessa's feet, the aroma of her perfume mixed with the wax and leather is too much for me. I try to ward it off desperately, but to no avail. My cock springs into a hard erection.

72

"Oh dear," says La Contessa with disdain. "It appears you cannot control yourself, slave. Now lick my boots," she orders, "I want every inch cleaned with your tongue."

I get down on all fours and bend over her feet. One of La Contessa's legs is stretched out for me and I nestle the boot in my hands. I start with the metal tip of the heel. I wrap my tongue around licking it fastidiously. I run my tongue along the sole of the boot, making sure I cover every inch. I work my way up the boot, ensuring I lick clean each silver eyelet and the tiniest triangle of leather between the laces. I do this in silence as La Contessa stretches back in her chair and observes each kiss and lick of the shiny leather.

When I've covered every inch of both boots, she orders me to stand. Unfortunately for me, I fear, my prick is still hard. She takes my cock in her hand. She runs her fingers along its length, and its throbbing veins.

"No control, no self-discipline. Take your cock in your hands and wank for me slave. Kneel before me and wank over my boots as an act of humiliation."

"Yes, mistress," I reply.

I take my cock in my hands and hold it over one of the boots stretched out before me and masturbate. By now, I'm desperate for release but doubt La Contessa will allow it. I rub my cock furiously to please her and feel the orgasm pulsing inside me. It's imminent and I don't think I can hold it back.

"May I have permission to come, mistress," I splutter.

"Yes, you may slave. But make sure your spunk falls on my boot."

I'm so relieved. I don't think I could have held it back any longer. I groan desperately as the pressure builds up in my cock and I can do nothing to hold it back. It spurts over La Contessa's boot. There's a copious volume of spunk in thick white globules. I continue rubbing to squeeze every drop out of my cock.

"Thank you, mistress. Thank you," I gasp in relief at my release.

"Thank you? Why are you thanking me? This is for my pleasure, slave. This is to humiliate you and teach you a lesson in discipline. I trust you know what you must do next."

Then it strikes me what penance there will be for allowing me to come in her presence. I understand automatically what I must do. I cannot leave her beautiful boots in this condition. I know I must clean the spunk off... with my tongue.

I undertake the task enthusiastically, licking the blobs of spunk from the boot and swallowing the thick, salty substance. And yes, it's gloriously humiliating. But I love every minute of it, love kneeling at the feet of this dominant mistress, carrying out this disgusting act at her command.

La Contessa puts her dressing gown back on and offers me a last word of advice, "You must understand, slave, carrying out deeds is all very well but servitude in its purest form is in the mind. You can do tasks for me with dedication and efficiency, but there is more. You must learn this to be truly submissive."

"Yes mistress. Thank you mistress."

"Now, let me turn to this afternoon's proceedings. I have my guests arriving soon and have laid entertainment on for them at which I need my slave's presence. Julia, would you do the honours for me in preparing him?"

Julia is standing with a garment made of leather straps and buckles. Under the watchful gaze of La Contessa, she starts by threading my, now flaccid, cock through a metal ring and then tightening a band around my waist with a buckle.

"You may try to arouse him if you wish, Julia, but he will incur my wrath if he gets another erection. My slave has had more than enough sexual gratification for the day."

Another two straps are passed through the crack in my arse and buckled to the waist strap. The leather digs into the flesh and serves to compress my backside, making my bum cheeks stand out; I suspect to make them a nice fleshy target for something... or somebody.

Further straps run diagonally across my body and are fastened to the waist band. By the time Julia has finished, I'm neatly trussed up in leather straps whilst leaving the most sensitive flesh exposed.

"Excellent, Julia. Now, my slave, you must go to my games room and await me and my guests there."

11: The Card Game

I make my way to La Contessa's games salon where I wait patiently beside the card table as I've been directed. The other household servants are not put out by having a naked servant wander around the house wearing no more than a collar and a few leather straps. I get the odd admiring glance at my manhood from the younger, female servants. But they know not to linger too long in admiring my physique or they'll get a reprimand from old Lucio.

The centrepiece of the salon is a billiard table, but there are also several card tables, one laid out for a game. There's a chair arranged on one side of the table and four on the opposite side. In front of each setting is a stack of chips fashioned from ivory, each with a distinctive coloured marking on it. There's a decanter of *malvasia* and glasses set out around the table at each place setting.

The table is set out for a game of *faro*, a hugely popular card game in Venice for many years. *Il Ridotto*, the gaming houses sanctioned by the Venetian state, are full of people playing *faro*. I once visited the largest of these gambling houses in Calle de Ridotto. It was an eye opener; a vast candlelit hall with over a hundred gaming tables packed with gamblers. It's hugely popular though I've never been tempted to partake. I've seen and heard of too many lives ruined from fortunes lost at the gaming table. I know how popular the game is with the aristocratic elite of Venice so it doesn't surprise me La Contessa should invite guests to play with her.

The green baize has a suit of spades set out in classic formation with a row containing ace to six, another row with eight to the king, and the seven to one side on its own. Faro is simple and fast moving, hence why it's so popular and how people lose so much money playing it. Basically, people play against the dealer by placing bets on the cards.

At the start of the game three cards are turned up from the pack. The first isn't used in the game and is discarded to the left of the pack. The next card is the 'loser' and is placed in front of the dealer whilst the card left face up on the pack is the 'winner'. 'Loser' cards win for the banker who takes the stakes from the card on the board while 'winner' cards win for the players who've bet on that card. After each 'turn' of the two cards the bets are settled and the stakes of the cards not turned over stay on the table.

I admit to being intrigued about the role I'm meant to play in the game. I imagine La Contessa will add a sexual twist to it, or maybe she wants me as a decoration to stand there naked in my leather straps.

I hear a commotion of chatting and giggling from the other side of the door before it's flung open by Lucio dressed in formal attire for the occasion. Lucio sees me standing by the card table and shoots me a disdainful stare across the room. La Contessa enters with her four guests.

They are a bizarre sight dressed with the formal extravagance of Venetian court life. Julia has done a remarkable job in transforming her mistress into the epitome of current Venetian fashion. The wigs are enormous, even by the standards of the day. It's as if they've entered a competition for the tallest wig, which, inevitably, La Contessa has won, as hers is several inches higher than the others. They are embellished with jewels and enormous feathers so that, even in the high ceiling of the salon, they nearly touch the roof. In fact, I believe the size of La Contessa's wig is so preposterous a parody of the fashion of the day, or even a mockery of her guests, is suggested. She has the statuesque figure and poise to pull it off but, though I'd dare not hint it to her, as a group they appear rather ridiculous.

It's not only the enormous wigs. Their faces are powdered white, their lips rouged and their faces adorned with false moles in the shape of hearts or spades. Their gowns are sumptuous; the quality of the material, their cut, and vibrant colours are stunning. They walk stiffly, encumbered as they are by their wigs, bustles, and layers of undergarments.

As they enter one of La Contessa's guests is nattering away to the others in good Italian with a strange accent, which I take to be English, "I'm enjoying Venice exceedingly. I must say, much to my surprise, so is Lord Rudston. I was most worried he'd be bored away from his estate and his hunting, but he seems to have taken such an interest in the architecture here. You know, he has taken to regular constitutional walks where he simply insists on going out on his own to explore Venice. I'm most delighted he's shown an interest in things other than his hunting, it's most refreshing."

I have to restrain myself from laughing. I catch La Contessa's gaze and we exchange discreet smiles. We both know where Lord Rudston's been! He's taken himself off to the brothels of the Cannaregio. He's probably fucked every prostitute in Venice by now without Lady Rudston suspecting a thing. Well, I say every prostitute; that would be some achievement given there are several thousand of them!

From the introductions made by Lucio I can identify La Contessa's guests. There's Lady Rudston, with a short round body and spherical face looking absurd in her massive wig. Apparently, Lord Rudston owns huge estates in a part of England I've never heard of called 'Yorkshire'. There's Archduchess Hofburg from Salzburg, who is tall, angular and pointed, Anastasia Petrova, allegedly a Russian Princess and finally, and most interestingly, Mademoiselle Marie La Tour, the wealthy heiress to the Gobelins tapestry factory in Paris, who is young and pretty. They make for a strange party.

Now, from the point of view of La Contessa's plans for her soiree, they have each come with a male servant, dressed like me in combinations of leather straps and thongs. I expect La Contessa has loaned this attire as I can't imagine this being normal dress in these aristocratic houses. They are directed to stand next alongside me at one end of the card table.

The ladies take their seats at the table and Lucio pours out a glass of *malvasia* for each of them. They unfold their enormous fans, decorated with hand-painted Japanese geishas, which must be the latest fashion. I appreciate it must be hot under the thick velvet and damask dresses but the salon is not so warm. I can only think the fans are an affectation or, it occurs to me, they might be used for coded messages if the players had conspired to cheat La Contessa, as I know fans are used in this way. But I consider this highly unlikely. Indeed, it's hard to imagine Lady Rudston having the wits to cheat anybody.

La Contessa explains the rules of her game, "I know you are familiar with the rules of *faro*. I shall play the role of dealer. You can bet up to five stakes for each turn. There is a delightful little twist to my version of the game though. After each turn your winning stakes are converted into punishments for our respective servants. So, if the dealer, that's me, wins, then I get to punish your servant. If a player wins, then you get the chance to punish my slave. So, there you are ladies, it's really win-win for you, either you administer corporal punishment or you watch it being delivered to another servant."

As La Contessa explains her rules I stand there mentally calculating the likely odds. Surely that means with four against the dealer I have four times more chance of being punished than the other servants? Oh well, I was expecting there to be a twist, and it doesn't surprise me La Contessa would load the odds against me.

"This is good. I am looking forward to game. Salons of St Petersburg do not permit such goings-on. We are not so, how do you say, opening of minds as in Venice," explains the Princess Anastasia in broken Italian.

"Oh my goodness! If only Lord Rudston knew what I'm getting up to whilst he's wandering around Venice looking at churches. He's such a stick-in-the mud," laughs Lady Rudston. "He'd never imagine I'd be doing anything as naughty as this whilst his back's turned!"

"I was once invited by the Comte du Conde to a masked spanking ball at the palace of Vaux le Vicomte," added Mademoiselle La Tour, "it was great fun. Thank you for inviting me Contessa, I'm looking forward to this."

The thin Austrian archduchess looks across at her haughtily, "I'm surprised Le Comte would invite a tradesman and commoner to his palace."

Mademoiselle stares daggers at her, "Money opens doors, as you'll no doubt discover soon Herr Hofburg. Nobody will talk to an impoverished aristocrat as I expect you'll soon find out after your husband has settled his debts at *Il Ridotto*."

This afternoon could be fun! But La Contessa has no time for this squabbling amongst her guests and rapidly pulls them back to the game at hand.

"Lucio, lay-out the instruments of punishment for me," she orders.

He fetches an armful of implements and arraigns them on the green baize of an adjoining card table. There is a collection of whips, riding crops, tawses, straps, slippers, and canes of varying sizes, materials, and flexibility all capable of delivering severe corporal punishment. The servants of the other aristocratic guests stare nervously at the tools arraigned before them.

"I will add a little more interest to the game by giving a value to the implements. I believe the canes are the harshest so they need two winning stakes before you can use them. For the overall winner, the player with the most winning stakes, I have a special treat. So, shall we begin ladies?"

La Contessa nestles into the dealer's chair. The ladies place their stakes on the cards. She shuffles the deck and places it face up in front of her on the table. The card showing is the first card, known as the *soda*, and this is discarded and placed to the left of the pack. The next card is the two of diamonds; this is the 'loser' and is placed between the discarded card and the pack. The card showing at the top of the pack is the eight of clubs, and is the 'winner'.

Lady Rudston has placed a stake on the two of spades on the board, this means she has lost to the dealer and, under the rules of this version of the game, La Contessa can punish Lady Rudston's servant.

She's in fits of giggles over it, "Oh, I'm so sorry, James. I was never any good at cards! Lord Rudston has always said I've no luck in card games and he's right. This is such fun."

I glance at the deck. Two guests, Mademoiselle La Tour and the Archduchess Hofburg have put stakes on the eight which means I receive one stroke from each of them. I think I might enjoy being whipped by the pretty French heiress and the Archduchess looks so feeble, I'd be surprised if she can even lift a riding crop!

Lady Rudston's servant, James, bends over dutifully to receive his punishment. La Contessa leaves him there as she adds another detail to the rules.

"I should have mentioned that a lady can opt to use her hand to deliver a spanking instead of the implements, if she prefers. I choose to use my bare hand."

She stands up, ceremoniously stretches out her arm and slowly pulls off her lace glove. She raises her arm and brings her hand sharply down on the servant's backside with a loud slap. The servant shouts out.

"Ouch! That hurts."

La Contessa looks at him with disgust, "It is a mere tickle. You'll find out what real punishment is later in the game. There is another rule. Servants must take their punishment in silence. If they make any noise, or if any one of the players think they have not accepted their punishment gracefully, then they can ask for another stroke."

La Contessa raises her arm again and brings her hand down even harder. James, having learnt his lesson, takes his punishment in silence.

Now it's my turn and I bend over and thrust my arse up invitingly into the air. Out of the corner of my eye I see Mademoiselle choose the riding crop, and the Archduchess a leather strap. The riding crop crashes on my backside. It's a hard stroke, and I can tell Mademoiselle means business. The cord at the end of the crop delivers a nasty little sting. The Archduchess strikes me with the leather strap. I'm surprised at the strength of the stroke. The impact and quality of the pain is wholly different as the flat leather strap whacks against one bum cheek.

"Contessa," Mademoiselle calls mischievously, "I heard him grunt when the crop whipped him, so I claim another stroke."

"Yes, I'm disappointed in him. He has been trained to receive punishment. Of course, Mademoiselle, these are the rules of the game, please go ahead."

I'm sure I didn't grunt, but I'm not going to argue. I steel myself for another stroke and this one is even harder. She's obviously determined to enter into the spirit of the game.

"That's not fair. I struck him harder than her, and I heard him grunt too. I demand another stroke," this from the indignant Archduchess who doesn't want the French woman to get one over on her.

"But yes, you are entitled to another stroke," replies La Contessa.

The heavy leather strap crashes on my arse again with a loud slap. This could be a long afternoon if the ladies compete for more hits like this.

La Contessa's card game continues in a similar vein. *Faro* is a fast moving game; turns last only as long as it takes to deal the two cards, hence why it's so easy to lose money in the state gaming houses. The guests quickly get used to La Contessa's rules and, as the game gathers pace, the turn-over of spankings, whippings, and beatings becomes faster and more furious.

La Contessa finds it highly entertaining. I can tell she's exercising restraint and refrains from delivering the beatings I know she's capable of to the other participants who are not as experienced in receiving punishment. Consequently, the shock of being struck by La Contessa's whip with its long leather thongs leads them to emit squeals, groans, and gasps leading to further strokes. But the other servants get off lightly. Somehow, I find it's me who gets the lion's share of the punishment.

La Contessa laughs with the other ladies, "I really don't know what's happening, I don't appear to be having much luck as dealer. The 'winner' cards are coming up for you so frequently."

We servants face the game as La Contessa considers it amusing for us to see the stakes placed and the cards as they are turned over so we can work out the punishments we can expect.

"I believe it adds to the anticipation and the fun for us." she explains, and they agree as they regard our shocked faces with amusement.

In fact, La Contessa's luck is so poor in this game I suspect she's manipulating it to make sure I receive the most punishments. I've been party to her games long enough to know it's likely. The other interesting point about *faro* is that stakes can build up on an individual card until it is turned up. It so happens twelve stakes have accumulated on the knave and, surprise, surprise, La Contessa turns the knave of hearts over as a 'winner' card, which means I have to take twelve strokes.

The guests find this highly amusing. They each make their choice of implement: the Russian Princess the riding crop; the Austrian Archduchess, a slipper; Lady Rudston, the leather strap, whilst Mademoiselle La Tour selects to use her bare hand. They have me bend over and stick my arse up in the air for them as they line up to take their turns. Three strokes of crop, two of the slipper, three of the strap in quick succession with barely time to take breath and finally, four slaps from Mademoiselle. After the beating my arse is red and throbbing. Strangely, I don't mind. I know how thin the boundary is between pain and pleasure, and I'm only too willing to join in the game. I'm convinced I take this punishment in steely silence but Mademoiselle, who I think is playing games with me, insists I let out an audible gasp and should, therefore, be punished further by both her and the other guests too. La Contessa acquiesces with her demand. This means a further twelve strokes.

They each have their different styles of delivery and, after downing several glasses of *malvasia,* they are soon tipsy and lose their inhibitions. The Russian's strokes are icy and determined, and the heaviest of the four.

The Austrian doesn't hit as hard yet finds a delivery which gives a nasty sting. It takes a while for the English lady to get going as to start with she's in such a fit of giggles she fails to deliver a proper stroke. As she warms up her hits become firmer. She looks a sight after delivering her three strokes, her round face flushed and bright red from the exertion. Mademoiselle is having the most fun. She's playing along with the spirit of the game and finds any excuse to administer me more punishment. It's Mademoiselle who's the first to exercise the rule of holding back on stakes to use the cane. She's the most successful player, much to the annoyance of the Archduchess Hofburg.

"Contessa," she says after winning with four bets on number nine, "I've four stakes with this win and I've saved another six from other wins, so I believe I have the right to use five strokes of the cane."

"Certainly, Mademoiselle," agrees La Contessa, "by all means make use of your stakes. We shall enjoy seeing my slave get punished with the cane."

"*Sacre bleu*, I'm looking forward to this. I had a lover once who enjoyed corporal punishment. When it was quiet, I used to tie him to a loom in the tapestry works and give him a good caning. It's such a shame, he's no longer my lover now, but they were happy days!"

"How wonderful," replies La Contessa. "Yes, there is nothing like caning a lover... or a slave. But Mademoiselle, I've had a wonderful idea for a commission. As you know, I've invited you here because I need tapestries to decorate my gaming salon. I propose you design a tapestry of me punishing my slave. It can be a permanent memento of our afternoon."

"Why, that would be wonderful, Contessa. The men in the works will have such fun designing it. And I will make sure you look magnificent in the tapestry. I will have them weave your dress in gold thread."

"Excellent, Mademoiselle. We will discuss details later."

The Austrian Archduchess has a face like thunder. I fear she has misjudged La Contessa. She only has to look at the outstanding paintings, sculptures, and tapestries in the palazzo to recognise La Contessa has an appreciation for fine arts.

"Now to the business at hand," smiles Mademoiselle with relish. "Stick your arse out for me. I want a decent target to aim at."

I do as I'm told and present myself for her. She circles around me flexing the cane. She drags it across my arse, raw from many beatings over the course of the card game.

She raises the cane high above her head and brings it down with a swishing sound to crack onto my backside. It stings. She's young and strong, and she knows how to deliver a severe punishment. I can hear the other women gasp at the ferocity of the stroke. I breathe heavily but hold my position.

She leans over so her face, topped by the huge wig balanced on top of her head, is pressed close to mine. I get a whiff her scent, sweet and flowery, the most expensive from her Parisian *parfumier* no doubt.

"Now, I don't want to hear the slightest whimper from you. And I'm listening… very carefully!"

The next stroke comes cracking onto my backside. There's a slight pause and then the next three in quick succession so I can barely draw breath. Do I let out a gasp? I can't help it. It may only have been faint, but if challenged I couldn't deny it.

"He makes breathe, I think," says the Russian Princess triumphantly.

"Yes, he definitely did," confirms La Contessa as she turns to me. "I'm disappointed in you, slave. I've been praising your ability to take punishment to my guests, and now you've let me down. I think Mademoiselle is entitled to another five strokes. And I will give you another five for failing to serve my guests adequately."

Mademoiselle has a wicked glint in her eye. She's enjoying this. I steel myself for the next five strokes. She knows how to use a cane and these are another series of hard strokes. La Contessa comes forward. I know she's cruel and will show me no mercy. The cane bears down on me with a swishing sound as it slices through the air and then hits my backside with a loud crack. Oh yes, La Contessa knows how to wield a cane with malice. Four more strokes of those whilst straining to the utmost not to expel the slightest gasp, knowing it will lead to further punishment, is as much as I can endure.

After she finishes, La Contessa adds to my humiliation by inviting her guests to inspect my arse with its deep red marks where the cane has slashed across the flesh.

They carry on playing to complete a round, working through the whole deck of cards. I do a quick calculation; there are twenty-five rounds within the deck, four players, each placing five stakes. A total of five hundred strokes of whip, crop, paddle, strap, slipper, and hand (and that's not even counting the extra ones given). On average there should be one hundred per servant, yet, though I've not been counting, I'm sure I've received more than my fair share of them. La Contessa, as the dealer, doesn't appear to have won anything like the odds she should have in a game of *faro*.

It's no surprise Mademoiselle is the overall winner, having won by far the highest number of stakes.

La Contessa announces, "I promised a special prize for the overall winner. Get onto the billiard table, slave," she orders.

The billiard balls are swept to one side to clear the table, and I climb face down onto the green baize. La Contessa distributes a coil of rope to each of her guests and instructs them to tie me to the corner pockets of the billiard table. Mademoiselle and the Russian undertake the task with relish. They expertly secure the ropes around my wrists, stretch my arms out and tie the other end of the rope around a pocket. The Archduchess is more reluctant as she's still smarting from the French heiress being the winner. Meanwhile, Lady Rudston is getting in a tangle with her knots and needs La Contessa to help her out. Once the knots are secured around my ankles, the four ladies pull my legs to stretch me across the table, tying the ends of the ropes to the corner pockets.

"You see ladies how sadistic domination is an art form. See how the slave's brown body looks spread-eagled on the green baize of the billiard table. Admire how the slave's balls are left exposed to us. He's all yours Mademoiselle."

"What should I do with him?"

"Well, there are the billiard cues," La Contessa suggests.

"Or the billiard balls," adds Mademoiselle clicking two of them together.

"Oh yes, what an excellent proposition."

My eyes water as I imagine what she might have in mind.

"Would anybody like to join me in a game of billiards?" asks Mademoiselle.

I hear the clunk of an ivory ball being laid on the table, the sound of cue on ball, and then feel the billiard ball slam against my balls left exposed on the baize. Mademoiselle has given the ball an almighty, and accurate, hit.

"My slave's balls are the pocket," announces La Contessa, "The aim of the game is to hit the pocket with the billiard ball."

"Oh what fun, Contessa. I must try this. Lord Rudston only allows gentlemen into his billiard room, so I expect I'll be hopeless."

"Here, let me help you Lady Rudston," says Mademoiselle.

I'm conscious of massive powdered wigs hanging over me as Mademoiselle leans over to show Lady Rudston how to hold the cue, helping her line it up with the ball.

"There, now slide the cue firmly between the bridge formed by your fingers," explains the French woman.

A billiard ball rams against my balls to squeals of delight from Lady Rudston at hitting the 'pocket'. My balls are now throbbing with the pain of being crushed by the heavy ivory.

Princess Anastasia makes her contribution by squeezing the sac of my balls against the baize with the tip of the cue. The four guests play 'billiards' with me in this way, much to their amusement. La Contessa looks on, satisfied her guests are having an entertaining time. She grasps a billiard cue from the Archduchess and asks them to stand back before raising it over her shoulder and bringing it crashing down on my backside. I'm not expecting it and let out a yelp of pain.

"You will suffer your punishment in silence, slave. Two more strokes for a lapse of concentration."

She whacks my arse with the cue another couple of times. I imagine those final strokes will add bruises to my already sore backside.

"I hope you've enjoyed your entertainment ladies. I think we shall retire for tea. Lucio, you can untie this slave for me now and dismiss him."

The four guests express their effusive appreciation for the different amusements La Contessa has provided before they leave the salon for her private waiting room, and tea.

12: Becky

A few weeks after the card game, La Contessa invites me to accompany her on a different venture. She's on a mission. She's searching for a loyal female submissive. She wants me to go with her to the Cannaregio again to make use of my contacts in the district to search the brothels for a young woman who can play the role of slave girl. This is how we find ourselves in a tavern I know in Campo di San Canciano where a madam I know specialises in procuring submissive girls. I wait attentively whilst she's deep in conversation with the madam.

La Contessa takes pleasure in visiting these places in Venice's dark underbelly, often in disguise. But today she appears as herself, dressed sumptuously in an indigo gown woven with pearls, her auburn hair swept above her head and held by two ivory combs. Over her shoulder is a black velvet cape. She wears a plain white mask over her eyes to disguise her identity.

All eyes in the tavern turn towards us. The brothels of the Cannaregio attract a diverse clientele, and it's not unusual to find noblewomen here searching for sexual excitement. They wouldn't normally attract a second glance, but La Contessa is a woman who commands attention wherever she goes. Her statuesque figure and voluptuous curves attract stares from everybody in the tavern.

"I think I've found what you're looking for," the matron of the house says.

"So, what makes you think she will be suitable?" La Contessa asks.

"I got a chance to speak with her. Her tale is a sorry one. She's had many unfortunate encounters. She says she's genuinely submissive, and I believe her."

"Do you think she understands what being in my service means?"

"I can't say for sure, your ladyship."

"I can procure plenty of girls who will prostitute themselves for me, who are only too willing to suck cock or offer themselves to be fucked at my masquerade balls. But I'm looking for someone special, a girl who's prepared to go further, who has the imagination to join in my games, and is willing to do anything for her mistress."

"All I can say, Contessa, is this girl struck me as being different. I see

85

plenty of pretty girls who come here to work, but this one isn't like the others."

"Hm," La Contessa ponders, "I'm definitely interested in her. Where's this girl now?"

"Ah well, there's a problem your ladyship. She's in the hands of a merchant from Syria who's been staying here. He asked for a private room where he could keep a girl. I found him a cell room in the cellars where he keeps her. I don't know what he does to her there; it's none of my business, your ladyship, I'm sure you understand, I don't interfere in anyone else's business. But I bring her food and get the chance to chat to her. She's a lovely girl, though I've got to say she's in a bit of a sorry state at the moment."

"Take me to her."

"Oh, it's difficult your ladyship, only the gentleman is with her now."

"Dare you cross me, madam?"

A fierce stare, a raised eyebrow and a few harsh words and the poor matron of the house is catapulted into a state of agitation.

"Of course not, your ladyship. I don't mean to contradict you. I'm sure I can arrange something. Come with me."

La Contessa has a satisfied smile on her face. We follow the matron down winding stone steps to the cellars where she points to a door hidden away in the corner and leaves us. My mistress gestures for me to be silent as we creep forwards. There is a metal grill in the door and La Contessa positions herself so she can see through the door without being seen herself. I take a position on the other side so we can both peep through the opening in the door.

The matron of the house is being coy about the purpose of the cell as it's obviously a service she provides in her brothel and is designed for clientele with more sadistic tastes. It's a dark cell fitted out with numerous chains and hooks. At first all I can see is a man's back, dressed in baggy light blue pantaloons and tunic, and a turbaned head. When he turns to one side, I see a pot-bellied Arabic man with a long black beard, who must be the merchant from Syria.

Looking past him, I see the girl. She's crouched in a corner, chained and shackled like a wild animal in a cage. The waves in her fair hair are matted, and her body bears the marks of physical abuse. There's a metal collar around her neck attached to a long chain fastened to a hook in the stone wall. At the moment this affords her some freedom of movement but her wrists and ankles have heavy metal shackles on, which have been used to secure her to the wall.

The merchant takes a pace towards her, slapping her hard across the face with the palm of his hand. He draws it back again, striking her other cheek with the back of his hand.

"Whore slut of Babylon," he shouts at her. "You're my slut and sex slave now. When I get you back to my land, you'll be made to service my family. I have seven sons, all of them randy. They'll take pleasure in having a little, white girl to fuck. You'll be my sex slave for life, what do you think of that?"

The girl remains silent, and the merchant slaps her violently across the face again.

"I said, what do you think of that, girl?"

"Yes, very good master," the girl replies quietly.

La Contessa watches intently. Will she intervene I wonder? At the moment she appears content to let the scene unfold, her eyes gazing with studied fascination. I try to gauge the girl's reaction to her abuse. Is she enjoying this treatment? I know that's possible. I've been tormented by La Contessa and have learnt to appreciate the blurred line between pain and pleasure. I stay loyal in my service to her because of, not despite, her treatment of me. But I see no hint of pleasure or engagement in the girl's face, only a blank stare. Her expression is resigned as if this is a fate she must accept.

The merchant pulls at the girl's bodice and rips it apart releasing her ample breasts. He bends down and bites her tits. I see the red marks he has left on her soft flesh. He reaches out for a whip from the floor and lashes her across the breasts. The girl doesn't moan or whimper, let alone scream. The act of striking the girl is arousing the merchant sexually because the outline of a hard cock pressing against his loose pants is obvious.

"Get on your knees bitch," he shouts at her. "I'll make you my bitch-dog, you fucking slut. Now, get on all fours."

With a clank of the metal shackles on her ankles and wrists on the stone floor, the girl clambers onto all fours as she's ordered. The Syrian merchant stands over her, pulling the chain attached to her collar so the rough edges of the metal dig into her neck. He grabs hold of her hair and yanks it hard. The girl lets out a gasp and, egged on by the reaction, the merchant twists her hair around his fist and pulls even harder. This time, the girl, anticipating what's next, doesn't react. He pulls her head around and puts his face close up to hers.

"I'm going to take you girl, like a bitch in heat. But I'll punish you first for being an insolent whore. What are you?"

"An insolent whore and a bitch slut, master," she answers obediently.

He releases her hair and, whilst she's still on her hands and knees, pulls up her skirt and sets on her backside with the whip. The blows rain down on the peachy flesh of her arse. The whacking sound of leather on skin fills the cell. The blows get harder until her backside is glowing red.

"Take that you bitch. What do you say?"

"Thank you, master."

He throws the whip onto the ground, drops his pants and kneels in front of her. He twists her hair around his hand again and pushes her head down onto his erect cock.

"Now suck on it, slut."

The girl responds to the command at once, takes the angry hardness in her mouth, and sucks. Her head bobs up and down as her lips run along the length of his throbbing member.

"Ooh, yes, suck hard you bitch, suck harder."

Still holding onto her hair he pushes the girl's head up and down his cock in fast rhythmic movements. He lets go of her hair and the girl continues the tempo of her sucking, her mouth moving in a frenetic pumping motions. The merchant looks as though he's going to burst, his face is bright red and he's moaning in ecstasy shouting, "suck me whore, suck me!"

He pulls his cock out of the girl's mouth and moves behind her. She's still in a doggy position and the merchant let's go of her chain lead to grasp her hips and ram himself into her cunt. He's so close to coming it only takes a few hard pushes before he releases his load into her. He moans in ecstasy. She pants for breath with the shock and force of the final penetration. She collapses onto the floor, no longer able to hold the position on her hands and knees, and the weight of the Syrian merchant's corpulent body falls onto her.

La Contessa and I gaze on the scene transfixed. I can see mistress is not interested in the cock sucking or the forced fucking. She's studying the girl's behaviour, her facial expressions, and her reactions, weighing up her potential to participate in La Contessa's more refined erotic play. The girl can definitely take punishment, but it's hard to judge if she's taking it because she has to or because she genuinely desires it. La Contessa will want more than a passive vehicle for the crude abuse the merchant administers; she will want a slave willing and open, who will be prepared to explore the sadistic fantasies La Contessa can offer her.

Having taken his pleasure, the merchant sits the girl up with her back against the wall of the cell, spreading her arms and chaining them to the wall Then he spreads her legs and locks them to rings set in the floor.

"I'll be back to take more pleasure from you later," he threatens.

It's at this point La Contessa decides to intervene. She pushes the door open and strides imperiously into the cell. She towers over the merchant, filling the small room with her feminine power and beauty. The merchant is startled. Before he can respond, La Contessa proclaims her intentions.

"You have a pliable young girl there. I am looking for just such a girl for my household. I will offer you good money for her."

The Syrian's brown eyes light up at the word money, but he's too experienced a haggler to sound overly eager.

"She's my sex slave now. She's mine. Why should I give up my slut-bitch to you?"

"I will give you a good price."

"How much?"

"Four silver *ducats*."

"No, six."

"No, four. Come, with four silver *ducats* in your pocket you can fuck every whore from here to Damascus five times over, and still have change."

"No, six," insists the merchant.

"I will offer you five. Besides, she's damaged goods. It's a good price and you know it. If you carry on treating her like this, she'll be worth nothing. Even fully fit you'd be lucky to get one *ducat* for her at the slave market. Five is my final offer."

The merchant pretends to ponder awhile but they both know he doesn't want to lose the sale.

"Ok, mysterious masked lady, you have a deal."

"Excellent, my servant will return with the money and collect the girl this evening. It's been good business for me."

"Likewise for me, Madam," says the merchant as he takes La Contessa's hand and plants a kiss on it.

She bristles, pulls her hand away, and throws him a disdainful glance before sweeping out of the cell. Her look throughout the brief negotiations for the girl is inscrutable, and I'm amazed she would hand over five silver *ducats* to the sadistic Syrian. Against my better judgement my curiosity gets the better of me.

"But mistress, are you going to pay the rat five *ducats*?"

"Idiot. Do you think I would hand over good money to a worthless serpent like that? I want the girl. I'm interested in the girl. She has potential. But I'm not paying five *ducats* for her. Take my signet ring and go to the *procurator* of the Sestiere di Cannaregio and demand he sends constables to arrest him. I have plans for him. You will go with them. Say the girl has been stolen from me and then bring her back to my palace."

I smile; how foolish of me to doubt La Contessa's determination and ingenuity.

"Yes, mistress. It will be a pleasure."

When I return with the girl, my instructions are to take her to Julia and report to La Contessa's salon. She's sitting on her throne, expecting me. She orders me to strip off and get on my hand and knees at her feet so she can use me as her foot stool. It's from this position I explain that the girl has been successively procured. La Contessa is pleased.

Soon after Julia arrives, beckoning the girl into the chamber. She looks forlorn and bedraggled; her hair is a tussle of fair waves, and her bodice and skirt are rough and torn. She has scratches on her cheek, bruises on her upper arm, sore marks around her neck, wrists, and ankles where the iron shackles have been. There are welt marks all over her, the results of her abuse at the hands of the Syrian merchant. But La Contessa has seen beyond her battered body and unkempt appearance to recognise the potential in her.

La Contessa rises, pushes me onto the floor with a booted foot. Stepping onto me, she pauses for a few moments as I try to support her full weight with the sharp heels of her boots digging into my back. Then she steps off. Two deep indentations are left on my back. She steps forward a few paces, her penetrating green eyes appraising the girl.

"What's your name girl?" she asks.

"Rebecca, madam, but I'm known as Becky."

"Becky, what a strange name."

"It's foreign madam. I'm from England."

They stand facing each other, La Contessa in her sumptuous indigo gown and the girl in tattered rags as if she's been dragged through the alleys of Venice; one imperious, the other forlorn, but with a quiet air of dignified resilience. La Contessa runs her painted fingers sensuously across the girl's face, gently straightening a few strands of tousled yellow hair.

"She's lovely," La Contessa says, turning to Julia. "I love her fair hair and pale skin. It's so unusual to see such a complexion even in a cosmopolitan city like Venice. My companions will love her; I think they will be attracted to her peachy complexion. When she is bathed and dressed, her underlying beauty will shine for all to appreciate. Tell me girl, how is it you find yourself in Venice."

"It's a long tale madam, but I'll try to be as brief as I can. I once served a master back in Norfolk in England. I submitted to him dutifully, and he dominated me like a true master but he lost his money when the wool trade collapsed and he sold me to a German merchant from the Hanseatic League. Much of his trade was through Venice and he brought me here with him as his sex slave. A few days ago he bet me as a stake in a game of dice to the Syrian merchant and lost. The Syrian was even crueller and abused me terribly as you have seen."

"I hear you are submissive, yet you speak of your abuse as if it were a trial for you?" La Contessa queries.

"This is true, but yet the German and Syrian did not truly dominate and control me madam, they used me abusively," Becky replies.

La Contessa nods quietly.

"Well-spoken girl. Yes, few men understand how to truly dominate. They think beating a girl up and raping her is sadism. They are wrong, true sadism is an art form. Don't you agree slave?"

"Oh yes mistress," I concur enthusiastically, "and you are its most skilled proponent."

La Contessa curls her red lips into a smile.

"To be a true sadist, you must have the artistry of a painter, the perception of a mind reader and," she lets out a wicked little laugh, "a cruel and twisted imagination. It is not brutal but subtle and refined. It takes a special person to possess it and a particular quality to receive it. Are you that girl Becky?"

At this, La Contessa runs her hands over Becky's neck and pulls her ripped bodice apart to expose her tits. She runs the tips of scarlet fingernails across the pale flesh of her breasts and takes a nipple between her fingers. The two women stare into each other's eyes. La Contessa squeezes the soft buds of Becky's nipples between her hard nails. Becky expels a gasp of air and the slightest shudder ripples through her body, but she does not flinch for one second, and her eyes stay fixed on La Contessa. She takes Becky's other nipple between her nails and squeezes them both simultaneously. I have been subjected to this treatment myself. I know how sharp La Contessa's nails are, how painful when she squeezes nipples so tightly. From my position crouched on the floor, I watch on fascinated. La Contessa is testing the girl and she, for her part, is showing her what she's capable of taking. Her eyes have glazed over with the effort of enduring the pain, but they are still locked onto La Contessa's.

"Do you know what it means to serve me, girl?"

"No, madam," Becky whispers.

"I am a demanding mistress. I am cruel and capricious. I expect my servants to obey my every word without question. I demand a lot from them. The nature of my household is, how should I say, bizarre and perverted. Yet for those who genuinely give themselves up to me and embrace their servitude the rewards are great. Isn't that so slave?"

"Oh, most definitely mistress," I reply with feeling.

La Contessa, still gripping Becky's nipples tightly with her nails, twists them suddenly and firmly. The girl's eyes flicker momentarily but then stare dreamily back into La Contessa's.

"Do you still wish to serve me?"

"Yes, madam. Yes please madam, I do. Very much."

"I don't accept anybody into my household. There must be a test, an initiation, to see if you are truly worthy to serve me. You have passed one little examination, but this will be a far more strenuous challenge. Do you still want to go ahead?"

"Yes please, madam."

La Contessa finally releases Becky's nipples. They are reddened and sore. I notice the deep impressions La Contessa's nails have made in the soft flesh.

"Very well, I will make the plans for your initiation ceremony. Julia," she calls to her maid, "this girl desires to join my household. As you can see she is in a poor state. I want you to care for her. Run her a bath and put rose water into it. I will have her smelling like an old fashioned English garden. Find a salve for her cuts and bruises. Then find some suitable clothes for her. Report back on her progress, I want her ready for me a week from today. You will bring her back as my little rosy-faced, fair-haired, submissive girl, dressed for her introduction into the perversions of the world of La Contessa."

With these ominous words La Contessa dismisses us from her presence with a wave of her hand.

13: Revenge

The week passes. It's not long before I'm waiting for La Contessa underneath the portico at the entrance to her palace, the imposing marble staircase fanning out before me towards the canal side. Becky is by my side having been bathed and dressed by Julia and the maids. She's wearing a crisp, white, cotton bodice, laced tightly, her fulsome breasts lifted up to display them in their soft, milky magnificence. I gaze at her breasts swelling with every breath she takes. Her skirt is decorated with a bright, rustic, floral pattern. Her lips have been painted a subtle pink, and her cheeks with the merest touch of rouge to set off her pale skin. The knots have been combed out of her fair hair, which tumbles in waves over her shoulders, and she smells fragrant. I see La Contessa's vision for Becky; she's been re-cast as a fresh and innocent peasant girl dressed in her finest clothes for a special occasion.

I have to say she looks lovely now she's been cleaned up and her wounds tended. At the sight of her, I have to control the swelling in my cock. I'd better be careful on two accounts; I daren't let La Contessa see any traces of an erection or I'll be in for a severe punishment. I also see Julia noting the looks I cast towards the new slave girl. She's looks askance at me with a fiercely quizzical gaze.

Becky looks calm and serene now, but I wonder if she knows what she's let herself in for. I have experience of La Contessa's wicked imagination and know the ordeal she'll devise for the night will be challenging.

There's a bustle of activity behind me as La Contessa, with a coterie of attendants, sweeps through the grand, marbled entrance hall of her palace. As always she looks stunning. She's wearing a low-cut, silk gown in bright scarlet with matching silk gloves. Over her shoulders is a huge hooded cloak, also in scarlet. Her hair is combed long and loose tonight. She wears a magnificent pair of knee length boots in soft Italian leather with silver buckles, white silk laces, and long stiletto heels capped with pure silver. They are a vivid reminder of my boot worship. She wears a simple *moretta* mask in black.

She glances across at Becky, and her red lips curl into a smile of satisfaction. One of the attendants puts a black cape over Becky's shoulders to keep her warm from the chill of the crisp autumn night, and then a *moretta* in white over her eyes.

"You look lovely my dear. You smell like an English rose, fresh and innocent, but ready to be picked," she adds ominously. "You know you must surrender completely and give in to the path I have laid out for you. I trust you are ready for your trial. Are you nervous girl?"

"Yes, madam, but I'm willing to submit to you."

"Good, that is how it should be. Now we must go."

La Contessa puts an arm through Becky's, and they descend the staircase together to the waiting gondola moored at the foot of the grand entrance to the palazzo. It's my task to transport them to La Contessa's secret destination. Her gondola of black lacquered wood with fittings of solid gold is a magnificent vessel as befitting her wealth and status. La Contessa takes up her position on silk cushions under the ornate gilded *felce*, the small gazebo structure in the centre of the gondola. It is fitted with curtains of red and gold damask, tied back so La Contessa can be admired. Night has descended, and the gondola is lit with lanterns hung from the *felce* which illuminate La Contessa. Becky sits opposite her, whilst I take up the oar at the stern of the boat. I push the flat bottomed vessel gracefully into the Grand Canal.

After we've been rowing for a few minutes, and whilst in full view of the crowds lining the canal, La Contessa gestures for Becky to come forward. She seductively parts her scarlet cloak to reveal her leather boots. No words are exchanged between them. Becky knows instinctively what she has to do. She gets onto her knees before La Contessa and licks her boots. She runs her tongue across the sole of the boot and then takes the silver tipped heel into her mouth and sucks. She kisses the toe of the boot, then runs her lips up its length cleaning the silver eyelets with delicate flicks of her tongue. I see everything whilst steering the gondola and feel a twinge of jealousy; how I wish it was me at La Contessa's feet.

This is the city of my birth, and I still marvel at its splendour. It's never more beautiful than at night time when the candlelight from the magnificent palaces lining the Grand Canal reflect on the water so ripples of light appear to dance on its surface. The Venetians are out in great numbers in their finery. I hear the bustle of street traders around Ponte Rialto and the mouth-watering smells of food vendors plying their trade. This is my city and I love it. I love that I serve La Contessa and am honoured she has chosen me to carry her along the canals of Venice on this special task. In my heart, I believe the girl will not let her down. The gondola glides under Ponte di Sospiri, and soon after La Contessa gives orders to turn the gondola into the network of narrow canals in the Sestiere di Santa Croce. It's nine o'clock at night and the bells from the hundreds of churches of Venice peal in unison across the city. I sense the bells are tolling for the sinister fate awaiting the girl.

The lanes in this part are less well-lit and the buildings close darkly in on the narrow canals. This is another aspect of Venice I love; its narrow canals and winding lanes, places where you get lost, places with dark secrets. We glide through just such an area, the atmosphere dark and oppressive, the buildings looming over us. La Contessa directs me to turn left pointing for me to navigate the gondola towards a small landing stage. I notice a sign by the side of the iron gates above the stone steps. 'Palazzo di Sadismo' it reads, and I know we have reached our destination.

I reach out my hand and help La Contessa up from her reclining position on the cushions of the gondola. She leads the way up a short flight of steps with Becky following her, and me at the rear. I see the tension in Becky's body as she climbs the steps to meet her fate. It's a sensation I know only too well from those occasions of being summoned into La Contessa's presence; a tingling fear of the unknown mixed with excitement and anticipation. I wonder if she sees the inscription on the building and understands its meaning.

There's an iron grille at the top of the steps and within it an unlocked gate which La Contessa pushes open, its hinges creaking ominously. We enter a vast stone room with a vaulted ceiling, formerly a wine cellar or store room, but now used for more sinister purposes. La Contessa is an exacting mistress and expects everything to be perfect; she's no doubt sent forward instructions as to how she wants the room set out, as it's already been prepared for her.

In the centre of the chamber are four huge, wrought-iron candlesticks arranged on the floor in a square, two either side of a wooden frame fixed to the floor. By its side is a large wooden chest. The glowing church candles cast a gloomy and atmospheric glow over the vaulted chamber; its flickering light casting shadows across the stone ceiling. The light does not penetrate the corners of the stone room but, as my eyes adjust to the dimness, I see the hazy outline of other pieces of metal furniture. It is equipment designed for torture, I'm sure, recovered from the chambers of Venice's mediaeval past. I'm reminded that Venice has not always been the liberated city state of this enlightened century. The outline of the equipment is indistinct in the gloom though it's obvious the room has been set out as a place of torture.

I see the girl is spellbound as an awed hush permeates the room. The only sound is the click of La Contessa's heels on the stone floor as they echo menacingly around the chamber. The vaulted ceiling is supported by a row of pillars and, on the pillar directly opposite the wooden frame, a fat bearded man is tied. It comes as no surprise to find the Syrian merchant there. La Contessa used me as intermediary with the procurator of the Sestiere di Cannaregio to arrange his arrest, and subsequent transfer into La

Contessa's hands. Her power and influence in the city is great and, with the offer of a small gift and the promise of an invitation to one of her famous balls to partake of their perverted pleasures, he was easily persuaded to do her bidding.

The Syrian has been skilfully tied. His whole body is covered in a criss-cross pattern of black ropes, an elaborate arrangement of knots pulled so tightly I can see the rope burn marks on his wrists and ankles from his struggling. He's gagged with a ball gag made of a wooden ball covered in leather and secured with leather straps. On La Contessa's arrival he struggles to shout abuse at her but only a muffled noise comes out. If this isn't the work of La Contessa, who I know is an expert at rope bondage, it's of a skilled practitioner of the art.

Becky looks fearful at the presence of the Syrian merchant.

"Yes, I have arranged for your tormentor to be here," announces La Contessa, "do you trust your new mistress, girl?"

Becky stands quietly and obediently, her arms behind her back, her breaths short and shallow. She relaxes her body, which bristled with tension on seeing her abuser, and gives an affirmative nod.

La Contessa turns to me and says, "Servant, you will not be required to join in the events of the night, but I do want you to observe. And I don't expect to see you getting aroused at any of the sights. You are here to witness only, do you understand?"

"Yes, mistress," I reply.

La Contessa's painted fingernails pull gently on the cords of Becky's bodice, loosening the laces until, with one tug, the bodice parts, and the girl's beautiful breasts bounce free. La Contessa runs a finger gently across the soft curve of her flesh and around her pert nipples, which stand erect. Becky expels a gasp of pleasure. She pulls the bodice off her shoulder, letting it drop to the floor. The tension of the moment is palpable; I witness the subtle interplay between the dominant mistress and her offering, her submissive girl. La Contessa squeezes her finger underneath the waist band of Becky's skirt, and runs it gently along her midriff, brushing the soft hairs over her sex before finding the hook holding up the skirt. As La Contessa releases it, the skirt slips over Becky's hips and drops to the floor. On La Contessa's instruction no doubt, the girl is not wearing any underwear. Becky quietly steps out of the skirt from around her ankles and kicks off her shoes. La Contessa brushes her pubic hairs with the back of her hand and Becky's body responds with a ripple of pleasure.

"She's perfect, isn't she?" La Contessa asks.

"Yes, mistress, she's lovely."

Indeed she's exceedingly lovely. Julia and the maids have carried out a remarkable transformation from when she was first brought to the palazzo. The welt marks on her backside, the sores on her ankles and wrists from the shackles, and the cuts and bruises on her face and breasts have healed. Her pale skin glows in the candlelight, and she is fragrant with the smell of the rose water from her bath.

La Contessa manoeuvres Becky into position. The girl quietly complies with every touch and unspoken command as my mistress raises each arm in turn and ties her wrists onto hooks on the wooden frame with black rope. She spreads her legs and pulls her ankles, which are also tied to the wooden frame. Becky is rendered helpless, and completely in La Contessa's control.

La Contessa goes back to the wooden chest and pulls something out. She walks back to the Syrian merchant, the clicking of the silver heels on the stone floor gaining in menace with each step. She dangles metal objects before the merchant's eyes. Although they're a type of clamp, I've never seen such a design before. She stares into the merchant's eyes, a powerful feminine presence. The gentle swelling of her breasts above the scarlet, silk gown and the aroma of her scent conspire to overwhelm him into submission. La Contessa's voice is low and full of menace.

"These are my newest toy. I know a trader of silks from China who, being aware of my special predilections, told me of these, and I asked him to bring them back for me. Ah, the Orient," she sighs wistfully, "now, there's a place where they know about torture. Perhaps one day I shall travel there and refine my art. But, in the meantime, I have these. They're called clover clamps and they are ingenious little things. When they close on your nipples they hurt but they tighten with every touch so that when a cord is attached to them, all I have to do is flick it," and she demonstrates by pinging the thin rope with her finger nail, "and it will increase the pain. So, what do you think?"

She's playing with him and relishing every moment of it. She's in her element, teasing with cruel words and suggestions. The look on the merchant's face is one of sheer terror, but all he can do is grunt into his gag. La Contessa squeezes one end of the metal clamp and the other opens. She stares into his eyes as she holds the metal object directly in front of him before releasing it onto his nipple. There's a grunt of agonised pain through the gag. She does the same to his other nipple. La Contessa deftly ties pieces of thin cord to the ends of the clamps and steps back to her new slave girl.

She faces the girl and wordlessly opens the clamp and holds it in front of her. From the shadows in the stone room, I watch Becky's reaction intently. She stares at the sinister metal object, transfixed. With her other hand, La Contessa plays with her nipple, stroking it, digging her nails in, squeezing,

97

and twisting. Finally, she reaches out to release the clamp on the girl's nipple. I notice Becky's body tense, and her lips expel a gasp of air at the moment the clamp tightens on her nipple. After the initial shock, her body melds into the pain. I watch, enthralled. I know these clamps to be severe instruments, capable of inflicting exquisite levels of pain yet the girl has taken them unquestioningly. I know La Contessa will be pleased with her. She repeats the process with a second clamp on Becky's other nipple.

She takes the cord in her hand and jerks it hard making the merchant squirm in pain before tying it to the clamps attached to Becky. La Contessa laughs. I too, from my place in the shadows, smile at this ingenious piece of invention. The cord is taut between the slave girl and her former tormentor. La Contessa pulls the cord, lightly at first, and the clamps close tightly on the two sets of nipples. She jerks the cord hard. The merchant lets out a muffled scream into his gag. Becky is silent, her eyes glazed into the effort of embracing the pain.

La Contessa turns to the merchant, "Do you see how the girl is stronger than you? She takes the pain without whimpering."

She takes out a whip with leather thongs from the chest and begins to strike the merchant's cock and balls with harsh strokes. His body pulls and twitches from within its rope restraints, which only causes the clamps to dig more tightly sending a ripple along the taut cord which tugs on the girl's nipples. La Contessa laughs wickedly at their predicament.

"Don't you see how you are two slaves joined in pain, and punishment. Each movement you make will cause the other to suffer."

This time she whips the merchant on the nipples, directly on the clamps, and once again he lets out muffled screams of pain. La Contessa turns to Becky and whips her right across her cunt. Her body jerks in reaction to the stroke. But Becky appreciates the game. She knows every movement of her body will send a ripple along the taut cord and inflict pain on the merchant. She knows her resilience is greater than his, and through her pain she can make the merchant suffer more. With each flail of the whip she jiggles her voluptuous breasts and sends a surge of pain through the cord. La Contessa finds this hilarious. She laughs wickedly as she continues the play, alternately whipping one of them or pulling on the tight cord to inflict the greatest torment. It's the Syrian merchant who suffers most.

"I could do this all evening," she smiles, "but there are many more torments I need to administer before the night is out. Servant, you can untie him now."

She pulls the nipple clamps off the girl first, and then off the merchant, but cannot resist the temptation of one final tweak with her fingernails. I do as La Contessa commands, unravelling the complex arrangement of knots. My youthful and muscular physique would always have been too much for the overweight Syrian, but in his current state he's in no position to offer any resistance. Once the ropes are released, I drag him across the cold, stone floor to the position La Contessa wants.

He is soon lying on the floor, his face directly below Becky's cunt, his wrists tied to the bottom of the wooden frame, and his ankles to a set of wooden spreader bars.

La Contessa stands over him. She's a magnificent sight. I'm almost envious of the merchant, staring up at her voluptuous curves, a stunning presence in her figure hugging silk gown. La Contessa shed her red cloak long ago, and now her slender arms and shoulders are bare. What a wonderful sight for the merchant, one he hardly deserves. Once again, I try to resist the swelling in my cock.

La Contessa rests one of her boots on the merchant's chest. The shiny black leather and the glittering silver buckles placed under his nose. She raises the silver tipped heel over his sore and tormented nipples, and presses hard forcing the full weight of her body onto the nipple. The Syrian grunts in anguish. She runs the sharp silver across his chest and across his stomach, leaving a long red scratch. Finally, she rests the silver tip on the end of the Syrian's cock, which lies flaccid and exposed on the stone floor. She presses hard, releases for a moment, and then presses even harder. The merchant's body jerks, his body twisting with the pain and pulling on his restraints. I see spittle oozing from the side of the ball gag as he tries to scream. La Contessa is not finished yet though. Becky stares into his eyes to witness his torment and humiliation.

La Contessa gives me an instruction to undo the ball gag. As the leather covered ball is finally pulled from the merchant's aching jaws, he starts to spew out angry words in his native tongue. La Contessa turns on him, her eyes fiery with anger.

"Shut up. I don't want to hear a peep from you. What you have experienced so far is a mere fraction of what I am capable of. You will suffer in silence. Let it be known La Contessa will extract her retribution. There is one final act of humiliation I need to witness before I banish you from my presence."

She gently strokes Becky's fanny and gazes into her eyes.

"Slave girl, this will be your final act of revenge on your abuser. I think you understand what I need you to do."

Becky nods. At first it's a trickle of golden water as she releases her piss over him. It's soon a torrent of hot water gushing from her cunt over his black beard, seeping into his mouth. It's as if Becky has been holding it in her bladder, knowing the use to which her golden waters will be put. When the girl's piss has been emptied over her tormentor's head, La Contessa finally looks satisfied.

"Now servant, I want you to take this one away. I have finished with him. There is a cell at the far end of the dungeon. You can lock him in there until he can be returned to the custody of the procurator." Turning to the girl, La Contessa proclaims, "Now, it is about you and your initiation, girl, to find out if you are fit to become my slave girl. I've extracted retribution on your behalf from your abuser. I'm pleased with how you have acquitted yourself but you must face more ordeals before I can fully admit you into my world."

"Yes Madam, I understand. I'm ready to submit to you."

14: Il Padrino

I lead the merchant, his wrists tied together, away to the cell. When I return I find La Contessa putting a blindfold of white silk over Becky's mask.

"Can you see girl?"

"No, madam," she replies, breathless and nervous.

La Contessa gestures for me to stand quietly in the shadows as she retreats into the darkness at the end of the chamber. The gloomy candle-lit room descends into silence. I can't tell if Becky is aware of my presence, but I see the tension building up in her as she waits; waits for an unknown trial. We both stand there in hushed silence, Becky on the wooden frame, me in the shadows. The sense of anticipation is great for me, and I'm only an observer, it must be agonising for poor Becky in the darkness, waiting.

I hear the click of heels on stone again. La Contessa returns. Four black shadowy figures follow her, dressed in tight fitting black suits displaying the contours of their well-formed male physiques. They're wearing elbow length black silk gloves. Each of them wears an animal mask: a lion, a zebra, a chimpanzee, and a jackal. Once again I'm in awe of La Contessa's inimitable sense of theatre. She circles Becky speechlessly but her presence fills the room, and the sound of metal on stone echoes around the chamber, building up tension. The black masked figures are silent, and Becky's not even aware of their presence.

One of the mysterious masked figures, the jackal, gently runs his silk glove across Becky's shoulder and down her arm. I watch intently, and her reaction is astonishing. You might have thought she'd received a stroke from a cane, not the merest brush of a silk glove on her bare flesh. The pent up anticipation has left Becky in a state of wild agitation. She must have been expecting the worst, so the merest touch triggers an extreme reaction in her.

La Contessa smiles; pleased at the response her mind games have elicited from Becky. Silk gloves run over Becky's naked body; on her back, across her arse, up her thighs, across her stomach and over her swelling breasts. It's a sensual overload for her as she sighs and moans contentedly. She must know pain will follow, but for now she wallows in the sensuous touch, knowing the severe torment is at least delayed. A hand runs over her pubic hair, it runs silken fingers across her mound. Becky moans. Silken fingers are inserted into her sopping cunt, first one, then two and then a third, and are gently manipulated inside her. Becky gasps. Gentle hands run over her bum cheeks and a finger inserted into her tight arse-hole. Becky groans.

It's at this moment, with hands all over her, and fingers inside her, La Contessa chooses to expose the shadowy figures toying with her. She pulls the end of the white silk of the blindfold letting it float gently to the floor. Becky looks around her bemused, disorientated. A lion's mask is in front of her, a jackal is on its knees at her crotch pushing fingers into her. At her shoulder with hands on her heaving breasts is a chimpanzee. Whilst behind her she can glimpse the zebra with silk-gloved finger in her arse and hand running across her backside. La Contessa steps back admiring her creation, and smiles. The tempo of the movements increases; a second finger is rammed up her arse. Her senses are in overload; her body tenses as it builds up for orgasm, but the hands keep her hanging on the edge.

Before Becky gets the release she desperately yearns for, fingers are withdrawn from her orifices, and hands removed from her tingling flesh. It's like they've sensed some elemental danger, their instincts warning them of an impending threat. Meanwhile, their victim, Becky, has to be left, strung out to face this new menace.

I'm concentrating so much on the shadowy animal-masked figures and Becky's reactions I too fail to notice another figure emerge from the darkness; black cloaked, leather-gloved, with wide, black-rimmed hat, and white mask in an upturned, sinister grin. A leather gauntlet closes over Becky's nose and mouth. She's shocked. She's not been aware of the shadowy figure sneaking up behind her. She can see La Contessa before her, no longer smiling, but severe, and realises there is another presence in the room. She struggles for breath as the hand closes tightly around her, gasping for every morsel of air she can suck from between the gloved fingers. Becky is on the point of expiring when the hand is taken away, and she draws in a deep draught of fresh air.

"La Contessa, it's always a pleasure to receive you as a guest in my dungeon. I admire your bizarre and exotic imagination."

La Contessa smiles appreciatively at the compliment.

"Il Padrino, you know how much I enjoy your dungeon, and sharing in our pleasure of the sadistic arts."

"This is obviously the girl you spoke of who needs initiating. Do you think she is ready and willing?"

La Contessa nods, "Yes, I believe so. I think she is naturally submissive, and can be trained to be my slave girl. Becky, you have come this far on a journey. You will not let me down now at the final stage of your initiation?"

"No, madam. No, I promise I won't."

"You see, Il Padrino, her answer comes from the heart. I think she is ready."

The dark figure emerges from behind Becky.

"Girl, this is a partner of mine in the arts of domination, Il Padrino, or The Master, as I believe you might say in your native tongue," La Contessa announces before turning to the mysterious cloaked figure. "She is lovely isn't she? Marvel at her pale skin like delicate porcelain. She's a little antique doll ready for us to play with."

"Yes, so fresh, innocent and fragrant."

"You should have seen her earlier when she was dressed as an English country rose. But, she's not so innocent; she's been rescued by me from abuse and savagery by a crude and ignorant male who does not understand our skill and art."

La Contessa and her companion work together to untie Becky from the wooden frame. They steady her as she adjusts her body weight to a standing position. La Contessa's attention to detail and artistry at creating her scenes is evident as Becky stands before them; La Contessa in her sleek scarlet gown and Il Padrino, in black, save for the unsettling white mask with its lurid grin.

Il Padrino pulls Becky's arms behind her back and binds her wrists with long strands of silky, black rope, twisting it two or three times around her slender wrists, before knotting tightly. He twists the remaining portions of rope up her arms. Becky remains passive and compliant, allowing him to bind her without a murmur of complaint.

As Il Padrino kneels to work on her legs, La Contessa threads a piece of rope under Becky's breasts and draws it under her bound arms and across her back where it's knotted. Mistress and master work silently and skilfully with concentration, each knowing what the other is doing, both working together to put the girl into a complete and tight restraint. La Contessa draws two long pieces of rope from behind Becky's back and pulls them between her breasts and then over her shoulders, pulling hard on the rope as she does. Meanwhile, Il Padrino, kneeling at her feet, ties her ankles together and winds the remaining lengths of rope round her legs up to the soft milky flesh of her thighs, supporting the weight of her body as he goes.

I gaze into Becky's eyes from the shadows and see a whole range of emotions in them; fear, anticipation, acceptance, and excitement are there as she relinquishes control to the two dominant figures. They finish their work. The girl is bound from toe to neck in a criss-cross pattern of black ropes. La Contessa's work on her breasts is especially artistic as she creates an intricate pattern of ropes around them, pulled tight so her bosoms bulge, bright red with the tension of the ropes. Her breasts will be sensitive to touch now.

La Contessa reassures her, "Are you alright girl? Are your ready to go further?"

"Mm, yes mistress," Becky replies dreamily.

Il Padrino ties more ropes onto the knots at her back and threads them into the hooks at the top of the wooden frame. As they both let go, Il Padrino pulls the rope supporting Becky, and her body is pulled into the air, her back suspended by the rope tied around her arms.

She whimpers, "Oh, please, no."

La Contessa reassures her, stroking Becky's face as she hangs at an angle, her feet barely touching the ground.

"Trust, you must learn complete trust in your mistress. Let your body go girl, and your whole being will drift into the experience."

Becky nods quietly. She releases the tension in her body, lets the weight of her body go, and allows the ropes to support her. Il Padrino pulls the rope pulley he has created within the frame, and Becky's body lifts into the air so she's suspended, supported only by the ropes. Her body rocks and sways gently as Il Padrino steps back to admire his work; a naked body given up to bondage, entwined in black ropes with a rosy-skinned arse exposed.

"How do you feel, girl?" La Contessa asks, gently stroking her face.

Becky can barely utter a word so absorbed is she in the world of bondage into which she's been placed.

Eventually she whispers, "Good. It feels so good to surrender myself to you mistress."

"Yes girl, I know. I understand. It's where you belong, isn't it? You know you must suffer for me if you desire to offer yourself completely."

"Yes mistress, I know."

Il Padrino moves alongside La Contessa.

"Is she ready to be punished now?"

"Yes, she is ready," replies La Contessa.

Il Padrino holds a flogger with long leather flails, its handle a golden lion, the symbol of Venice.

"Kiss the implement of your punishment, girl," he says, as he puts the gilded handle to Becky's lips.

The girl, still swaying on the wooden frame, reaches her head forward to gently touch the golden lion with her lips. Il Padrino runs the leather thongs of the flogger across her masked eyes, and down her cheeks. Without the need for any order Becky instinctively knows what she must do as she touches the strands of leather with her lips.

"How many strokes should we give her?" he asks, "I think a round hundred would be good."

Becky's eyes widen to the size of saucers as she hears this proposal, and she lets out the merest whimper of protest.

La Contessa laughs, "You think you can't take a hundred; one day you will for your mistress, girl. Cruel though I am, even I regard that excessive for an initiation. Tell me girl, how many strokes do you want?"

Becky goes silent for a moment as she contemplates her answer. I can guess what's going through her mind. It's a loaded question; choose too many and she'll inflict a punishment on herself she may not endure, but choose too few and the mistress and master may not be satisfied it's enough and, perhaps, insist on the full hundred. I've acquired an instinct into how La Contessa's mind works. Becky announces her decision in a clear voice.

"I will accept whatever mistress decides I must receive."

La Contessa laughs again, "Excellent girl, you learn quickly. Then I declare that you should take fifty strokes, forty with the flogger and the last ten with a cane. Don't expect any restraint with the force of the strokes, and there will be no mercy given even if you plead. La Contessa has chosen and you must submit to her judgement."

"Yes, mistress."

Il Padrino runs the leather gently across the cheeks of her backside, which stick out invitingly from her suspended position. The first stroke hits with a loud slap which echoes around the dungeon. The master is true to La Contessa's warning; it's a powerful stroke. The girl lets out a grunt of pain and her body rocks in the rope swing with the force of the hit. Will she be able to endure fifty of these? The next four strokes come down, building up in power with each successive stroke.

"How many is that, girl?" Contessa asks.

"Five," Becky whispers, through gritted teeth.

Il Padrino gives her a short rest and gently runs his hand across Becky's arse, following the red marks he has made on her flesh with his finger. Becky moans with pleasure from the little respite she's given. He delivers the next five strokes in quick succession. The punishment is heavy. The girl's suffering; her breathing is heavy, and she expels little grunts with each stroke but does not flinch or plead for mercy. La Contessa takes up the flogger now. It's her turn to administer the girl's punishment. The ornate golden lion handle nestles comfortably in her experienced hands. She fits the role of the severe dominatrix perfectly. The thongs of the flogger dangle menacingly against her silver-buckled boots.

She puts her mouth to Becky's ears and whispers, "Your new mistress will deliver the next ten strokes."

Becky mumbles an acknowledgement. If she thinks she'll get any respite from La Contessa's hand then she'll be sorely mistaken. She's skilled in this art, and can deliver a stroke as hard as any man. The flogger strikes Becky's backside hard three times. I see the soft flesh of her arse wobble with the force of the stroke, and her bound body sway back and forth. I get aroused from watching the spectacle. The sound of the flogger on flesh, her moans and whimpers, and the sight of her beautiful rounded bottom in the air receiving punishment is giving me a hard-on under my breeches. La Contessa glances across at me knowingly. She misses nothing, and I expect there'll be a reckoning to face for this lapse when I return to the palace.

I see Becky is going deep into herself, and her own ordeal of pain and pleasure. The force of the strokes, along with the rocking of the suspension, takes her into a trance-like state as she prepares to receive each new stroke. The punishment continues; the stinging whack of the flogger interspersed with the occasional gentle stroke of La Contessa's or Il Padrino's palm on her throbbing arse. By the fortieth stroke with the flogger, her backside is glowing red and imprinted with darker lines where the implement has created an impression on her skin.

There is a swishing sound now as Il Padrino stands in front of Becky wielding the cane. He offers the cane up to Becky's lips and she kisses its tip. Il Padrino and La Contessa administer their five strokes, each one hard and relentless. Becky grunts at each stroke, but accepts them bravely. The cane leaves a criss-cross pattern of red lines across her arse. The fifty strokes have been delivered, and the girl has survived them.

A heavy silence fills the air. The audience of the men in their animal masks look on in admiration and respect at Becky's powers of endurance.

"Well girl, have you anything to say?" La Contessa asks angrily.

Becky has drifted into her own world and looks confused at being brought back to earth.

"Well!"

A light of realisation switches on in her brain.

"Thank you, mistress. Thank you, master."

"Yes, I should think so too. For forgetting to thank us without being reminded you will be given another five strokes of the cane."

La Contessa sets upon poor Becky with another five heavy strokes. Becky, thinking she had endured the punishment, lets out a squeal with the shock of these extra, unanticipated, strokes. I believe these are the hardest for her to take.

"Thank you mistress," she gasps after the final hit; she won't make that mistake again.

"Good, I am satisfied with what you have taken girl; and you Il Padrino?"

"Yes, Contessa, she has taken her punishment well."

La Contessa signals for me and the chimpanzee masked man to untie Becky's arms and legs and help her down. As the two of us untie the carefully constructed arrangement of knots, we support Becky's body as we drag her from the suspension frame. The other men return with another piece of torture equipment; a rack, which they place in the centre of the vaulted room in the middle of the cast iron candlesticks. Surely Becky won't have to endure more?

Becky has drifted off into her own sub-space. The movement has still not returned to her legs, and she needs to be supported. Il Padrino stands before her. He brushes her bush of fair, pubic hair with his hand and runs fingers across her cunt lips.

"Oh," moans Becky.

"Look, she's wet Contessa. She's sopping. I think she's been aroused by her punishment."

"Is this true girl, are you turned on?" La Contessa demands.

Il Padrino pushes a second finger into her pussy and moves them both around inside her in a circling motion. Juices ooze from her cleft.

"Oh, I think I must be," Becky replies guiltily.

"So, you get pleasure from receiving pain?"

"Mm, yes, I must do madam."

"Hm, it's lucky for you you're not a male slave because I don't tolerate them getting sexual pleasure," she tells Becky, casting a meaningful glance across at me, "but in a girl slave, well, if you get aroused, then I can't possibly let you go without allowing you satisfaction."

La Contessa has a wicked gleam in her eyes.

"Assist her onto the rack," she orders.

We help Becky, now unbound except for the ropes still wrapped tightly around her tits, climb onto the rack. She lies and waits for the next stage in her initiation. Leather cuffs are attached to her wrists and ankles. Her arms are stretched out on the rack whilst her legs are pulled over the wood frame with chains attached to the cuffs, so they are splayed into the air, her wet cunt exposed to view.

The girl is tied to the rack. The four animal masked figures stand beside her, two at either side, with La Contessa and Il Padrino at either end. La Contessa leans over her, her cleavage thrust into her face as she first caresses and then gently nips the girl's swollen, and reddened breasts. She produces the wicked metal clamps again and closes them around the girl's nipples. Becky simpers with pain. La Contessa goes to each of the masked figures in turn and unbuttons their black suits at the crotch and pulls out four erect penises. The scene is bizarre; Becky spread out on the rack, the dark masked figures of lion, chimpanzee, jackal, and zebra, now with erections protruding from their shadowy black bodies, illuminated by the candlelight.

La Contessa gestures. The zebra takes up a position between Becky's legs. The zebra's nostrils lean over her crotch, and a sliver of tongue slips out of the mask as the figure goes down on Becky, licking her pussy. He thrusts his tongue inside her licking her sex with fast little flicks,

"Oh, yes, please, yes," moans Becky.

The girl is being driven wild, her body bucking and twisting on the rack. La Contessa has other plans for her. She pushes Becky's head to one side and firmly holds it in place against the wooden rack. Facing Becky is another hard cock, this one belonging to the jackal. What happens next is inevitable as the rampant, hard flesh is threaded between her soft lips. She sucks on the cock enthusiastically. The animal figures take it in turns to pleasure her and take their pleasure from Becky's body. She is stretched out and powerless, having surrendered herself into La Contessa's perverted game. They insert black-gloved fingers into Becky's cunt and tug on her clitoris with their lips, skilfully keeping her on the edge of ecstasy.

Becky's body thrashes wildly on the rack as the four masked beasts inflict their animal yearnings on their helpless victim. She groans with pleasure even when her mouth is full of cock. She sucks hard and enthusiastically, revelling in the combination of ecstasy and humiliation. The lion pulls his cock from her mouth, its tip glistening with a mixture of his pre-cum and Becky's spittle. La Contessa looks on in amusement at the scene she's created.

"Oh, please make me come, please," Becky begs.

"But your ordeal isn't finished yet girl."

La Contessa stands by the side of the rack, a leather strap-on, thicker and wider than any of the men's cocks, sticks out from the scarlet silk of her gown.

"Take it girl," she urges, as the object is pushed into her mouth.

Becky can barely breathe as the strap-on fills her mouth and is pushed deeper. But she still finds the energy to suck on it determinedly, knowing she must submit to this act of humiliation for her mistress.

Il Padrino has been watching attentively on the side-lines at the actions of his four apprentices, but the moment has come for him to enter the play. He unbuttons his breeches and pulls out is cock, aroused from watching the torment to which Becky has been subjected. La Contessa withdraws the strap-on from Becky's mouth so she can turn her head and watch as Il Padrino mounts the rack. His black-rimmed hat and sinister white mask loom over her as he rams his rampant cock into her sopping cunt.

She groans desperately as she receives her master's cock, and arches her body to take it deeper inside her. Il Padrino starts pounding into her. He's already aroused and Becky has been on the edge of coming for ages. It takes only a few minutes of hard thrusts before Becky lets out a scream of ecstasy as the waves of orgasm wash over her. Il Padrino reaches his orgasm soon after her, shooting his cum into her eager cunt. La Contessa releases the clamps from Becky's nipples and she lets out a final gasp of pain and pleasure as blood rushes back to sensitive nerve endings. Becky looks spent and exhausted, but there's also a euphoric glaze in her eyes. She's left in silence for a few minutes to recover.

"So, now do you understand what it means to serve La Contessa?"

"Yes, mistress."

"You have completed your initiation into my service and I am pleased with how you have acquitted yourself. Are you ready to give yourself up to me?"

"Yes, mistress."

"Now you have offered yourself into submission, know my name, La Contessa di Nemesia, the ruler of fate and distributor of justice and retribution. I wanted a slave girl, and my command of fate brought me to you. It was I who rescued from captivity and ignorant brutality for a purpose. You were destined to serve me, my slave girl. Do you believe that?"

"Yes, I do, mistress."

15: Allessandro Fernasse

It's the middle of the night before La Contessa's gondola weaves its way through the torch-lit canals back to her palace. I'm exhausted, and I've only been an observer. Becky, the slave girl, must be aching all over after the attention she's received. Yet, I know from my own experience of La Contessa's domination that this extreme fatigue produces a euphoric feeling. She did well, and La Contessa is delighted with her performance, commenting on how good it is to have a girl slave who truly understands the meaning of submission. I can't wait to relate the exploits to Julia, as I usually describe the scenes La Contessa creates to her in great detail… and there's plenty to tell her about the night!

But it's a few days later when we get a chance to meet up. She comes to my room to inform me La Contessa will need me in her private sitting room later in the day. I'm ready to tell Julia about the torture of the Syrian merchant, and Il Padrino, but she's in an uncharacteristically strange mood. At the mere mention of Becky, she fires back an acerbic response.

"Yes, it's all I've heard from my mistress over the last couple of days. How perfectly submissive Becky is, how well she took her punishment, how lovely she is. I'm sick of hearing about her. And did you enjoy fucking her, Roberto?"

I pause to let the last comment sink in. Surely it must be a misunderstanding?

"But Julia, I only assisted La Contessa. I never joined in any of the play, and I never fucked Becky."

"That's not what La Contessa says. She's described in graphic detail how she let you take Becky whilst she was tied onto the rack, and the pleasure you got from it."

I'm confused now, and I can only think La Contessa is playing a game with Julia.

"I promise you, Julia. I didn't fuck the girl. Your mistress is messing with you. You've said yourself how manipulative she can be."

This remark causes her to reflect and temper her rage.

"Well, I don't know what to think," she mumbles.

"I didn't, but besides," I add, "if mistress ordered me to fuck her, I would have. You know that, Julia, it's what I'm here for. I'd have carried out her instructions to the letter. You explained this from the start."

"Yes, yes. I know, you're right Roberto. It's just that… since she's come to the palazzo all I hear about from La Contessa is her slave girl. She's so beautiful, she's so lovely… she's never called me these things in all my years of service. Do you think Becky's so pretty?"

I grasp Julia by the shoulders. I choose my words carefully.

"Yes, she may be Julia. I'd be lying if I said she wasn't attractive. But that's not the point. She's not as beautiful as you Julia and, believe me, I feel nothing for her. She's La Contessa's slave girl. Nothing more. And do you really expect La Contessa to praise you all the time. After all, Julia, you're her maid."

As soon as the words spill out, I know I've said the wrong thing. I see tears welling up in her eyes.

"I'm only a maid am I? You think that's all I am to her?"

Shit. I don't know how to respond. The honest answer, harsh as it may be, is yes. Whatever rapport they may have built up over the years, Julia's role will always be to serve La Contessa. What else can I say? I've seen the intimacy of the relationship she has with her mistress at first hand, but it's still one of mistress and servant… what more can Julia expect from it? What strikes me about this exchange is how jealous Julia is of Becky. Her presence seems to have exposed Julia's doubts… about her relationship with La Contessa, about me, and about her place in the household. I take her into my arms and console her.

"I can't guess why La Contessa wants to give the impression there might be something between me and Becky, but I promise you it's not true. I love you, Julia. Becky means nothing to me. I want you and wish you had time to stay with me now so we can make love."

I pull out a handkerchief and gently wipe the tears from Julia's eyes.

"Yes, I know you're right. I know my mistress plays mind games with people, but she's never done it with me before, not in such a hurtful way. It's upset me that she would treat me that way."

"Well, I know it's no consolation, but she treats everybody else the same," I say trying to make light of it. "Perhaps you shouldn't take it too much to heart, Julia."

"Anyway, I've got to be going. We'll meet up as soon as I can. And don't forget, madam's sitting room at 4pm. And naked, naturally!"

I have a few domestic chores to complete and the rest of the day goes quickly until I have to make my rendezvous with La Contessa. I knock on the door, and she invites me to enter.

I take in the scene before me. Given my recent conversation, the first thing to strike me is the presence of both Julia and Becky, the latter standing with her arms behind her back next to the chair where La Contessa sits.

She's dressed plainly and modestly in a simple knee length cotton chemise buttoned all the way down the front with a leather belt around her waist. Well, I say modestly. You can see the outline of her nipples protruding from the material. She looks every bit the obedient submissive. She does, it must be said, look lovely. With each week serving at the palazzo she looks more and more ravishing. Her hair, a natural and striking blonde, so distinctive to see in Venice, is thick and rich. She has put on a bit of weight since being rescued from the hands of the Syrian merchant, but it's no bad thing as it's enhanced the voluptuousness of her curves. Julia, looking pensive, is serving La Contessa and her guest coffee from a silver pot engraved with naked nymphs.

La Contessa gestures for me to take up a position at the opposite side of her from Becky.

She's dressed formally, in her wig, a rich embroidered gown, and as much make-up as I've seen her wear. She's dressed to impress, and when I see her guest, I understand why. His gown is grand, its hood lined with ermine. But it's the cane, capped with a silver winged lion, which provides the vital clue for me. Nobody would openly carry such an iconic symbol if they were not part of Venice's ruling elite. The ensuing conversation confirms my suspicions.

"May I speak frankly to you, Contessa?"

"Yes, these are my servants. I trust them not to allow any report of our conversation to go beyond this room. They know the severity of the punishment if they do."

"This is a delicate matter, Contessa. As you know the trade through Venice of late has declined, and the Doge and Council of Ten are, let me be frank, in straightened circumstances."

"Allessandro Fernasse, I'm perfectly aware the interest on my loans to the Doge is due for payment in a matter of days. No doubt you've been sent here to crawl on behalf of the Council of Ten to renegotiate the interest payments. And, knowing the perverse lecher you are, I don't doubt you'd also like to avail yourself of the entertainments I offer. You will see I have acquired a new slave and slave girl since you were last here. The girl is especially delicious don't you think... and very willing."

The corpulent representative of the Council of Ten squirms uncomfortably in his seat, sweat dripping from his forehead. I'm intrigued by this exchange. It explains a lot. Venice is a place where money rules. This must be the hold La Contessa has over the ruling elite of the city, making her untouchable in whatever she does.

"Yes, Contessa, on behalf of the Council I'm here to ask for a rescheduling of our debts."

La Contessa raises an eyebrow, "Ask? You mean beg, surely."

"Well, to discuss what mutually beneficial arrangements we might come to," splutters Fernasse.

"Ha! You mean beg. And yes, I will make you beg! Get out of the chair onto your knees and crawl towards me."

"But, Contessa, is it your intention to humiliate me?"

"Yes, indeed it is. Do as I say and get on your knees or there will be no negotiation. I will simply insist on the repayment of my loan. You know the consequences."

Offered no alternative, Fernasse heaves his body out of the chair and gets down on his knees. He crawls the short distance to where La Contessa sits, her hand outstretched ready for him. He takes it in his hand and kisses it. There is a pause.

"Yes?" prompts La Contessa.

"Contessa, I beg you on behalf of the Doge and the Council of Ten to extend the period of your loan to the city for six months. We are expecting a fleet of merchant ships to arrive from the Far East by then with goods we can trade. I beg you to grant us this favour."

"That's better. And tell the Doge, next time he wants to reschedule his debts, he must come himself, and I will make *him* get down on his knees and crawl. I am minded to agree to an extension but I do have further conditions; a few trifles to satisfy my whims."

"Yes, Contessa; let me know what they are. I'm confident we will be able to accommodate them," said Fernasse, still on his knees.

"The first stipulation is that, on the final day of *Carnevale*, I will expect my barge to lead the procession along the Grand Canal, and for the ball to be held in my palazzo."

"Why yes, Contessa, we would be honoured for you to host the *Carnevale's* masked ball," he says, relieved at the relative modesty of the request.

"Then there is the question of the travelling theatre troupe, the Gelossi. Their plays are lewd, and they have a rather good line in political satire too. They amuse me, and it would give me great pleasure to see their work performed in Venice. It appears they are having difficulties obtaining a licence. I trust this is a matter you can smooth over for them."

"Well, possibly Contessa." Fernasse replies with obvious discomfort. "Though the Doge may object to this stipulation as this theatre troupe are known for their bitter attacks on him and the Council of Ten. Their satire ferments discontent in the city."

La Contessa's eyes flash with anger. She leans down and lifts Fernasse's

113

chin up with her finger so she can stare, unflinching, into his eyes. He tries to avert her gaze, but she grips his chin in her hand.

"So, Allessandro, are you not entrusted to negotiate on the Doge's behalf?"

"Yes, madam."

"Is it not clear to you what will happen if you do not accede? It amuses me that this theatre troupe ridicules the rulers of Venice, and I will have my way. I am sure you understand."

"Yes, Contessa."

"So, I can take it the matter is settled then."

"Yes, Contessa."

"There is one last tiny thing," she says releasing his face from her grip.

Fernasse's body slumps; what next, he must be thinking.

"I am holding a piece of theatre, a puppet show, and it would please me if the Council of Ten attend. I am sure they will find it amusing."

"Yes, we would be honoured to attend such an entertainment."

"In particular, I want the Archbishop to attend."

"The Archbishop? Can I ask the nature of this puppet show? Will it be of sexually perverse nature?"

La Contessa waves her hand, "I have a reputation to maintain Allessandro."

"You know only too well how many of us enjoy Contessa's soirees, but the Archbishop is very pious... and may be offended at the activities on display."

"Yes indeed, pious... and a hypocrite. Does the church not benefit from the generosity of my loans?"

"Yes, madam, of course it does."

"Then it should be an easy matter for you to convince the Archbishop it is in his, and the city's, interests to indulge my whims, should it not?"

"Yes Contessa, I'm sure I can persuade him to attend."

"Excellent. So, our business is concluded then. I will have my procurator draw up the agreement to extend the period of interest on my loan."

She holds her hand out, and the deal is sealed with a kiss.

Allessandro Fernasse is effusive in his thanks, "Thank you, Contessa. We will forever be indebted to you for your fair mindedness and generosity to us."

I'm fascinated by this exchange. It explains the power La Contessa holds over the rulers of Venice. I can't help but smile inwardly at the manner in which my mistress controlled the meeting. She played with him, humiliated him, and manipulated him. Her conditions are designed to show off her prestige and influence whilst insulting the Doge and the ruling elite. I gaze on in admiration at the domineering qualities displayed by my mistress in the exchange.

"So, now our business is concluded, I expect you want to avail yourself of some sexual pleasure whilst you are here."

"Yes, madam, you know how much enjoyment I derive from your entertainments."

Now he has concluded the business part of the meeting, his eyes twinkle with expectation. I imagine that, despite the humiliations he has been subjected to, he willingly volunteered for the task, knowing he might be invited to take part in some sexual debauchery.

La Contessa invites Fernasse to take his seat with a flourish of her hand, so he gets up from his knees and nestles his vast backside into the plush velvet of the chair. His heart is racing in anticipation at what my mistress might be planning for him.

"Let me introduce you to my new slave girl," says La Contessa, taking her hand and leading her to stand in front of Fernasse. "I rescued her from the clutches of a cruel master and brought her to my palazzo. She's beautiful, is she not?"

"Yes, Contessa, she's lovely," he gasps.

I can tell he wants her. I see the lust in his eyes. I hear his little brain whirring as he sits there imagining the filthy things he could do with her.

"And she's submissive and willing... she'll do anything I ask, won't you girl?"

"Yes, mistress. I serve you in everything, mistress," Becky responds.

"Yes, of course you do, my dear. My guest looks rather hot and bothered. Perhaps you should relieve him of his clothes."

Becky steps forward in front of the chair. Fernasse breathes heavily at the presence of the girl as she stands close to him, drawing in her exotic scent as she divests him of his fur-lined gown. Becky passes it to Julia, who takes the robe nervously, folds it up, and places it carefully on a table. She's waiting anxiously to see how this play will unfold, no doubt wondering what my role in it will be.

Becky gets down onto her knees. She loosens the cords around his flabby waistline. Fernasse instinctively lifts his arse up enough to allow her to pull his breeches and knickerbockers down until they are wrapped around his ankles. His already erect penis jumps into the air as soon as it's released. Becky looks at it with curiosity, as if she's never seen a man's cock before, and runs her fingers along its taut flesh. Fernasse groans with pleasure at her touch.

Becky gets to her feet again. She stands directly in front of him, her crotch at eye level. Sensuously she unbuckles the leather belt, pulls it from her waist, and allows it to drop to the floor. Her chemise hangs loosely around her, the candlelight silhouetting her curves through the thin cotton. She unbuttons the shirt as Fernasse looks on open-mouthed. Button by button the material parts slightly to offer a glimpse of the soft lines of her cleavage. He fidgets in his seat, mesmerised by her seductive performance. More buttons are unfastened until the bush of her pubic hair is exposed, and when all the buttons are undone Becky pulls the chemise apart to reveal her sexy body. Fernasse's cock involuntarily twitches with need. He reaches his hands out to grasp her fleshy breasts in his fingers.

Before he can touch, his hands are met with the sharp snap of a flogger. He recoils in pain. He looks to one side to see La Contessa with the implement of punishment in her hands.

"No Allessandro, you are not allowed to touch."

"Please Contessa, let me take her breasts in my hands," he pleads.

"No, you can only watch. Sit there and gaze upon what you can never have. She is my special girl, my very own. Do you think I will see her fouled by your grubby, fat mitts?"

"Oh, but please Madam, let me touch her, let me have her," his voice desperate with desire.

"Since it's clear you are unable to control your lusts, I will have to take further measures to ensure my girl is not corrupted by your filthy fingers… and filthier mind."

She gestures to bring her coils of rope from a nearby table. Quickly, with an effortless speed and before Fernasse can protest or resist, La Contessa pulls his arms behind the chair and ties his wrists together. She takes his cock in her hand, wraps her fist around it and squeezes so hard I can see it brings a tear to Fernasse's eyes.

"There," she smiles, "all you can do now is enjoy the show. You can't even masturbate. You have to sit there whilst my slave girl taunts you with her sexuality."

"You are so cruel, madam," he gasps.

But secretly he's enjoying every minute of this display. There's no doubt he loves being tormented by the girl, and her mistress.

Becky removes the shirt from her shoulders. She runs her fingers along the pale flesh, squeezing the pair of orbs together. She holds the nipples of one breast between two fingers and squeezes, expelling a squeak from her lips… whether from self-inflicted pain or pleasure it's hard to say. Finally, she lets the chemise slide from her body until she stands in front of Fernasse, entirely naked.

He emits a groan of appreciation.

"She's lovely isn't she?"

"Yes madam, she is."

"And she's mine... all mine, aren't you girl?"

"Yes mistress, I submit myself to you and your desires... completely," she replies softly.

"You will never have her," La Contessa taunts, "never be allowed to touch her. You can only sit there and admire her feminine beauty. You will be tormented by what you can never have. And when you get back to your palazzo, you think you'll go straight to your chambers and wank yourself off."

"Yes, madam."

"I even permit my male slaves to play with her," she says, gesturing with a nod for me to approach Becky.

Oh, oh, I don't like the sound of this. Julia watches proceedings from across the room, silently seeing how the scene develops. I cast a glance over at her, see her eyes widen, and a face like thunder. She does not look pleased. But I have to obey of course. I've pledged my service to La Contessa. I have to carry on regardless of Julia's feelings.

La Contessa leans forward and whispers in my ear, "Touch her, run your hands over her. Kiss her. Bury your face in her crotch. Arouse her. Make her wet for me. You have your mistress's permission."

La Contessa has set me a task I can relish. Is there any way I can hold back to show my loyalty to Julia? Not really, my mistress's directions are clear. And I understand the game she's playing. I appreciate the nature of the torment she wants to inflict on Fernasse. She wants me to do the things he would love to do to the girl, but which La Contessa will never allow. I enter into the role with enthusiasm, much to Julia's disgust.

I start by standing behind her, pressing my bare flesh against hers and nuzzling her neck and shoulders as I wrap my arms around her chest and fondle her breasts. Fernasse, his wrists still tied behind the chair, is in paroxysms of frustration. I plant kisses on her sweetly scented flesh, I take her nipples in my lips, and roll my tongue around them. I have her turn around and bend over so her beautiful arse is sticking up in the air, then get down on my knees to lick her. He squirms in his chair, his cock still standing erect, desperate for release. I kiss her thighs and bury my face in her bush. I seek out her bud with my tongue.

La Contessa taunts him, "You see, even my slave can touch her, even my slave has access to her most intimate orifices. Yet you are denied."

"Please madam, release me. Let me touch her. Please, I beg you."

"No. No, she is not for you. She is my special slave girl. She is beyond your reach, and always will be. What a shame, my loveliest toy, and you will never get the chance to play with her."

Oh yes, I warm to my task. Becky is aroused. She pants and gasps at every touch of fingers and lips as I explore her body whilst the desperate and frustrated Fernasse can only look on. I make her wet. I eagerly lick the juices oozing from her cunt. Becky participates in the game. Her moans and groans as I pleasure her are genuine, but exaggerated. Like me, she's putting on a performance for La Contessa to make sure her guest is tormented. And my cock is hard. I hope my mistress is not displeased with me, but it's impossible not to get aroused. Meanwhile, Julia is looking uncomfortable at the sight of her lover giving sexual pleasure to her mistress's slave girl. And La Contessa doesn't hesitate in teasing her.

I overhear what La Contessa says to Julia, "See how my slave is enjoying his task. See how hard his cock is. I should punish him, but I am inclined to indulge him on this occasion as he is carrying out my wishes, and doing such a good job. See how frustrated Fernasse is! It's most amusing. I'm enjoying this. And they make such a good couple don't you think Julia?"

"What do you mean?" she replies tersely.

"Why Roberto and Becky? They are so suited to one another. Roberto understands the girl's body; he knows how to pleasure her. It's a joy to watch. See how deeply his tongue penetrates her; she will come soon."

"It's a game, isn't it? You're playing with them."

"Playing with them? Well, yes, I suppose so... and yet." She pauses to call out a command, "Stop now Roberto. I don't want her to come... not just yet."

"Yes, mistress," I reply.

I see her leave Julia's side and glide towards the table. She lifts her sumptuous gown and appears to adjust something before she turns back.

La Contessa surveys the scene. Becky is panting, on the verge of climax, whilst Fernasse is tied to the chair, his cock sticking up; and me, my cock also erect.

"Hm, two hard cocks. Do you want her Allessandro? Do you want your prick up her cunt? Or should I let my slave fuck her?"

"Oh yes. Please, madam. Release me and let me take her," he exclaims, his hopes raised by La Contessa's suggestion.

"You know I will not allow that. Besides, I need a final guarantee for the fulfilment of your promises. Julia, bring me what I need," she calls to her maid.

Julia retires to the rear of the room and returns carrying a metal object which she passes to her mistress.

Fernasse's eyes widen in shock when he realises what it is... a chastity device.

La Contessa nestles the fearsome object in her hand. It's a cage for a cock, constructed in strips of cold, hard iron, with a padlock hanging from it.

"Yes, it is an intriguing little toy, is it not?" she taunts, "Made to my design by my blacksmith."

"But madam, surely you don't mean to lock me in that?" Fernasse splutters.

"Indeed, I do. You see, now you will have a personal stake in ensuring my demands are complied with. I don't know what you are fussing about; the *Carnevale* is only in a few weeks, after I return from my hunting lodge. I will release you at the ball when you have delivered on your promises. Besides, it will be a good discipline for you to refrain from sexual release for a while… and it will amuse me to think of your cock in the cage."

The threat of being put into chastity has dented Fernasse's arousal, and his penis has subsided into a soft, flabby object. La Contessa takes it into her hands. She puts the metal cage around it and closes its two halves, manipulating his cock to fit tightly into the device so the hard iron presses against the flesh. She threads the padlock through a metal loop, clicks it shut and then removes the key from the lock. She dangles the key from its chain in front of him.

"Madam, please…" pleads Fernasse, but to no avail.

"I will take care of the key, though should I mislay it I'm sure my blacksmith will find a way to break open the iron with his hammer and anvil. The design is ingenious. Should you start to get an erection then the metal will dig into your cock."

He looks broken and humiliated, sat there tied to the chair with a fearsome cage around his cock.

"Now, where was I?" says La Contessa. "Oh yes, my slave girl. Should I let my slave take her? What do you think Julia?"

Julia squirms in discomfort at her predicament. She daren't say what she really thinks.

"Whatever you wish, madam," she mutters.

No, I don't think so… not today, anyway. I have other plans for you girl. Do you want to come?"

"Yes mistress; if you'll allow me. If it will give you pleasure, mistress," gasps Becky.

"Oh yes, it certainly shall. Get down on all fours girl."

Becky climbs onto the floor.

"Now, make yourself ready. Lift your arse up, girl," she orders.

La Contessa stands in front of Becky, who glances up at her in adoration. Shuffling, her mistress adjusts her gown. She lifts up the folds of the billowing velvet and reveals a huge strap-on cock, secured to her waist with a leather strap. Becky gasps. It's made of smooth wood and is long and broad.

"This is going inside you, girl. Do you want it?"

"Yes, mistress. Yes please, mistress."

"Allessandro, I'll let you watch whilst I take this girl with my strap-on."

"Thank you, Contessa," he mutters, resigned to his fate, but still desiring to see the performance.

La Contessa kneels behind Becky. She runs laced-gloved fingers along her crack and Becky, already aroused from my attentions, gasps. Her mistress parts her cunt lips with her fingers and inserts the fearsome strap-on into her. She's wet, and it slides in.

"Take it for mistress. Take it all in for mistress," she says as she pushes it deeper inside her.

"Oh, yes," groans Becky "Thank you mistress. Thank you. Take me mistress! Fuck me mistress!"

La Contessa pommels hard into her now. Becky struggles to keep steady on her hands and knees, whilst still lifting her crotch up to receive the strokes, which get stronger and deeper. She squeaks and squeals in ecstasy as mistress pushes into her. It's the first time I've seen the slave girl lose control, I mean really lose control. I've seen her punished before but her reactions are usually controlled. She submits willingly, almost dispassionately. Her response to her mistress taking her is wild and unrestrained. Her mane of fair hair shakes as her whole body works with La Contessa's thrusting motions to impale herself on the strap-on.

I have to say the whole scene is a massive turn-on. My erection is throbbing, though I daren't do anything about it for fear of offending my mistress, who hasn't given me permission to come. Fernasse, even though he can't get release, gets his own perverted pleasure from watching La Contessa fuck the girl. I peer across at Julia. It's hard to read the expression on her face. What emotions are there; shock, desire, jealousy... arousal? Her hand strays under her dress. She's masturbating. The vision of seeing her mistress with a strap-on fucking the girl is turning her on.

The whole scene reaches a climax. Becky screams out in ecstasy as she climaxes; unable to stay up on all fours her head and torso collapse onto the floor. Her mistress collapses onto her, the wooden strap-on still being thrust into her as waves of orgasm come over Becky again and again. Quietly, I hear Julia murmur gasps of pleasure as she discreetly comes to her own climax. I ought to say I'm frustrated at not getting release myself, but I'm too intrigued by the scene in front of me to be bothered.

La Contessa withdraws the strap-on from Becky's cunt. It's glistening with her juices. I'm expecting to be ordered to suck them off, but I'm not. She calmly adjusts the vast hoops and smooths her dress. There's the slightest curl on her lips. She's had fun, I can tell.

Becky is sprawled on the floor panting, "Thank you, mistress," she gasps. "Thank you so much. It's been a privilege to have you inside me, mistress."

"Well, of course it is girl. Get up and tidy yourself up. Allessandro, I will see you on the night of my puppet show... and your chastity will help you focus on the conditions of our agreement."

"Yes, Contessa. And thank you, madam. I've had an incredible afternoon, madam. You are a truly remarkable woman."

At this compliment La Contessa calmly marches out of the chamber leaving her servants and guest panting with exhaustion from their exertions. I untie Fernasse. He pulls his breeches on over the chastity device and the bulge at his crotch is obvious.

I run over the events of the afternoon in my head. Julia is already in a strange mood; I wonder how she feels about my fondling of the girl, and what am I to make of her masturbating to the scene La Contessa created?

16: The Archbishop

My worst fears about Julia's reactions to the afternoon's activities, in particular La Contessa's command for me to fondle her slave girl, are not realised. Indeed, the whole episode turned us both on. Luckily she has no use for either of us for the rest of the evening so we retire in secret to Julia's room. It proves an ideal opportunity to connect after the frostiness of our exchanges earlier in the day. Watching La Contessa take Becky with the strap-on has made us both horny. When we get to Julia's room we strip off and go at one another with an enthusiasm fuelled by our arousal by the whole scene.

I nestle Julia in my arms after a session of frantic fucking. I take the opportunity of this post-coital, mellow mood to raise the subject of the slave girl.

"You know, I don't have feelings for Becky, don't you? I do what La Contessa requires, and I do it with commitment because it's what she expects. But that doesn't mean I want to be with her. We both serve La Contessa, and we do whatever she commands. But when I lie with you it's because I want you, not because a mistress has ordered me to," I explain.

"Yes, I know, Roberto. I know it in my heart, I just find it hard thinking of you getting pleasure from her. But you're right, I know the rules of madam's household better than anyone, and I've no right to be angry at you for fulfilling your position."

I'm relieved to hear she understands this.

"You know Contessa is playing with you. Whatever she's said, this afternoon was the first time I've laid hands on the girl. I promise you."

"No, I believe you Roberto. I think my mistress is toying with me, and I don't know why. It's cruel."

"So, you're not jealous of Becky, because there's no need to be?" I ask.

"Yes I am, but not because of what you did with her. Did you see the pleasure Contessa got out of fucking her with the strap-on? I... no it's ok, I don't want to say."

"No, go on Julia, I want to hear, what?"

"I wish, I really wish it was me she took with that thing. I'd love her to fuck me like that... to give me that attention. Oh... I'm sorry I don't mean anything against you, my love... it's just..."

How intriguing. I expect I should be shocked, jealous, insulted maybe, but I'm not. I noticed the expression on Julia's face as she watched La Contessa pleasure Becky. She was aroused by it, so much so she could not resist the temptation to masturbate in front of us. I don't know if La Contessa saw her though she misses nothing. I doubt if Becky did, so focused was she on her own sexual needs.

"Are you shocked, Roberto?"

"Not really. With the stuff I've done on the streets of Venice or in the service of La Contessa, I'm not easily shocked! It's fine. She's a remarkable woman; it doesn't surprise me you'd get turned on by her. Honestly, it doesn't bother me... I don't take it personally."

"Thank you, my love. I want you, Roberto."

And it's true, it doesn't particularly bother me. I'm blissfully happy, both with my service to La Contessa, but also laying here with Julia in my arms. I plant a kiss on her lips, and she smiles, touching my cheek tenderly with her hand. We lie there for several minutes in companionable and affectionate silence. It's Julia who speaks next.

"What do you make of Becky?" she enquires.

"To be honest, I've hardly exchanged a word with her. You have to remember, whenever I've been with her La Contessa has always been there too, so we've never spoken to one another. She's pretty inscrutable. It's hard to know what's going through her head, other than her need to be submissive. How about you? You must have talked with her more, after all you looked after her when she first arrived."

"I agree with you; I find it hard to make her out. She was quiet but grateful for everything we were doing for her, and so pleased to be taken in by La Contessa. Although she's deferential to me and the staff, she has an air of calmness and determination about her too."

"I know what you mean. I think she's truly submissive. When she's with mistress, it's as if she enters another world. She glazes over, submitting to whatever La Contessa throws at her. I think she's naturally submissive... in a way I'm not. I mean, I get a thrill out of serving La Contessa I admit, but I'm not naturally submissive like Becky is. Look, if I was, I'd hardly be lying here with you, would I?"

"No, the risks we take bother me. I'm convinced Lucio is spying on us. He definitely suspects something, but whether he's found enough to go to La Contessa with, I don't know. And I don't want to lose my position here, Roberto. I can't. Contessa's world is the only one I've known since I was a child."

"Well, we have to be careful. Perhaps we can pull it off, have each other and still serve our mistress."

The next day, La Contessa summons us to her bureau for a meeting about the puppet show she's planning; the one she ordered the Archbishop to attend as a condition of renegotiating the terms of her loans. Julia is there, along with Becky and me and, to my surprise, old Lucio, plus other members of her household who will act as 'puppeteers'.

La Contessa introduces us to Vincenzo, who she describes as the 'artistic director' for her soiree. I know him well as he's only a few years older than me and I've chatted to him on many occasions whilst polishing mistress's statues. He's responsible for the presentation of La Contessa's table, makes many of her masks and has a flair for the visual, so he's a natural choice. Vincenzo is enthusiastic and excitable. He's beaming from ear to ear, delighted at having been chosen for the role, and keen to make a good impression on his employer.

"Contessa, I promise you the performance will be beautifully choreographed, and extremely funny and lewd, as I know Contessa desires. I assure you, your guests will go away amazed… and disgusted!"

"Excellent. Now, I have briefed Vincenzo of the story outline. What I have in mind is an erotic homage to the *Commedia d'arte*. My slave, Roberto, and my slave girl, Becky, will play the role of the lovers, the *inamorati*, and they will be puppets attached to strings controlled by the puppeteers."

I glance across at Julia. She's agitated about the direction the performance is going. I can't help but agree that her mistress is playing with her.

Lucio, you shall play the part of Scaramouche, the *vecchi*, the girl's cruel guardian.

"Madam, far be it from me to criticise but I believe I'm unsuited for a role in the theatre, and I fear it is unbecoming of the head of the household to act in such an unseemly way."

Oh dear! I know Lucio is a senior member of La Contessa's household but nobody, and I mean nobody, however important, can be critical of any decision she makes, especially in front of other staff.

La Contessa fixes him with her coldest, most penetrating stare. I've been in receipt of it on numerous occasions, and it's withering. You know you've done something to *really* anger her when you get one of those, and you just want to hide!

"Lucio," she spits, "you are playing the role of the *vecchi*; the matter is not one for further discussion. Vincenzo has made a splendid mask for you."

"It's very good," interjects Vincenzo, amused at getting one over his master, "It has a crooked nose and warts."

"And besides," La Contessa adds dismissively with a wave of her hand, "you are perfect for the role of a cruel and morally upright disciplinarian, are you not? And my maid is having a part, aren't you, Julia?"

"Am I madam?" she says, surprised, before realising not to cross her mistress. "Oh, yes, madam."

"Yes, Julia will play the part of Pantalone, the *zanni*."

"The clown, madam! Can I not be one of the *amorosi*, alongside Roberto," she probes.

"Certainly not. Besides, you will make an excellent clown Julia. You will bring chaos and mayhem to proceedings. It's the funny role, my maid. You will get all the laughs!"

I know I should sympathise with Julia's plight, but I must confess I find the idea of Lucio and Julia playing the *vecchi* and *zanni* amusing and, unfortunately, I can't suppress a smile forming on my lips at the image of it. Mistress pounces on it.

"Yes, you see, even Roberto finds it amusing, don't you my slave?"

"Yes mistress, your casting is perfect."

Well, what else can I say! Lucio is fuming, and Julia stares daggers at me. Meanwhile, Becky stands quietly with her hands behind her back, but even her inscrutability can't hide the amused sparkle in her eyes. The girl is relishing the role of *inamorati*.

"Well it's all settled then. The rest is in the hands of Vincenzo who will direct you. There must be plenty of lewdness and debauchery in it. After all, I want my puppet show to impress the Archbishop."

La Contessa dismisses us, and we disperse to carry out the various household tasks without any opportunity to gossip about the impending performance.

I'm expecting lots of rehearsals, but there are few. Vincenzo briefs me on the outline of the story, explaining that the detailed instructions will be given to the puppeteers, who manipulate mine and Becky's actions. We do have a practise in La Contessa's theatre so we can both get the hang of how the puppeteers will control our movements.

The day of the puppet show soon arrives. There's a buzz throughout the palazzo. I'm excited about it, though Julia is more anxious. The performance is preceded by a reception; the 'actors' are permitted to attend so we can be introduced to the guests before we disappear behind the scenes to prepare.

There are familiar faces here including guests from La Contessa's card game.

Mademoiselle La Tour is friendly and gracious towards me.

"How is your arse, *mon ami*. Is it still throbbing?"

"Yes, mademoiselle, you certainly entered into the spirit of the game."

"And I am so looking forward to this afternoon's entertainment."

And Lady Rudston is here with what I presume is her husband; a round, balding, ruddy-faced man. The pair of them make a good couple. She introduces me to Lord Rudston as one of La Contessa's favoured servants, which amuses me, and I engage in conversation with him.

"I understand you have an interest in Venetian church architecture, your lordship?"

"Hm, yes, that is so," he splutters.

"There are many hidden gems in Venice. Have you been to San Canciano in the Cannaregio. The frescoes in that church are magnificent, amongst the best in the whole of Venice."

"Yes, indeed, they are," he mutters.

I know there are no frescoes in San Canciano!

"And the Cannaregio is such an interesting district, don't you think? It's one of the liveliest parts of Venice. You should take Lady Rudston there, I'm sure she'll enjoy it."

"Oh yes, you simply must take me there, my dear," says Lady Rudston.

Lord Rudston looks flustered, and his face goes even redder. La Contessa, who overhears this exchange, looks across at me with a knowing smile. I'm enjoying this party.

"Well the boy has come up in the world, hasn't he, Lucretia?"

"We said he'd go far, didn't we?"

I recognise the voices and swivel round in surprise. It's Lucretia and Viola, as I know them, though who these two transvestites really are, in their extravagant satin gowns and beneath the layers of make-up and clouds of perfume, remains a mystery. They must be rich and important to have been invited to La Contessa's soiree.

"It's good to see you again, albeit in different circumstances," I reply. "As you can see, I'm now in the service of La Contessa di Nemesia."

"Yes, and I'm sure you give her good service."

"Yes, we can vouch for the quality of service the boy gives, can't we Viola?"

"Yes, and I expect La Contessa is a demanding mistress," Lucretia adds.

"Yes, but the rewards of service to her are considerable," I reply before La Contessa catches my eye and beckons me over.

She's curious, "How do you know them?" She asks, "Were they clients of yours?"

"Yes, mistress, I was with them the night Julia found me in the Cannaregio."

"Well, I suppose I should not be surprised. Have you any idea who they are?" she asks.

"None at all, mistress."

She leans forward and whispers in my ear, "Keep this quiet, slave, but they work for me on special schemes. I keep their secret and allow them to indulge in their fantasies when they attend my palazzo."

This is how I end up standing next to La Contessa when Allessandro Fernasse arrives with the Archbishop of Venice. Fernasse, relishing another afternoon of La Contessa's particular brand of entertainment, is bumbling but enthusiastic as he introduces the primate of Venice to La Contessa. The Archbishop, tall and angular with a pointed nose and haughty expression, looks distinctly uncomfortable. His discomfort is accentuated by La Contessa's dress for the occasion. She has foregone her formal entire in favour of an embroidered indigo gown in silk, decorated with pearls, and tight corsetry which enhances her voluptuous figure. The cut of the bosom in particular is designed to emphasise La Contessa's breasts and leaves nothing to the imagination. The lascivious Fernasse slavers over mistress's tits whilst the Archbishop, his face etched with the strain of trying to ignore them, cannot resist gazing at the magnificent orbs of white flesh decorated with false moles, one on each breast, in the shapes of a crescent moon and a sun.

My mistress greets him generously, "Archbishop, I'm delighted to meet you. I do not believe I've had the pleasure. I do so hope you enjoy the entertainment I've laid on for you…"

"The correct form of address is 'Your Grace'."

La Contessa ignores his interjection, "…It will be an amusing and instructive piece of puppet theatre for you."

"I hope this will not be the kind of debauchery for which you are renowned. The morality of the city is disturbingly low, and the church would look to its most important citizens to uphold public morals."

La Contessa's elegant eyebrows raise, a forced smile spreads across her lips, and the *assassina* mole rises like an accusation.

"Indeed, Archbishop, I couldn't agree with you more about public morals. At least I can provide the assurance that audience and performers are of consenting age, which I believe is more than you can claim… *your grace.*"

The last two words are spat out with bitter irony. The Archbishop's angular features screw up into a face like thunder.

"I've no idea what you mean, Contessa," he replies angrily, but with extreme discomfort.

But the statement is out there for everybody clustered around the two figures to hear. So, the rumours spreading through the city are true then; the Archbishop uses his influence to procure young girls… and boys from local orphanages for his priests, and for himself. I don't believe La Contessa would have been so explicit if it were not so.

La Contessa continues, "The moral turpitude of *La Serenissima,* and the hypocrisy of its mother church, runs deeper than anyone can imagine, does it not? Come Archbishop, you are obliged to sit through my puppet show, as you know."

She turns away to speak to somebody else, leaving the Archbishop red faced and speechless. So, was it always La Contessa's intention to use her afternoon's entertainment to expose the dark seam of corruption running through the church in Venice?

17: The Puppet Show

Soon after La Contessa's encounter with the Archbishop, I'm summoned to the changing rooms behind the theatre to prepare for the performance. I put on the mask of the *inamorati* with its lovelorn expression, puckered lips, and bright red, painted cheeks. I strip off so the puppeteers can attach the complex arrangement of wires that will manipulate my movements. One wire is tightened around the base of my cock. I'm aware it's important for the story to maintain an erection, though I don't have any fears on that score. The wires allow for the limited manoeuvrability necessary to perform the role effectively though to the spectator it will appear as if my movements are being controlled by the puppeteers. I slip on a turquoise silk robe which also has wires attached to it.

Becky, having foregone the chance to join the reception for La Contessa's guests, is in position when I appear. She looks stunning. Her mask also depicts the expression of wistful lover but with a beatific smile, rosy cheeks, and exaggerated eyebrows and eyelashes painted on it. She's in a yellow silk kimono, hers decorated with lotus flowers, which hugs the curves of her breasts and hips seductively. Looking at her, there's no chance of me not getting a hard-on when I need it!

"Are you ready, Becky?" I whisper.

"Mm, yes Roberto. It feels good to be trussed up in wires," she purrs.

I see the far-away glaze in her eyes through the holes in her mask. Yes, she's already in the zone and ready to perform. She too is secured by a maze of wires. They are manipulated by the crew of puppeteers hidden in the rafters out of sight from the audience, holding control bars with wires attached to them. It looks complicated, but I trust them not to get the wires in a tangle and mess-up the show. Having been given this opportunity to demonstrate his skills, Vincenzo will want to impress his mistress.

From the other side of the curtain I hear La Contessa's voice, muffled by the barrier of thick velvet.

"Welcome to my theatre. I have laid on a special puppet show for you. This is a tale of two lovers, and the vicissitudes they encounter in pursuit of their love in the face of a cruel guardian."

There's polite applause as the curtain rises.

I've a moment to take in my surroundings. The theatre is magnificent. Its façade is decorated in rich reds and gilded wood in baroque style. Fixed to the top corners are two solid-gold masks modelled on Greek theatre depicting comedy and tragedy. Smaller golden masks with various dramatic expressions: joy, sorrow, anger, quizzical and confused, cover the columns of the theatre. I take a peek at the audience arraigned in rows on luxurious, velvet-covered seats. At the centre of the front row in pride of place are La Contessa with an expectant and mischievous smile, her breasts bursting out of her dazzling, indigo gown, and her principal guest, the Archbishop, looking thoroughly miserable and uncomfortable.

I feel the tug of the wires pulling me around. It's a strange sensation, one of being led rather than a complete loss of control. Whilst the wires direct my movement, I have to relax my whole body to allow them to do their work, creating the impression of being manipulated by the puppeteers to the audience. My actions are jerky and quirky as you'd expect with a real puppet.

I find myself facing Becky. My arm is raised and lifts up to touch her cheek. My hands are pushed down to brush against her shiny silk robe. The touch of the sleek silk is exquisite. As my hands are directed to run over her breasts, I finger the hardness of her nipples pulling against the tight material. I hear Becky gasp. Our roles are meant to be played out in silence, but it's a barely audible expression of her arousal the audience can't hear. And I'm turned on too. My cock instantly swells until it presses against the sensuous silk. Surely the audience must be able to see my cock tugging at the robe as it becomes erect?

The puppeteers raise Becky's hands to make them run against my robe. I hadn't noticed how erotic the silk was to touch when I put it on as I was focused on getting ready. But now, with the girl's fingers running across the silken material, the sensation is erotically mind-blowing, especially as her fingers stretch towards my groin and touch my hard cock through the silk. I sense the anticipation in the audience as they watch the display of fondling, and the erotic tension building up between us.

The puppeteers execute a swift manoeuvre so the next thing I'm aware of is my arms being wrapped around Becky, and hers around mine as the wires thrust us together. I feel the pulse of her heart racing with sexual excitement as her breasts press against my chest. Then the wires gradually pull our faces together until our masks touch. Through the holes in the masks our lips brush against each other's. Her tongue reaches out into my mouth, and we kiss through the masks. On her lips I taste the sweet *malvasia* wine she drank before the show to calm her nerves. I wonder what

Julia is thinking. I haven't seen her costume yet, but I know she'll be waiting in the wings watching every moment.

The masks part, and our bodies are twisted around by the stiff cords to face the audience. I watch as the ingenious arrangement of wires allows Becky's robe to slip from her body into a crumpled heap on the floor. There is a collective gasp from the audience as La Contessa's slave girl is revealed, standing naked, waves of blonde hair tumbling over her bare shoulders with only the mask of the *inamorati* to cover her face.

There is a tug on the wires securing my robe and I realise the costume is cleverly designed to split into parts so the puppet wires don't impede the silk's stately progress as it slides over my flesh. There's one anxious moment when the robe snags on my erect cock, and the puppeteer has to jerk a wire so it can slip onto the stage. There's another gasp as my hard-on is shown to the audience. Through the eye-holes in the mask, I see Lady Rudston swooning into a faint. Now, I'm not one to boast… well no, that's not true! I know my cock is a great asset, and when it's fully erect, as now, standing out proud, thick, and hard, I know it's a magnificent tool. Far from being embarrassed at having my cock exposed to a crowd, I revel in it, and get turned on by it.

So the scene is set. The two *inamorati* stand naked on the stage. The audience is expectant, waiting to see if their love for each other will be consummated. The wires push Becky onto the floor so she's on all fours. One jerks her bottom up into the air, her cunt lips hanging there waiting to be penetrated. The puppeteers tug at the wires to pull me onto my knees and pull my arms forward under Becky so I can grasp her tits. My penis hovers tantalisingly over her crack. The puppeteers use the wire secured to my erection to adjust the angle of my cock. It's a manoeuvre requiring deft skill and precision. If the slant of my cock is only a fraction out, then my penis will miss its target. Vincenzo has trained his performers well. My cock probes the entrance to Becky's vagina, and at just the right moment I've the freedom of movement to push my member inside her. Her cunt tightens around my cock, and then I thrust into her harder, taking her doggy style before the assembled guests. I warm to my task. The movement of the wires guides me, but I can add my own force to it. What the audience see, to their delight, is one puppet fucking another.

As I push myself into Becky, my thoughts turn to Julia. Although she claims she's not jealous of the girl, it must be hard for her to see her lover fucking another woman in such a public spectacle.

Whilst I pump my cock into Becky trying to hold back from coming inside her, I hear a splutter of laughter. I should explain that the set is designed in the style of an Italianate garden, and at the back of the stage is

131

a row of bushes. As I glance out the corner of one eye, I realise the audience is amused at the antics of Julia. She's dressed as the *zanni,* a clown in a harlequin suit of blue, red, and yellow triangles, white stockings, a tall white hat, and a white mask with a shocked expression. I must say she looks great in the part and, I have to hand it to her, whatever her misgivings, she's entering into it with gusto. She's hiding behind a bush spying on us, and then every so often, indeed in time with my fucking motions, her head pops out from above the bush. Then she dances behind another bush and sticks her head out from its side each time my cock thrusts into Becky's cunt. We have to pretend we haven't seen her and carry on with our lovemaking, regardless of the *zanni's* antics at the rear of the stage.

La Contessa loves it. She's laughing, as are her guests, except for the Archbishop who sits there po-faced. At one point Julia does cartwheels to the front of the stage jumps up, points at us feigning shock, and then runs out to stage left. We continue our fucking throughout her performance. Becky rolls her backside into me and, as my cock pushes into her, she emits quiet grunts. We aren't meant to climax, but it's obvious we are both turned on. It's an effort for me to hold back from ejaculating, and poor Becky is straining her whole body to prevent herself from collapsing into orgasm.

Relief comes with appearance of Lucio dressed as the *vecchi,* the girl's cruel guardian. He's dressed in tunic, stockings, tri-cornered cap, and mask, all in black. Vincenzo has gone to town with the mask. It's black with a bulbous nose and decorated with lines and huge warts. He's made to look incredibly ugly. I should add that he's carrying a fearsome whip with leather thongs in his hand. Julia, who has gone to her master to report what she's seen in the garden, is bouncing up and down excitably pointing at us whilst we carry on screwing.

Lucio marches forward, grabs my ponytail, pulls me out of Becky and throws me to the ground. Becky's juices on my cock glisten in the glow of the candles used to light the stage. The *vecchi* aims a few carefully aimed strokes with the whip across my backside. They sting. Old Lucio, who out of the staff, has never particularly taken to me, uses his mistress's puppet show as an opportunity to vent his hostility with a severe whipping. My arse is smarting, and I can feel the welts swelling up out of my flesh.

But I'm lucky compared with Becky. I guess it's in keeping with his role in the play as the girl's master and guardian, and probably with instruction from La Contessa. My pain threshold is high, and after these months of service under the La Contessa it has increased, but her slave girl's levels of endurance are outstanding. Lucio sets about her with the whip and I can see he's not exercising any restraint. The tongues of the whip slash against her backside with heavy slaps. There is a collective gasp from the guests at the

132

punishment Becky takes though all I can see from La Contessa is a sadistic glint in her eye. Do I also detect a certain pride in what her girl can take? Becky receives it with resigned silence, never allowing a moan or whimper pass her lips.

The performance moves on apace. A cage is lowered onto the stage and puppeteers use the wires to drag Becky into it. In the meantime Julia surreptitiously helps Becky change her mask from the *inamorati* to one showing a sad face. I'm banished by the master and retreat out of sight behind the bushes for now, where a stage hand passes me a mask exactly the same as Becky's. So, now the lovers are parted. I've been expelled never to see my love again whilst the girl is imprisoned by the *vecchi* as punishment for succumbing to her lusts. Lucio attaches wooden, sprung clamps to her nipples, pulls them tight and ties them to the bars of the cage, so any time Becky moves, the cords tug at them.

The *vecchi* leaves the stage to a cacophony of boos and hisses from the crowd. Julia, sorry for having betrayed the two lovers and the punishments she has unleashed, changes her role to one of intermediary between them. She prances around the stage in a comic pose, looking around her to make sure the master is not watching, and passes paper and pen to Becky to write a message. She takes the slip of paper and, putting her hand over her eyes, does an exaggerated search in the bushes for me. At this point the wires lift my head over the bushes. She excitedly does cart wheels across the stage, leaps up and hands me my lover's message. I'm impressed. I never realised Julia was such a good gymnast! Maybe a career on the stage beckons her.

The play follows the *zanni's* antics in acting as intermediary between the two lovers until Lucio returns. He comes to get his ward out of the cage but as he leans over to close its iron gate, the *zanni* pushes him inside and locks the door. Now the two lovers are re-united the sad masks are replaced with the masks of the *inamorati* again. The irony of Julia playing the role of bringing Becky and myself together as lovers is not lost on me, and neither will Julia have missed it.

We now come to the climax of the performance where the love of the re-united *inamorati* is consummated. The puppeteer's wires manipulate Becky onto the stage, lowering her onto her back in full view of the audience, and lifting her legs up so everybody gets a view of her puffy labia, red and swollen from its earlier attention. It's a brazen show of Becky's sex, flaunted for all to see. The Archbishop looks especially disgusted at the performance. The wires lead me towards Becky. I stand over her, framing her cunt between my legs. Then I'm lowered down and my cock manoeuvred into position. I get the chance to fuck Becky again, but this time I know we have permission to come, providing a fitting climax to the entertainment.

133

Becky lies there helpless, held into place by the puppeteers' wires, her legs splayed, her cunt wet and inviting. The puppeteers tug my cock closer and closer towards Becky's waiting sex. She's gasping with anticipation, urging the puppeteers controlling me to feed my member into her. My arse is directly facing the audience. I try to visualise their admiring looks at my muscular backside. The tip of my penis brushes against the folds of Becky's cunt lips as the puppeteer's manipulate the wires to line it up to the exact spot. When my cock's in the right position, they release the tension on the wires holding me back and I pound into the girl with one long push. Becky squeals in delight. She wants it. She needs release by now as urgently as I do.

When I'm finally nestled deep inside her and start fucking her there's a ripple of applause and calls of encouragement from the audience. They've come to see a performance, and they want to see La Contessa's slave girl fucked. Lucio, still in the cage as the *vecchi,* is forced to watch whilst Julia, still in character as the *zanni,* jumps up and down in her harlequin suit clapping as I fuck Becky senseless. Unable to control herself any longer, Becky squeals with pleasure as she takes the frenetic strokes of my cock. The wires are slackened so she can move in time with my thrusts, and to allow her hips to buck and twist as, reaching her climax, she screams out in ecstasy. I respond, and empty my seed into her. At this moment the curtain starts to lower and the audience break into applause.

We listen to the clapping and whooping of appreciation from behind the curtain as we disentangle ourselves. The wires are fully slackened now so we can stand up. Julia is alongside us, as is Lucio, now out of the cage, and we are joined by Vincenzo and his puppeteers. When the curtain rises, we take a bow. I see La Contessa on her feet applauding, a beaming smile across her face as we receive a standing ovation. Her guests shout out, "Bravo, Bravo Contessa, Bravo." Even the Archbishop, not wanting to be the odd one out, stands up, however reluctant his applause.

La Contessa climbs up the steps at the side of the stage to join us. She kisses Becky on the lips and gives Julia, Vincenzo, myself and even old Lucio a hug. Believe me it's a rare tribute to receive from a strict mistress and dominatrix. I try not to look too pleased with myself, as I don't want to be guilty of vanity, but inside I'm glowing with pride for myself and the other performers. It's rewarding to please your mistress.

"What a splendid entertainment," calls La Contessa above the applause. "I'd like to thank Vincenzo for his artistic direction, the puppeteers, and my servants, Becky, Julia, Lucio, and Roberto for entering into my little production with such enthusiasm, and bringing it to a fitting climax. There will be champagne and patisseries served in the reception room after the performance."

When La Contessa returns to the floor she's greeted by her guests congratulating her on such a fun, erotic and delightfully disgusting piece of theatre!

The performers are buzzing with the thrill of delivering a performance. We are chatting excitedly amongst ourselves. Even Becky, who is often detached, is smiling, and gratefully accepting compliments from the staff. Even Julia is excited, and seemingly unphased by my role. I tell her she was brilliant in the part of the *zanni* and praise the exuberance of her performance.

18: The Hunting Lodge

As soon as the excitement over La Contessa's puppet show has died down, the household is plunged into another whirlwind of activity. It's Julia who catches me in the kitchens one morning and excitedly explains.

"La Contessa's announced that we are going to her hunting lodge in Piedmont. She goes every winter and returns to Venice in time for the *Carnevale*. This year she's sprung it on us suddenly. We're to make preparations and leave in a few days-time!"

"Is this to her country estate?"

"One of them," Julia explains. "She's a villa overlooking Lake Garda I've been to and various other estates. The hunting lodge is one of the highlights of the year. You'll love it there, and she's sure to come up with interesting ways to entertain herself! And, with a bit of luck," she looks around to make sure nobody else can hear, "we should get time to ourselves."

She winks at me. Julia has lovely hazel eyes, which complement her olive skin and chestnut hair perfectly, especially when she's animated. They light up the room. I'm pleased to see her in such a bright mood. The puppet show has lifted her spirits. There's been no adverse reaction to my fucking of Becky in full view of La Contessa's guests. Indeed, it seems mistress was full of praise for the enthusiasm with which Julia entered into the role. This has restored her confidence, making her less paranoid about how La Contessa is treating her.

Julia explains we are to be part of an advance vanguard to prepare the lodge, with La Contessa and her slave girl joining us when everything is ready. Mademoiselle La Tour, who has become a confidante of La Contessa since the card game, has also been invited as her guest. This means we'll get a few days together on our own, and no Lucio snooping around after us.

Julia's role is to prepare La Contessa's wardrobe for the trip. It can't take too long I think, naively. Several days later I stand at the landing stage surrounded by a mountain of trunks and hat boxes, watching the fleet of gondolas hired to carry them. I realise this is more like a military expedition. The gondolas convey staff and luggage across the lagoon to the mainland where a line of coaches await us for the arduous journey across country. The trip, along the bumpy roads of northern Italy, is made pleasurable by the opportunity to share the journey with Julia. We snuggle up together in the coach. Along the way we stop at coaching inns where, though we have separate rooms, we contrive to spend the nights together for sex.

Eventually we arrive at Villa Perosa, La Contessa's hunting lodge. I'm surprised at the modesty of the house. I say this in relative terms, making comparison with both the Palazzo Cavelli in Venice and other hunting lodges of the Italian nobility, which I know can resemble palaces. At the heart of the estate is a handsome single-storey log-built lodge. It's a commodious rural retreat containing a great hall with its fireplace, a study, other reception rooms, and suites for La Contessa and her guests. It's more homely and welcoming than the luxuriously grand I expected and know she could afford. There are smaller wooden lodges at the rear, the accommodation for her household staff, along with stables and kennels. The lodge itself is nestled in a dip and surrounded by pine woods and woodland paths. To reach the hunting lodge, we take an avenue running through the farm and olive groves. This must be where La Contessa produces her olive oil, which I've seen in rows of bottles in the kitchens at the palazzo decorated with her livery of the black swan.

Julia immediately sets to work directing the other staff in unloading the coaches, and I muck in by helping carry the trunks to La Contessa's suite. Julia is on a mission to get the work done as soon as possible so we'll get time to ourselves before La Contessa and her entourage arrives. The staff waste no time in fetching logs and lighting fires in the rooms to warm the place up. By early evening, the lodge is comfortable, the glow of the fires giving it a homely atmosphere.

Julia's pleased. The other staff are busy with chores, and it's her place to unpack La Contessa's trunks containing her clothes and personal effects. I'm nestled in a most commodious armchair in the corner opposite La Contessa's four poster bed as Julia unpacks.

"How long are we staying here?"

"It depends," says Julia, "two to four weeks usually. La Contessa is capricious; if she gets bored I've known her leave at a moment's notice. That would be bad, Roberto, after all you and her slave girl are here to entertain her so if we leave early it'll reflect badly on you," she scolds.

"She needs all this stuff for a few weeks!" I exclaim, as I get up to drag another trunk along the floor for Julia to unpack.

"Roberto, have you learnt nothing? Of course, she needs it all! She has to look magnificent at all times as you know. Each garment is carefully chosen and has its place."

Julia empties a trunk containing La Contessa's underwear. There are silk knickerbockers, satin corsets, and lace stockings. She dangles a shiny, ivory basque from her fingers.

"You ought to try it on!" I suggest.

"Oh no, I shouldn't. If she were to find out she'd be furious. Maybe *you* should try it on," she taunts.

Julia picks up a pile of knickerbockers in various colours: white, cream, red, black, and purple, buries her nose into them and breathes in their aroma.

"Julia! That's a bit kinky."

"No it's not. They're freshly laundered. They smell delicious. They smell of roses and lavender, and her."

I can't help thinking it wouldn't bother her if they were soiled, and she inhaled the odour of dried piss. She'd still be waxing lyrical about her mistress's scent.

"No, really, wear La Contessa's undergarments whilst you unpack. Go on. You'll look sexy in them. Thinking about it is giving me a hard-on."

"Oh, you're incorrigible, Roberto! Ok, just for you."

She slips out of her servant's clothes, the smart skirt, and the blouse with La Contessa's livery embroidered on it. She chooses black satin knickerbockers and wriggles them up over her hips, tying them with a lace cord.

"Oh, that feels so nice," she gasps, "so smooth against the skin and sensuous compared to the starchy linen ones I wear. But then you know all about wearing sexy women's underwear don't you, Roberto!" She says, reminding me of the occasion La Contessa dressed me as a noblewoman.

"You look fabulous, Julia," I say, encouraging her. "Try one of the corsets on."

She picks up the corset with purple and black satin panels and stiff whale bone stays.

"I'll need your help to lace it up," she calls.

I oblige her and, as she bends over for me, I pull the laces tight. She looks fantastic.

"God, I feel great. I can see why La Contessa dresses like this. It makes me feel so powerful... and sexy. Come over here and fuck me!" Julia exclaims.

It's tempting... so very tempting. And I can't deny how turned on I am by Julia parading in La Contessa's sexy undergarments, looking every bit the dominatrix in them. But I exercise restraint, deciding I'd prefer to spend time watching her in them.

"No, not now... not yet. Carry on unpacking whilst I watch you. I reckon if you carry on I'll cream in my knickers!"

"Oh Roberto, that's disgusting. No masturbating! You're only allowed to watch. I don't want you wasting your spunk. I want that in my cunt."

This sexy game is turning us both on.

Julia carries on with her work. She empties the trunks of gorgeous silk evening gowns, sumptuous velvet dresses and tantalisingly teasing costumes. I've seen La Contessa wear this full range of clothes during my service as she dominates all, from collared slave to the ruling elite, with her commanding presence fuelled by a wardrobe designed to enhance her considerable physical attributes. Who wouldn't wish to kneel before her!

"I love this," says Julia. "I've always enjoyed unpacking at the lodge, but it's even more exciting having you here watching. And I'd never dared try anything on without your encouragement. You're a bad influence on me, Roberto!"

She handles each item of clothing with loving care, caressing the folds of material as she smooths creases out, before hanging them up in a massive *armoire* of polished Piedmont pine. She's relishing every moment, and I appreciate watching her fetishistic pleasure at handling La Contessa's beautiful wardrobe.

Eventually, she comes to the last trunk which is packed full of coats, cloaks and over-garments.

"Oh my god, look at this," she exclaims holding a fur coat in the air for me to admire. "I've never seen this before, it must be new."

She holds up a coat which has to be wolf fur. It's magnificent; the pile of the fur is thick and lush, and its silver-grey hue shimmers in the fire-light.

"You must try it on."

"Should I? I can't, it's my mistress's. Do you think I ought?"

"Do it Julia. It's magnificent. See the quality of the pelt. You'll look stunning in it."

"Oh well, ok. I suppose it can't do any harm, and we're alone. Contessa will never know, will she?"

She threads her arms into the sleeves and wraps the luxurious fur around her, revelling in the touch of it against her skin.

"It's gorgeous. And it's so heavy, like it's dragging me down."

"You look amazing," I exclaim.

She walks towards me seductively; a wolverine glint in her eyes making her appear feral and sexy as if she's actually taken on the qualities of the creature the fur came from. By now I'm sitting back in the chair, admiring every step. She stands before me, and then gently parts the heavy pelt to reveal her lovely legs and seductive curves.

"On your knees," she whispers, the command sounding natural coming from her whilst enveloped in silver-grey fur.

I do as I'm told. The months of training in La Contessa's service making me submit instinctively to any command from a female voice.

"Un-lace my knickerbockers and pull them down."

I carefully untie the laces and gently pull the black satin over Julia's hips and down her thighs and legs. When they're on the floor, she steps out of them and kicks them to one side. When I glance up, I'm eye level with her crotch. I bury my face into the downy, brown hair of her bush, feeling the warmth of her against my cheek and smelling the juices oozing from it. My tongue seeks out her cunt, lapping wildly at her like a wild wolf on heat. I find her clit, and she moans.

"Fuck me, Roberto. Take me whilst I'm wearing the fur."

Julia jumps onto the bed and spreads herself onto the embroidered coverlet, parting the coat slightly so I see the crack of her sex winking invitingly at me through the slit in the fur. I waste no time in discarding my clothes and joining her. The silver-grey fur is wrapped around her and I run my hands over it; the pelt is thick and soft. Julia moans in pleasure at my touch through the animal skin. I kneel over her, pulling the coat apart to uncover her shapely breasts with their pert nipples, pushed up by the corset, and her cunt. Julia splays her legs for me, inviting me to enter her.

"I want you inside me," she whimpers.

Julia, turned on by the touch of fur on her skin, the flaunting of her sexiness in front of me and, dare I add, the illicit, wanton behaviour of wearing her mistress's clothes, is sopping. Risk is always a turn on; a lesson I learnt in my time in the Cannaregio. It's why the wealthy choose a prostitute when they could have the pick of many girls. I waste no time in satisfying her needs.

I thread my cock into her and she's ready for it, desperate for it! It's a relief for both of us to be joined, and now I'm inside her, the urgency of our desires is satisfied and we take time over our lovemaking. I gently slide into her, and her body arches to receive me. The wolf fur becomes a tool, enhancing the sensuality of our union. I pull it up to Julia's cheek as I kiss her, run it along the curves of her breasts and brush it against her nipples. She pulls it over us so we become enveloped in its luxuriousness. Our orgasms have a long, slow build-up, but they are all the more explosive for that. The pace of Julia's heart quickens against my chest, I hear her breathes as they deepen, and savour the desire on her lips. Her moans become incessant and full-throated as her climax builds, until she has to let go with screams of release and pure physical pleasure.

It's not the end of our lovemaking for the evening. The corset and wolf skin fur get discarded, tossed aimlessly onto the floor. If La Contessa could see the careless way we treat her precious things, she'd be furious, but by now we are beyond caring. We're focused only on each other, and our mistress's presence recedes into a dangerous oblivion. Tired and satiated after a night of great and fulfilling sex, we crash out on La Contessa's bed, curled up in one another's arms, and fall into a deep sleep. When we merge from our slumber, it's Julia who brings us back down to earth.

"Shit, look at the state of this bed, Roberto! It's a mess."

I admit it's rather dishevelled. Our lovemaking has pulled the sheets, rumpled the coverlet, and dented the pillows with the impressions of our heads. The bed oozes with the odour of great sex; of sweat, spunk, and cunt juices. I love it.

"Don't worry, Julia, we've plenty of time. She's not expected to arrive till later in the day."

"Yes, Roberto, but I've no time to get this lot laundered."

"Straighten it up, smooth the sheets and bolster and it'll be fine," I reassure her.

We get out of bed and set about tidying up. We throw the cover back, tighten the linen sheet and tuck it in before putting the coverlet back on. Whilst doing that I notice a spunk stain on the embroidered cover where we made love. There's no mistaking what it is, a white stain on bright turquoise textile. I don't want to panic Julia by drawing her attention to it. So, whilst she hangs the wolf skin fur in the *armoire* and her back is turned, I try to wipe it off with spittle and a handkerchief.

"That looks better," she says with relief as she plumps up the pillows. "But open a window and let some fresh air in, it stinks in here."

"I know. It smells of us. It smells of dirty sex."

"Sorry Roberto, not now. It was a great night, but it's back to work for us now. We've got to make sure everything's right before La Contessa arrives."

19: La Contessa's Arrival

Later that morning Julia summons me and the other staff. La Contessa has arrived earlier than expected; she's been spotted in the distance riding along the sweeping avenue leading to the hunting lodge. Julia hurriedly assembles the domestic staff to greet her. It seems she has taken two horses, one for herself and another for Mademoiselle La Tour, to ride on ahead of the carriage. As a group of us emerge from the house. La Contessa has already dismounted, and strides towards the wooden portico at the entrance of the lodge, leading a splendid black stallion by its reins. Julia hastily hustles the staff into a line and we bow or curtsey to La Contessa.

Her face is flushed red, and her chest is heaving with the exertion of the gallop down the drive. Her horse, its body still steaming, is a magnificent beast, as imposing as its mistress. She towers over us, both because she's tall, also because her bearing and presence enhance her stature. She's dressed in hunting attire, a smartly tailored black jacket, which spreads out over her hips to accentuate her hour-glass figure, and a top hat with a pheasant feather in it. In her hand is a riding crop. My eyes are drawn to her fawn jodhpurs clinging tightly to her thighs, and her riding boots, knee high with silver spurs on them. The leather is splattered with mud. I remember polishing these boots and getting turned on by handling them. To see them on their owner, worn with such power and elegance is a sight to behold. The scowl on her face betrays her displeasure.

"What sort of rabble do you call this, Julia? Do you think this is the greeting I should expect after a long journey?"

In a fluster, Julia replies, "No, madam. I'm sorry, madam. We've been busy getting things ready, and we weren't expecting you until later."

"You should know to expect me at any time. I trust everything is prepared for me and my guest," she says, as an assumption more than a question.

"Yes, madam, everything is ready," Julia says, and luckily it is.

La Contessa's piercing gaze bears down on Julia, "You seem flushed, maid."

"Well yes, madam, I've been busy with finishing touches to make sure everything's perfect for you."

"No, I don't mean it in that way. I mean flushed like you've had a good fucking, my maid. Look at your rosy cheeks, you're positively glowing."

Julia looks horrified, and guilty.

"I'm sorry, madam, it must be because the last few days have been hectic," she mumbles.

La Contessa glances up at the rest of the staff to gauge their reaction. What do they know... or suspect? They appear uneasy. Is it because they know about me and Julia, or because their mistress is angry?

Her gaze is directed at me, stood behind Julia in the line with the other staff.

"You slave, come here," she orders.

I move forward and offer a sweeping bow.

"Welcome, mistress. I hope you've had a pleasant journey," I don't expect to sweet-talk her out of her foul mood, but it's worth a try.

"Oh well, at least one of you is ready to greet me properly," she says with sarcasm. "But don't think mere pleasantries will get you out of trouble slave. You are getting above yourself. A bit of praise and it goes to your head. That needs to be corrected, my slave. And what do you think you're doing here with clothes on? Strip off! And where are your manners, can't you see my guest wants help to dismount. She needs a foot stool to help her get down."

I contrive an appropriately contrite expression as I take my uniform off, but inside I've the lovely gut-wrenching feeling of submission. I love it when she's like this. Love the tone of controlled anger in her voice. Once naked, I walk over to Mademoiselle La Tour and get down onto all fours.

Mademoiselle, still sat upright in the saddle of her panting brown mare, looks on the scene with an amused glint in her eye.

I hear the crunch of riding boots on gravel as La Contessa follows me to Mademoiselle's mount.

"That's better, slave."

There's a swishing sound behind me as La Contessa slices the air with her riding crop using such force I feel the air blast against my backside like a winter squall. I know what will follow. The next stroke slices down on my arse with unrelenting power. It stings... it really stings! It's as if her irritation has been channelled into one stroke. I use all my powers of control to hold my position and stop myself from screaming in pain. Another three hard hits strike the flesh of my backside. The stiff wood of the riding crop delivers a severe stroke.

"I've been waiting to do that, my slave. You've grown complacent in my service and you need to be taught a lesson."

"Yes mistress, thank you mistress."

"Don't think this hunting trip is a holiday for you... or any of my servants," she adds fiercely, so they can hear. "You will be put to work and I will use you how I see fit."

"Yes mistress, of course mistress," I say, and I mean it. I want her to punish me. I want to submit to her.

La Contessa reaches her hand out to Mademoiselle, and the French woman slides off her horse, resting one of her booted feet on my back. The leather sole presses on me, but I strain to keep my position. Soon after, the second boot comes to rest on me so she balances precariously on my back. Mademoiselle may be petite but I'm still supporting her entire weight. I struggle to bear her as the riding boots press down on me, and the stones of the drive dig into my hands and knees. I daren't give way as, if I collapse, Mademoiselle will go tumbling onto the ground, and I'll be in serious trouble. At the moment when my body is about to give way, Mademoiselle steps off my back and I get relief. I maintain my supplicant position though.

Mademoiselle is dressed in riding attire in the same fashion as La Contessa. I've only seen her in formal dress and preposterous bejewelled wigs before. Viewing her today with subtle make-up and her black hair tumbling loose from under a top hat, I appreciate what a natural beauty she is.

"I think he rather enjoys the crop, Contessa. I recall how I used it on him during your card game."

"He's not meant to enjoy anything, Mademoiselle. He is there to suffer for me and serve me. Is that not so, slave?"

"Yes. mistress," I concur.

"I think he should have more strokes," Mademoiselle says.

"Whatever gives you pleasure, my friend. He is yours to use how you please."

The crop whips down on my arse in a succession of severe strokes, some using the stiff body of the crop, others the leather loop at its tip. Mademoiselle may only be tiny, but her hits pack a punch. She stops to tease me, running the crop gently against my backside. The leather loop is soft against my flesh, but it's only a short relief as the crop cracks on my arse. It's sore now, and tender to touch.

There's a crunch of boot on gravel as Mademoiselle takes her place in front of me. I keep my head down to maintain my supplicant position. I'm conscious of the brown leather of her riding boots and the fawn moleskin stretched over her thighs. From here I can peek under her riding jacket to spy her crotch where I see a damp patch, whether from the sweat of being in the saddle or arousal at punishing me, it's hard to say.

Mademoiselle settles her riding boot before me. I know what's expected and lean forward to lick the specks of moist mud off the leather. I work my tongue up the boot to the knee. I suck in the glorious earthy taste of soil mingled with polished leather. Whilst my tongue is at Mademoiselle's heel something sharp digs into my throbbing backside. It takes me a moment before I realise what it is… the riding spurs from La Contessa's boots. She pushes the spikes deep into my skin. I sense the indentation marks forming in my flesh as she digs hard into my bum cheek. The spurs run agonisingly across my skin, and it doesn't take me long to realise where they're heading. In this position my cock and balls hang invitingly for her. Sure enough I soon suffer the sharp spurs digging into my sac.

"Stop squirming, slave. Marie will you give me a hand. Hold this slave to stop him wriggling so I can dig my spurs into him."

"That looks fun. Can I have a go when you've finished with him?"

"By all means, Mademoiselle."

The French woman uses her hand to push on the small of my back whilst La Contessa leans on her as a support to gain greater purchase with the spurs. In this position she works the spurs across my balls. The metal digs deep into the sac and presses on my testicles. It's a sharp and spiky pain. I can't help but squeal.

Mademoiselle laughs at my predicament, "I think you've got to him. But he has a hard-on, Contessa. You shouldn't allow that."

"Certainly not, I'll have to do something about that. I can't have him getting any sexual pleasure out of his torment."

Contessa runs the spurs along the length of my erection and the pain of the spikes digging into my cock is soon enough to dent my arousal. She pushes one of the spurs into the end of my penis, and it's excruciating.

"You can have him now, Marie."

La Contessa rests the sole of her riding boot over the small of my back and presses, the spurs digging into me again as Mademoiselle kicks my balls with a few staccato swings. This comes as a surprise as I'd prepared myself for the sharp tingling pain of the metal. I groan and collapse, falling onto the stone drive. This is the position Mademoiselle wants me in, flat on the floor with the sole and heel of my mistress's boot pressing on me. It's only then she starts to work on my cock and balls with the spurs. I recall from the card game how Mademoiselle enjoys administering punishments. She takes pleasure from this, as does La Contessa, and between them they make a formidable pair. The French woman pushes my cock hard against the ground with the spike of one of the spurs. She works the sharp tip into the hole at the end of my cock.

"*Zut alors!*" exclaims Mademoiselle, "This is where they belong; under our boots, tormented by powerful women."

"Yes indeed, Mademoiselle. It's such a pleasure to work with such a natural sadist as yourself."

"Ah, *ma Cherie*, but the pleasure is all mine. To watch an expert in the arts of domination at such close quarters is a privilege."

"Thank you. What an exceedingly nice compliment, Marie."

The two mistresses look up as they hear La Contessa's carriage approaching. From my position on the ground I see the coach, pulled by four black horses and mounted by two horsemen in La Contessa's livery, rumbling down the incline towards the hunting lodge. As you'd expect, her carriage is lavish, decorated with vermillion paint, gold leaf and carvings of black swans. It pulls up outside the lodge where the staff stand, having witnessed my humiliation at the hands of La Contessa and her friend. Julia still looks pensive but relieved her mistress's attention is diverted off her and onto me.

"Ah, I wonder how your slave girl has fared?" asks Mademoiselle.

"Yes, we left her in an entertaining predicament, hog-tied and strapped into the carriage. I suppose I ought to check how she is," added La Contessa with a nonchalant wave of her hand.

She climbs into the carriage. There's a shuffling sound as La Contessa releases Becky from her confinement. It's the girl who emerges first. She's naked, naturally. She's also gagged with a metal bit like those worn by the horses. Around her forehead is a headdress with black and white feathers, so she's adorned exactly like the horses pulling La Contessa's carriage. Her arms are secured behind her back with two leather cuffs chained together and she has a collar around her neck. As Becky steps down from the carriage, mistress follows holding a lead attached to the collar. When the girl reaches Mademoiselle, she gets down onto her knees and looks up at her with adoration.

"Ah, my sweet," she says stroking Becky's hair like she's her pet. "We've had such fun in that carriage. You're such an attentive slave. What a journey. I've never had so many orgasms! Your tongue, your fingers, they are simply everywhere. Here, with your mistress's permission, let me release you from your bit."

La Contessa nods her approval, and Mademoiselle removes the metal from the girl's mouth. She stretches her jaw.

"Thank you Mademoiselle. It's been a pleasure to serve you…"

"…To service me, *ma cherie*," corrects the French woman. She bends over, taking Becky's face between her palms and kisses her.

"Do you see girl?" La Contessa says, pointing to me lying on my front in the dirt. "He has disgraced himself. I believe he needs more punishment," she adds, handing her slave girl the riding crop.

And I thought my torment was over for the afternoon. Becky sets about me with the crop with a fearsome determination that surprises me.

"That's it girl, give him a good beating," La Contessa encourages.

And she does, raining a series of savage strokes on my backside and top of my thighs. By the end of it my arse is raw and throbbing.

"It's been a long journey, girl. Do you need to relieve yourself?"

"Yes please, mistress, if I have permission."

"Then you may use my slave as your piss-pot, girl," La Contessa says, gesturing to me lying flat on the ground.

"Thank you, mistress."

With a flick of the lead Becky steps forward, stands over me and spreads her legs. It starts as a warm trickle over the back of my head but soon becomes a gushing torrent of hot piss flowing through my hair, down my face, and into my mouth. I drink it in greedily. It tastes fresh, warm, and salty. It's humiliating to be subjected to this, especially in front of the household staff, some of whom stare open-mouthed, as not all are familiar with the intimacies of La Contessa's techniques of domination. I confess to being rather partial to the bouquet of fresh pee. Besides, I'm thirsty by now too! So, I try to suck the warm fluid into my mouth rather than see it spilt on the ground and wasted.

After Becky has emptied her bladder over me she tightens a collar which mistress has passed to her, around my neck, and hands the lead to La Contessa. I'm told to get down on all fours again whilst Becky is ordered to get down alongside me. Mademoiselle takes her lead. The pair of strict mistresses stroll along the drive pulling Becky and myself behind them like their dogs.

"Julia, follow me," La Contessa commands. "Let me see if everything is in order."

Julia looks worried... very worried.

147

20: The Hunt

La Contessa is in a mean mood. She's come to the hunting lodge determined to inflict her particular brand of discipline on her servants, and in Mademoiselle La Tour she's found an enthusiastic and equally sadistic accomplice.

She finds fault with everything Julia has done. The pine wood furnishings haven't been buffed well enough, there's still dust on the floors, the plates, and cutlery haven't been polished and, perhaps most significantly, her clothes and undergarments should have been pressed before being hung in the *armoire*. Oh dear, all I can think is, it's lucky she doesn't know what we really got up to! Julia is as penitent and apologetic as she can be, but her mistress will accept no excuses.

I overhear her scolding Julia, "You lack focus lately, my maid. You seem distracted when your whole attention should be directed at serving me."

Julia is upset. She rarely gets such treatment and prides herself on making things perfect for her mistress, so takes the criticism badly. She looks fraught by the end of the day.

As for me, well, there's no let up for the punishments. In the evening my wrists and ankles are tied together and I'm strung up from the beams of the hall as a plaything for La Contessa and Mademoiselle. I'm subjected to further corporal punishment with whip and paddle and nipple torture from mistress's teeth. I have my cock and balls tied with cord and drizzled with hot wax to the delight of the two women. The mindset of a dominant's slave is a strange one, and I've come to understand it. Yes, my treatment is humiliating, and the punishments inflicted on me excruciatingly painful, but it doesn't mean I don't get a perverse pleasure from them, I certainly do. I understand my role and enter into it with dedication.

Naturally the slave girl forms a significant part of the entertainment. The bond she's established with Mademoiselle over the course of the coach journey develops. Becky is her pet. She spends the evening on a collar and lead being led around the hall, petted and stroked, and pleasuring Mademoiselle with her tongue. She's strung up from the beams opposite me where she's also subjected to punishments from both women. At one point the nipple clamps are attached to each of us by a cord, so each time one of us wriggles or flinches in response to the whip it tugs on the nipples of the other, much to the mistresses' amusement.

I don't see anything of Julia during the night. She gets up ridiculously early to make amends for the deficiencies La Contessa pointed out and ensure everything is in order by the time her mistress rises. Lucio arrived the previous evening. He's here to check the farm and olive groves are being well managed.

By the next morning I'm relieved to hear La Contessa and Mademoiselle are going hunting, so I might get respite from their attentions.

"What does she hunt?" I get the chance to ask Julia after she's finished dressing her mistress.

"There are boar and deer in the forests around here, and they hunt for smaller animals like rabbits too."

"Wolves?" I ask, thinking of the magnificent fur coat.

"No, not around her. You've got to go into the Alps to find wolves."

"Do you join La Contessa's hunting party?"

"No. I've never been on the hunt itself. But the staff gather outside before it sets off. There's a great atmosphere and, as you can imagine, La Contessa always looks fabulous for her hunting trips, as you'll see."

After a hearty breakfast, La Contessa, and Mademoiselle congregate outside the lodge with a group of servants who will attend the hunt and the rest of the household staff who are there to see them off.

Today the pair are dressed for show. They wear woollen overcoats in olive green, lined around collar, sleeve, and hem with black fur, and matching fur hats. They look like they've stepped out of the Russian steppes. The knee length leather boots and riding crops are obligatory!

The horses; La Contessa's sleek black stallion and Mademoiselle's brown mare, are especially handsome. They stamp their hooves on the stones and shake their manes, impatient for the impending ride. They are surrounded by La Contessa's hunting dogs. This is a pack of *spinoso,* a dog bred in Piedmont for hunting and retrieving. They gather around mistress yelping excitedly. They are square built dogs with long heads and white, wiry coats with orange or brown markings.

"Let us toast our host," announces Mademoiselle La Tour as she produces a flask, and glasses are handed round. "The finest French cognac, an aperitif to warm us up before we ride out. *Bon appetit!*"

The staff are in better spirits today as they share in Mademoiselle's toast to La Contessa.

"And what will our quarry be today, *ma Cherie*. Deer, boar, bears?!"

"I have a more interesting sport planned, Mademoiselle."

"More interesting than bears!" she laughs.

"Indeed, for the animals we hunt today are of the human variety."

"Contessa, you are incorrigible. But we won't be able to have our catch for dinner!"

La Contessa arches an eyebrow as if to say *why not?*

And there was me thinking I might get a quiet morning and respite from La Contessa's attentions. But it's Becky who's led out from the lodge with only a fur cape around her naked shoulders. She must be freezing as winter in this part of Italy is chilly. So, it's the girl they plan to chase?

"Slave, come here," she orders me to come forward. "Why are you still dressed? I don't care how cold it is, you should make yourself available at all times. And if the girl can stand the chill then surely you can? Besides, a little exercise will soon warm you up."

I don't like the sound of that.

"Yes, mistress," I say, as I strip off, handing my uniform to Julia, who looks at me in sympathy for my impending plight.

"Let's make this interesting shall we?" announces La Contessa. "Mademoiselle and I will hunt you both. We will give you a half hour head start to make it interesting, and the pack a good run. Neither of you know the woods, so it will be fair. Whoever is caught first will be subjected to humiliation and punishment, and whoever wins will be permitted sexual pleasure. Marie, we can have another couple of glasses of your excellent cognac whilst we are waiting. How does that sound?"

I don't know why she's asking, as if I have any choice in the matter.

The dog pack is allowed to gather around Becky and myself to sniff us. There are five *spinoso* gathered around me with their muzzles like drooping moustaches sniffing at me. Once the dogs get the scent they become over-excited and have to be hauled back by their tethers.

"Are you ready, my slaves? You may set off at the sound of the horn."

"Oh, Contessa, you are so wicked. I can't wait to join the hunt," says Mademoiselle before downing a glass of cognac in one gulp.

I might as well enter into the spirit of it. It could be fun... but then again? I glimpse across at Becky, who acknowledges me with a nod. She's a determined look on her face. I fear she'll be a formidable adversary. She's focused on victory, and the promise of pleasure. I can imagine she'd love Mademoiselle to lick her clit and make her come, if it were offered as a reward for victory.

La Contessa is handed a horn, fashioned out of a stag antler.

"Are you ready?"

"Yes, mistress," we reply in unison.

150

She puts the hunting horn to her lips and blows. The rasping sound echoes around the lodge. The household staff, who are thoroughly enjoying the spectacle, let out a loud cheer as Becky and I set off.

We head off into the woods in different directions. I run at a steady pace because I don't want to tire myself out. It might be tempting to set off at speed and build up as big a distance as possible from the hounds until they are released, but I want to conserve energy. It's hard running on the forest floor with the undergrowth and foliage digging into the soles of my feet. We're both sent off into the wild entirely naked. There's something exhilarating and primaeval about it to be honest, like acting out an ancient ritual hunter and animal have been part of for millennia.

After I've covered a fair bit of ground, I pause to get my breath back and reflect. The person who gets caught will be the one whose scent the dogs pick up first. I reckon the route to victory is to make sure the dogs don't pick mine up, and the only way to do that is find water. Unfortunately, the city of Venice has been my home for all my life and I know nothing of rural ways, how to disguise my tracks or even where to find a water course. I plunge forward into the woods. The half-hour before La Contessa sets the dogs loose gives me time to put more distance from them.

I plunge further on into the woods, heading downhill in the hope I'm more likely to find a stream there. The pine trees tower over me, and in the direction I take they close tightly in on me, making my path claustrophobic. As I run forwards, the branches flick against my naked skin. I no longer feel the winter chill as my steady pace has warmed me up by now. I come across a ledge with a steep incline, and at the bottom is what I'm looking for, a bubbling stream weaving its way through the forest. I scramble down the slope, slipping onto the forest floor, and the bed of pine needles covering it. Spiky pines. That's all I need sticking in my sore arse right now. Unable to stop myself, I crash through a thorny bush on the way.

Once at the bottom, I'm encouraged. My plan now is to run along the length of the stream in an attempt to put the pack off my scent. The water is icy. I shiver at its touch as it flows as high as my knees, but I'm convinced this is the right course. I plunge forward as fast as I can whilst wading against the fast flowing water and stumbling on the slippery rocks on the brook's floor. At one point the stream narrows into a channel and the waters reach my groin, enveloping my cock and balls in an icy chill. I carry on through them, anyway. I stop again to take stock. I'm panting with the exertion now. I consider myself fit, but the exercise I take to tone my body has not prepared me for the sustained stamina needed for this. I've lost track of time but can only assume the dogs have been released by now. I wonder how Becky is getting on. I must have an advantage as I've seen nothing from her time at the palazzo to suggest she's stronger than me. Dare I allow myself to speculate on what sexual pleasure might be permitted if I emerge as victor?

I'm brought back to earth by the sound of the hunting horn. It's in the distance and faint, but proof the chase has begun. I understand La Contessa's thinking, she will want us to know how close the pursuit is because it will make the hunt more interesting for her. I decide it's time to get out of the stream, climb up the other side of the bank and start running again to put distance between myself and the pack. The horn blows. It sounds closer. Does this mean the dogs have picked up my scent? I run ahead with greater urgency.

The horn blows again. There's no question it's getting closer. I've scrambled up the bank. I notice scratches from thistles and thorns all over me, though I've barely noticed them. The horn is louder still. Looking across the valley I see her on the brow of the hill as her black horse crashes through overhanging branches into a clearing. She's way off still, and the steep incline of the valley divides us, but the pursuit is on. I duck behind a tree and peek from behind it. I should continue my escape, I know, but I can't resist the temptation. She's a figure to admire even from this distance. She's riding side saddle and looks imperious in her olive green coat and its fur. She gazes out across the valley. Mademoiselle joins her with the dogs panting and yelping around her horse. I see the two women exchange words and La Contessa point into the distance. They daren't try to take their horses down such a steep incline. They send the hounds crashing down the slope whilst they gallop off, presumably to find another route across the valley.

This is the moment of truth. Will the barrier of the stream be enough to put the dogs off the scent? The pack plunges down the incline into the stream. At first the signs are good. The dogs are confused and scurry around sniffing in the water and along the bank, but then one picks up on a scent and barks. The others gather round and they start scrambling up the hill. It's steep and they're struggling but it's only a matter of time before they make it to the top. I set off at a dash through the trees now. My instincts tell me I'm done for now, but I can still put further distance between me and the dogs to at least delay the moment of reckoning. Perhaps they've already captured Becky?

There's nothing to do but run as fast as I can. The horn blows. The sound comes from my side of the valley. The net is tightening around me but I keep on running. I can't give up, La Contessa will expect the thrill of a chase and some sport. I crash through the branches of the trees. I hear the gallop of hooves in one direction and the yapping of dogs in the

152

other. I see a flash of black, brown, and green through the trunks of the trees. La Contessa pulls the reins of her horse to bring it to a halt and Mademoiselle comes to a stop behind her. They both peer through the trees.

Mademoiselle points, "Look madam, through the trees. I saw a shadow. I think we have him."

"Yes, Marie. I see him. The hunt is on!" she calls.

The end is inevitable, but can I extend the pursuit? Looming before me is a bank of thorny bushes, *prinus spinoso*. Perhaps I can hide in there for a while. The horses won't pursue me through there and the dogs will surely be put off by the thorns. I clamber through the blackthorn. My feet are cut and bloodied by now, and there are scratches all over my body. I crouch within the brambles and consider what to do next. The dogs are sniffing at the entrance to the barrier of brambles. The thorns are no impediment to their progress as I can hear their panting getting nearer. I break out of the bushes into open land and run as fast as I can. The first dog wriggles out of the thorns and starts barking at its prey. The other dogs soon join him and they begin the chase after me. Suddenly the horses emerge from the trees at a gallop.

"Good boys," La Contessa shouts at the dogs. "Get him!"

My heart is pumping, and blood coursing through my veins. I sprint, but I know the game is up. Exhausted and unable to run any harder, I stumble and collapse to the ground. The dogs are on me in a second, jumping over me and barking. I'm thankful *spinoso* are not an aggressive breed of dog or I would fear being bitten to shreds. They clamber over me, slaver dripping from their muzzles. La Contessa rides up. She doesn't call the dogs off. She enjoys the spectacle of them jumping on me, their muddied feet pawing over me.

La Contessa throws raw meat onto the ground as a reward for the dogs and they leave me to take chunks from it. I'm still panting, my dark hair a matted mess, my feet bloodied and sore, and my body covered in scratches. I glance up. She looks magnificent. Her cheeks are flushed from the fresh air, whilst her breasts swell rhythmically with the exertion of the chase. She stands upright side-saddle on her horse, towering over me with a triumphant smile on her face. Mademoiselle trots up beside her.

"What excellent sport, madam," she says.

"Indeed, mademoiselle. It was most amusing, especially at the end to see him running away from us in desperation. You thought to hide in the *prinus spinosa* and hope the dogs wouldn't follow you? How foolish," she spits disdainfully, "the clue is in the name of the breed, *spinoso*. They are thick skinned, coarse haired, bred to pursue their quarry in thorny bushes.

Well, we've seen no sign of the girl, so you are the first to be captured, my slave."

La Contessa slides off the stirrups of her horse with effortless grace despite her long dress and heavy coat. She offers a kid-gloved hand to Mademoiselle to help her down.

"The others will join us soon; then we will go in pursuit of the girl who seems to have disappeared into thin air. In the meantime, let us amuse ourselves with this hunted slave."

She retrieves ropes from her saddle bag. She has me leaning against a tree, pulls my arms behind it and secures my wrists, and then ties my ankles together. I'm too tired to care, almost thankful for a sit down. She strolls back to the blackthorn bushes and snaps a couple of branches off. Their spines are long, tough and sharp as a pin. La Contessa bends over me. She takes a glove off and touches the spine with the tip of her finger.

"Ouch! Yes, these are suitably cruel implements of torment. Imagine what pain these spines will cause on a nipple…"

She digs the thorn hard into my nipple.

"…or on a tender cock."

She drags a branch along the length of my penis scraping it with a row of sharp spines and digs a thorn into its tip. I flinch and gasp with the pain. When I look down, I see a spot of blood on my nipple where the thorn has pierced the skin.

"Oh come now slave, don't be so timid about receiving pain. It seems you've been saved from further punishment, but I will take these nasty, spiky thorns back with me."

The rest of the household servants, who have been following La Contessa on foot, have caught up. She goes over, points at me, and issues directions.

"We have to prepare our quarry to carry it back to the lodge," I overhear her explain.

They approach with a long wooden pole. Released from the tree, my ankles, and wrists are now tied to the pole. I'm going to be carried back as if I'm a dead deer, hanging from a pole. Four servants lift me up, resting the pole on their shoulders. We march off, La Contessa and Mademoiselle, who have re-mounted their horses, in the lead with the pack of dogs and me, swinging from a pole, at the rear. Of all the humiliations La Contessa has inflicted whilst I've been serving her, this is the worst. Tired, cold and scratched to shreds I'm now treated like a hunted animal, which of course I am.

La Contessa knows the forest paths, so it doesn't take too long to re-trace our steps. She sends out the dogs to hunt for Becky's scent, but it's not until we get near the hunting lodge they appear to pick up anything. At one point they get excited and start sniffing around, but they find no trace of the girl. We're about to set off again when there's a plaintive call from the undergrowth.

"Mistress, please mistress, do I have permission to come out now?"

"What, where are you girl?"

There's a rustle, a head emerges from a pile of pine needles and then Becky's naked body, covered in needles and leaves, her fair hair hanging in a dishevelled tangle over her breasts. She looks comical, especially seeing her upside-down as I do from my position.

"Have you been there all the time, girl?"

"Yes mistress. I rubbed myself with rosemary leaves and then made a shelter to hide in, and covered it in pine needles to disguise my scent, mistress."

"*Ma cherie*, you are such a clever girl," applauds Mademoiselle.

La Contessa's reaction is more restrained, torn as it is between admiration for her slave girl's ingenuity, and the possibility she's been made a fool of.

Becky, seeing her mistress's ambivalent look, tries to make amends. She approaches La Contessa's horse and kisses her boot and then the fur hem of her coat.

"I only mean to please you, mistress."

"Don't ever think you can outwit me, girl, or you will get a harsh reckoning," scolds La Contessa.

Mademoiselle, who has dismounted her horse, wraps her coat around the girl, and springs to her defence.

"Do not be so harsh on her, madam. She has played your game in the right spirit and emerged as the victor. And besides, she looks so sexy covered in leaves, and she smells divine. I could eat her up right now!"

Mademoiselle's hands are all over Becky, fondling her under cover of brushing the leaves and pine needles from her body. She kisses the girl on the lips.

"Then she is your prize, Marie. You can pleasure her however you desire."

"You are most generous, madam."

"Thank you, mistress," echoes Becky.

Before we return to the lodge La Contessa sends the dogs out to hunt for rabbits, which are tied up and slung over the arms of the men carrying me.

"So, it's rabbit stew for dinner," says Mademoiselle, "I know an excellent recipe."

"Yes, that... or roast slave," replies La Contessa with a sadistic ring in her voice.

The entourage returns to the hunting lodge, and I'm paraded through the entrance porch into the hall where the fire has been burning all day. La Contessa and Mademoiselle retire to their chambers for a hot bath, and to get changed. The rabbits are taken off to the kitchen to be skinned and stewed. I'm taken off the pole but with the dire warning my punishment for being hunted has barely started.

I sit there quietly as the hustle of the activities of the staff buzz around me. When the two women return, they emerge refreshed and changed into stunning new outfits. They both wear jerkins and pantaloons in black leather. La Contessa leads the way with Mademoiselle behind her, Becky on her arm, now bathed and tidied up from her adventure in the woods. Her hair is pinned up, and she wears a golden tunic, short enough to leave her solid thighs exposed. Mademoiselle settles into an armchair with the girl at her feet. She unbuttons the front of her leather pants. One hand strays to her crutch, whilst the other playfully twists a curl hanging loose from the obedient girl's hair.

"You must lick me out, my sweet, like you did so deliciously in the back of the carriage Then I shall return the compliment, as your reward for being victorious in the hunt."

"Yes mistress," says Becky, nestling herself up against Mademoiselle's leather clad thigh.

"Should I put more logs on the fire mistress?" asks one of her servants.

"No, not yet. Those burning embers will suit my purpose well. I said we would have roast slave, did I not? And so we shall."

My eyes widen in shock and fear. Surely she can't be serious? Yet when servants enter the hall carrying a cast iron spit, I realise she is. I'm ordered to lie on the floor on my front. The spit is laid along my back and then with my arms and legs stretched out along its length I'm tied onto it. The fireplace, the focal point for the hall, is huge. It's used for roasting boar and pigs... so this is what La Contessa has in mind for me. The spit is heaved up by servants, placed on its stand, and a handle attached.

"Madam!" squeaks Julia, unable to refrain from expressing her concern at the unfolding scene.

"Keep silent, maid."

"But..."

"Do you think I don't know how to judge my punishments?" La Contessa scolds, as her hands run along my buttocks, stroking my skin as I stare into the fiery embers. "Besides, he looks so content in that position, don't you, my slave?"

"Mm, yes, mistress," I reply, squirming on the spit.

My body is enveloped in the heat of the rising currents. It's hot, uncomfortably hot, but not dangerously so. I stare into the embers, mesmerised by the glowing ashes.

"The fire is dying down, I believe it needs more tinder," says La Contessa as she selects branches from a wicker basket at the side of the fireplace.

As soon as she throws the dry wood onto the burning embers, flames leap up in fiery tentacles. My breathing intensifies and my heart races. I can do nothing but stare back powerless into the flames as they curl and spark upwards. The heat spreading over my body intensifies. I endure it on the tip of my cock as it dangles towards the fire. La Contessa's torment is ingenious. I notice she chose not to use the massive logs, but the branches used for kindling with the intention of delivering a scare, but not of roasting me alive... at least I hope so. The smoke wafts up into my nostrils making my head spin.

"Is it the pine wood, madam?" asks Mademoiselle, breathing heavily. "He'll smell delicious once you've finished roasting him."

Through the heat haze and the blur of the smoke, I see the French woman reclining in a tapestry upholstered chair, her leather pants around her ankles with Becky at her knees licking her fanny like a demon.

"Is it getting hot for you slave?" my mistress asks, a wicked smile spreading across her lips.

I'm in too much of a daze even to reply. La Contessa takes hold of the metal crank and turns the spit. It's a disorientating sensation as my body slowly gets turned 180 degrees so I'm now facing up, staring into the sooty tunnel of the chimney. I'm swung around to complete a 360 degree rotation and then back up again. La Contessa stands grinning over me, her hand gripping the spit's crank. Through the heat haze she looks even more stunning. The leather outfit clings tightly to her figure and, from my upturned position I have a view of her cleavage hanging over me.

She bends over to put more wood on the fire. There's a hiss and crackle and then a surge of heat on my back and arse. I try to wriggle in discomfort but I'm too securely tied to the spit. La Contessa retires to a comfy chair and nonchalantly sips from a glass of brandy whilst the waves of scorching heat creep over me. From my precarious position I catch the gleam of satisfaction in her eye as she revels in my predicament, and the spectacle of Mademoiselle and Becky pleasuring each other.

The two women are on the rug in the centre of the hall in a '69' position with the French woman on her back reaching out with her tongue to lick Becky's clit. The slave girl is on top, her face buried in Mademoiselle's crotch, her backside sticking up in the air. The French woman squeals in ecstasy as she approaches her impending climax. The sight of Becky's pale arse sticking out from under her tunic is too tempting an invitation for La Contessa. She takes up a whip with leather thongs and, from a sitting position, whacks her behind. Becky whelps in pain, but it only encourages her to go down on Mademoiselle with even greater enthusiasm. La Contessa continues to whip her slave's arse, until both Becky and Mademoiselle come to simultaneous orgasms. The room is engulfed with the groans and screams of their euphoric climaxes. Mademoiselle pulls Becky towards her, and they curl up into each other's arms and kiss deeply, the sweet taste of their juices on their lips.

La Contessa turns her attention back to me. I've been so drawn into the erotic scene being played out that for a moment I've forgotten my own discomfort. But the heat is overpowering now. Sweat trickles from my forehead. I sense my whole body glowing red.

"Is it getting hot for you slave?"

"Yes mistress," I gasp, hoping she might have had her fun.

"Being roasted alive for your sins by a powerful woman and strict mistress? Do you think this is what hell must be like?"

Somewhere in my heat induced daze I find the wherewithal to reply, "No, I think this is what heaven must be like."

She laughs. "Indeed! But don't think your wit will earn you escape from further punishment."

She leans down and holds another twig in the fire for a minute and then lifts it out. She waves it across my face.

"Do you see this slave?"

I nod. She's taunting me with its glowing tip. I fear she will to press it into my flesh.

She moves into position over my crotch and holds the burning branch over me. She flicks it and a shower of golden sparks falls onto my cock. I scream out in a strange amalgam of agony and ecstasy. She flicks the twig again and glowing cinders float onto my balls. I've experienced many kinds of cock and ball torture at mistress's hands, but this pain is sharper than any I've felt before. I can't see if the sparks have burnt me, but La Contessa is ingenious; she's planned on inflicting the severest torment to my tackle without causing any permanent damage. She takes the branch and, pressing it against my side, rubs it against my flesh to burn the surface of my skin with three short lines in the shape of an 'N'.

"There, slave, that is my mark," she says, as she runs her finger across my skin and scrutinises the trail of scorched skin she has left. "'N' for La Contessa di Nemesia. It will leave a red mark on you as a reminder of your servitude. One day, I should brand you properly. I should like that. Then you would have a permanent reminder of who you belong to."

"Yes mistress," I mutter, too bamboozled with smoke, heat, and pain to protest at her declaration of intent.

"Well, we shall see. Julia, summon servants now and get him down. What a satisfying day; the hunt, stewed rabbit, roast slave. I've enjoyed it immensely!"

The servants haul the huge iron spit, with me tied onto it, out of the fireplace and untie me.

I flex my aching limbs, run my hands along my hot, glowing skin and admire La Contessa's mark etched into my side. I'm woozy and unsteady on my feet but, as is always the case with mistress, there's a glow of satisfaction and euphoria at having been used in such an extreme way. I'm tired now. The strain of the day having caught up with me, all I want to do is sleep.

Julia is concerned and attentive.

"Are you ok, Roberto?"

I nod.

La Contessa's eyes flash, "And what do you care, Julia? You show an undue consideration for this slave. Do you care for him?"

"No, madam," she stutters. "I just thought he looked unduly stressed."

"Stressed," she sneers. "What do you mean, *girl*?"

Julia prickles. I've never heard La Contessa use the expression before... Julia, maid, servant, but never *girl*; she usually reserves that for Becky.

"You're both dismissed," she says with a contemptuous wave of her hand.

21: Discovery

Julia takes my arm to aid me as I walk unsteadily out of the hall.

"That looked ghastly. Are you alright Roberto?" she asks, concern etched over her face.

"I'm fine, just a bit woozy. It wasn't as bad as it looked."

"She roasted you! And she's burnt your flesh. I'll get some ointment to put on it."

"Well, I suppose so. But she knew what she was doing. And besides I'm rather proud of the mark."

"You're a masochist! You actually enjoy this stuff, don't you? I don't know what to do with you."

"I guess so. It's hard to explain. I'm sore and knackered, and my skin is like it's on fire, but I feel alive."

Julia takes me to her room; brings a jug of water to quench my thirst, which I guzzle down in seconds, and a supper of bread, cheese, and grapes with red wine. I'm ravenous as I've had nothing to eat since breakfast. When I've finished eating Julia puts a cooling herbal unction on the burn.

"It's oil from the aloe vera plant. It's good for burns," she explains, carefully rubbing the soothing ointment onto the mark and the surrounding flesh. "It will leave a scar. Is it painful?"

"It throbs a bit, but the burn is only on the surface."

Julia traces the 'N' with her finger, "She's put her initial on you to mark that she owns you."

I can't argue with her observation!

I'm too tired for sex but we curl up together on her bed and embrace, Julia caressing my throbbing, glowing flesh.

Julia's room adjoins La Contessa's so her maid is available to her at all times.

I don't know, maybe we've got too complacent. During the journey and whilst waiting for our mistress's arrival, we've got used to sleeping together. We're too tired and lazy to move from the comfort of Julia's bed so we doze off there.

When I wake up in the early hours of the morning, I have a massive erection, which desperately requires attention. Julia looks so peaceful laying there, her luscious, ruby lips curled into a beatific smile. It seems a shame to disturb her, but my need is urgent. Her chestnut hair is tousled around her shoulders. I prefer to see it loose like this than when it's neatly brushed and pulled up into place by ivory combs. I can't resist reaching out and curling strands of it around my fingers. It feels full and lush and has the aroma of her perfume and fresh bed linen. My gentle touch is enough to rouse her. Her eyelashes flicker and she looks at me adoringly through narrow eyes, encouraging me to pursue my attentions. Her eyes close again. She's sleepy, but pliable and willing. I caress her cheek with a finger and she emits the slightest of moans. I put my hands under the coverlet and run them over the warm flesh of her breasts down to her sex. She groans and her eyes flicker open again.

"I want you inside me Roberto," she whispers.

I roll on top of her. My finger searches for her slit and parts the fleshy folds. I scoop up the moisture in her cunt and use it to rub her clit. Her groans are louder now. I put my hand over her lips.

"Sh," I whisper.

Maybe she's forgotten where she is, but I'm mindful La Contessa is sleeping in the adjoining chamber. In the morning, I'll have to smuggle out of Julia's room without being seen, but that's a problem for later. Right now my attentions are focused on Julia. I part her legs and probe her entrance with my hardness. She offers no resistance. Her back arches, inviting me to enter her. I'm gentle as I know she's still half asleep. I slide the stiffness of my cock into her slippery hole, she gasps through my fingers, my hand still over her mouth to muffle the sounds of her pleasure. I start slowly. This will be one of those leisurely, early morning screws. Besides, I can't fuck Julia too energetically as I daren't risk the noise of squeaking bed springs rousing La Contessa. It's a slow, luxurious fuck. My hand has moved away from Julia's lips but, as her moans get louder, I realise the only way to stifle them is to kiss her. So I put my lips to hers and my tongue seeks hers out. In this position my movements get stronger as I work myself up to my climax. I want her so much. I want to come inside her.

The sound of footsteps distracts me and I glance to one side. *Shit. Oh shit!*

In front of me there's an expanse of vividly coloured silk and the patterns of two fire-spewing dragons, clinging to voluptuous, feminine curves. It's La Contessa's dressing gown. I stop my fucking motion. My cock instantly loses its erection.

"So, my maid and my slave; finally caught in the act." Her tone is disdainful. "Get out of bed."

Julia's eyes spring open. She's wide awake now.

I slide my cock out, roll off Julia and scramble out of the bed. Julia looks mortified. She follows me, too stunned to utter a word. We both stand there, naked and guilty.

La Contessa's imposing presence towers over us. She has Lucio with her, looking smug and triumphant. It wouldn't surprise me if he'd been spying on us all along, reporting our activities back to mistress, as he's always possessed a disliking for me. There are a couple of other servants who look sheepish. The staff may or may not know what Julia and I have been up to since I arrived at the palazzo, but we are both popular and they don't appear to be taking any pleasure in our exposure.

La Contessa moves into the armchair. She beckons us both over and, with one imperious movement of her hand, gestures to us to get down on our knees before her. She nestles herself in the chair making herself comfortable, preparing for an interrogation of her two hapless victims.

"So is this what you call servitude? You repay the generosity of your mistress with a flagrant disregard for my rules and standards?"

There's silence. Julia looks shell-shocked at having been caught in the act, her brain calculating the terrible implications for her. There's nothing we can say. Denials are useless and false. We've been caught red handed.

"Have you nothing to say for yourselves?"

Her tone is forceful but calm, which is actually scarier. She never loses her temper, never loses control. I can sense her calculating what terrifying punishments she will inflict for such a gross betrayal of her trust.

"Did you really believe I never knew what was going on? Do you take me for a fool? You think I didn't know what was happening in my own household, under my very nose?"

Her words sink in.

My curiosity overcomes me, "You mean you knew all along?"

"Why, you fool. It is my business to know. I know everything. I am La Contessa di Nemesia. I am the strictest dominatrix in Venice. Do you think I can't rule my own household?"

"But when? When did you know?" I pursue.

"From the start. From the first time you had one another on the gondola when my maid picked you up from the streets. Her flushed cheeks, the enigmatic glow; I know when my maid has been fucked. Do you think the pair of you has been discreet?!"

A disdainful sneer spreads across her lips.

"The creeping into her room at night, the going out into the alleyways of Venice to find a hidden corner where you can make love, fucking her on the kitchen table; I know all of this. Some has been reported to me, the rest is instinct. I could give a list of the times you've been together. But in my bed... in my own hunting lodge? Do you think you can make a fool out of me? Well, believe me, you are mistaken. Lucio, show him."

Lucio presents the cover off La Contessa's bed from the night Julia wore the wolf skin coat and we made love in mistress's bed. She thrusts it under my nose triumphantly. It's still there, the stain from the other night.

"Spunk stains. You leave your disgusting mark on an antique tapestry cover." She turns to Julia, "You wear my fur coat. You try on my undergarments. What were you thinking of girl? I bring you into my household, I give you a home, a job, feed you, look after you. Is this how you repay me? With disrespect and deception."

Julia cracks. Her face is in her hands and she's sobbing.

"I'm sorry," she wails through the tears. "I'm sorry... *so, so sorry*. I'm sorry, madam. I didn't mean it. Really, I never meant it like that. I'm truly sorry."

"Sorry is not enough. I want punishment and retribution."

I can't help myself. I have to ask this question. I'm in so deep causing further offence to mistress will make no difference now.

"But why? If you knew all along why didn't you stop it? Why didn't you summon us before you and punish us, rather than let us continue?"

"Because it amused me, my slave. The thought of you scurrying around imagining you were being secretive and clever when I knew what you were up to all the time. This is a test of loyalty and discipline for you both, and you've been found wanting. I've been waiting to see how far you would go, merely waiting to choose the right moment to expose you. Do you really have nothing to say for yourselves?"

"Nothing mistress. What you say is true. Only that I'm prepared to submit myself to your judgement."

She narrows her eyes and her stare bores right through me, "And so you shall slave... so you shall."

Julia is in a pitiful state, collapsed on the floor sobbing. I feel sorry for her, I truly do. She has far more to lose than I. But we both knew the risks we were taking for our sexual pleasure, and for consummating our love.

"Stop your snivelling, and get up girl," La Contessa snarls.

Julia heaves her naked body up from the floor her head bowed, unable to look either La Contessa or me in the eye.

"The question now," La Contessa muses, "is what to do with the pair of you. Now there's an interesting quandary... let me see. I know, I have the perfect place to inflict my punishment for your disobedience. Lucio, take them to the olive press."

22: The Olive Press

Lucio leads Julia and I away from the hunting lodge to the stone farm buildings clustered behind the main house. He unlatches the wooden gates to the olive press and pushes us into the building.

I find it strange there's no effort to bind us. I'm strong and know I'm capable of overwhelming Lucio to make an escape, though I've no wish to do so. It's not because I expect La Contessa would recapture me and drag me back anyway, I've been fairly caught out and should face my punishment. Another thought occurs to me; am I secretly pleased to get caught? Is my behaviour, knowingly taking such risks under La Contessa's nose because I subconsciously want to be exposed? I can't deny that possibility. There's another reason for not fleeing; I don't want to leave Julia to face the situation alone. Whatever my confused emotions about my servitude to La Contessa, I do love Julia, and have a lot of affection for her. I'm furious with myself in allowing those feelings to drive us into this predicament.

Julia looks distraught. I try to catch her eye but she appears to be in her own world of guilt and misery, oblivious to anything. How quickly things can change. Only minutes ago I laid at her side admiring her beauty and, here she is now, eyes reddened and face etched with a profound sadness, unable to even exchange a glance with her lover.

We sit in silence waiting for La Contessa's arrival. Lucio is prowling around preventing any contact between us. He's gloating, I can tell. Indeed, he can't resist commenting on our plight.

He mocks me, "So, you thought you could get away with it? Fucking mistress's maid. I made sure she knew what you were up to. Now your arrogance and lust will get their just reward."

"Ah, young lady," he says disdainfully, turning towards Julia, "you have become mistress's confidante but now you are undone, betrayed by your desires and stupidly falling for this young fool. Now with you gone, I'll get complete control over the household."

Bastard. So, it seems Julia, and I have been caught up in another agenda, the web of Lucio's palace politics. I wonder if La Contessa knows of his ambitions, or his plotting to bring poor Julia down. Mind you, he's the fool if he believes he'll ever control La Contessa. Julia couldn't care less. Lucio's words have no impact on her. Her misery runs deeper than Lucio's pathetic household power struggles.

But Lucio has played his hand; in his moment of victory he has shown his ambitions whether he is wise or not remains to be seen.

Whilst waiting for La Contessa there's a chance to take in my surroundings. The olive press is an open-planned stone building, the equivalent of two storeys high, with white-washed walls. Rough wooden beams run across the building, some at ceiling height and others at what would be first floor level. In the centre, and dominating the space, is a huge cast iron frame and stone press with its cogs and wheels. Underneath it there is a large, shallow stone bowl used for gathering the oil once the olives have been pressed. The various implements used for the process: stone weights, wooden ladles, cast iron slatted spoons, funnels, and stoneware flagons are scattered around the building. There's a gallery at one end where barrels and jugs of oils are stored. My imagination is running away at the torment La Contessa can inflict with this stuff!

La Contessa arrives. She has changed out of her dressing gown and is wearing the same one-piece leather suit she had on last night. The gleam in her eyes is harsh and determined. Becky is behind her, naked with coils of rope hung over her shoulder like a human spindle, looking inscrutable as ever. Mademoiselle has come to watch the display too though her demeanour is subdued. She doesn't appear to be taking any pleasure out of this turn of events. For her, bondage and domination are a tool for sexual fun, but for La Contessa they're a serious business. She means it, it's part of who she is.

La Contessa's eyes flit around the olive press building, mentally noting its potential for sadistic punishment. She starts with me. She directs me to stand inside the stone bowl where the oil is gathered, with the press itself looming in front of me. The surface of the stone has a slick, oily texture. Lifting the coils of rope off the girl's shoulders, she begins by tying my ankles together. Then she ties my wrists and, throwing one end of the rope over a beam, she steps back and tugs at it until my arms are raised into the air. She pulls hard so the soles of my feet just touch the floor, and my arms are stretched. The rope is tied to one of the cast iron cogs used to turn the stones which crush the olives.

I'm compliant and offer no resistance. I understand why I need to be punished. I've no complaints. Indeed, dare I say I'm only too willing to submit to La Contessa, and accept whatever chastisement she desires to inflict.

She takes a narrower piece of rope, kneels in front of me and grasps my balls in her hand, pulling at them viciously. I let out a yelp.

165

"This is only the beginning, slave!" she exclaims.

She squeezes my balls and separates the two testicles with her fingers, running the cord between them, then threads the rope back around the base of the sac and pulls tightly. My balls are squeezed into two bulging blue-veined sacs. She holds one of them between her red painted fingernails and squeezes my testicle, her nails digging into the taut flesh. The pressure on my balls is intense and, again, I squeal at the intensity of the pain. She takes the loose end of the rope and secures it to a winch, part of the mechanism of the press. This enables her to pull the cord which in turn stretches my aching balls even further. She's not finished yet. La Contessa pulls the rope securing my arms and stretches them even further, forcing me onto tip toes. I'm in an awful predicament. She can cause untold agony by manipulating the ropes. My shoulders are aching, and I wonder how long I can hold this position.

La Contessa says nothing but, leaving me in this position, strides across to Julia. She takes her face between her hands and forces her to stare at me.

"Do you see your lover now? Observe the predicament he is in. You can watch him suffer, and then it will be your turn."

She removes more coils of rope from Becky, and secures one around Julia's ankles and ties her wrists with another, throwing the rope over a beam to haul her arms into the air. Julia does nothing to resist. Her eyes are blank and her body limp like a sock puppet. La Contessa could do anything with her and she wouldn't care. She takes one of Julia's nipples between her fingernails, squeezes it and then twists. There is a whimper as she finally gets a reaction from Julia. I feel sorry for her. I'm used to this treatment, after all, it's what La Contessa uses her slave for, but being naked and strung up is a new experience for Julia.

La Contessa strides over to one side of the building, the silver tips of her boots clicking on the stone slabbed floor. It's here where an array of tools is mounted on the wall, most of them fearsomely intimidating. Her back faces me so I can't see what she's selected. She returns with an armful of implements, dumping them into the circular stone trough with a clatter.

Her first act is to add to her ingenious cock and ball torture. She takes up a stone used as a counter-balance for the pulley of the press, and threads rope though a hole in the weight. She ties this onto the sac of my squeezed and stretched balls. She bends down in front of me whilst supporting the heavy stone, assessing its weight as she nestles it in her hand, the striking scarlet of her fingernails like flames against the dull grey of the stone.

"Do you see this slave?"

"Yes, mistress," I mumble.

"Can you see how heavy this stone is? You know I don't think I can hold onto it for much longer. And when I let go, imagine how the weight will pull on your balls."

I nod, acknowledging her taunts, and wait for the fateful moment when La Contessa releases the stone. She smiles a cruel smile.

"Oh, I'm only a feeble woman, the weight is simply too heavy for poor little me!"

She parts her hands and lets the stone go. It drops swiftly. The rope tugs on my balls and I expel a grunt. The pain is excruciating. The stone swings to a stationary position but it's a dead weight stretching my balls causing a relentless aching in my groin.

"Oh yes, that made you squeal. Was it painful slave?" she asks as she rests one hand against the press and raises a boot.

Even in my current predicament, I notice La Contessa is wearing my favourite pair of boots of hers, the ones with long silver-tipped heels and laced eyelets.

She kicks the stone weight with her boot.

"Ah," I scream as the weight swings from side to side, dragging my throbbing balls with it.

She lets the stone swing into a stationary position again, pauses a moment for effect, then kicks it again, this time harder.

"Oh," I shout.

"Your moaning and groaning is distracting, slave." She turns and calls behind her, "Mademoiselle, Would you do me the honour of lending me your knickers to gag this slave."

"*Mais oui*, madam. It would be my pleasure," she replies.

She hitches up her indigo velvet dress and wriggles her hips as she shuffles out of her knickers, and tosses them over to La Contessa.

"Mm. Look at these. Real silk, how delicious. And they are in the French style, see how petite they are."

She dangles them up before my eyes. They are beautiful, ivory silk with dainty lace trim. She pushes them up against my nose. They reek of Mademoiselle's French cologne.

"Smell them," she commands. "These are no Venetian bloomers. They are so small and tight, the material must have worked its way up into the crack of Mademoiselle's arse, and into her slit... and you know how wet she gets. Seeing you get tormented will be turning her on. Oh yes, see the damp patch where the crotch is. Open wide slave."

I obey and stretch my jaw open. She rolls the knickers into a ball and shoves them unceremoniously into my mouth. The silk is smooth on my tongue. They taste both sweet and salty, a delectable concoction of

Mademoiselle's perfume and body fluids. La Contessa ties a short length of rope around the back of my head and across my mouth to keep the gag in place. I'm conscious of my vulnerability, stretched out, every part of my body exposed to La Contessa's ministrations.

"Hm, now what can I use next," she ponders. "Ah, perhaps a little corporal punishment would be in order."

She chooses from the selection of implements. She selects a ladle, a large wooden spoon with a long handle used for mixing and blending the olive oils. She smacks it against the palm of her hand.

"Yes, that should cause a nasty sting."

She positions herself behind me and swings the wooden ladle against my backside. It hurts. My arse is already sore from being scratched by brambles from the hunt and roasted during the evening. La Contessa's first stroke is strong, vicious and heart-felt. The cup of the ladle makes a satisfying slapping noise as it strikes my flesh. She continues with another seven or eight heavy strokes and then pauses.

"Mademoiselle, would you like to take over?"

"*Mais perdone.* I hope you don't take offence but this punishment of your slaves is madam's business. It would not be right for me to interfere. I am content to watch an expert in the art of domination, madam."

"Very well, Mademoiselle, as you wish, but you are missing out on delivering exquisite pain. I know my slave girl will have no such reservations."

"No, mistress. I'll do anything you ask, mistress," answers Becky.

La Contessa continues with another series of powerful whacks with the ladle. Now my arse is sore and aching as well. It's funny how the pain of my stretched balls has receded as mistress switches her attention to my backside. They are a dull background throb now compared to the sharp pain of the ladle lashing across my bum.

She chooses another implement, this one nastier looking than the wooden ladle. It's a cast iron slatted spoon with a huge shallow bowl. It's used to run across the surface of the oil to pull out any detritus from the pressed olives. She rubs the underside of the metal against my chest. Its surface is rough with jagged edges of metal which dig into my nipples. I grunt into my knicker-gag.

"Oh yes. This is a nasty little thing. It's rather crude and, being only a tool, the blacksmith has no need to smooth its surface. As you can see, slave, it has nasty pointed edges."

She raises the metal spoon high in the air and crashes it against my arse. It stings horribly. It's not only the jagged edges digging into my skin, but also the slats of the spoon which hit with such force they make an impression in my flesh. She hits me again... and again. The strikes are so powerful they

168

cause the stone weight hanging from my balls to swing in time to the strokes and pull on my balls. After she finishes with the object, she runs her hand across my throbbing backside.

"How satisfying," she says. "The slats have left a pattern across your arse, and the points have pressed into your flesh and left little indentations. How artistic. Mademoiselle, you must come and admire the pattern when I've finished with him."

"I can see them from here. As you say, madam, you are an artist."

La Contessa still hasn't finished with me. I wonder what implement she will use next. She picks up a reddish stone flagon and removes its stopper. She smells the oil inside.

"Extra virgin olive oil, the purest blend produced on the farm. It seems a shame to waste it on a slave, but on the other hand..."

Shit. What's she planning?

She beckons Becky over and whispers in her ear. Many of the ropes coiled round her have been used to tie up Julia and I; she pulls the rest over the girl's head. Removed of her coat of coils, she's now naked. La Contessa passes her the flagon of olive oil.

Becky steps behind me, her bare feet padding on the stone slabs. The next thing I notice is a strange sensation. There's something slimy and oily being drizzled across my backside. It's the olive oil. The oil is cool against the red, throbbing flesh. It trickles down my arse and runs into the crack. It's a pleasant sensation, the slickness is disarmingly comforting on my skin, and over the exposed orifice of my anus. Becky rubs the oil over my backside, working it over, and into, the hole. I sense the touch of something hard being inserted into my arse, the oil allowing Becky's finger to slide into the hole with ease. I've got to confess, I love the sensation of anal play. It's so intimate and disgusting to have your most vulnerable orifices explored in the way Becky is doing. There's the perfect balance between the pain of being stretched, and delectable pleasure.

"What are you doing, girl?" La Contessa's voice is harsh, "This is meant to be a punishment for him. Look at his eyes, he's enjoying it girl. Here, give me the oil."

She grabs the flask of olive oil off Becky, and steps behind me.

"It is a nice picture though. If only you could see it my slave. Red spots on glowing bronzed skin, with dark green oil, and the girl's finger stuck up your hole. You can take your finger out now girl. Pass me the funnel."

I remember seeing this object hung on the wall. It's one of a series of funnels of varying sizes used for decanting the oil into storage vessels. My instincts tell me La Contessa would have chosen the largest one. I'm not wrong. She does not stand on ceremony. It's thrust right inside me and pushed hard. I gasp into the gag. Then I experience the most bizarre sensation, an oily sensation not on my skin but inside me. The oil oozes out of the funnel into my anal passage. La Contessa pours the olive oil out of the flagon into me. The viscous fluid is filling me up and stretching my anus. She pulls the funnel out.

"Hold it all in slave. I don't want you to squeeze any oil out until I say so. Girl, pick up the ladle. You know what to do with it."

Becky slides the long handle into my arse. My hole is so well oiled and slippery there's no resistance. It doesn't stretch me though I can feel its length inside me. The girl pushes it in and out, and twists it around. I might have found the sensation comforting, except I notice the new object of torment La Contessa has taken up.

It's a long metal tool with a handle at one end and a hook at the other. I've no idea what it's used for, but I've a pretty good idea where it might be going. La Contessa pours olive oil over my cock. I can see it now. The oil is thick, slimy, and green. As she said, it must be the highest grade of oil produced by the farm. She takes my cock in her hand and rubs its tip, working the oil into the hole. She carefully inserts the hook end of the tool into my penis. Tying more rope around the handle she secures the implement to one of the beams. The hook stretches my urethra and tugs the end of my cock. La Contessa kicks the weights hanging from my balls. My instinctive reaction is to flinch from the pain, but doing this has the effect of making the hook tug inside me, causing yet more agony. La Contessa has created a devilish piece of predicament bondage.

"Girl, pull the handle out and use the spoon now," she orders

The thin piece of wood Becky's been using to probe my anal canal slips out. I'm still filled with olive oil so it slides out easily. I endure the pressure of being stretched as she pushes the wide end of the ladle past my sphincter, and the sense of relief when it passes through the tight hole into my anus. She twists the ladle. I try to keep relaxed and let the wooden object do its work, knowing that if I react, I will only pull on the ball weights and hook. It's not an enviable position to be in!

"Take it out now, girl. You have permission to empty your bowels slave."

Becky eases the ladle out of me. The critical and most painful point is when it's passed back through the narrow channel of my sphincter again. There's a sense of relief when the object pops out. I push my bowel muscles and let the olive oil squeeze out of my backside. It runs down my legs, no longer cooling, but hot and oily. Some of it gushes out onto the stone basin where I stand. The thick fluid oozes between my toes. But I have to say it's a massive relief to empty my bowels.

Whilst Becky is doing this, La Contessa steps over to the miserable, fearful Julia to taunt her. Meanwhile, Mademoiselle reclines on the edge of a stone gulley wide-eyed and open-mouthed, appreciating her lesson in extreme bondage and domination.

"Ah, your poor lover. See the hook up his cock. He had better not make any sudden movements or his cock won't be fit for anything, it will be rendered useless for fucking you, my maid."

All the time La Contessa teases Julia she tweaks her nipples, making her writhe and wriggle against the ropes.

"It will be your turn soon. What object will I use on you maid," she taunts gesturing to tools hanging from hooks on the wall. "Look, there are scythes for cutting the olive trees, they have a sharp point. The funnels and ladles. They would be fun to insert up your cunt. Oh, yes, it will soon be your turn to squirm and squeal. I'll keep you wondering for a while longer though, because I haven't finished with my slave yet."

I don't like the sound of that. La Contessa slips the hook out of the end of my cock, much to my relief. It's red and sore but there's no sign of any lasting damage.

"Put your hands out girl," she orders Becky.

She dutifully cups her hands and holds them out for her mistress. La Contessa takes up the flagon of olive oil again and pours some into the girl's waiting hands.

"Use the oil to make him hard."

I ought to like the sound of that, but I suspect La Contessa has a sinister motive for encouraging me to get an erection. I see the pool of green oily liquid in Becky's cupped hands. She pours it over my cock. It's cool and soothing against my red raw member. She rubs the oil over my cock, working it from a tortured, flaccid object into a hardening piece of flesh. It takes only a few short minutes of Becky manipulating my cock and running her fingers along its oily length before I get a hard-on.

"Is he hard yet?"

"Yes, mistress."

"I expect you'd like to suck him, wouldn't you girl?"

"Yes, mistress, if it pleases you mistress."

"No, it does not. I've no intention of letting you pleasure him. He's had too much pleasure lately. As I loosen the rope, I want you to pull him forward and lay his erect cock on the press."

Throughout my ordeal I've been stood in the round stone trough in which the oil is gathered, with the olive press looming in front of me. I suddenly realise the ingenuity of La Contessa putting me in this position. As she slackens the rope holding my arms in the air, the soles of my feet return to the ground, a huge relief as my calf and thigh muscles are stiff. Indeed, I wonder how I've been able to keep this position for so long. Becky pulls my groin forward and rests my erection onto the stone.

This is scary. I see La Contessa's intent clearly. The stone forms the base where the olives are laid. Before me, a full four feet above, and reaching up into what would be the second storey of the building,

is the olive press. There's a huge wheel with metal cogs at the top, linked to a smaller wheel and a spindle. The mechanism turns a thick corkscrew which moves the upper half of the stone press downwards. The olives get crushed between the two stone wheels with the oil being forced into a grooved channel into the stone bowl where I'm standing.

La Contessa laughs sadistically. "Ah yes, I can see from your expression you know what I plan."

Old Lucio, who has been quietly watching proceedings from the side, sniggers.

"Oh, my punishments amuse you do they?" she snaps.

"No mistress," he splutters. "I've only tried to serve your interest dutifully, mistress."

"Be careful, my friend, or it will be you strung up there. Don't think I haven't noticed what your game is. I know you've tried to make an enemy of my slave, and you've long been jealous of Julia's influence. Perhaps, Lucio, my whole household needs shaking up because I will hold for no petty rivalries amongst the staff in my palazzo."

Yes. That's wiped the smug look off Lucio's face. She's seen through him. My respect for her has never been greater, despite the dastardly torment she's about to inflict on me.

"So, see how it works my slave. I turn this handle, which turns the spindle that turns the small wheel which turns the big wheel that turns the screw which pushes the stone down. You watch the stone get closer and closer until your penis is caught between the two stones. Then the top stone is turned against the bottom stone, the one your cock is resting on, as if I need to remind you. So, like the olives from the plantation, your cock gets crushed. Wicked, is it not?"

I'd already worked it out for myself, and yes... it's wicked.

La Contessa turns the handle and sets the whole process in motion. The well-oiled thread works the press and pushes the stone, slowly but inexorably, downwards.

"The technology is simple but effective, don't you think?"

I watch the stone as it's lowered by the press; the stone which must way a ton and is used to crush a whole season's crop of olives. It's soon only inches away from cock, still erect and helpless. I feel the touch of the cool, rough stone on my member. La Contessa inspects it.

"Yes, it can lower a fraction more."

I gasp loudly, surely audible even with the gag. La Contessa is in her element, loving every moment of her sadistic punishment.

"Ah, here's the donkey to turn the stone," she announces.

I glance across in trepidation. I hadn't noticed Becky leave the building. She returns now with a bridle on, a metal bit in her mouth and a leather harness on her body. She's been turned into a human donkey. La Contessa attaches her harness to hooks in the side of the upper stone. With Becky in position she takes a horse whip from the wall and cracks its cord against her arse.

"Come on girl, get to work!" she calls as she whips the girl again.

Becky struggles hard to shift the heavy stone. She moves it a few inches. It's enough, more than enough, to suffer the crushing weight of the stone rubbing against my cock. The pain is excruciating, a combination of pressure and the rough surface of the stone inflicting agony on my hard cock. La Contessa laughs. Mademoiselle applauds.

"*Incroyable*!" she exclaims.

La Contessa holds the whip high above her head and slashes it against her rump. I see a dark welt mark forming on her pale flesh. Becky bites onto the bit and strains to pull the stone a few more inches. There are several more severe lashes before she realises the girl can't shift the stone another fraction.

"How wonderful my maid," says La Contessa turning her attention to Julia. "What a perfect punishment. To have my slave girl crush my slave's cock! Don't you find it amusing maid?"

Julia says nothing.

"What's wrong? Oh dear, have you lost your sense of humour? Are you worried about what happens next? Cheer up. Who knows, I might not be as cruel to you as to my male slave."

She takes hold of one Julia's nipples between her finger nails and gives it a nasty twist.

"Or I might not punish you at all, but dismiss you from my service," La Contessa says turning away from her.

"No! Please no. No!" Julia screams.

We look over in surprise. Julia has stood quiet in her misery for so long that, coming out of nowhere, her piercing scream is shocking. I know Julia is not used to being punished but surely the tweak of her nipples is never enough to explain this heart-rending wail.

La Contessa, her back to Julia, cocks her head to one side, "What's wrong with you girl, can't you take a little punishment?"

"Punish me! Punish me, madam. Punish me all you want. But don't send me away. Please, anything but that. I couldn't live without you, madam. Please, not that. I owe everything to you. Don't you see... I love you! I love you more than anything. I live for you. I love every second serving you. Please. Punish me. Whatever it takes. But give me another chance. Please don't dismiss me."

La Contessa stops in her tracks.

She has her back to Julia so I can see the expression on her face. She doesn't know. She's never realised. In all those years Julia has worked for her she's never understood what her maid really feels for her. Julia's outburst doesn't surprise me. I've been aware of it the whole time I've been in the palazzo. It's obvious whenever I've seen them together that Julia adores her mistress. I've noticed the way she talks about La Contessa, how she hangs on her every word and, more recently, how jealous she has become of the attention her mistress has given the slave girl. Of course she loves La Contessa.

La Contessa stands motionless digesting this turn of events.

I try to read her expression. There's shock, confusion, indecision. I've never seen La Contessa look so uncertain as in those fleeting seconds. I wait to see if she recovers her composure, but she remains shaken by Julia's revelation. She's used to people doing whatever she commands, complimenting her, and worshipping her, but I wonder if anybody has told her they love her. Love her with the honesty and passion Julia does.

She takes a deep breath and turns to face Julia.

"You say this word 'love' Julia, but what does it mean to you?"

Breathless and sobbing, Julia composes herself to reply to La Contessa, "Don't you see madam, I live for you. I love every minute in your presence. I love serving you, helping you, touching you, being part of your world. I can't help it. You took me in and were the first person to show me kindness. I owe everything to you, madam. Please madam, please don't throw me out on the streets. I don't know what I'll do without you."

"That is as maybe but you repay me by disobeying my rules and going behind my back. You know who I am. I am La Contessa. I am the strictest dominatrix in Venice, yet you take these risks knowing the likely consequences."

Julia breaks down again, "I know, I know. I'm sorry mistress. I'm so sorry. I don't have the words to say what I feel. I have sexual needs, I know. If I could never have you, I had to express them somehow. But what I really wanted was you."

"What do you mean?"

"I wanted you to touch me, to have me, and I so desired to give myself to you. All those years that's what I've wanted. And then Becky came along. You know when you took her up the arse with the strap-on; well I wished it was me. I so wanted you to be inside *me*."

La Contessa is wide-eyed and shocked. She never realised she was an object of Julia's desire.

"You wanted to be my submissive?"

"No. Not really," she sobs, "that's not who I am. I wanted you. I know it sounds silly and I know it can never happen but, I wanted you... as a lover."

"Oh... and the boy, Roberto, do you love him?"

My ears prick up. This will be interesting.

"Yes. Not like you, not in the same way. I don't know. It's just different. But yes, I do love him."

"But you see why he needs to be punished?"

"Yes, madam. Of course he does. I do too, I know. Do It. Do it now. I'll take anything from you, but please madam, please don't send me away. I'm sorry. I'm truly repentant. Please give me another chance."

There's silence. La Contessa appears to be taking it all in. It's hard to read her expression. Suddenly she springs into action.

"Lucio, get these two down," she orders, her manner brusque and business-like. "And prepare for our return to Venice. They can go on ahead... in separate carriages."

"Mademoiselle, I apologise for our sudden return but I have business to attend to, aside from dealing with my maid and slave. I promise I shall make it up to you, by inviting you to be my special guest for the *Carnevale*."

La Contessa marches out of the olive press with a bemused Mademoiselle following her. What an abrupt end to proceedings, and strange turn of events.

23: The Reckoning

The return journey from the hunting lodge is long and miserable. Julia and I are kept apart, so we both face the long hours along the bumpy roads alone, left to speculate La Contessa's next move. The abrupt ending of her punishments in the olive press, and the sudden departure of her entourage for the palazzo, has provided no hint as to how she will deal with either of us.

Back in the palazzo we are confined to our room under the strict instruction there can be no communication between us until La Contessa returns to Venice. The curious thing is we are not kept as prisoners; my room is not locked. When Vincenzo brings a tray of food for me the first evening after our arrival he explains that Julia and I are permitted no contact but are both entirely free to leave if we choose. I question him about this.

"You mean I can walk out the palazzo at any time?"

"Yes, my friend, that's how I understand it. If we see either of you leaving, we've been told not to stop you. It's been made clear you're not to be kept against your will. So, what will you do?"

"Oh, I've no intention of leaving," I reply. "I have to face La Contessa's judgement, and I can't leave Julia to face this on her own."

"I thought not. Good luck Roberto. I know it cuts no ice with the mistress, but the other staff are behind you. They don't want to see you or Julia thrown out of the palazzo."

"Thanks Vincenzo. Your support means a lot."

I keep to the confines of my room for two days after which La Contessa arrives back from the hunting lodge. In the evening I receive message of an appointment with her at eleven the next morning.

I'm despondent. If she dismisses me, which I'm expecting, then I'll be upset not least because my own arrogance and carelessness has betrayed us. I've loved my time in the palazzo, loved serving mistress, and I will miss being part of her twisted sexual games. But it's Julia I feel for. She's spent her adult life serving La Contessa. To lose all this will be devastating for her. And where this leaves me and Julia, I don't know.

The next day I'm taken to La Contessa's chambers. When I enter she's sitting at her bureau, her back turned, deep in conversation with two flamboyantly dressed men. Julia is already there. She looks terrible; her hair dishevelled and her eyes blood shot as if she's been crying the last couple

176

of days. It's heart-rending to see her in this state as she usually has such an uplifting disposition and always looks well-presented and beautifully made-up. Becky is there too. The three of us are wearing our uniforms in La Contessa's livery, which is unusual for the girl as she usually wears no clothes.

La Contessa finishes off her business and, as the two men turn to one side, I recognise them. It's Viola and Lucretia, as I know them.

"Yes, Contessa, piracy is a terrible thing," says Viola.

"I know, it's simply shocking," echoes Lucretia.

"Such a shame. A whole ship's worth of goods too. The value of the cargo must have been enormous," says La Contessa.

"A veritable fortune, my dear."

"What will the Doge and the Council of Ten do now? They have such massive debts," says Lucretia.

"Indeed, they do," La Contessa smirks. "And the interest on them is considerable... and will need to be paid."

"My dear, you should dress as a pirate for the *Carnevale* Ball," suggests Viola.

"That would be deliciously daring, darling," Lucretia adds.

La Contessa laughs. "Perhaps I will. You are coming then, I take it."

"Oh we wouldn't miss it for anything, would we?"

"It's the highlight of the Venetian social calendar, my dear, and I believe this year's will be especially entertaining."

"Until then my friends," says La Contessa concluding her business.

What a double act they are! It's strange to think back to my chance meeting with these two transvestites only to find they act as her nefarious agents.

When they turn around they instantly recognise me.

"Well, look who it is?" says Viola.

"I hear you've been a naughty boy."

"A very naughty boy!"

Lucretia turns to La Contessa, "If you've no use for him, we'll take him off your hands."

"Yes, we can find plenty of uses for him, my dear."

I nod to acknowledge their good humoured banter.

After Lucretia and Viola leave, La Contessa spins around from her bureau to confront us. She's dressed, demurely for her, in a simple velvet dress with a cameo broach at its neck, her hair piled on her head, and held in place by two ivory combs. She's dressed for business, but is no less a formidable figure for that. The doubt and confusion of those final moments in the olive press are gone; there's clarity in her eyes and her voice is calm and authoritative.

"So, my slave, you have knowingly gone behind your mistress's back to indulge your own sexual desires with my most trusted personal maid. Why should I not throw you back into the alleyways of the Cannaregio where I found you?"

This is the moment of reckoning. In the days since our return to the palazzo I've been running through my head how I could reply to this very question. There's no answer I can give. I would dearly love to continue serving La Contessa but I have to face up to it; when I see it from my mistress's perspective, my behaviour has been abominable.

"I have no excuses mistress. From the moment we met there was a spark of attraction between me and Julia and, it's true, neither of us has been able to control it, despite knowing it wasn't permitted. I understand how my behaviour offended mistress and I can only say I will accept whatever judgement you reach. I do love Julia, I can't help it. But, despite what I've done, I respect mistress, and this time I've spent in the palazzo as your slave have been special. I would dearly love to continue serving mistress but acknowledge the matter is entirely in your hands."

There, I've said what I needed to. Her expression betrays nothing.

"So, Becky, I know you are not guilty of any deception, but you have unwittingly found yourself a protagonist in this episode. Do you have anything to say for yourself?"

"Only that my desire is only to serve you mistress. I do whatever mistress requires from me and surrender to her will and, in doing so, I bear no ill-will to Julia or Roberto. It's a privilege to submit to such an awesome and cruel, but fair, mistress. The staff of her household have only ever treated me with kindness and respect."

"Ah, now I turn to you my maid. You have had time to reflect. Is there anything else you have to say?"

"There's nothing I can add, madam. I've opened myself up to you and expressed my innermost feelings. I love you and would do anything to continue serving you. There's nothing else I can do or say to change that, so I can only submit to your judgement," Julia explains with dignity despite the emotional turmoil she's obviously in.

La Contessa turns back to Becky, "What would *you* do my slave girl? How do you think I should deal with my disobedient servants?"

Becky looks wide-eyed and startled. I doubt anybody's asked her opinion about anything before!

"Oh... me, mistress? You really want to know what I think?" she stammers, flustered because the person she submits to so completely, the person she's so used to obeying, wants to hear her view.

"Yes girl. I want your opinion on this subject. Contrary to what you might think, I listen to my servants. After all, I have to understand them to come up with the most fitting punishments for them," she smiles.

"Oh, well." she stutters hesitantly before growing in confidence. "I do have a view, mistress. You see, I've spent much of my life trying to find out who I am, trying to come to terms with my submissive nature. It's taken me into dark places and I've made poor choices or circumstances have driven me into bad places, but now I've found the mistress I can truly give myself up to. But the lesson I've learned is to stay true to who I am. Now, if Julia and Roberto truly love one another, and I believe they do, I believe they should be given the chance to express those feelings. I can see in what she says and does that Julia is devoted to you mistress. She lives for you, far more than I. If you sent me away from you I would be bereft, but I would find another master or mistress to serve because that's my nature. I've observed her, and I believe she needs you, as a benefactor and... as a friend even."

I steal a glance across at Julia. She has turned to Becky with a look of open-mouthed amazement. Neither of us expected her view to be canvassed, let alone to find such an articulate ally in her.

"And I've observed Roberto and I think he too is devoted to you, mistress, in his own way. He may not have the same submissive nature as I, but he is willing to do anything to serve you mistress. So, I believe it would be sad if they had to give up their love for one another and a shame, and loss to mistress, to lose them as servants. But, I understand mistress's dilemma. They have disobeyed you and gone behind your back and, for that, they should be punished. But whether the punishment should be expulsion from mistress's household, only mistress can decide."

I don't think I've heard Becky say more than two sentences in the time she's been serving in La Contessa's household, yet here she is with such an eloquent summing up of the situation.

La Contessa sits at her bureau, concentration etched on her face. Julia looks pensive. Now is surely the moment of truth. What will her mistress decide?

La Contessa composes herself. She stands up, the heels of her boots click ominously on the tiled floor as she takes up her position in front of the three of us, the imposing dominatrix she is.

"Julia...," she pauses for what seems like an age and Julia looks as though she's about to burst. "I took you into my service many years ago when you were a young orphan and you have served me loyally since then. There are times when I have truly valued your companionship over those years though I may never have said so. For that reason I cannot find it in my heart to dismiss you. You may stay as my maid."

There is an outpouring of relief and emotion from Julia, "Oh, madam. Thank you. Thank you so much. Thank you for your forgiveness."

"Wait, there is more. I have listened to what you say and respect that you have exposed your innermost feelings for me. You may love me if you wish, my maid, but I cannot vouch the love can be returned in the way you desire it. I can involve you in my play perhaps, but you must understand you cannot be an equal; you must always be subservient to my needs. Do you understand that?"

"Yes mistress, I accept what you say. I'm so relieved mistress has given me another chance."

"And the boy," La Contessa says waving her hand dismissively at me, "do you still love him?"

"Yes mistress, I do, though in a different way."

"Listen to me Julia. I will not have any jealousy or rivalry in my household. I will use my slaves however I see fit, and for whatever tasks I wish. So, such envy of my slave girl you hold must be cast aside. Can you do this?"

"Yes, yes, madam, I can find it in my heart to do that."

She flings herself at Becky and throws her arms around her. The girl doesn't know how to respond, but eventually closes her arms around Julia to give her a hug.

"Thank you, Becky. I shall always be indebted to you for your generous words. I see you never intended me or Roberto any harm."

Becky looks bemused, "My mistress asked me and I gave an honest opinion. What else would I do?"

I smile. Now, that's the mark of a true submissive, to define all you say and do in terms of servitude to your mistress.

"Ah, now we come to my slave, Roberto. What am I to do with you? You are too cocky for a slave; which is a lesson you will have to learn for the future…"

"…for the future," I gasp.

"That is an excellent example, interrupting your mistress before she's finished! Yes, despite all, I have rather come to enjoy your company. You amuse me. Also, I am pleased with the rapport established between my slave and slave girl. So, yes, I will retain you in my household."

"Thank you, mistress. Thank you so much. I'm speechless."

"Well, that will make a change. There is one final thing. I have toyed with you over these last months. I could have brought your liaison to an end at any time but I chose not to. I do not object to sex as such. There are lessons I will take from this whole affair. Consequently, I will allow you and Julia to continue your relationship, though of course your needs must be subservient to your mistress's at all times. Is this clear? And to be fair I will extend this relaxation of my rules to the rest of my household staff."

"Madam. I don't know what to say…"

"I've made my judgement; I need no fawning exclamations of gratitude. Let us draw a line under this episode. I want us to move on in the context of this new understanding of my wishes. There is the *Carnevale* to prepare for. I want my staff and slaves focused on that. You will all have a role to play. Julia, I will give you and Roberto this afternoon off as you will, no doubt, wish to share your reactions to my decisions. But I want you back this evening to discuss my costume for the *Carnevale*. I like the idea of a pirate… a debauched, dominatrix pirate. It amuses me… though I doubt the Doge will enjoy the joke. You are dismissed for now."

With a wave of La Contessa's hand we troop out of her boudoir.

Once outside, Julia is jumping up and down, ecstatic with joy.

"I can't believe it! I was expecting the worse. I can still serve her and keep my lover. I thought I'd end up with nothing."

"I'm shocked. I don't know what to make of it," I reply.

"I'm pleased for you both," interrupts Becky. "I did not want to see your chance for love taken away."

"We are the best of friends, Becky," says Julia. "I understand you are only ever serving madam as loyally as I do. I see you did nothing to drive a wedge between me and Roberto. I'm sorry if I've ever treated you badly. But why did she have us back? Why would she let us carry on seeing one another?"

"Julia, you have to remember she was playing with us all along, watching us carry on like we did amused her. I think your declaration of love shocked her though. I was watching her reaction, and it was like a jolt went through her. She didn't realise… and she didn't know how to react. In a strange way, I actually think she's grown fond of us."

Julia grabs hold of my hand and pulls me along the corridor.

"Enough talking! Sorry Becky," she calls back, "if you'll excuse us, Roberto and I have got an afternoon to do some catching up, if you know what I mean…"

24: The Grand Canal

Life at the palazzo has returned to its bizarre normality. La Contessa remains in complete control of her household. Lucio's ambitions having been exposed, he now keeps a low profile and astutely confines himself to his previous spheres of power in the palazzo. Meanwhile, Julia is restored to her former place of influence as La Contessa's personal maid and confidante. I remain as her slave, available to her at all times for her sadistic pleasure. Becky continues as her slave girl though since the recent events I've noticed she's acquired a new confidence and ease with herself. Without anything further being said since La Contessa's meeting, we are aware a new understanding as to our roles has been reached.

The main beneficiary of the arrangement is Julia. Those few days of misery and uncertainty have been put to one side, and she has returned with a reinvigorated dedication, an expression of her gratitude to her mistress. Her service to La Contessa, her determination to fulfil every command to its exacting detail is back. It's a delight to see her breezy good nature and enthusiasm return. I do wonder if La Contessa ever intended to dismiss Julia. I've observed them together, and Julia is a good companion to her mistress. She would have been missed, there's no doubt about it. There's also a positive effect on Julia's physical appearance too. She looked terrible at one point, wan and dishevelled, but now she is lovelier than ever. Her olive skin is glowing, her rouged cheeks are flushed with good health and her whole demeanour exudes positivity.

The sex under the new arrangement with La Contessa is amazing. The demands on our time from our mistress are such that we see one another no more than before, but when we are together, it's liberating to know we're no longer doing anything behind her back. Our proclamations of respect and desire to serve her are, and always were, true, so to be released from any sense of going against her will is a burden lifted. We can be open about our feelings for each other. No more creeping around the corridors of the palazzo looking over our shoulders to see who might be watching. Lucio might not like it, but La Contessa has spoken so he must put up with it. Although it's likely the household always knew what we were up to, now our shows of affection are more public.

The staff are pleased with the outcome. We know we always had supporters and friends amongst them. We are doubly popular now because La Contessa has relaxed rules about relationships, including sex, for everyone. The consequence is that previously suppressed emotions can be expressed with a resulting release of tensions. The impact is immediate as the household has never been more relaxed, nor its service to its mistress more enthusiastic and heartfelt.

The mistress has noticed this, commenting on one occasion, "I believe more sex has been beneficial for the household. As long as they serve me with such enthusiasm, I do not care. Perhaps it was a mistake to enforce a rule of celibacy."

Julia has taken La Contessa's instruction on board and shaken off any jealousies she had of Becky's role. Make no mistake La Contessa has tested her, deliberately creating scenarios where I've been made to play with the slave girl, having me penetrate her in view of Julia to test her reaction. Julia's been helping Becky with her dress and make-up, choosing items from La Contessa's vast wardrobe of corsets, tight leather, boots, and other fetish wear for Becky to wear, so she can please her mistress. And Becky has responded to Julia's kindness; she's been telling Julia about her misadventures across Europe with the various masters she served.

It's as well the palazzo is in such a harmonious state because it's a busy time. The preparations for *Carnevale* occupy the household's time, and there's a regatta to plan. La Contessa's barge will lead the flotilla along the Grand Canal, which was one of the conditions imposed for extending the interest of her loans to the Doge and the Council of Ten. Then there's the grand finale, the spectacular *Carnevale* ball, which will be held in the grand ballroom of Palazzo Cavalli. I can't wait. The ballroom is the one room of the palazzo I've never seen as it's only opened up for such special occasions, though talk of its opulence is rife amongst the household.

There are deliveries to the palazzo on a daily, indeed hourly, basis: orchids and other flowers to decorate the rooms, barrels of oysters, kids, lambs, and calves for the banquet, boxes of fine wines and *malvasia*, breads and patisseries from the confectioners. The palazzo is a hive of activity. Julia is in constant demand helping her mistress with the arrangements.

La Contessa is making other preparations though these are more secretive. I've an insight into how ruthlessly she's manipulating the ruling elite and get further evidence of this one day. I find myself strung up in La Contessa's boudoir having been subjected to various forms of cock and ball torture for her entertainment when she has a visitor. It's Allessandro Fernasse again. He heaves his corpulent body into the room. He takes up a seat by the bureau alongside La Contessa where the pair hold an intense discussion.

183

They talk in whispers so I only hear snippets of the conversation, but what I do hear confirms my suspicions.

"We are in a desperate plight, madam. Please, is there nothing you can do to help us?"

"Yes, indeed, it is most unfortunate your cargo should be taken by pirates. Regrettably it is one of the risks of trade these days. But I can see a way out of your difficulties if you can persuade the Council of Ten to accede to my demands..."

At this point La Contessa's voice goes quieter. Usually, she's not bothered what her slaves hear, but there's something going on she wants to keep secret. I pick up more of the conversation later.

"If you persuade the Council to ally itself with me, then an accommodation is possible. So, now you know my conditions."

"This is unprecedented, Contessa. I hear your demands but the Republic of Venice would have seen nothing like this in its long history. Personally, I'm sympathetic to your cause, but you must appreciate my difficulties in persuading other members of the Council."

"The matter is perfectly simple, my friend. If they do not agree, I have the power to bankrupt the Doge and the Council. The Ten can save themselves from impoverishment if they disown the Doge and align themselves with me. The argument must be persuasive."

"Yes, I know, Contessa. But what you ask will turn the governance of Venice upside down."

"Yes. Obviously, this is my intention. My ambitions are clear. You must use your considerable political wiles to persuade them they have little choice. No banker will lend them money now, not at an affordable interest rate. Make no mistake, Alessandro, I will call in my debts if you do not agree to my terms."

"I will do what I can, Contessa. I would agree to your terms. I have no wish to end my days in poverty. I will muster my powers of persuasion to convince a majority they have no choice. The decision will be made one way or the other by the finale of the *Carnevale*. I understand you and appreciate the sense of theatre you want to bring to the ball."

"Come, you will love it, Alessandro," smiles La Contessa. "Released from the shackles of the Doge and the church, *La Serenissima* will enter a golden age of perversion and debauchery!"

"Indeed, madam, indeed. I can believe it."

"I trust you are still wearing your chastity device?" asks La Contessa. "The moment of your release fast approaches, and the rewards for you are considerable if you can achieve this last thing for me."

"Yes madam, I'm still wearing it, though several people have commented on the bulge in my breeches. I would not dare contravene a command of yours, Contessa."

She laughs. "Excellent. Imagine the relief from all the pent up frustration when it comes, should you be successful."

I listen intently, despite being hung up to the ceiling in rope bondage with nipple clamps, ball weights, and a butt plug shoved up my arse. What's she plotting? What demand did she put to Alessandro that could be so radical? I'm intrigued.

So, what with plans for the *Carnevale* and her political intrigues, La Contessa is exceedingly busy.

The excitement in the palazzo builds to a crescendo. *Carnevale* is the highlight of Venice's social calendar. I remember fondly from my childhood joining the throngs of people who filled the city. The whole city comes onto the squares and canal sides during *Carnevale,* and it attracts thousands of visitors. It's a raucous, licentious event. The lanes are filled with jesters, snake charmers, jugglers, conjurors, and fire eaters. Music and dancing go on throughout the day and late into the night. Everybody wanders the streets masked whether with a simple *moretta* or an elaborately decorated mask. The social order is turned upside down. Noblemen dress as country bumpkins, great ladies as milk maids, whilst maids dress as great ladies and butlers as gentlemen... men dress as women and women as men. *Carnevale* is a glorious statement of the Republic's tolerance, debauchery, and unique style. And we will be at the centre of it.

La Contessa's giant ceremonial barge will lead the regatta, and we will be on it. By we, I mean Julia, Becky and myself, and Mademoiselle La Tour as La Contessa's special guest. We will be alongside her as a 'decorative accompaniment' and have a central role to play as part of the entertainment for the grand ball. I can't wait. Whatever she has planned, it will be wonderful.

The flotilla of barges, *fellucas,* and gondolas assembles on the banks of the Canale di San Marco. It will take a route past the Doge's palace, with the backdrop of the campanile of San Marco and the domes of the basilica; then follow the length of the Grand Canal. It's at the moorings in the canal basin where we join La Contessa's barge, which I see for the first time.

It's magnificent. The barge is vast, the largest and grandest in the whole flotilla which comes as no surprise. Its black-lacquered hull is decorated by a line of gilded, golden mermaids with naked breasts. Its prow is in the shape of a black swan's graceful neck and head with golden beak, and red rubies for its eyes. At the stern a *felce* is supported by columns carved as gold dragons with a gilded throne upholstered in scarlet velvet on a dais. It takes forty gondoliers, twenty each at the port and starboard sides, dressed in La Contessa's livery, to propel it.

La Contessa has us dressed in complementary costumes consisting of silk cloaks in azure for me, scarlet for Julia, and white for Becky. She explains that, by chance, she's come into the possession of dazzling silks from the Orient and has decided to make use of them by having these cloaks specially made for the occasion. They are designed to accompany the spectacular and beautiful masks created for us.

Julia's is an ornate mask decorated with long plumes of feathers in red, orange, yellow, and gold. She looks wonderful, like a phoenix rising out of the flames. The bright fiery colours complement her skin tone perfectly. I'm wearing a peacock mask with its exotic feathers and eyes in bright azure and turquoise feathers. Between us we look like two exotic birds. Becky's is pure white and made with swan feathers to match her pale skin. The masks and their respective colours have been chosen for a purpose, which is not lost on us.

The three of us take up positions on the *felce*. Mademoiselle is already waiting. She's pleased to see us, especially Becky.

"Ah, it's good to see you, *mes amis*. I'm glad to hear the difficulties with your mistress have been resolved, and to see you still in her service. Such willing and enthusiastic servants must be hard to find, especially for such a demanding mistress. I would take you all back to Paris with me if I could, but you belong with La Contessa, I know."

She turns towards Becky, "Ah, *ma cherie*, you are lovelier than ever. The kohl on your eyes makes them look so lovely. I could gobble you up."

"Thank you, mademoiselle, Julia has been helping with my make-up."

Mademoiselle pulls the girl towards her and French kisses her, whilst allowing her hands to stray underneath the girl's cloak to finger her crotch.

"*Sacre bleu.* But what's this *ma cherie*?" she exclaims as her hand grasps something hard.

Becky parts the white silk to reveal the costume La Contessa has dressed her in. It's a studded silver plate engraved with vine leaves covering the girl's crotch with only a slit through which she can pee. It's attached to a belt which has a delicately wrought keyhole in it. This in turn has bars attached to silver plates over Becky's breasts with tiny indentations for her nipples. These are kept in place by a bar bending around her back and secured by another lock. She's locked in a frame of gleaming silver.

"It's a chastity belt mademoiselle."

"But why *ma cherie*?"

"Mistress says I've been getting too much pleasure and wants to lock me away until she's ready to offer me up to her guests tonight. It's mistress's wish. I rather like it mademoiselle," she says running the tips of her fingers longingly over her silver encased crotch.

"Oh, how frustrating, for me as much as for you," exclaims mademoiselle. "Patience, my sweet, when your mistress deigns to release you from the device, I promise I will ravish you!"

There's a commotion on the quayside and the sound of gasps and then laughter. La Contessa arrives. She marches up to the reception party consisting of members of the Council of Ten, the Archbishop, and various dignitaries. They stand outside the Doge's palace, ready for the formal proceedings to launch the regatta.

She's dressed in a pirate's costume.

She looks fantastic as you'd expect. Her black tunic, decorated with gold brocade, is tucked in at the waist to enhance her figure. Hanging from her wide leather belt is a cutlass on one side and a pistol on the other. She wears a pirate's hat decorated with skull and crossbones, and there's a brightly coloured, trained parrot sitting jauntily on her shoulder. I recognise her boots, having had the task of polishing them for the occasion. They are a pair of pirate boots, knee high with the leather turned back at their top. La Contessa makes a daunting pirate.

By now it's common knowledge that the Council's ship, laden with expensive material, china, and spices from the Far East, has been captured by pirates off the Turkish coast. I wouldn't dare hazard a guess as to what part La Contessa had in the endeavour, though my suspicions are that she, and my two old friends, Lucretia, and Viola, had a part to play in it.

As the Council approach, the parrot spreads its wings and blasts out an angry squawk. Despite the pointed humiliation directed at the ruling elite, they welcome La Contessa fawningly. They are all over her; bowing and scraping, kissing her hand, and showering her with flattery. The Council members are effusive in their welcome even though she mocks them by inviting them to compliment her choice of costume. It's only the stern Archbishop who goes through the motions, whilst looking distinctly uncomfortable. La Contessa is milking the attention as much as she can and is thoroughly enjoying herself.

It's strange that the Doge himself is not there. It's customary for him to launch the flotilla but it appears Alessandro Fernasse is taking the lead. Perhaps the Doge is indisposed?

La Contessa crosses the gang plank and boards her barge. She strides past the rows of gondoliers, steps up onto the elevated *felice*, and waves at the crowds with a flourish of her pirate's hat, to great applause. She takes up her chair on the dais. Mademoiselle stands at her side, beaming with delight, as Julia, Becky and I take up a lower and more subservient position in front of them.

"Come here girl," orders La Contessa, beckoning Becky forward.

She unfastens the cords at the neck of the cloak, allowing the white silk to glide onto the ground to show off Becky to the crowds in her silver-clad glory. She spreads her fingers over the girl's shining metal crotch.

"You look magnificent, girl. If I am the pirate, then you are my exotic booty, captured from a far-away civilisation, and brought back to serve her mistress."

Mademoiselle is gushing in her appreciation, "Thank you so much for the invitation, Contessa. You costume is fabulous, madam. You make the perfect pirate!"

"Thank you, Marie."

"This will be marvellous. What tales I will have to take back to Paris with me!"

I'm surprised to see it's Fernasse who starts the celebrations for the finale of *Carnevale*. He raises his hand and instantly fireworks set off from San Marco behind him to mark the start of the regatta.

The rows of gondoliers set the vessel going with graceful pulls of their oars. The barge glides away from the quay-side into open water, and the flotilla of boats sets off behind us. It's a splendid sight. The cupolas of the Basilica gleam in the midday sun. We pull away from the Doge's Palace and San Marco and head for the entrance into the Grand Canal.

Who would have thought? Was it only a few months ago I was on my knees sucking cock in the alleyways of the least salubrious district of Venice? Now, here I am, at the head of a grand procession of barges, feluccas, and gondolas, in the service of the most powerful, not to mention richest, woman in the Republic of Venice. Whatever twists and turns my journey has taken, and whatever punishments and travails I've had to endure, it's with great pride I take up my place alongside my mistress. Julia is beaming. This is a landmark for her. In the many years La Contessa has participated in the regatta, Julia has never been invited to attend her on the ceremonial barge. She's taking in the whole spectacle and loving every moment of it. Even Becky is smiling, but then she does have Mademoiselle's hand fondling her arse, which is not encased in silver.

As we enter the Grand Canal we are greeted with a roar from the throngs along the canal side or leaning from the windows of the palaces lining the canal. Of all the spectacles Venice has to offer, a regatta is the finest. The Grand Canal is still the grandest waterway in the whole world. It represents Venice at its best and has not suffered the decay of the city's hidden districts.

It looks at its shimmering best today. Brightly coloured tapestries hang from the balconies of the magnificent palaces. Venetians make an effort to look the part during *Carnevale,* so the crowds are dressed in their finery, and there are spectacular masks everywhere I turn. I glimpse back to the flotilla of boats behind us. There are the magnificent barges like La Contessa's, and the gondolas decorated for the occasion. The sun reflects off the black lacquer, golden-gilded ornamentation and scarlet canopies. It's a sight to behold. Seeing it makes me proud to be a son of *La Serenissima.*

The barge continues its stately progress along the canal. As we approach Ponte di Rialto, masked crowds hang from the bridge waving flags and shouting. La Contessa raises her hat to acknowledge the adulation of the crowds. She's loving every second. Here she is, Venice's most notorious dominatrix, for few in the city are unaware of her reputation, leading the flotilla. It's a pinnacle of her achievement to have the elite of Venice following *her* in the regatta, have the crowds adulating *her.*

We soak up the experience. It's exhilarating. It's dazzling. And La Contessa is there at the forefront of it.

The barge rows the length of the Grand Canal when the flotilla disperses. The vessel is taken back along the canal to drop us off at Palazzo Cavalli. We have spare time to relax and get ready for the evening's ball.

La Contessa is pleased, "It was a splendid occasion. Now you must prepare. For I want this ball to be the most debauched public event Venice has ever witnessed and, as you know, you have a role to play in it. You will be on show to the people of Venice. Naturally, I demand complete subservience from you."

25: The Carnevale Ball

All is prepared. The guests have finished their banquet and file into the ballroom to wait in excited anticipation for their host's appearance. We follow them to take up our allotted positions, still dressed in the silk cloaks and peacock, phoenix, and swan masks. I'm excited. I've heard much about the palazzo's ballroom, and now I'm finally getting the chance to see it.

It's like walking into a dream. There's so much happening it's hard to take it in. The overwhelming impact is one of opulence. The ballroom is vast, accommodating hundreds of guests with ease. I'm surprised at how light and airy the room is. I was expecting baroque grandeur, but the panelled walls are in pastel shades of blue and green, decorated with delicate filigree patterns of foliage in gold. Along the length of the ceiling are candelabra of Murano crystal with candles set in them, making it rain sparks of rainbow light on the revellers. It's an architectural delight, and beautiful because it has a sense of restraint. This glorious light filled space is a delight. I stand there open-mouthed looking around.

Then there's the art work, all by renowned artists and tasteful. Well, it's extremely explicit but executed in a tasteful manner! There are huge canvases on the wall between each set of window frames. The overall theme is classical, specifically classical love stories; more specifically love stories involving perverted sex. The ballroom is bursting with rosy buttocks, bouncing breasts and rampant penises.

I recognise the stories they depict. Zeus features prominently, but then he was a horny god. There's Zeus as a cuckoo proposing to Hera, seducing Europa in the form of a bull, fucking Leda in the shape of a swan, and abducting Ganymede as an eagle. There's a definite bestiality and shape-shifting theme going on. There's one shockingly explicit painting of a god peeing. It takes a while for me to work it out until I realise the painting depicts Zeus seducing Danae as a shower of gold though in this depiction the golden shower is painted literally. I hope to examine them more closely in daylight, but for now I scan the room transfixed as I appreciate the rich colours of the oils as they glow in the candlelight.

To my surprise I get a gentle nudge from Becky; she glances across at me and mouths, "Wow!"

The ballroom alone is enough to take the breath away, but the revellers packing it out add yet more colour and magnificence. Venetians dress up for *Carnevale* and, given the room is full of people from La Contessa's inner circle and many of the city's wealthiest inhabitants, it's hardly surprising to see an array of outrageous ball gowns, tunics and masks. My flamboyant peacock mask looks restrained compared to others. There are silk, damask, and velvet dresses with extravagant collars and lace ruffs. The jewellery on display is breath taking in its opulence. The guests glitter with silver, gold, pearls, and precious stones, an abundance of diamonds, rubies, and emeralds being on show. There are embroidered masks of white, black, silver, and gold decorated with exotic displays of feathers. There are *panniers* so wide the women can barely fit through the door. Mademoiselle is wearing such a gown made of emerald silk decorated with orange flowers with a massive golden bow. The ballroom is filled with a rainbow of colours, blinding in their dazzling brilliance.

The atmosphere is raucous and licentious. They're drunk on wines and brandies, and ready for a party. They want entertainment and, this being the decadent republic of *La Serenissima*, and these being amongst of its most liberated citizens, they want debauchery. Their eyes turn to the centrepiece of the ballroom, a large platform in its centre set out as a dungeon, with a rack, metal chair, suspension frame, St Andrews cross, swings, and ropes. The steps leading up to this stage are where Becky, Julia and I wait, expectant, like lambs for the slaughter.

The guests cheer as the gilded doors of the ballroom swing open. Leading the way is a procession of belly dancers in silver masks with glass candelabras mounted on their heads. La Contessa follows them, riding across the dance floor on a pure white horse, the guests parting for her to form a passage to the centre of the ballroom. The horse's bridle and stirrups are made of solid gold, diamond jewellery hangs on its brow, and on its head is a headdress of ostrich feathers. La Contessa pulls the horse to a halt at the point where we stand, and surveys the throng of revellers in their gorgeous costumes and spectacular masks.

Her mask is magnificent. It's golden, decorated with pearls and golden feathers; arms of golden material stretch out from it like the rays of the sun. Her cheeks and lips, visible below the mask, are dusted with gold. In her hand she wields a sceptre topped with a silver moon. She is the sun and the moon. She is a celestial being descended from the heavens to appear amongst the revellers.

Whilst La Contessa sits on her mount towering over the crowd, another figure mounts the platform. He's dressed in a multi-coloured harlequin costume with a preposterously huge, false phallus, which masks the bulge in his crotch, and matching harlequin mask. From his bulk, I realise it must be Alessandro Fernasse.

"If I can have your attention," he shouts, and the crowd silences to an expectant hush. "It is an honour to be a guest of La Contessa in her magnificent palazzo. It is an apt finale to *Carnevale* to have it hosted in the most stunning ballroom in the Republic. It is apt because I have a most important announcement to make this evening, and it is fitting you should be the first to hear it. The Council of Ten met yesterday and took the momentous, but necessary, decision to depose the current Doge of Venice. In his place the Council has taken the unusual step of appointing a female Doge. I bid you welcome the new Doge of Venice, La Contessa di Nemesia!"

There's a momentary silence as the guests absorb this shocking information, and then a roar of approval and raucous applause to welcome their new Doge.

So that's her game. She's after power, and she's manipulated the Council of Ten into giving her the ultimate prize, the ceremonial head of the city. The conversation I overheard makes sense now. They are in her control. Whatever offer she made, perhaps to write off their interest payments, was impossible to reject given their straightened circumstances. The repercussions are enormous. A woman as the leader of the city... it's unprecedented. Never in all the centuries of the Republic has such a thing been countenanced. But she's brilliant and formidable. Trust La Contessa to pull this off!

The crowd quietens to a murmur when La Contessa, still sat in the saddle of the white horse, begins her speech.

"Thank you my friends. I am a daughter of *La Serenissima*. I love the city of my birth. I love its liberated people, I love its extravagant pleasures... and I love its decadent licentiousness. I represent all that is great about this Republic. Under my rule your political... and sexual freedoms shall be upheld. I shall free you from the last vestiges of oppression by church and state. These are my first acts: I shall put an end to the censorship of political views, published works, the arts and theatre; I declare brothels, bawdy houses, and prostitutes to be working legally, and not subject to harassment from either state or church. Lastly, I declare sodomy to be legal and, forthwith, sexual acts between members of the same sex shall be tolerated by the state."

The guests shout and cheer. She's awesome. I find myself applauding wildly, caught up in the enthusiasm of the moment. I notice Lucretia and Viola amongst the crowds gathered around La Contessa and her horse. It was hard to spot them at first because, at this occasion, their flamboyant dresses and masks merely blend in with the other revellers. But at the announcement of the legalisation of sodomy, they jump up and down waving lace handkerchiefs to catch La Contessa's attention, signalling their approval for her declaration.

"Welcome to the *Carnevale* ball, my friends. You are Venice at its glittering best. The wine is flowing, the music will start playing. The whole palazzo is at your disposal. You must feel free to do whatever you desire. My dungeon is here for anyone who cares, or dares, to use it and my slave and slave girl are available to any of my guests. Enjoy the ball!"

Spontaneously, the whole crowd raise their glasses and toast La Contessa di Nemesia, the new Doge of the Republic of Venice.

I offer my hand to help La Contessa down from her horse. Her dress stands out, not because of its extravagance, but because it's so distinct. She's decided not to compete with the other women in their magnificent and elaborately decorated ball gowns. She wears a jerkin and skirt in white kid-skin leather with subtle swirls of golden thread sewn into it to match her sun mask. The jerkin is sleeveless and strapless, and she wears golden shoulder clasps and a torque in a Celtic design. The top is cut low and the curves of her breasts, a fake mole on each one, squeeze out above the leather. It's simple, but strikingly different and sensual, making her standout from her guests. She needs help to get out of the stirrups, as the dress clings tightly to her hips, so I step over to help her. I gently support her waist, the kid-skin jerkin being the softest leather I've ever touched, so she can slide off her horse.

"Mistress, may I congratulate you on your elevation to high office so ingeniously achieved, and ruthlessly executed."

"Thank you, my slave. Yes, you may. How do you like my ballroom?"

"It's spectacular, mistress, and the works of art are astonishing." I point to a painting of Andromeda chained between rocks with the sea crashing at her feet. Her rosy arse glows as the sea creature Cetus bears down on the ancient Greek princess, ready to penetrate her with its monstrous phallus, "Is it a Titian?"

"Why yes, well spotted slave," replies La Contessa.

"Well, you can't beat a Titian arse, mistress."

She laughs. "No, indeed, you cannot."

She gathers us around her.

"Julia, you can stay with me. Though you will be needed, I don't intend to have you used by all and sundry. But my slave and slave girl, you must make yourself available to any of my guests for any debauched activity they demand. I know you understand this."

"Yes, mistress," we reply in tandem.

"So, you can remove your cloaks but it is the etiquette of the *Carnevale* ball for masks to be worn at all times. Prepare yourselves. The fun is about to begin."

Becky and I unknot the ties around our necks and let the silk cloaks slide off our backs. Underneath the cloak I wear a collar and outfit consisting of no more than criss-cross leather straps in azure leather matching my mask, whilst Becky still wears the silver chastity belt and breast plates. La Contessa attaches leads to rings in our collars, and has us crawling behind her, up the steps onto the podium which acts as the ballroom's dungeon area. Julia, still cloaked, helps Mademoiselle, in her huge *pannier,* up the steps. A dark shadow of a figure follows. From his build and the set of his jaw, I recognise him as Il Padrone from the warehouse dungeon where the Syrian merchant was taken. He's dressed in a mask and cloak made of black raven feathers.

"Oh, the whole spectacle has made me so horny," gasps Mademoiselle. "I can't wait any longer, I have to come. Get under my dress, *ma cherie,* and lick my cunt."

Mademoiselle lifts up a panel of silk at the front of her dress to reveal the arrangement of willow hoops forming the structure of the *pannier,* and invites Becky to crawl inside. The girl disappears and gets to work on the desperate French woman. Mademoiselle leans against the side of the rack gasping as the girl works her tongue into her cleft.

"Oh, that's so good. You are so good at pleasing me. Make me come *ma cherie,* make me come!"

Whilst Mademoiselle is being brought to a climax, La Contessa, and Il Padrino lead me to the suspension frame. My wrists are tied and pulled up, my legs spread-eagled and bound to the frame.

"Excellent," exclaims La Contessa, "I see every sensitive part of your anatomy is exposed for my guests. Hopefully in a few minutes they will join us up here. I will go and encourage people to make use of the equipment I've kindly provided. Let me see, who can start proceedings. Ah, Julia. You love your mistress, yes? So, you will do whatever pleases her?"

"Yes, mistress," she concurs.

Handing Julia a flogger made in red leather to match her costume, La Contessa continues, "Besides, I know how much you enjoyed punishing him on the gondola. So, let me observe how you do it, let me see you whip your lover."

"Yes madam, anything you ask of me."

Julia grasps the handle firmly in her hand. She faces me, her hazel eyes behind the red and orange feathers of the phoenix mask staring into mine. She runs the strands of the flogger across my shoulders and neck. The leather is tantalisingly soft. She takes one of my nipples between her scarlet-gloved fingers. The silk is sleek and smooth, but the twist of my nipple bites. I squirm against my restraints. Julia runs the flogger along my chest until its leather tongues brush my pubes.

"Madam wants me to punish you. Do you recall when I spanked and whipped you on the gondola when we first met? Well, I'm going to punish you again, and this time you're tied up for me so there's no escape."

Her words are calm and seductively threatening. My heart is racing. La Contessa has been giving her lessons or maybe Julia has learnt from observing her. Yes, I remember the corporal punishment she administered when we first met. Then she was hesitant, but looking into her eyes now, there's a glint of sadistic pleasure in them which reminds me of La Contessa.

My cock is starting to swell. Julia takes it into her hands and runs the flogger across it. She releases my cock, now fully erect, and steps back. She raises the flogger over her shoulder and slashes it across the hard flesh. She lashes the leather thongs against my cock again and again. It retains its hardness but throbs with the pain, but it's an exquisite pain.

"What do you say?" asks Julia.

"Thank you," I gasp.

She arches an eyebrow through the eye-hole in the mask in a familiar gesture.

"Thank you... mistress," I add.

She smiles, "That's better."

La Contessa gazes on approvingly. I wonder if she's been training Julia for this. Perhaps she's introducing a sadistic little twist to the understanding between her, her maid, and her slave, for her own pleasure. I settle into my bondage and wait for more... yearn for more.

The tension between Julia and I is momentarily broken by the screams of Mademoiselle's delight as she reaches her climax. She grips onto the side of the rack as her whole body, hidden in the preposterously large gown, spasms with her orgasm. Her work done, Becky emerges from the willow frame supporting the billows of material, Mademoiselle's cunt juices dripping from her lips.

"Thank you *ma cherie*. God I needed that," she pants.

As soon as Becky is on her feet, La Contessa offers her a flogger, this one white. She steps forward to take up a position alongside Julia, and in front of me. The two women turn to face each other. The phoenix and swan masks face up to one another; Julia's the fiery red of passion and Becky's the cool, dispassionate white of submission. Julia reaches out to touch the girl's cheek. Immediately they are locked into an embrace, their lips pressed together in a passionate kiss. La Contessa demanded all jealousies be put aside, and here's the evidence they have. They kiss with the ardour of lovers.

La Contessa is amused, "Very good, perhaps the three of you should engage in a little *menage a trois*... with your mistress's full approval, naturally. But you should be focusing on the slave's pain rather than your own pleasure."

Hearing La Contessa's words their lips part.

"Yes, mistress."

"Of course, madam," echoes Julia.

Julia is behind me and sets to work flogging my backside, whilst Becky stands before me slashing the red tongues across my cock and balls. The two women work in tandem, one strike following the other. They are hard strokes. I noticed this on the gondola, for a woman with a delicate build Julia can wield a whip with force.

By now the guests are starting to fill the platform, either to watch the spectacle or join in. Il Padrino has a woman tied onto the rack, her arms outstretched, legs apart and gown rolled up to expose her cunt. He runs his fingers along her crack making her squirm and squeal. A naked man, save for his white mask with a leering grin, is being paraded around the stage by a lady in a vivid purple gown and mask, wielding a whip. A lady dressed as a mediaeval maiden in a tall, conical hat is tied to the St Andrews Cross as a group of men dressed in golden crusader costumes emblazoned with gold Maltese crosses and gold masks line up to penetrate her. La Contessa watches proceedings approvingly, conducting the action and supplying her guests with the tools for sexual pleasure and torment from her vast array of equipment.

There's a group clustered around the frame where I'm strung up. It's obvious they are keen to join in so, being good hosts, Becky and Julia hand their floggers to the guests. One is taken up by a stunning, black-haired woman wearing a striking scarlet gown in a devil mask with black horns. She takes the lead in punishing me, slashing me with powerful strokes, revelling in the opportunity to administer severe punishment on a willing subject. My back and buttocks must be covered in welt marks by now. Whilst the devil woman whips my arse another reveller dressed in an azure gown, her lips dusted with ground lapis lazuli, is on her knees before me, threading my cock into her mouth. She devours me with gusto, leaving blue flecks of dust sticking to the saliva and pre-cum on my cock by the time she's finished.

Other guests want to use the suspension frame I'm hanging from, so La Contessa unties me to free the equipment for them.

"I think you're ready for a change of scenery," she explains, strapping me onto a whipping bench with leather straps.

Whilst being secured I glance to one side to see a naked lady tied onto the rack with ropes, and Il Padrino orchestrating her torment. She has a massive dildo inserted into her cunt whilst at the other end her head is enveloped in a vast indigo ball gown as, underneath it, she's licks out the cunt of one of the revellers. Whilst she's doing this Il Padrino is drizzling hot wax over her breasts.

I'm on my front, my knees bent, arse in the air, and head locked in a wooden yoke so I can't see what's going on behind me. In front of me is another guest in a golden mask with red flames around it, her ball gown and undergarments discarded, wearing only a strap-on secured around her waist with a leather belt.

"Take this for me," she exclaims, threading the false cock into my mouth.

The strap-on is broad; I open my mouth wide to receive the smooth wooden object. She pushes it deep into my throat and, taking my face between her hands, rocks her hips back and forth pushing it inside me. It's only then I see the ingenuity of the design of this strap-on. It's carved in such a way that a protruding piece of polished wood fills her cunt so with each thrust into my mouth, she's penetrated as well. The harder and deeper she pushes into me the greater the pleasure she gives herself.

"Take it deeper for me," she gasps, penetrating my mouth with hard thrusts.

Before she comes, she slides the object out of my mouth. But there's no respite for me. She steps around to the rear of the bench. She runs her hands over my backside, covered with red marks from my earlier whipping, then probes my anus with the fearsome strap-on. She pushes it inside me. It stretches me but soon pushes past the tight ring of my anus deep into the passage. It's a strange sensation being filled, yet oddly comforting. She gets to work on me. Her thrusts are deep and powerful and, as the pressure on her own sex mounts, she groans and whoops with pleasure.

"Well, he's in a bit of a predicament, isn't he my dear?"

"Yes, and there's nothing he can do about it."

It's Lucretia and Viola.

"We can add to it though, can't we?" suggests Lucretia lifting up the folds of his gown to show silk stockings no knickers, and an erect cock.

I'm soon filled at both ends. Lucretia and Viola take it in turns to force me into sucking their cocks whilst the strap-on penetrates me harder and deeper. The activity is frenetic, and the excitement of the guest taking my back passage is evident from her screams as she reaches climax. There's one final animalistic scream as she comes. The pace of the strokes slows.

Viola withdraws my cock from his mouth and with Lucretia masturbating him; he comes with a squirt of jism which leaves globs of spunk splattered over my face. Viola returns the compliment and adds to the mess of come over my eyes, in my nose and dribbling down onto my lips, where I lick it off.

The woman returns to the front of the bench and kneels before me, taking my spunk covered face between her two hands.

"That was delicious," she whispers. "La Contessa's parties are wonderful. She's lucky to have such willing slaves, and it's generous of her to share them with her guests."

She sticks her tongue out, and proceeds to lick every drop of spunk off my face and smoothly shaven cheeks, relishing the feel and taste of each morsel.

Seeing a lull in the activity around the whipping bench, La Contessa comes over to unstrap me. Alessandro Fernasse follows in her wake, his eyes like a forlorn puppy. It's obvious what he wants. His demeanour is one of frustration bordering on desperation. Although he daren't ask La Contessa outright for fear of angering her, he is trying to draw himself to her attention.

"What a wonderful day it's been Alessandro. And what a fitting climax this ball is."

"Indeed, madam. And is Contessa satisfied her conditions have been met?" he probes.

She hesitates for effect, "…Well let me see. Yes, I must take pleasure at my new position at head of the Republic."

"And is madam satisfied with the part her humble servant has played in achieving her ambitions?"

La Contessa's eyes flash with irritation, "Do not crawl to me. It's obvious what you want. You want to be released from your chastity so you can join in the debaucheries, do you not?"

"Yes please, madam. If it pleases you, yes, I plead to have the cage removed from my cock."

She retrieves the key from a hidden pocket in her skirt and taunts Fernasse by dangling it in front of him, "Yes, it's true you have met all my conditions yet, on the other hand, it might amuse me to keep you in chastity for the rest of the night."

Fernasse says nothing but his eyes plead for release.

"…But I am generous in victory, so I suppose it is fair I unlock you from my cage. Drop your breeches, my friend. But be warned, my slave girl is off limits to you. You may watch her and you make wank yourself off to her, but you must not touch her. Is that clear?"

"Yes madam, perfectly. And thank you, madam. It has been an honour to serve you and assist you in realising your ambitions."

"Thank you Alessandro," La Contessa replies as she inserts the key into the padlock and turns it. She removes the lock and the two parts of the iron cage separate, much to his relief.

Fernasse departs to seek out his pleasures.

La Contessa turns to me, "Look around you slave. See how my guests are entering to the spirit of my ball. See how much they are enjoying themselves. This is what I take pleasure in… seeing the Republic in this most liberated and decadent state."

I do as La Contessa asks and cast a gaze around me. The dungeon space is packed with guests making use of the equipment. The sound of screams of pain… and pleasure fill the ballroom, drowning out the gentle background sound of the chamber orchestra. There are whips being flailed and canes cracked. There are squeals and groans of pleasure as revellers reach orgasm after orgasm.

I cast my eyes wider, away from the platform. The vast expanse of the ballroom floor has been transformed into a massive orgy. The activity in the ballroom is more vanilla than the bondage and corporal punishment being conducted on the raised platform. The floor is littered with discarded ball gowns, undergarments, and wigs as guests divest themselves of these encumbrances to indulge in all manner of sexual pleasure.

In accordance with the tradition of the *Carnevale*, people still wear their masks. They may be in various stages of undress but the masks remain, adding an aura of mystery and disguise to the ball. Couches have been brought out for the guests so they can make love on them in comfort, though when these are occupied couples, threesomes or more, fuck on the ballroom floor. The whole ballroom is awash with jiggling tits, rampant cocks, and sopping cunts as the revellers descend into a lascivious, perverted paradise. I'm intrigued that La Contessa doesn't actively engage in the perversions on display. She appears content to stay in the background orchestrating them.

My eyes flit back to the platform. There's the slave girl tied onto the suspension frame where I was earlier with Il Padrino using the cane on her backside whilst a male guest with a harlequin mask is on his knees fondling her silver belt.

One thing does occur to me though. I haven't seen Julia since the start of the night.

La Contessa hands me over to Mademoiselle, now divested of the encumbrances of the pannier hoops and preposterous ball gown, and wearing nothing but her mask and a simple cloak. She looks flushed and dishevelled.

"*Sacre bleu!* This is fabulous, madam. You know how to hold a party. And your guests are so debauched… and randy. It's all a blur. I must have been fucked at least five times tonight by different men… and that's not counting the women who've gone down on me!"

"Thank you, Marie. I wanted a raucous climax to *Carnevale*, and a fitting celebration of my elevation to power. You must take my slave. The bondage chair is free."

Mademoiselle takes my hand and leads me over to the cast iron, mediaeval looking bondage chair before anybody else claims it. She sits me down. The iron is rough and cold on my beaten backside. Metal bands clamp around my wrists. My legs are spread and other metal bands secured around my ankles. A metal collar is closed around my neck. The piece of equipment is dark and daunting. It reminds me of the atmosphere in Il Padrino's dungeon.

My cock is hard. It has been for much of the night. There's been so much sexual stimulation going on around me I have a permanent erection. Once locked in the metal bondage chair, Mademoiselle kneels in front of me and takes my cock in her slender fingers, running them along my shaft.

"Ah, your mistress treats you so cruelly. It's such a shame."

She squeezes the tip of my cock between two fingernails. The touch of her fingers on my erection is exquisite. I fight to resist coming over her fingers. But Mademoiselle has other plans. To my surprise, and delight, she leans forward and takes my cock between her lips. The sensation is wonderful as the moves her lips up and down over my shaft. The movements get faster and faster. She pulls away to take in breathes before starting again. The touch of her tongue as it curls around my cock, and her lips as she slides along my shaft, are exquisite. She pulls away as I'm on the point of coming.

She's distracted by a touch on her shoulder. It's La Contessa, dangling a pair of silver keys from a chain before her.

"I do not wish to spoil my guest's fun for too long," she smiles.

She cocks her head to one side to indicate Becky. The girl is now strapped face up on the whipping bench, her legs spread and pulled up, leaving the latch on her chastity belt exposed.

She snatches the keys from La Contessa's hand.

"*Merci,* Madam. Look at *ma cherie* there. She's ready for me. I must find a strap-on, unlock her, and take her. I'm sure these ladies will amuse your slave while I'm gone," she says gesturing to a group of revellers who gaze on.

There are three of them and they have come as a group because they have matching gowns, fans, and masks in vivid shades of orange, red and blue. They eagerly take up Mademoiselle's invitation to play with me. The one in orange parts the material of her gown to reveal a pair of long legs and no underwear. She raises a foot onto the seat of the iron chair seductively running her fingers up her leg as she puts her orange slipper over my cock and presses down. The girl in blue takes up a position behind the chair and reaches over me to clasp my nipples with her fingers. Meanwhile the one in scarlet goes to fetch candles, in the colours of red, blue, and orange to match their costumes. They proceed to torment me with simultaneous cock torture, nipple play, and hot wax.

By the time they've finished with me, I'm coated in a rainbow mixture of orange, red, and blue wax, whilst my cock and balls are caked in it. The three anonymous women take it in turns to grasp my wax coated hard cock and masturbate me to the point of climax.

Amongst all this activity I catch glimpses of Mademoiselle, now wearing an enormous strap-on, leant over the girl. She turns the key in the lock and peels the silver device away from Becky's crotch to uncover her sex. She inserts the other key into the band between the two breast plates, and releases her breasts. The three women having left me, I watch as Mademoiselle climbs onto the bench. She parts the lips of the girl's cunt and pushes the strap-on into her. Becky expels a gasp of ecstatic pleasure.

"Ah, *ma cherie*, but you are so wet for me. Do you want it? Do you want me inside you? I have your mistress's permission... to take you, to fuck you, to make you squeal!"

"Yes please, Mademoiselle. Please, I want it... I want you!" the girl moans.

A group has gathered around them to watch, amongst them Alessandro Fernasse, his cock, now released from its bondage, grasped in his fist. He wanks frantically whilst watching the two women fuck. Mademoiselle pounds into Becky, and her breasts jiggle in time to her thrusts. It's too much for Fernasse. He's too desperate to time his climax with theirs. His pent up frustration from weeks of chastity has to find its release... and soon. His cum spurts from his cock in sticky jets. His relief is palpable.

Mademoiselle presses her body against Becky's. She brushes strands of her fair hair dangling from under the swan feather mask, and kisses her. Their breasts squeeze against one another as the French woman grinds into the girl's crotch.

"Um, my sweet, come for me." Mademoiselle pants.

It's too much for Becky. She lets herself go, screaming and twisting on the bench as she climaxes. It's quite a performance from the pair of them.

I'm still locked in the chair when the crowds milling on the raised platform part for La Contessa. I don't know where she's been, perhaps mixing with the guests on the ballroom floor. I see she's leading Julia by a red leather collar and lead to match the flamboyant phoenix mask and scarlet silk cloak. Julia's lips below the mask are also scarlet, and they are pursed in an expression of expectation, even anxiety. I see her eyes behind the mask swivelling around, noting how she has become the centre of attention.

La Contessa stands her in front of the whipping bench. The bench is directly opposite the metal chair which means I have a full view of the pair of them. I wonder if it's deliberate, and La Contessa wants me to see what she's going to do to Julia. She loosens the ties around Julia's cloak and pulls it off, letting the silk rub seductively against her skin until it drops onto the floor. Julia is dressed in a similar outfit to the one worn by Becky except the leather straps on hers are in red. The straps criss-cross between, and around, her breasts making them burst out. I recognise Julia's body; it's so familiar, her olive skin, the curve of her hips, the chestnut brown bush above her sex, her pert delicate tits. She looks beautiful. She also looks as if she's being treated like a sacrifice. La Contessa does nothing without purpose, and her flaunting of her maid in this way before the crowds is deliberate.

La Contessa runs leather gloved hands through Julia's chestnut hair, runs a finger across her cheek, and between her lips for Julia to suck. I understand this. This is a place I've been often whilst serving her. You're mesmerised. You feel a tinge of fear, of the unknown, of not knowing where you are about to be taken, but also of acceptance. You desire it. Even if you know pain or humiliation will follow, you want it so badly. I can read this in Julia's expression as she stands quietly, expectantly, not knowing what depths of her psyche will be challenged and explored. But Julia will go anywhere for her. I know that. She loves La Contessa, as I do, as Becky and Mademoiselle and her closest followers do. And Julia will do anything to serve her.

La Contessa still wears her white costume and sun mask. She puts her fingers behind the waist band of the leather skirt and seeks out her crotch. When she removes them, they glisten with the juices from her cunt. She puts them to Julia's mouth making her lick each drop of her from the kid-skin glove, which she does with relish. It's a performance of sadistic seduction, and Julia revels in it. She brushes her finger nails across her maid's pert nipples and dark areola. She squeezes a nipple between her finger, and Julia flinches and emits a tiny whimper. La Contessa stares at her harshly, and Julia takes a deep breath to steel herself as the same attention is paid to the other nipple. This time her maid is able to control her response.

La Contessa takes hold of Julia's shoulders and guides her onto the rack where she's laid on her back. She pulls her arms above her head and ties her wrists together. She ties rope around her ankles, lifts her splayed legs up and ties them to the top of the wooden frame at the end of the bench. She's bound-up and powerless. Julia's cunt is spread out for everybody to see. Her puffy vulva and cunt lips are visible and they glisten with the moisture of her desire. I know what Julia must be feeling; a little fear, anticipation, excitement, and a desperate need and longing. You don't know what will happen, but you want it...whatever it is, because you want to surrender yourself. It's the response I have when I'm in La Contessa's presence, and what Julia's experiencing now.

La Contessa runs a finger along Julia's cleft and inserts a finger, a second finger and then a third finger, moving them inside her in a slow circular motion. Julia moans with pleasure. La Contessa removes the fingers and puts them to her maid's lips, making her lick the juices of her own desire from them. She leans over her helpless victim and kisses a nipple, rolling her tongue around it. But there's a sadistic twist to her sensual play as she takes the nipple between her teeth and bites on it. Julia gasps. It's pain, but beneath the surface of the pain is an underbelly of want and need. I envy her.

Who would not want to give themselves up to this sadistic torment at the hands of such a skilled dominatrix?

Mademoiselle passes an object to La Contessa. It's another strap-on, this one covered in the same soft white leather as her dress and attached to a matching belt. The French woman helps her adjust and tighten it. It's long, gnarled, and curved like a real cock. La Contessa climbs up onto the rack. She kneels over Julia's face, the huge strap-on hanging over her. Julia's eyes are wide. She wants it, I can tell. She wants to suck it. She wants it inside her. Perhaps of all people, I understand what Julia feels about her mistress and I know how much she wants this. And I want her to have it too. I may be her lover but I'm not a jealous one and I understand Julia's need only too well. The white cock is threaded between her lips. Julia sucks it, gorges herself on it, as La Contessa pushes it into her mouth.

The strap-on is pulled out of Julia. La Contessa leans right over her face. The golden sun mask, and brightly coloured red, yellow, and orange feathers of the phoenix face one another. Julia lifts her head up as far as her bondage allows her, to offer herself. Gold and red lips touch as La Contessa kisses Julia. They stay joined for ages as they kiss with passion and desire. I smile. La Contessa wants her. As a spectator looking on at this performance, there's no doubt in my mind; she desires Julia as much as Julia wants her. I'm convinced of it. And what La Contessa wants... she gets!

La Contessa shuffles her leather clad body along the rack. This is the moment of truth. Now is the time for the consummation of a maid's love for her mistress, no longer unrequited. La Contessa grips the leather phallus with one hand and, parting Julia's cleft with the other, she guides the object into her. Julia gasps. How much has she desired this? How often has she dreamt of this moment, never believing it might be possible? La Contessa pushes inside her, thrusting into Julia's cunt with urgency. Her voluptuous arse, a beautiful curved mound wrapped in tight, white leather, is bobbing up and down as she forces herself into Julia, grinding their hips and the nub of their sex together.

An audience of revellers gathers to watch the sight of their host fucking this lucky girl. The air is expectant. The guests sense there's significance in this act. After all, for most of the night La Contessa has kept aloof from the debauchery, happy merely to orchestrate. Yet this girl has been chosen for her attention. The significance is not lost on me... neither will it be lost on Julia.

The fucking gets more frantic as La Contessa grinds herself into her maid's crotch. Julia's moans of pleasure get louder and louder as her pleasure mounts, and she gets ever closer to her climax. Even La Contessa, usually so controlled, is panting and moaning as her thrusts get deeper and stronger. Then there's release. Julia screams out in ecstasy, her mouth below the mask contorted with pleasure, and La Contessa, she keeps thrusting until she comes. Her leather clad body writhes as, unable to hold anything in, she moans with the euphoria of climax.

The audience applauds. They may not know the background of La Contessa's centrepiece for the ball, but they understand it must be significant for their host, so they show their appreciation for this climactic moment. La Contessa's performance having come to an end, they disperse and continue their perverted orgy into the early hours of the morning when a breakfast of champagne and eggs benedict is served for the revellers.

Julia is untied from the rack, whilst Mademoiselle releases me from the metal chair where I've had a front seat view of La Contessa's ravishing of Julia.

We catch up with each other soon after. Her phoenix mask is askew, and she looks sweaty and dishevelled, but all the sexier for that. I kiss her on the cheek.

"Lucky girl!" I say with a smile.

"Yes, I certainly am!"

26: The Doge's Palace

I look around me in awe. We are on a tour of the state apartments of the Doge's Palace. We emerge from the chamber with ceiling panels depicting scenes of the good governance of the Republic, the renowned masterpieces of Veronese, and head for the Chamber of the Great Council.

It's known by reputation throughout the city though few get the chance to see it. La Contessa's ballroom is splendid but this is opulence on a different scale, on the scale of a nation state. It's allegedly the largest room in the whole of Europe, which I can believe. La Contessa belongs here. It embodies the magnificence of *La Serenissima* as a wealthy Republic built on the trade passing through its canals. Here are the walls painted with episodes of Venetian history, the ceiling depicting the classical virtues and the frieze of the portraits of the Doges by Tintoretto. I gaze from wall to ceiling, and back to wall again, mesmerised by the glowing colours.

I'm suddenly brought back down to earth.

"Stop staring at the murals, slave, and pay attention," snaps La Contessa.

"Will you move into the Doge's Palace, madam?" asks Julia.

"No, Palazzo Cavalli is my home. But now I have two palaces in Venice to run, not to mention my civic duties, so you will be kept busy my maid. I can keep the palace's staff here, but I still need to reorganise my household to accommodate my new responsibilities."

A group of us gather around La Contessa in the Chamber of the Great Council. There's old Lucio, Julia looking stunning in a sumptuous damask dress, myself in mistress's livery and Becky with no clothes on. La Contessa finds it amusing to parade the girl around the Doge's Palace naked, claiming it will set the tone for her reign. There's also Lucretia and Viola in extravagant wigs, opulent gowns and heavily made up, openly flaunting their transvestism.

"I think the palace staff may be in for a shock, my dear," says Lucretia.

"There is a new regime in the palace, and they will have to do their new mistress's bidding," asserts La Contessa. "Now I have brought you here to assign your new roles. Lucio, I want to place you as administrator and procurator of the Doge's Palace. I need somebody I can trust to investigate how everything is working and suggest what changes are needed to meet with my particular requirements."

"Thank you, madam."

He looks both surprised and thrilled at his new appointment, "It's generous of madam to offer these new responsibilities, and I promise I will not let you down."

"Lucretia, I want you to be in charge of the civic finances. I need you to investigate how the former Doge built up so much debt, and your advice on what actions to take to avoid such a thing happening again. The Council cannot act against me. They still owe me a considerable sum of money; I have merely cancelled interest payments to give them a respite in return for their support in electing me the new Doge."

"Yes, I will poke around into everything, my dear."

"Yes, I know I can count on you. Viola, I want you to be in charge of the Republic's moral welfare. It amuses me to have a sodomite in charge of that."

"Oh, thank you! You can trust me to uphold the moral affairs of Venice in an appropriately debauched manner, madam."

"Julia, my position will mean you will have extra responsibilities. You will stay my trusted and loyal servant, but I need you as my secretary and confidante, so I propose to appoint new maids to take over your domestic duties. There will be things you miss, I know. But you must not take this as a slight, my maid. You will be in a position of power, and will have to keep close at all times."

"I'm honoured, madam. I only ever wanted to serve you."

Turning to me she says, "Now, you will continue to be my slave and will need to be available to amuse me whenever I require. However, I consider your talents to be wasted on polishing my boots, whatever erotic pleasures you may get from the task. I want to make use of your knowledge of the arts so I will make you my advisor on these matters."

I'm astonished. I can barely believe the offer La Contessa has made.

"Mistress, I'm overwhelmed by your generosity."

"There is much work to do. I will be looking to fashion the rooms, though not the state apartments of course, more to my personal tastes, which I know you will understand. I will want you to purchase paintings and sculptures, and to commission new works for me."

"Yes, mistress. You'll need a new portrait of yourself in the robes of the Doge to sit alongside the other paintings of the city's former rulers."

"Excellent. Yes of course. I must have a new portrait."

"You can have the winged lion of St Mark in the background," I propose.

"And a whip in one hand…" Lucretia chips in.

"…And an enormous dildo in the other," adds Viola.

"Yes, what splendid ideas. Yes, my slave, you must commission a suitable artist straight away."

"Finally, I come to my slave girl. You will keep this role in my household, but I want to offer you a reward for your dedication and loyalty. Do you like Paris?"

"Paris, mistress? I've never been," says Becky.

"Well you have been invited by Mademoiselle La Tour to stay with her there for a few weeks. You must understand that you are on loan to her and do all she requires. Indeed, as you do for me, though I expect Mademoiselle will treat you less cruelly than I, and look after you rather well. I shall miss you."

"Thank you, mistress. It shall be a wonderful experience, and I shall enjoy servicing Mademoiselle. But mistress, you must know you can treat me as cruelly as you wish and I'll submit to you."

"I am content. I am embarking on a new adventure. It is important for me to have people around me who understand me and who, in their hearts I know love, revere and obey me."

* * *

Julia and I are curled up in bed. We're using the room in the Doge's Palace Julia has been allocated, which adjoins La Contessa's suite of private chambers. A sense of the grandeur of the room is conveyed by the fat, rosy arse looking down on us. It's a painting of Venus, by Titian no less. As I lay enveloped in the soft duck-down bolster, I'm still grappling with my new surroundings. This is a servant's room, but it has a masterpiece by one of the great masters on its wall. How the fuck did I end up here?

We're both exhausted but with the lovely tired, fulfilled feeling you have after great, energetic sex. It's been a frenetic session. Becky slopes back to her own room. She's been an enthusiastic participant, her fingers, and lips have been everywhere to pleasure Julia and myself. It's symptomatic of the changed pattern of relationships in her household for La Contessa to permit such a thing, and for Julia to embrace it without a hint of jealousy.

Julia sighs, "Can you believe this Roberto?"

"No. It's like a dream. Our lives have been transformed by her, haven't they?"

"Yes, they have. I love her... and I love you too Roberto. I have everything I desire, my mistress to serve, and my wonderful lover to share my bed. I've never been happier.